FORTUNE'S LADY

Trembling with terror, Suzanna clung to him, desperate for the strength he offered. "Oh, Jared," she whispered, not even certain she had said the words aloud.

But Jared heard them. "It's all right, sweet lady. I'm here," he said against her temple. His breath was soft and warm, his body hard and strong, and she needed him so badly.

"I'm scared," she said, and the confession covered far more than the bullets crashing around them.

"I know," he said, and for some reason Suzanna truly believed he understood the pain and the loneliness and the fear.

"Jared?" The word held a thousand questions, but he answered none of them. Instead, he pressed his lips to hers, hungrily, urgently, desperately. For a few wild seconds they were alone in the world. More shots were fired, farther away now, but neither of them heard as their bodies spoke to each other in the language older than words.

FORTUNE'S LADY

VICTORIA THOMPSON

AVON BOOKS • NEW YORK

AVON BOOKS
A division of
The Hearst Corporation
105 Madison Avenue
New York, New York 10016

Copyright © 1990 by Cornerstone Communications
Inside cover author photograph by Jim Thompson
Published by arrangement with the author
Library of Congress Catalog Card Number: 89-91358
ISBN: 0-380-75832-6

First Avon Books Printing: January 1990

AVON TRADEMARK REG. U.S. PAT. OFF. AND IN OTHER COUNTRIES, MARCA REGISTRADA, HECHO EN U.S.A.

Printed in the U.S.A.

RA 10 9 8 7 6 5 4 3 2 1

To Jim, the wind beneath my wings.

Chapter 1

"**H**e sure is a cold-eyed son of a bitch, ain't he?" Maisie remarked as they watched Jared Cain stride across the dance floor to his gambling table.

Suzanna nodded grimly. The two women sat silently on their bench for a moment, admiring his aristocratic features and the way his fine hands shuffled the cards as he arranged his faro layout in preparation for the evening's activities.

Behind them, on the stage at the other end of the long hall that comprised Dodge City's Comique Theater, Gambling Saloon, and Dance Hall, the five musicians who composed the 'orchestra' tuned their instruments in squawking cacophony. Soon the cowboy customers would begin to arrive, the minstrel show would commence, and the gamblers would start their games. Suzanna and Maisie and the other 'hostesses,' as the dance-hall girls were euphemistically called, would begin to circulate, shilling drinks and flirting in preparation for the dancing which would occur during the first intermission of the show.

"It's a pity he's so handsome," Suzanna sighed, noting the perfection of his face. Black brows arched over equally black eyes which were graced with lashes any woman would have killed to own. A long, straight nose complemented his lean cheeks and accentuated his beautifully sculpted lips. Everything about him spoke of class and good breeding. Clad in a sober black

1

suit and conservative vest, with his chestnut hair combed severely back from his broad forehead, he might have passed for the minister of a prosperous congregation.

Only the lack of expression in his dark eyes betrayed his true vocation. In fact, in the three months she'd been working at the Comique, Suzanna could never recall having seen him show any emotion at all, regardless of the circumstances. "When a man is good-looking enough to make women want to fall at his feet, he ought to at least have a heart," she remarked.

"Are you wanting to fall at his feet?" Maisie asked, interest lighting her plain face.

Suzanna grimaced and shook her head vigorously. "I learned the hard way not to fall for a man just because God gave him a pretty face."

Maisie smiled wisely. "I know what you mean. A girl can't be too careful." Her gaze drifted back to Cain, and she studied him for a moment. "Just between us, I'd almost decided he was one of those men who doesn't like women."

"He doesn't like *anybody*, male or female."

"No, I mean one of those men who likes men *instead* of women."

"What are you talking about?" Suzanna asked, frowning.

Maisie rolled her eyes. "Sometimes I forget what a hayseed you are, Suzie. I reckon that farmer you was married to never told you nothing about life, or maybe he just didn't know hisself. Anyways, there's some men who only like other men, even for . . ." She lowered her voice, ". . . sex."

Suzanna blushed furiously. Even three months in a dance hall had not destroyed her innate modesty. "You're crazy," she scolded. This wouldn't be the first time Maisie and the other girls had played on her innocence to tease her with tall tales. "Men can't . . . not with *each other*," she insisted, feeling her face heat again.

"Oh, yes, they can," Maisie insisted.

"How?" she scoffed, unwilling to be taken in by any more of Maisie's windies.

Maisie leaned close to Suzanna's ear and whispered.

"Good heavens!" Suzanna breathed, shocked beyond belief. "How horrible!"

"It's a sin, all right," Maisie agreed, "especially when there's lots of women'd give their right arms for a man. And I thought our Mr. Cain was one of 'em, mainly because he'd never paid no attention to any of the girls who work here . . . until last night when you sat down at his table."

Suzanna snorted contemptuously. "He's never noticed me. He never sees anything but his cards."

"Oh, he snuck in a peek every now and then when he thought you wasn't looking."

"He was just angry because he didn't want me there."

"Why'd you sit at his table so long then? You missed almost every dance. You must not've made any money at all."

"One of my partners wanted me to stay with him. He said he had a big ranch down in Texas, and he said I reminded him of his late wife. He thought I'd bring him luck, so he talked Mr. Cain into closing down his faro game and playing poker with him."

Maisie groaned. "You're too softhearted for your own good. Did you forget you've got a kid to support?"

Mention of Andy brought with it the usual clutch of guilt, but Suzanna pushed the thoughts of her son away. If she allowed herself to think of Andy sleeping all alone in their tiny home she would never be able to muster the necessary charm to perform her duties as hostess.

"I actually made more money than usual," she told Maisie with a forced smile. "Mr. Smith—that was his name—he paid me for all the dances I missed, and he bought me a drink every time the call came to go to the bar. I had so many checks in my pocket, I could hardly stand up.'' For each drink and each dance, the patron paid the sum of one dollar and the girl received a brass token which she turned in at the end of the evening to receive half of the payment as a commission. ''When he left, he gave me a fifty-dollar tip, too.''

''The hell you say!'' Maisie exclaimed, making Suzanna wince. Suzanna hoped she never became accustomed to hearing women swear. ''He must've won big.''

''He won more than he lost, I suppose. He seemed awfully happy.''

''And Cain didn't, which means he lost. Maybe that does explain why Cain was looking at you the way he was, although maybe he lost because your beauty took his mind off the game,'' Maisie teased.

Suzanna smiled. She had no illusions about her 'beauty.' At twenty-two, she was the oldest of the 'girls' who danced at the Comique. She was only fortunate that five years as a farm wife hadn't robbed her of her youth. If she'd been too work-worn to dance at the Comique, she and Andy would have starved because there simply were no respectable jobs in Dodge City for Suzanna, not after her fall from grace.

''And all those drinks!'' Maisie continued in feigned amazement. ''Wasn't your Mr. Smith afraid you'd get drunk?''

''He wasn't any greenhorn. He knew the girls' drinks are only tea. I guess he was just willing to pay the price to keep me with him, although I can't imagine why he wanted me.''

''Will you hush that talk? How many times do I have to tell you you're the best-looking girl Springer has working here?''

Self-consciously, Suzanna touched a hand to her honey-blonde hair. ''You ought to tell Springer. He never misses a chance to mention I'm too skinny.''

''Well, most Texans do like their women to have a little meat on their bones,'' Maisie said, proudly straightening the calico stretched tightly across her buxom figure, "but some men like their women delicate, too. Don't listen to Springer. He just has to have something to gripe about, and since you already dance every dance and get more drinks than anybody else, he's a little hard-pressed to think of anything to gripe about."

"Thanks, Maisie." Suzanna squeezed her friend's arm gratefully. Maisie had given her support since the very first night she had walked into the Comique, frightened out of her wits to be entering such a den of iniquity. Yet here she had found not only the job she needed to keep her and her son from starving but also the kindness and understanding the 'good' people of Dodge City had denied her.

Maisie had no patience with gratitude, however. "And another thing, you oughta buy yourself a new dress with Mr. Smith's money. That one is starting to show its years."

Suzanna glanced down at the faded gingham and grinned her agreement. "You know, when I used to hear about dance-hall girls, I imagined they wore silks and satins."

Maisie snorted her disgust. "Silk wouldn't last two minutes with these crazy Texans even if we could afford it," she said, referring to the cowboys the hostesses had been hired to entertain. After spending several months driving their cattle to Dodge City to market, the Texans had a tendency to be overenthusiastic in their revels. "I had me a silk dress once, though," she added wistfully.

"What color was it?" Suzanna asked obligingly, recognizing one of Maisie's moods.

"Red, of course," she said, as if silk came in no other color. "Lester bought it for me. I had it nigh on a month before we ran out of money again, and he had to sell it."

Suzanna bit back the words trembling on her tongue. She barely knew Maisie's husband Lester, yet she would have cheerfully strangled the man. Even Suzanna's own Andrew, with all his faults, would have died rather than put his wife to work in a dance hall to support him. In point of fact, only Andrew's death— and a few other events too horrible to recall—could have brought Suzanna to the Comique, and only her love for her son could keep her here. She would never endure this humiliation just to keep an able-bodied man in whiskey and cigars. "Maisie, you're . . . you're too good for Lester," she blurted, unable to restrain herself any longer.

Maisie sighed. "I know, but where am I gonna find anybody better?"

Suzanna thought about the men she met each night, the wild Texas cowboys not yet out of their teens, the bluff ranchers and sly townsmen who had left their wives and children safely at home, the hard-eyed gamblers like Jared Cain. Maisie was right: none of them exactly fulfilled a woman's dream of the perfect mate.

"I can't stand the thought of going home to an empty house," Maisie was saying. "Not everybody's strong like you are, Suzie. I need a man."

Strong? Suzanna blinked at the sting of tears. If only Maisie knew how many nights she cried herself to sleep in her empty bed, so lonely she would have welcomed poor, worthless Andrew back from the dead and gladly endured again all the heartache he had caused just for the luxury of having someone to hold her. Many times she felt as weak and helpless as a babe, and at those times she could almost understand why Maisie would tolerate a man like Lester.

"Here come the first customers," Suzanna said with false brightness, glad for an opportunity to change the subject. "We'd better get to work before Springer catches us loafing."

Maisie looked over at the doorway where a small crowd of young men had clustered hesitantly. "At least these ones took time for a bath," she said with a weary sigh.

The two women rose from their seats and strolled over to greet the cowboys.

Jared Cain glanced up from his work to watch the woman called Suzanna cross the floor to where the cowboys waited expectantly. His eyes narrowed in contempt even as his pulse quickened at the sight of her slender figure, graceful even in the clumsy boots she and the other girls wore to protect their feet from the Texans' stomping enthusiasm.

Damn her to hell! Why did she stir the longings he had successfully suppressed for so long? Hadn't he learned his lesson the last time? But he really should be grateful that a dance-hall floozy was the one who had made his celibacy unendurable. When he finally spoke to her, he knew he'd find her shallow and common behind her angel's face. Her crassness would repel him, then he would quickly tire of her body.

Just like the last time, he thought with a weary sigh.

Yes, he should be grateful someone like her had caught his eye. He would never dare involve a respectable woman in the wreck his life had become, but the women who worked in the Comique had no illusions about 'happily every after.' He would use this Suzanna to cool the raging passion he could no longer control, pay her handsomely for her trouble, and walk away without a twinge of guilt.

At the other end of the hall, the orchestra launched into a rousing tune, heralding the beginning of the show. Some of the cowboys drifted over to the benches where they could watch, while others allowed the hostesses to lead them toward the gambling tables.

"Have you come to buck the tiger? Get your money down, gents," Jared urged, slipping easily into his role of professional gambler as he lured the rubes to his table. Although Jared prided himself in running one of the few honest faro games west of the Mississippi, the odds in every game of chance greatly favored the house, and even if Jared lost, Springer paid him a hundred dollars a week just to run the table. His sangfroid was not so much a gambler's studied pose as genuine assurance of his ultimate success.

Turning his attention to the dealing box, he began the rapid ritual of selecting cards and collecting and paying bets, a ritual he repeated twice every minute when the game was in full swing. Fortunately, the task required his complete concentration, so the woman called Suzanna faded from his consciousness, at least temporarily.

On the stage, the actors in blackface strummed banjos and made jokes Suzanna had heard dozens of times. As young Eddie Foy questioned Mr. Bones and Mr. Tambor about their trip to the big city and the marvels they had seen, the cowboys roared their approval.

Momentarily without a companion, Suzanna stepped over to greet Sam, the Comique's bouncer.

"How are you doing tonight, Sam?"

Sam Goodwin looked down at her from his great height and grinned in delight. "Mighty fine, Miz Prentice. How's that boy of yours?"

"He's growing like a bad weed. I can't seem to keep him in clothes. Why don't you come by for a visit some evening before work? Andy would love to see you, and I'd even feed you supper."

When Suzanna had first come to the Comique, the red-headed giant had terrified her, but the other girls had warned her to get on his good side if she wanted her personal safety ensured. To her surprise, Suzanna had discovered that Sam Goodwin's massive body contained a spirit as gentle as her four-year-old son's. Chosen for the job because of his size, Sam hated ejecting rowdy cowboys. Only his sense of chivalry to the women he protected made his task bearable.

"That sounds mighty fine, but my time ain't exactly free no more," Sam said, and to Suzanna's surprise, he flushed crimson.

"Is something wrong, Sam?" she asked in alarm.

"Oh, no, it's just . . . I, uh . . ." He glanced away in an agony of embarrassment. "I'm seeing a young lady and . . ." He gestured vaguely.

"Oh, Sam, how nice," Suzanna exclaimed, genuinely pleased. "Who is it?"

"Polly Evans," he admitted shyly.

Suzanna fought to keep her smile in place. "Polly? I . . . I never would've guessed," she murmured, wondering what the acid-tongued dance-hall girl could possibly want with gentle Sam Goodwin. Suzanna couldn't imagine a more mismatched couple, but considering the debacle of her own marriage, who was she to judge? At least Sam seemed happy. Now if only Polly didn't break his heart.

"She's something, ain't she?" Sam asked, his hazel eyes glittering with affection. "I can't figure what she sees in me, though."

"Any girl would be lucky to have you, Sam. Polly knows that, too."

Sam didn't look too certain, but he wanted to believe her. Suzanna smiled encouragingly.

"She don't like working here," he said, as if feeling Suzanna out on the subject. "I wouldn't want no wife of mine dancing with cowboys."

"None of the girls likes working here," she reminded him, thinking she might have discovered what attracted Polly to Sam in the first place. Perhaps the girl saw him as a ticket out of the Comique. "Just don't go getting married until you're sure she feels the same way you do. Remember what I told you about my marriage."

Sam nodded sagely. "She likes me all right, but I ain't too sure if she loves me or not."

"Then wait until you're sure," Suzanna advised, patting his arm. "Uh-oh, there's Springer, and he doesn't look too happy. I'd better get back to work."

"See you later," Sam said as she walked away. "I'll come by sometime to see Andy."

"Bring Polly if you want to," Suzanna offered,

searching the crowd for a likely partner. She knew from the flow of the jokes that the second act was winding down. When the dancing started, she'd better have a cowboy on her arm.

"Balance to the bar!" Eddie Foy yelled, as if he were announcing another dance step and the cowboys surged toward the back of the room where several bartenders waited to serve them.

Suzanna sank wearily onto a bench as her latest partner fought his way through the throng to buy her the required drink. Instinct told her the night was almost over. At about 4 A.M. the orchestra would squawk to a halt, and Foy, who had been calling the steps since the show ended around midnight, would announce the last dance. Surely, it was almost four now. After three months, she could judge the time by how badly her feet ached, and her feet were saying at least three-thirty.

Vaguely aware of a man standing before her, she smiled mechanically and looked up, expecting to see her partner returning with her drink. Instead Jared Cain stood staring down at her out of his impassive brown eyes. "I'd like the next dance," he said.

Suzanna blinked in surprise, then glanced automatically over to his table. His faro layout had been carefully folded and stacked, the game shut down for the evening. How odd. Cain never closed down early. "Of course," she mumbled, too surprised to ask any of the questions buzzing in her mind.

Her partner returned, a gangly, bucktoothed cowboy. He glanced uncertainly at Cain who stepped back politely. The boy gave her the drink and the brass token which she slipped into her bulging pocket as she thanked him. "You said you were from Victoria," she said to him as she sipped the cold tea in the shot glass. "That's such a pretty name for a town."

"It's mighty pretty country down there. I bet you'd like it a lot better'n Kansas."

She made some noncommittal reply, acutely aware of Cain hovering expectantly.

From the stage Eddie called for the gents to find a partner, and when the bucktoothed cowboy pulled another token out of his pocket, Suzanna had to shake her head regretfully. "I'm spoken for, I'm afraid. Maybe next time." Ignoring the aching protests of her feet, she rose from the bench and turned to Cain who led her out to the floor.

Suzanna could have groaned aloud when she realized the dance was a waltz. She certainly had no desire to be held in Jared Cain's arms. Still she managed a professional smile as she took the token from him, dropped it into her pocket, and placed her hand in his.

She should not have been surprised to discover he was an excellent dancer: men like Cain did only those things at which they excelled. Because he stood almost a foot taller than her own five feet, three inches, she concentrated her attention on his collar button and waited for him to begin the conversation.

After a while he said, "I don't want you to sit at my table anymore."

She jerked her chin up, instantly defensive. "Mr. Springer gave me permission."

"*I* didn't give you permission, and I don't want you there. You cause too much of a distraction."

"I'd think a gambler would be grateful for a little distraction."

"Not when I'm the one being distracted."

Once again she blinked in surprise, but before she could do more than react, he said, "I want to buy your services for the night. How much?"

She stared up at him in confusion. Did he want to buy all her dances so she couldn't come to his table? But that would be a waste of money, since he'd already closed down for the night. And surely he didn't want to dance. In all the months she'd worked here, she'd never once seen him dance with anyone before tonight. But why else would he want to buy her services?

"I . . . I don't know," she stammered. "You'd just have to pay for the rest of the dances, and there probably aren't more than a few—"

"No," he snapped, his dark eyes glittering with barely suppressed fury. "I want to go home with you for the night, or what's left of it. How much do you charge?"

As a dance-hall girl, Suzanna had been propositioned many times and many ways, but none of her would-be swains had ever grown angry *before* she turned him down. If the mere act of asking her irritated him so much, why on earth had Cain approached her in the first place?

Unwilling to probe too deeply into this mysterious man's motivations, Suzanna gave him the small, regretful smile she used in such situations. "I'm sorry, but my 'services' aren't for sale," she explained gently.

But Cain was having none of it. "No, of course not. You're a virtuous, churchgoing woman who only works here to support her widowed mother," he said impatiently. "I'll give you thirty dollars. You can buy your mother a lot of biscuits with that."

Suzanna gasped, not certain whether she were more outraged or amazed. Thirty dollars was a month's pay for a cowboy, and Cain could have had almost any of Dodge City's whores for a dollar or two. Perversely, she felt flattered; but mostly she could not recall ever wanting to kick someone so badly in her entire life! Controlling her anger with effort, she said, "Mr. Cain, I am not a harlot."

His finely molded lips curved into the parody of smile. "Which means thirty dollars is not enough. Forty, then, but I'll expect my money's worth—"

"*Oh!*" Suzanna cried in disgust, wrenching free of his embrace.

"Miz Prentice, you having trouble?" Sam asked, beside her in an instant.

Too choked with fury to speak, she glared at Cain for a moment, gratified to see the crimson stain stealing up his neck. Still, his voice was perfectly calm when he said, "Not at all. I was just leaving."

He turned on his heel and strode from the dance floor as if nothing untoward had happened, while Suzanna muttered imprecations at his back.

"Miz Prentice?" Sam tried again.

"It's all right, Sam," she managed to say, swallowing her outrage. "Mr. Cain and I just had a small disagreement."

"I never seen you get mad like that," Sam marveled, shaking his head.

Suzanna drew a calming breath and let it out in a long sigh. "No one ever *made* me mad like that," she told him with a frown. "Do you know what he . . . ? Well, never mind. I don't think he'll bother me again. Thanks for stepping in, Sam."

"Just doing my job." Sam glanced over to where Cain was gathering up his equipment. "Looks like he's leaving now, but if you want, I'll walk you home tonight."

Suzanna studied the stiff set of Cain's shoulders and tried to judge whether he were the sort of man to lie in wait and seek revenge on a woman who had spurned him. Unfortunately, she had no idea whether he was or not. "I'd appreciate your company, but I don't want to get you in trouble with Polly."

"She won't mind," Sam assured her, although Suzanna doubted this was true. "Besides, your place is on the way to hers."

"Thanks, Sam," she said, turning to leave the floor. She came face to face with her former partner, who was grinning expectantly.

"Are you free now, miss?" he asked with reassuring deference.

"Yes, I am," she replied, taking the offered token and slipping gratefully into his arms.

Just as Suzanna had expected, only a few dances later Eddie Foy announced an end to the evening's revels. As soon as all the customers had retrieved the firearms they had checked at the bar and dispersed, the girls lined up outside Mr. Springer's office to collect their pay for the evening. Maisie nudged her way in behind Suzanna.

"What happened between you and Cain?" she whispered the instant she was close enough.

Suzanna sighed, knowing Maisie probably wasn't the only one who had noticed the incident. "He offered me thirty dollars if I'd take him home with me," she whispered back.

"Thirty!" Maisie cried, discretion forgotten. "God in heaven."

Suzanna decided not to mention he'd raised the offer to forty. "I tried to tell him I wasn't interested, but he wouldn't take no for an answer."

"No wonder he looked so mad when he left."

"He was mad before he even asked me."

"Really? Why?"

"I can't imagine. It was almost like he was mad about asking, but if he was, why did he do it?"

Maisie's thoughtful frown slowly cleared. "I know! He really is one of those strange kind of men, and he figured out that people had guessed. He was trying to change people's minds, so he picked the one woman he was sure would turn him down so he wouldn't really have to do anything and—"

"Maisie!" Suzanna scolded.

She shrugged. "It *could* be true."

"Have you counted your checks yet?" Suzanna asked to change the subject.

Obediently, Maisie dug the brass tokens out of her pocket and began to count.

When her turn came, Suzanna laid the pile of her own tokens down on Springer's desk so he could double-check her count. "Sixty-five," he announced when he had finished.

"That's what I got, too," she verified.

His gimlet eyes glinted critically. "You're down a

little tonight. You'd do better if you didn't waste so much time talking to the other employees."

Suzanna could have pointed out that she had made more than most of the other girls, but no good would come of correcting the boss, not when she needed the job so badly. As unpleasant as he was, Springer was better than most, and the Comique didn't have curtained alcoves where the girls were required to 'entertain' customers the way some of the dance-halls did. So she held her tongue and waited patiently while he counted out thirty-two dollars and fifty cents.

The small handful of coins felt absurdly light in her pocket as she made her way to the bar where she had checked her purse and the derringer inside it. On the infamous South Side of Dodge City, men had been murdered for far less than thirty-two dollars, and Suzanna had been advised to carry a gun when she walked home at night with her earnings. At least tonight she wouldn't have to hold the small pistol in her hand as she made her way down the lonely alley to her house.

Big Sam was waiting for her by the door. Beside him Polly Evans looked absurdly tiny by comparison. Polly stood five feet tall and weighed no more than a hundred pounds. Next to her, Suzanna felt tall, and she couldn't help wondering how Sam must feel. Why, if he sneezed, he might blow her away!

Smiling at the silly thought, she greeted the two of them. Polly did not return her smile. "Sam said he promised to walk you home."

The words sounded like an accusation, and Polly's china-doll face was screwed into a frown. Suzanna recognized the jealousy she had so often seen among the girls competing for a man one of them considered desirable.

"He was just worried because one of my partners behaved a little strangely—"

"Yeah, he told me all about how Jared Cain insulted you. He should've known better than to pick on Miss Goody Two-Shoes."

Hating the heat she felt rising in her cheeks, Suzanna refused to take offense. "You're right, Polly. You know how little use I have for men," she said firmly, willing Polly to know she had no romantic interest in Sam or any other male. "Now let's get going. I know you two are anxious to be alone."

Although the street outside was hardly cooler than the dance hall, the evening air felt blessedly clean after the smoky interior of the Comique. On the sidewalk they encountered two men who stood in the circle of light coming from the open door. One of them was James Masterson, brother of Sheriff Bat Masterson and co-owner of the Comique. His deputy marshal's badge shone dully on his lapel. Masterson merely nodded an acknowledgment of their passing, but his companion smiled a greeting and tipped his hat.

" 'Evening, Miz Prentice."

"Good evening, Mayor, although I guess it's probably closer to morning now."

Dodge City's mayor, James Kelley, laughed appreciatively. "I reckon you're right." Kelley was a slope-shouldered man with a drooping mustache, but his Irish charm more than made up for his homeliness. Suzanna didn't care what he looked like or even what other people said about the corruptness of his administration. He would always hold a special place in her heart because of what he had done for her and Andy.

"Andy just worships that dog you gave him."

"I know," Kelley said with a grin. "I saw them the other day playing in the alley. Every boy should have a dog."

Suzanna glanced meaningfully down at the two greyhounds lying expectantly at Kelley's feet. The mayor always took several of his dogs with him wherever he went.

"That's right, Dog," Masterson crowed, calling Kelley by the nickname his devotion to his purebred hounds had earned him. "If a boy should have a dog, I reckon a man should have at least a dozen."

"That's right, and the more of a man he is, the more dogs he should have," the mayor replied, making them all laugh as they recalled his kennel full of hounds.

"Did I miss a joke?"

Everyone looked toward the woman who had just joined the group. Of only medium height, she still gave the impression of stateliness, even standing on a shadowed sidewalk in front of a saloon. Suzanna supposed many years on the stage accounted for Dora Hand's commanding presence. Long past the first blush of youth, Dora still radiated an earthy sensuality that brought men by the hundreds to hear her sing every night at the Comique. Suzanna had met her there, and the two women had found they shared many common interests.

"What's been keeping you, Dora?" Kelley demanded. "I've had to stand here listing to Jim Masterson complain about the Texans for half an hour."

"You poor dear," she clucked, patting Kelley's cheek affectionately.

"You ought to feel sorry for *me*," Masterson said, "after he stole my best singer for that sorry excuse of a saloon of his—"

"I only borrowed her," Kelley insisted.

Dora laughed, a sound almost as melodic as her singing voice. "It's only for two hours a night," she reminded Masterson. "You don't even miss me."

"I know," Masterson grumbled, "but they'd sure miss you over at the Alhambra. Why, if it wasn't for your singing, nobody'd have any reason to go to Beatty and Kelley's at all."

"Now wait a minute—" Kelley began, pretending offense.

"I'm too tired to listen to you two fight. Jimmy, take me home, please," Dora commanded, slipping her arm through Kelley's. As they turned, she caught sight of the others.

"Suzanna! I didn't recognize you." She squinted at

Polly and Sam and greeted them, too. "Heading home, are you?"

"Yes," Suzanna said. "Sam and Polly are walking with me because I had a little trouble with a customer this evening."

"No use going out of your way," she told Sam. "Suzanna can walk with us. She and Jimmy are neighbors, you know."

"Well, uh . . ." Sam began, but Polly cut him off.

"Thanks, Miss Hand. We're much obliged. Come on, Sam."

Before he could protest, the tiny girl was dragging him away. Dora stared after them in amusement. "How long has *that* been going on?"

"Not long," Suzanna said. "Sam's smitten, I'm afraid."

Dora shook her head. "I hope he doesn't get hurt."

"Me, too."

"Well, if you've finished solving the world's problems, shall we be getting on?" Kelley inquired. "Good night, Masterson."

They started down the sidewalk toward the Great Western Hotel which, like the Comique, stood on the south side of Front Street facing the plaza and the railroad tracks. The two greyhounds followed silently at their heels.

This was perhaps the quietest time in Dodge, after the saloons and dance halls had closed and before the respectable townspeople were up and about. The Front Street Plaza—really nothing more than a three-hundred-yard-wide strip of unimproved land divided by the railroad tracks that separated the respectable North Side from the disreputable South Side of town—was nearly deserted. A tumbleweed skipped forlornly in the hot July wind, and a stray dog sniffed a pile of trash.

Dora Hand's sigh broke the silence. "What was Jim saying about the Texans?"

Mayor Kelley shook his head. "Same thing he always says. He never had any love for them *before* they killed his brother and since they shot Mac McCarty last week . . ."

Kelley didn't have to explain. Both women knew how Ed Masterson had been killed in an altercation with two drunken Texans in early April. Then, nine days ago, Deputy Sheriff McCarty had been killed by a half-wit cowboy who stole his gun and shot him with it as he stood conversing with the bartender in the Long Branch Saloon.

"I suppose Jim can't help but think what a good target he makes every night out there in the streets with that badge on his chest," Dora remarked, and then sighed again. "I just hope that when I die, I get the same kind of send-off they gave Ed Masterson. Imagine being so well-loved that every business in town closed down for your funeral." She turned to Suzanna for agreement, but Suzanna shuddered at the thought.

"I hope I'm so old when I die that most folks have forgotten all about me," she replied. "Honestly, Dora, you think about the strangest things."

Dora shrugged. "Life is strange, but if you insist on changing the subject, go right ahead."

"Yes, please do," Mayor Kelley said acerbically, giving Dora a disapproving glance which she ignored.

"Well, I *have* been wondering how you talked Mr. Masterson and Mr. Springer into letting Dora sing in your saloon, Mayor," Suzanna ventured.

Kelley chuckled. "All I can say is being mayor has a few advantages. Of course, I'm sorry I gave her the job now because she throws all her extra wages away on charity, and she's so busy visiting the poor and needy, I never get to see her anymore."

"She's here right now," Suzanna pointed out as they turned down the alley beside the Western Hotel toward the row of two-room shacks lined up behind it. Here, where the light from the street did not penetrate, total darkness closed around them.

"You're wrong, Suzanna. She's not here," Kelley

said lightly. "No respectable woman would be going to a man's house with him in the middle of the night."

"You're absolutely right," Dora agreed, and Suzanna smiled in spite of herself. A few short months ago she would have been appalled to hear of a man and woman living in sin. Now she understood only too well how two people could be desperate enough to clutch at whatever small joys life tossed their way.

"Are we going visiting tomorrow?" Suzanna asked Dora.

"No, she isn't," Kelley replied for her. "You women spend too much time taking candy to those snot-nosed Mexican kids down by the river. Tomorrow, I'm taking Dora out hunting."

"Jimmy," Dora protested, "little Pedro still has the mumps, and I promised . . ."

Suzanna covered a smile at Mayor Kelley's exasperation, as he said, "All right, you can go see him, but no one else! The rest can wait a day or two."

"But some of them need food and—"

"Mrs. Prentice'll take it to them by herself, won't you?" Kelley prompted.

"Of course," Suzanna said with a grin. "Dora, you mustn't offend the mayor. He's a very powerful man."

Dora looked him over appraisingly. "He certainly is," she replied archly.

Kelley made a choking sound, and Suzanna looked away, embarrassed by such a frank sexual reference. In her experience, sex was not a joking matter.

Fortunately, they had reached the end of the alley. Suzanna's house, one of the tiny shacks behind the hotel, stood on the corner, two doors down from Mayor Kelley's. These dwellings faced the river, or would have except for the tents scattered about the river's edge where prostitutes plied their trade. At this hour, even the tents were dark and quiet.

"Thank you both for walking me home," she said, pulling her key from her purse.

"You never did say what kind of trouble you had tonight," Dora recalled.

Suzanna didn't really want to discuss Jared Cain anymore, not even with Dora. "Just the usual—a man who didn't want to be refused."

"Oh, yes," Dora sighed. "Men hate to be refused."

"They hate to be kept waiting, too," Kelley remarked, making both women smile.

Taking the hint, Suzanna hastily unlocked her door. Through the wooden barrier she could hear the click of running paws on the plank floor. "It's me, Pistol," she called softly to keep the dog from barking.

"Hell of a name for a dog," Kelley remarked.

"Don't swear, Jimmy," Dora chastened fondly.

"Good night, and thanks again," Suzanna said, slipping inside. She closed the door behind her and slid home the bolt before turning the key in the lock.

Pistol nuzzled her skirt, whining softly until she reached down and scratched behind his ears. As always, she felt a flood of gratitude for the animal who now stood guard over her son while she worked.

One evening Mayor Kelley had seen her crying as she walked to the Comique and learned she wept because she had to leave the boy alone all night. The next morning, to Andy's great delight, the mayor had delivered one of his prize greyhounds and presented it as a gift to the boy. Suzanna later learned the hound would have been worth three hundred dollars had Kelley chosen to sell it, but everybody knew Kelley never sold his dogs. Sometimes he traded and occasionally he gave one away. And because he had given this one away, Suzanna need no longer fear leaving Andy unprotected.

"How is everything?" she asked the dog, who stared up at her through the darkness with eyes so intelligent she almost expected him to reply.

With the dog at her heels she hurried through the front room to the bedroom. Sweeping aside the curtain in the doorway between the two rooms, she looked eagerly toward the cot standing against the right-hand wall.

Moonlight illuminated the scene, and for one long minute she studied the small form huddled in the center of the cot. Holding her own breath, she waited until she heard the reassuring sound of her son's untroubled breathing. Only then did she allow the tension and worry of the last eight hours to drain out of her. Slumping wearily against the door frame, she indulged herself in the luxury of watching Andy sleep for a while, until her own fatigue reminded her she should be in bed, too.

Silently, she stole over to his bedside and smoothed his flaxen hair away from his forehead. Then she bent down and placed a mother's kiss there, inhaling his sweet, little-boy smell. "I love you, Andy," she whispered as tears welled in her eyes.

He stirred and muttered something, but he did not awaken. Carefully, so as not to disturb him, she stepped back and watched him a little longer. She really should go to bed, she knew. Andy would awaken in a few short hours, ready to go about his business and unable to comprehend why his mother preferred to sleep. Still, she couldn't resist the impulse to simply look at him.

Andy was more precious to her than her own life, and if her death could have helped him in any way, she would have gladly sacrificed herself. Dying was a simple solution, however, and life was never simple, as Suzanna had learned. No, life demanded that mothers sometimes sell themselves in dance halls and other places, she thought, recalling the pathetic women in the tents nearby, women only a little less fortunate than she.

Instinctively, she felt in her pocket for the coins Springer had given her earlier. Their substance reassured her. As unpleasant as her job was, at least she didn't have to live in one of those tents and . . .

The memory of Jared Cain's invitation sprang unbidden to her mind. She hadn't even considered accepting his offer, but she knew her strength of character came from a pocketful of tokens worth fifty cents apiece. If she had been hungry, if *Andy* had been hungry . . .

She shuddered, unwilling to contemplate a situation in which she might be forced to sell more than her company in order to keep her son alive.

As if sensing her disturbing thoughts, Pistol whined again. Absently, she patted his head. "Go to bed now," she said, and the dog hopped up on the cot beside his young master. He lay his noble head on his front paws, but his eyes continued to watch until she had undressed and slipped into her own narrow bed on the other side of the room.

She was just dozing off when Pistol's ears pricked and he sat up alertly. Alarmed, Suzanna strained to hear what had disturbed him and caught the sound of footsteps in the alley beside the house. Her heart raced as she reached for her purse which hung just out of Andy's reach, but before she touched it, Pistol relaxed and lay down again, satisfied the footsteps were receding.

Outside, Jared Cain strode quickly up the alley, silently cursing his own weakness. What had possessed him to stand in the shadows of the hotel porch and wait until she came down the street so he could see if she was going home with another man?

The way Sam Goodwin had come to her rescue, Jared had thought perhaps . . . But that was ridiculous. It was Sam's *job* to protect the girls from trouble. Still, Jared had known one moment of jealous rage when he saw Suzanna come out of the Comique with the huge bouncer, and another when the two men on the sidewalk had spoken to her.

He'd felt absurdly relieved to see her walking with Dog Kelley and Dora Hand. Everyone knew the two were lovers, although no one spoke of it openly out of respect for Dora, so Jared had no reason to be jealous of Kelley.

But what had compelled him to follow them down the alley? Knowing where she lived wouldn't do him any good. He certainly wasn't the sort of man to force a woman when she had already turned him down. Except for the one lapse with Claire back in Wichita, for the past five years he hadn't even been the sort of man who *asked* a woman, for God's sake.

During those years he'd worked his way across Kansas from one cattle town to the next, gambling in the most notorious saloons and dance halls in the country. Pride forbade him to relieve himself with the common whores who worked the line, and only once had he succumbed to temptation and taken a mistress.

What a mistake that had been! Although Claire had done her best to satisfy his physical needs, their relationship was only an empty mockery of the closeness he craved. She'd sensed that he was holding back from her and begun to delve into his past, trying to discover his mysterious secret. By then he'd been glad for an excuse to end the affair that had magnified his loneliness instead of ending it. He'd been alone ever since.

Jared made his way through the shadows into the hotel and down the long hallway to his room. After lighting the gaslight on the wall, he glanced at the window, briefly debating whether to open it and endure the dust from outside or keep it closed and endure the overheated stuffiness. In a compromise, he lifted the window a few inches and then stripped off his clothes, hanging them carefully on the pegs on the wall.

Naked, he stood before the washstand and splashed tepid water over himself in a vain attempt to cleanse away the sweaty stench of the dance hall. Tomorrow he'd go to the barber shop across the plaza for his daily bath. For now he only wanted to cool off enough to sleep.

Without bothering to dry off, he went to turn out the light, but with his hand on the valve, he hesitated, taking one last look around the room. He'd slept here for months, yet the barrenness of it had never struck him so forcibly before.

A bed, a washstand, his clothes hanging on pegs. Except for the set of silver-backed brushes and a leather shaving kit, both of which he'd won in card games, the room contained no personal items at all. *Anyone* might have lived here.

Or no one at all.

In spite of the heat, he shivered and hastily put out the light. The iron bedstead creaked as he stretched out full-length upon it. He wouldn't allow himself to grow morbid or, worse, sentimental. There was nothing wrong with being alone. He'd always been a solitary person. Even now he could hear his mother chiding him for staying in his room so much.

"It's not natural," she would say. "Go outside and play."

Of course she'd known he was avoiding his father, but she'd been loath to see him become a hermit, all the same. Still, he'd liked being alone, and certainly when he'd left home with nothing except the clothes on his back, he'd known what sort of a life lay ahead for him.

Jared had thought he was used to his solitary existence until the other night when Suzanna Prentice sat down at his table. He'd seen her before, just as he'd seen all the women who worked at the Comique, but he'd never paid her any particular attention. As a general rule, he didn't pay any of the women particular attention, but last night he'd had no choice. That damn cattleman had kept her right there beside him through the whole game, so Jared couldn't help but notice her sweet smile and her cornflower-blue eyes and her golden hair and her . . .

Jared groaned at the tightening in his loins. Sleep wouldn't come easily tonight, he knew, but at least his dreams were likely to be of the elusive Suzanna rather than the usual nigh*mares of the past. If she could keep those spectres at bay, he might forgive the inner turmoil she had created.

Besides, tomorrow was another day, and a dance-hall girl's greed would eventually overcome whatever quirk had caused her to turn down his offer tonight. He'd have Suzanna Prentice . . . and soon.

Chapter 2

"Mama? Mama, wake up."

Suzanna struggled to consciousness as her mother's instinct overcame her body's resistance. "Andy?" she croaked, unable to open her eyes more than a crack.

"Mama, Pistol needs to go outside."

Andy's sky-blue eyes reflected his disapproval of her laziness. She managed a moan and flexed her fingers experimentally to see if she was still capable of motion.

"I wouldn't have to wake you up if you'd let me take him out by myself," he reminded her in what was becoming a familiar litany. Her baby was growing up; he just wasn't quite as big as he fancied himself.

"I'll be up in a minute."

"That's what you said before, but you went back to sleep," he informed her testily.

Suzanna moaned again, realizing she had no recollection of the conversation. "This time I mean it," she said, forcing her eyes completely open.

Andy's cherubic face was only inches from hers, his bow mouth turned down in irritation. Beside him, Pistol stood patiently, watching her, too.

"Pistol doesn't like to do his business in the house," Andy reminded her, "and you don't like to clean it up."

"I know," she sighed, pushing up on one elbow. Every muscle in her body protested, but she'd learned

27

from many such mornings that strength of will could overcome even exhaustion. "Will you bring me a wet rag, please, sweetheart?"

Andy raced to do her bidding, Pistol at his heels. In an instant he returned with a dripping piece of cloth which she slapped on her burning eyes and held there until the coolness was gone. By then her blood had begun to circulate again, and she was able to work her legs over the side of the bed until she was sitting up. After a few more minutes of titanic struggle, she was washed and dressed and as ready as she could ever be for Pistol's morning walk.

The bright sunlight sent a shaft of pain through her head, but she pulled her bonnet brim a bit lower and forged on, out into the blinding light. Ahead of her, Pistol pulled Andy along by his leash, a length of rope Mayor Kelley had provided. They walked down the alley to a vacant area that lay between the rear of the hotel and the row of dwellings. Suzanna refused to think of the two-room hovels as 'homes,' although she had to admit she preferred her current residence to the prairie dugout where they had lived when Andrew was alive. At least here she didn't have to worry about snakes and the other varieties of creepy-crawlies that had inhabited the dugout.

When Pistol had finished his 'business,' Suzanna and Andy strolled on down the alley to the Great Western Hotel. Leaving Pistol tied up outside, they went into the dining room for their breakfast. The proprietor's wife, Mrs. Galland, greeted them warmly.

"You're up awful early this morning," she observed.

Suzanna smiled grimly. "Not by choice, I promise you."

"Can I have an egg this morning, Mama?" Andy asked as they took seats at a table near the kitchen.

"You may have whatever you like," she replied, feeling extravagant because of the large tip she had received from Mr. Smith the other night. "You'll need lots of energy today because Mrs. Hand wants us to help with her visits later."

Mrs. Galland shook her head in wonder. "That woman is a saint. I don't care if she does sing in a saloon, and I don't care what the church folks think of her either. She's done more good than all of them put together. Of course, who am I to talk? Those same folks look down on me for keeping a hotel on the South Side."

"You keep a mighty respectable hotel, no matter what side of town it's on," Suzanna pointed out. "You're the only place south of the tracks that doesn't sell liquor."

"Not quite," Mrs. Galland reminded her wryly. "Ham Bell doesn't sell liquor at his livery stable."

"My mistake," Suzanna replied cheerfully. "Oh, by the way, speaking of Dora Hand, did you know Reverend Wright asked her to sing at the church on Sunday evenings?"

"Do tell!" Mrs. Galland exclaimed. "I imagine he'll be hearing from some of the ladies in his congregation."

"He figures Dora's singing will bring in the sinners who need to be in church most."

"He's right, too. I never saw a preacher so willing to try new things. Reverend Wright isn't afraid of anything."

"At least he's not afraid of the good ladies. He proved that by letting me come to church," Suzanna reminded her.

"Oh, pshaw, they wouldn't have turned you away. Nobody really believed . . ." She caught herself, glancing at Andy to see if he were paying attention. Fortunately, he was busy trying to discover if Pistol was visible from where he sat. "What I meant was, anybody who knows you knows the kind of person you are and would never believe anything bad."

Suzanna had good reason to doubt this, but she

smiled her gratitude. "You're a good friend, Mrs. Galland."

Mrs. Galland shrugged off the compliment. "Well, young fellow, how would you like your egg fixed this morning?" she asked, recapturing Andy's attention.

"Sunny side up, with toast and fried taters."

"And milk," Suzanna added. "I'll have toast and coffee, *lots* of coffee."

"Coming right up," Mrs. Galland said, hurrying off to the kitchen.

"Where are we going today, Mama?" Andy asked when they were alone.

"First we'll go to Wright and Beverley's," she said, naming the largest mercantile store in town.

"To put your money in the safe," Andy guessed.

Suzanna nodded. Because Dodge City had no bank, Wright and Beverley's safe served the purpose, and their bookkeeper, John Newton, kept track of everyone's account. Suzanna smiled when she thought of the money she had managed to save already. By the end of the summer she might have as much as fifteen hundred dollars, more than enough to take her and Andy back to Georgia and set them up in some respectable business. Maybe a boardinghouse . . .

"Then where will we go?" Andy prompted impatiently.

"Next we'll find Mrs. Hand and find out who she wants us to take food to."

"We'll be done in time to meet the train, won't we?" Andy asked anxiously.

"Oh, yes," Suzanna assured him. Meeting the noon train, the *only* train, was the high point of the day for most people in Dodge City. Virtually everyone turned out to see who arrived and who departed.

"I hope somebody good comes today, like Mr. Foy. He said such funny things that day, even Mr. Springer laughed. I sure wish I could see his show sometime."

"I told you, they don't allow little boys in the theater."

Andy sighed dramatically. "I know, but since Mr. Foy's your friend, I thought maybe . . ." He shrugged, giving her a look she'd seen in Pistol's eyes when he was begging for a treat.

"The show is much too late, and you know it," Suzanna reminded him, trying to sound stern. If there had been any way at all, she would have allowed Andy to see the show, even though she couldn't stand the thought of taking him into the Comique where he would see the drunken cowboys and know exactly how his mother earned their living. Better he miss out on a treat and continue to believe her job was something glamorous.

"What are we gonna buy at the store?" he asked, deciding to pursue a more promising course.

"Oh, a candy stick for any good little boys I see," Suzanna teased. They chatted for a few more minutes until Mrs. Galland brought them their food.

Suzanna accepted the plate guiltily. "I still can't get used to having somebody serve me my meals."

"Oh, pshaw, you work too hard to have to cook. Besides, if you made a fire in that place where you live, you and Andy would both roast to death. Those shacks aren't big enough to whip a kitten in."

"Why'd you want to whip a kitten?" Andy asked.

Mrs. Galland winked at Suzanna. "Ask Pistol. He'd probably like to gobble it right up."

"Pistol don't eat cats," Andy scoffed, picking up a piece of toast to dip into his egg yolk.

Suzanna grabbed his wrist, stopping the bread halfway to his mouth. "And only heathens eat before they ask the blessing."

"Oops," Andy said, lowering the bread with a sheepish grin.

Mrs. Galland withdrew discreetly while Suzanna said a brief prayer. When they had finished their meal, they set out across the Front Street Plaza for Wright and Beverley's store, located directly across from the Comique Theater. Its position north of the tracks put it in the respectable part of town where men were forbidden by law to go armed and women could walk without fear of being accosted.

At this time of day no one would ever guess Dodge City was anything more than a thriving rural community. In the wide plaza, teamsters vied with farm wagons and horsemen for the right of way while pedestrians walked carefully through the clouds of dust churned up by hooves and wheels and carried by the relentless prairie wind. The carousing drovers, the slick gamblers, and even the lawmen were still abed.

Suzanna scanned the plaza, realizing with a start that she was watching for Jared Cain. How silly! she chided herself. She had never before encountered him on any of their morning excursions. Like most people who worked all night, he probably didn't rise until noon or even later. In any case, she had nothing to fear from meeting him, certainly not in broad daylight on a public street.

Calling herself a fool, she took Andy's hand. "Be careful crossing the plaza and don't let go of me until we're on the sidewalk," she cautioned.

Andy rolled his eyes in disgust. "You tell me that every time. I'm not a baby anymore."

"I know you aren't, but I feel better when you hold my hand. Don't let go of Pistol's rope, either."

Andy didn't bother replying to such a ridiculous remark. They made their way carefully through the crush of morning traffic, across the tracks and toward the sidewalk on the north side of the street. Pistol trotted along on his leash, sniffing and snorting at all the strangers.

With her free hand, Suzanna pressed a handkerchief to her nose to block out some of the dust. She couldn't help but think how the current drought would have affected their farm. If Andrew hadn't died, if they had remained on their homestead, they would have gone bust this year for sure.

Only the buffalo bones had saved them up until now.

Andrew had gathered the bones by the wagonload and carried those last remnants of the great slaughter to Dodge to sell. Shipped back East, they were used to make bone china and fertilizer. Now even the bones were growing scarce. Without a crop this summer . . .

Suzanna didn't want to contemplate what might have befallen them. And for all the good they brought, the bones had also given Andrew the cash he needed to buy liquor.

On that thought, Suzanna stopped reminiscing. No good would come from thinking of things she couldn't change. They walked into Wright and Beverley's store, and Suzanna forced herself to think about the present.

"Why don't you go pick out some candy while I find Mr. Newton?" Suzanna suggested, sending her son and his dog over to the glass counter filled with every imaginable goody while she went in search of Dodge City's unofficial banker.

When Suzanna and Andy returned home later, they found Dora Hand waiting for them. Dressed in a smart riding outfit, she was ready for the hunting trip Mayor Kelley had planned. She turned her heavily laden market basket over to Suzanna and gave her instructions on whom to visit while Kelley waited impatiently.

"Come on, Dora. The day'll be gone, and you'll still be here gabbing," he said.

"I'm coming. We'll see you later," Dora promised, giving Andy an affectionate pat on the head. "We might even bring you back a buffalo. What do you think, Jimmy?"

"If there's one left in Kansas, we'll find it," Kelley promised.

"I liked that antelope you got last time," Andy hinted.

"Then antelope it'll be," Dora agreed, hurrying off to join Kelley, who had already walked away. "We'll see you after supper."

Suzanna and Andy made their rounds, delivering Dora's gifts. After joining the rest of the townspeople at the station to meet the noon train, they ate a sumptuous dinner at Delmonico's Restaurant, Dodge City's most prestigious eatery, and wound their way back to their tiny home.

"I'm getting too old to take naps," Andy announced as they walked through the front door.

"What makes you think so?" Suzanna inquired, having heard this argument before.

"Because I am, that's why. I'm almost five. I bet five-year-olds don't have to take naps."

"All children do what their parents tell them, and your mother says you have to take a nap," Suzanna informed him.

"But I'm not sleepy."

"Well, I am. Remember, Mama has to work at night, so I have to sleep sometimes in the daytime."

"I don't have to work, so why do I have to sleep, too?"

"Because I can't trust you to stay out of trouble while I'm asleep," Suzanna replied, holding back a smile with difficulty. "Now, march into the bedroom and take off your clothes."

Even when they didn't light a fire or cook in the tiny house, the noonday sun turned it into a hotbox. Suzanna couldn't blame Andy for his reluctance to come inside on a day like this, but she desperately needed some rest. She would never make it through a night of dancing on the few hours of sleep Andy had allowed her this morning.

In deference to the heat, Andy stripped down to his underdrawers, and Suzanna to her chemise. Suzanna fell asleep almost instantly, and after considerable squirming, Andy finally dozed off, too.

He awakened less than an hour later. Taking great care not to disturb his mother, he dressed and withdrew to the front room where he pulled out the set of toy soldiers his mother had bought him at Wright and Beverley's. He and Pistol set up an elaborate battle and fought it to the last man. Several times the sounds of gunfire grew loud, but Suzanna didn't stir.

After what seemed like hours to Andy, he went back into the bedroom to check on his mother, shaking his head when he found her still fast asleep.

"She's no fun, is she?" he asked Pistol, who licked his face in reply. "I'll bet you need to go out, and she wouldn't wake up even if the whole house fell in."

Andy returned to the front room and plopped down among his soldiers again, considering the situation. "She thinks I'm a baby," he complained to the dog, "but I'm not. I could take you out just fine."

He glanced at the curtain separating the two rooms, then at the front door which Suzanna had securely bolted, and then at the dog. "Do you want to go outside, boy?" he asked hopefully.

Pistol's tale swished, and his wide mouth opened in what Andy interpreted to be a grin of agreement.

"You really do want to go out, don't you!"

Pistol's tail went berserk. He skittered over to the door and gave a woof.

"Shhh! Don't wake her up. Wait, first I gotta see if I can reach the lock."

He scrambled to his feet, grabbed one of their two straight-backed chairs, dragged it over to the door, and clambered up. When he stood on tiptoe, he could just reach the bolt, which he released with a triumphant whoop. He covered his mouth guiltily, but he heard no sound from the back room. Climbing down with more discretion than he had climbed up, he took the leash down from the nail where it hung and slipped the noose over Pistol's head.

"Come on, boy. We'll go out and come back and then we'll tell her she don't have to worry about us no more!"

Andy had a little trouble with the key, especially because Pistol kept nudging him excitedly, but soon he had the door open, and the two fugitives made their escape.

* * *

"It sure is a scorcher today," the barber remarked as Jared paid him for the shave and the bath he had just enjoyed.

"We could certainly use some rain to settle the dust," Jared replied.

"That's what I always think until it does rain, then I'm sorry I wished for it when I'm wading through a foot of mud on Front Street."

"A foot?" Jared asked dubiously.

"Or more," the barber assured him. " 'Course you only been in town a few months, and it hasn't rained to speak of, so you wouldn't know. Take my word, when a good rain comes, a fellow could lose a horse out there if he's not careful."

"I'll be careful," Jared promised soberly as he left Koch and Kelly's Pioneer Barber Shop. He paused on the sidewalk, pulled the heavy gold watch from his vest pocket, and checked the time.

Who, he wondered idly, had decreed there must be twenty-four hours in a day? Whoever it was had obviously never been at a loss as to how to fill those hours. Sighing, Jared tucked the watch away and scanned the plaza in hopes of seeing someone who might be interested in a poker game to while away the hours from now until it was time to go to work.

On the other side of the tracks he could see the Comique Theater, but he knew it would be deserted this time of day, as would most of the South Side. With another sigh, he started down the sidewalk toward the Long Branch which lay on the 'respectable' north side of Front Street. Surely there he would find someone equally anxious for a little distraction.

Closing the door softly behind them, Andy and Pistol raced around the corner and down the alley toward their favorite play area. Andy found a stick and tossed it. Pistol charged after it and proudly retrieved his prize, his rope dragging and catching in the brush.

Andy considerately slipped it off his neck and tossed it aside.

The game went well for a while, until Pistol's energy began to lag in the heat. Panting, he dropped the stick at Andy's feet and plopped down for a much-needed rest. Andy sat down beside him and scratched the dog's ears.

"Mama'll be real proud when she hears how good we done without her," Andy remarked. "She still thinks I'm . . . What is it, boy?"

Pistol's attention had strayed. For several seconds he stared alertly at something in the alley, then he bounded to his feet and barked sharply.

"What is it? What do you—? *Pistol!*" Andy cried as the dog charged down the alley. Andy took off after him, calling frantically. Ahead of them he glimpsed a streak of orange that he recognized as one of Mrs. Galland's cats. "Pistol, come back!"

Oblivious, the dog raced on, quickly outdistancing the boy. "We aren't allowed in the street!" Andy screamed as the greyhound darted between two wagons and lunged into the plaza. "Pistol, come back!"

Without hesitation, Andy squeezed between the wagons and ran right into the churning mass of animals and vehicles and dust. For a moment he lost sight of the dog. "Pistol!" he called, stumbling to a halt.

"Haw! Haw!" a man yelled, and Andy jumped back as a team of mules thundered past. "Watch where you're going, boy!"

"Pistol!" Andy ran on blindly, dodging a horseman who cursed him roundly. "Pistol!"

"Look out!" someone shouted, and Andy darted out from in front of a buggy and straight into the path of a team of oxen.

Andy had never seen anything so huge, and he froze, terrified by the giant hooves, the clanking chains, the roar of men's voices. The ground shook, and dust rose up and up, choking him as the beasts thundered closer and closer.

"Mama!" he cried in the last second before he felt a solid hit and was carried to the ground by a crushing weight.

Churning, turning, whirling, he saw sky and ground, and sky again as the unseen mass rolled and tumbled along with him. Then quite suddenly, everything went still.

"Are you all right, partner?" somebody asked him.

Andy blinked a few times to get the dirt out of his eyes. When they were clear, he saw a face he did not recognize, a man, and he was very close.

"Are you hurt anyplace, sonny?"

The man was all covered with dust, and he was hatless. And why were they both lying on the ground?

"Where . . . Where's my dog?" Andy managed.

The man smiled, a funny, crooked kind of smile. Andy wanted to smile back, but he didn't know where Pistol was.

"Anybody hurt here?"

"What happened?"

"I seen the whole thing . . ."

Suddenly, they were no longer alone. Men seemed to come from everywhere, closing in around them the way the dust had done, and for a second Andy was afraid again. The man with the crooked smile put his arms around him, though, and then he wasn't afraid anymore.

"He seems to be all right," the man said, sitting up and pulling Andy into his lap. "Did anybody see what became of the dog he was chasing?"

Andy looked around, but the men's legs were blocking his view in every direction.

"I seen the whole thing," one of the men was saying. "The boy ran out into the plaza, right smack in front of that freight wagon. Scared him senseless, I reckon, and he just stuck right there, so Cain here, he runs out and knocks the boy out of the way, slick as slobbers."

A lot of the men started speaking at once, talking

loud and saying bad words. Andy's lip started to quiver, and he felt the burning in his nose that meant he was going to cry. He didn't want to cry in front of all these men. They'd think he was a baby and tell his mother.

Andy looked at the man who was holding him to see if he was still smiling. He wasn't, but when he saw Andy's face, he pulled him closer and struggled to his feet, still holding Andy in his arms. "Let's see if we can find your dog, partner," he said.

"Here's your hat, Mr. Cain," a boy said, handing him a somewhat battered bowler.

"Thanks," Mr. Cain said, shifting Andy to one hip so he could have a hand free. When he had placed the hat on his head, he reached into his pocket and pulled out a silver dollar. "For your trouble," he said, tossing it to the boy who thanked him profusely.

"I saw the dog," another boy said, obviously hoping for a reward for himself. "He ran down thataway."

"Pistol!" Andy cried, trying to peer over the crowd.

"Pistol? Is that your dog's name?" Mr. Cain asked.

Andy nodded, not willing to trust his voice.

"It's one of Dog Kelley's hounds," someone said. "Big gray one."

"Look, here it comes now."

The crowd parted, and Andy saw Pistol trotting wearily across the plaza, skillfully dodging wagons and horses as he came.

"Pistol!" he cried, wiggling free of Mr. Cain's hold. The man set him on his feet just as Pistol lunged for them. Andy grabbed the dog around the neck and hung on as Pistol slathered his face with an affectionate tongue.

"Looks like everybody's fine now," Mr. Cain said. "Show's over, boys."

"I'll buy you a drink, Cain," someone offered.

"As soon as I find this boy's mother," Mr. Cain replied. "Anybody know where she is?"

"Don't even know *who* she is. What's your name, boy?" a strange man asked.

Andy opened his mouth, but everybody was looking at him. Their faces seemed huge, and an enormous lump lodged in his throat, blocking all sound.

"Maybe you'd better leave us alone," Mr. Cain suggested, and the others nodded and drifted away, leaving Andy alone with Mr. Cain.

"Do you know where your mother is?" Mr. Cain asked gently.

"Yes, sir," he replied, swallowing the lump and trying to sound grown-up.

"I'd better take you to her, don't you think?"

"Y . . . yes, sir," Andy admitted reluctantly.

The man's lips twitched the way Mama's did when she was trying not to laugh at something he said. "Well, then, you'll have to tell me where to find her, won't you?"

"I . . . uh . . . Are you gonna tell her what happened?" he blurted.

Mr. Cain's dark eyes narrowed thoughtfully. "No, but I think maybe you'd better tell her yourself."

Andy swallowed hard. "She'll be awful mad, and I didn't get hurt or nothing. I don't wanna make her cry."

"She's bound to hear about it sooner or later. Don't you think it would be better if she heard it from you first?"

Andy thought this over for several seconds and then nodded reluctantly.

"Then tell me where your mother is. She must be getting worried by now."

"Oh, no, she's still asleep," Andy said, scrambling to his feet.

"Asleep?"

"Yes, sir. We take a nap in the afternoon because Mama works at night and she gets tired. I woke up early, and Pistol wanted to play, so I took him out but . . ."

Mr. Cain was looking at him strangely. "Did you say your mother works at night?" Andy nodded. "Where do you live?" Andy pointed toward the South Side. Mr. Cain frowned but only for a second. "Well, then, let's get you home before she wakes up and starts to worry. Will your dog follow, or should we get a rope?"

"He follows good unless he sees a cat. I left his rope down behind the hotel. We can get it on the way."

Jared nodded absently. What a tragedy that such a fine boy belonged to one of the South Side whores. At least he didn't look neglected. Underneath the dust he had acquired rolling in the street just now, he was clean and his clothes were new and fit him well. He wore no shoes, but most boys went barefoot in the summer. Jared had done so himself in spite of his family's wealth. Jared only hoped the boy's mother was really asleep and not lying in a drunken stupor.

"What's your name?" Jared asked as he swatted the worst of the dirt from the boy's clothes and his own.

"Andy. That's short for Andrew. My papa and me had the same name, but we don't get confused 'cause he's dead now," the boy explained ingenuously.

"I see," Jared said, absurdly glad to know the boy had known his father.

They started down the alley beside the hotel. Andy easily located Pistol's rope and put it back on, although the exhausted dog had shown no further inclination to bolt.

"Mrs. Galland said Pistol liked to eat cats, but I didn't believe her. Do you know Mrs. Galland?"

"Yes, I live at the hotel."

"That's funny. I never seen you there. Me and Mama eat there almost every day."

"Do you?" he asked, wondering how a prostitute managed to afford such a luxury. "I often eat elsewhere."

"Maybe that's why," Andy supposed. "We're neighbors, though, 'cause this is where I live."

Jared stared at the little house in disbelief. "Here?"

Andy nodded. "It's kinda small, but I like it a lot better'n the house we used to have. It was dark, like a cave. From outside, you couldn't tell it was there at all except for the stovepipe."

"You lived in a dugout?" he asked, trying to piece together the facts Andy had revealed.

"Yeah, I mean, yes, sir. We had a farm before Papa died. I'm glad we moved here. I like living in town. I'm not old enough for regular school yet, but I get to go to Sunday school, and Mama says—"

"Who lives here besides you and your mother?" Jared asked, cutting him off.

"Nobody," Andy replied hesitantly, confused by the intensity of his question.

"Does your mama have any . . . friends?"

"Oh, sure. Mrs. Galland is our friend, and Mrs. Hand, and Mr. Kelley. He gave me Pistol. Did I tell you that?"

"Does she have any men friends?"

"Mr. Kelley is a man."

"No, I mean men who come to visit her here."

Andy shook his head. "She said we wasn't never to let men come in the house. Some men aren't very nice, did you know that?"

Jared nodded, feeling the strangest mixture of relief and panic. Suzanna Prentice hadn't lied to him after all. She really wasn't a harlot, and he need no longer endure the torment of jealousy of thinking her with another man. On the other hand, if she wasn't a harlot, she also wasn't the kind of woman to indulge in a casual affair. If he pursued the attraction he felt for her, she would expect the type of relationship he simply could not risk, not if he was to keep his secrets.

Jared glanced down at the boy, knowing it was already too late. The instant he had run out into the plaza to rescue the child, he had broken his cardinal rule never to become involved in other people's lives. But how could he have known the boy was Suzanna's son?

Andy had paused, his hand on the doorknob, his reluctance to face his mother painfully apparent.

"I'll go with you," Jared offered. He knew, even as he spoke, that he was only digging himself in deeper, but he couldn't resist the compulsion.

"I told you, Mama don't allow men to come in."

"Your mama won't mind," he lied. "We're friends. I work at the same place she does. Her name is Suzanna Prentice, isn't it?"

Andy's blue eyes widened in surprise. "Yeah, it is! I guess if you're friends, she won't mind, and she . . ." He looked down, embarrassed, and dug his bare toe in the dirt. "She won't yell too much in front of you either."

"Exactly what I was thinking," Jared replied with a wink.

Convinced, Andy opened the door and led Jared inside. The curtains had been drawn against the afternoon heat, but Jared was able to see the small room plainly in the dim light. Sparsely furnished with just a stove, a table, and two straight-backed chairs, it still bore the unmistakable mark of the people who lived here.

Suzanna had decorated the walls with pictures from old calendars and samples of Andy's artwork. The tablecloth had been carefully embroidered with roses, a design copied onto the chair seats and the muslin curtains. In marked contrast to his own barren room, this was a home.

Pistol immediately made for his water dish where he lapped noisily for a minute, then collapsed in a weary heap.

"Don't step on my soldiers," Andy warned in a whisper as he tiptoed across the room to the curtained doorway.

Walking carefully through the scattered toys, Jared followed him, knowing he was leaving behind the last of his good sense when he pushed aside the curtain and entered Suzanna Prentice's bedroom.

"Mama," Andy said softly, shaking her shoulder.

Jared caught his breath at the sight of her. She lay sprawled on the bed, her honey-colored hair spread out in a golden tangle, her luscious body thinly concealed by the single garment she wore. Dewed by the heat, her skin seemed to glow against the brightly colored patchwork quilt on which she lay. His mouth went dry as he watched her breasts gently rise and fall beneath the thin cotton of her chemise.

"Mama."

Suzanna heard the call dimly at first, but as always, her mother's instinct overcame her desire for sleep, and she pulled herself forcibly out of the netherworld to consciousness. "Is it time to wake up, sweetheart?" she asked hoarsely, not quite able to open her eyes yet.

"Mama, something happened."

The tone of his voice jarred her awake instantly. Her eyes flew open, taking in every detail of his appearance in a flash. "How did you get so dirty?" she asked, pushing herself up on one elbow to get a better look.

"I fell down," he said, not quite able to meet her eye.

"Where? You couldn't have gotten so dirty in the house. . . . Andy, did you go outside?"

Andy cast a desperate glance toward the doorway. Following his gaze, Suzanna at last caught sight of the man standing there. She cried out in surprise, grabbing for the corner of the quilt to cover herself. "What are you doing here?" she demanded furiously, clutching the quilt to her breasts.

He exchanged a look with Andy who turned back to face her with renewed resolution. "He bringed me home after I fell down."

"Where . . . how . . . ? All right, start at the beginning. How did you get out in the first place? The door was locked."

"I climbed up on a chair. I'm growing real big, Mama."

"So you took Pistol out after I told you not to," she

said sternly, resisting the urge to look at Cain even though she could feel those dark eyes on her still.

"Yes, ma'am. I was only gonna take him to play a little. Then I was gonna tell you so you'd know I was big enough to take him out alone." He hesitated.

"What happened?" she prompted.

"Pistol saw one of Mrs. Galland's cats and took off after it. They ran out into the plaza and . . ." Once again he cast an imploring look at Cain.

"Do you want me to tell the rest?" Cain asked with surprising gentleness.

Andy nodded, his blue eyes filling with tears.

"Andy ran out into the plaza after the dog. I guess all the wagons frightened him."

"There was this real big one, Mama," Andy continued. "It had *cows* pulling it, only they was bigger than any cows I ever saw! They was running, and I was right in front of them. I tried to run away, but I got so scared I couldn't move, so Mr. Cain, he grabbed me and got me out of the way."

Suzanna stared at her son in stricken horror for a moment as she relived the scene he had described and realized how close disaster had come. "Oh, Andy," she cried, reaching for him.

He scrambled up onto the bed and straight into her arms.

"Oh, darling, oh, baby," she crooned while he wept out his terror against her bosom. "It's all right now. Everything is all right. Mama's here. Don't cry," she urged, heedless of the tears running down her own cheeks. "I hope you understand now why Mama tells you not to go out alone."

"I do, Mama; I do," he sobbed. "I'll never ever disobey you again, not ever in my whole life!"

She smiled through her tears at the rash promise, and her gaze met Cain's. For one brief second they shared an understanding before Suzanna remembered who he was and what he had said to her just the night before. Then she realized she was clad only in her chemise. No wonder the man was looking at her!

"Uh, maybe you'll wait in the other room while I get dressed, Mr. Cain," she said, feeling the heat rise in her face.

"Of course," he replied with maddening unconcern. He stepped back and let the curtain fall into place.

Suzanna spent a few more minutes comforting Andy and eliciting promises from him never to go out without her again. When he was calm, she told him to go entertain their guest while she made herself presentable.

Not bothering with underwear, Suzanna threw on a loose-fitting dress and hastily brushed out and pinned up her hair. When she pulled back the curtain, she found Cain hunkered down on the floor beside Andy examining the set of toy soldiers.

He rose instantly, pulling off his hat—which was slightly the worse for wear, she noticed—in a belated gesture of gallantry.

"I . . . we'd like to thank you, Mr. Cain." Now she noticed other things she'd been too startled to notice before. His suit bore the same yellow blotches as Andy's clothes, as if they had both been rolling around in the dirt. "I see Andy's rescue was even more dramatic than he described," she said, indicating his suit.

Cain glanced down at his clothes. "After I grabbed him, we both fell down."

Suzanna doubted this explanation conveyed the extent of his heroism, but she was glad for an excuse not to feel overly grateful to the man. "I don't know how to thank you. If there's anything I can do for you . . ." She paused in alarm when she realized what she was saying.

Cain's eyebrows lifted, and for the first time in all the months she'd known him, he smiled. "Don't look so scared. I'm not going to suggest what you apparently think I am."

"I . . . I don't know what you mean," she murmured, knowing her crimson face gave her away.

His eyes called her a liar, but he just continued to smile. Her heart began to thud alarmingly, although she wasn't exactly sure if the reaction came from apprehension or something else.

"Andy, have you thanked Mr. Cain?" she said to break the uncomfortable silence.

"Thank you, Mr. Cain," Andy parroted. "I'm sorry you got all dirty."

"Just be sure to obey your mother from now on so nobody else has to drag you out of harm's way," he said, turning his disturbing smile on Andy who returned it cheerfully.

"I will, I promise."

Cain reached down and ruffled Andy's hair with easy affection. Startled by the uncharacteristic gesture, Suzanna could only stare. Before she gathered her wits, Cain was leaving.

"Thank you again," she called after him, knowing she owed him far more than thanks for having saved the most precious person in her world.

He paused in the doorway and looked back. Once again his eyes were devoid of expression. "I'll see you tonight," he said.

When Suzanna arrived at the theater, the show had already begun. She saw Springer standing in a corner, frowning at her late appearance, but she pinned on her professional smile and approached the first cowboy she saw.

After the excitement of the afternoon, Andy had been much too keyed-up for bed and had refused to fall asleep even after a bath and a story and a back rub. Unwilling to leave him while he was still awake for fear of what mischief he might create, she'd had no choice but to stay with him even though she knew she'd incur Springer's wrath.

Later he would lecture her on how many other girls

would give their eyeteeth to have her job and how he only kept her on because he felt sorry for her and her kid. For two cents, she'd tell him to keep his lousy job, except she knew it wasn't a lousy job at all and she'd earn almost two thousand dollars during the two months still remaining of the cattle season. Even if she could save only half of it, she and Andy would have more than enough to start their new life in Georgia.

On stage Belle Lamont, billed as "The Queen of Song," warbled the sentimental "Silver Threads Among the Gold." While Suzanna's companion listened, enraptured, Suzanna surreptitiously glanced around to find Jared Cain watching her over the faro table while his customers placed their bets. Their gazes met for no more than a second before he turned his attention back to the game, but Suzanna's heart accelerated the same way it had this afternoon when he'd looked at her.

It was only apprehension, she told herself sternly, and she really had nothing to fear from him. A word to Sam Goodwin and Jared Cain wouldn't be able to stand up straight for a month, much less do her any harm.

But was she really afraid he'd do her harm?

Fortunately, her duties kept her too busy for further contemplation. After Belle's song came the first intermission when the dancing began. The remainder of the night passed in a blur of faces, some the familiar cowboys who spent most of the summer in Dodge holding herds outside of town for fattening, and some strangers whom she would never see again.

Near the end of the night, Sam Goodwin caught her eye between dances and motioned her over.

"I got a message for you, Miz Prentice," he explained.

"Andy?" she asked in alarm. The boy hadn't been far from her thoughts all evening.

"Oh, no, nothing like that," he assured her hastily. "I reckon you're right to worry, though. I heard what happened this afternoon. If Cain hadn't've been there . . ." Sam shook his head solemnly.

"I'm just thankful he was," Suzanna said, not allowing herself to dwell on it. "What message did you have for me?"

"It's from Mr. Cain. He wants you to save him the last dance."

"He does, does he?" Suzanna snapped, furious to think that Cain had decided he could take advantage of her gratitude.

"Now don't get mad," Sam said in dismay. "He didn't say it like that at all."

"How did he say it?"

"He said . . ." Sam wrinkled his brow as he tried to recall. "He said, 'Ask Mrs. Prentice if she would do me the honor of saving the last dance for me.' "

"Oh," Suzanna said, feeling foolish. "I . . . Of course I will."

She glanced around, but Cain was absorbed in his game and did not look up. What now? she asked herself as she wandered back toward the dance floor in search of another partner. She didn't have to wait long to find out. At the end of the next reel, Eddie Foy announced the last dance, and Jared Cain appeared out of nowhere to claim it.

Suzanna waved away the offered token, but he pressed it into her hand anyway. "You might as well take it," he said. "It's paid for, and I certainly have no intention of dancing with anyone else in this place."

She went warily into his arms, unusually conscious of his closeness. Ordinarily, she felt little or no physical reaction to her partners unless one of them particularly repelled her. With Cain things were entirely different. He was no faceless customer, no partner to be forgotten as soon as the music ended. Now he was a person she knew, and someone to whom she owed a debt. Suzanna didn't like to be indebted.

"How is Andy doing?" Cain asked.

"He's fine, although he was still so excited, I could

hardly get him to sleep. I was late because I didn't dare leave him alone for fear of what trouble he might get into.''

"You leave him alone while you work?'' Cain asked, frowning in disapproval.

She felt a twinge of guilt, but she refused to let Cain see it. "I don't have any choice,'' Suzanna defended herself. "No woman in town is willing to take care of a child whose mother works in a dance hall.''

"I can see you've tried to find someone,'' he said sympathetically.

Suzanna didn't need any sympathy. "Andy and I have discovered we can get along very well without help,'' she said stiffly.

"Like this afternoon?'' he inquired, reminding Suzanna of the debt she found so galling. Her conscience pricked her.

"Mr. Cain, I—''

"Before you thank me again, I believe I owe you an apology,'' he said.

"You do?''

"Yes, I . . . uh, I made certain incorrect assumptions about your character. I was insulting, and I apologize.''

Suzanna stared at him in astonishment. Was this the same Jared Cain who had been so obnoxious the other night? Of course, three months in a dance hall had taught Suzanna a man would say anything to get his way with a woman. She frowned skeptically. "Why have you decided I'm not a harlot, Mr. Cain? Just because I have a child?''

"Many of the women on the South Side have children. It's a natural consequence of their work,'' he pointed out with a hint of the smile she had seen this afternoon.

"Then why?'' she insisted, ignoring her burning cheeks.

"Andy told me you weren't.''

"What?''

"Oh, not in so many words," he assured her. "I merely made some discreet inquiries, and he gladly told me your whole history. You're the widow of a homesteader, and you don't allow any men to come into your house."

"I'd be more flattered if you said my ladylike behavior had changed your mind."

"Ladylike behavior? You make your living by cheating cowboys out of their hard-earned pay."

"I don't cheat anyone! Men come here to dance and enjoy themselves, and they pay for the privilege. If anyone cheats them, it's the *gamblers*," she said perversely, even though she knew Cain ran an honest game.

He nodded to concede her point. "You're a difficult woman to apologize to, Mrs. Prentice."

Once again Cain had managed to prick her conscience. Good heavens, the man had saved her son's life and was trying to tell her he was sorry for having misjudged her. Why was she being so ungracious? "I . . . I'm sorry. I guess I'm still a little upset about what happened this afternoon."

"Perfectly understandable."

"But it's no excuse to be rude after what you did. I accept your apology, Mr. Cain. Will you accept mine?"

"Only if you promise not to thank me again."

She smiled in spite of herself. "Agreed."

The music stopped, and the Texans whooped exuberantly as they dashed for the bar to retrieve their firearms. Most of the girls were already heading for Springer's office, lining up to get paid. In a moment, Suzanna and Cain were the only couple left on the floor.

Suzanna studied him, trying to decide if she had misjudged him. Until today she had seen only his emotionless gambler's facade, but this afternoon he'd been gentle and friendly with Andy, and tonight he'd been courteous and had even apologized for having insulted her. If anyone else had saved Andy's life, she would have already made some effort to show her gratitude. She'd hesitated to properly thank Jared Cain because she feared he might try to take advantage of the situation. Somehow, she no longer feared that possibility.

"Mr. Cain, if you won't let me thank you, the least you can do is allow me to fix you a home-cooked meal. I'm a very good cook and—"

"No, thank you," he said quickly, stiffening. "I don't think that would be a very good idea."

"Why not?" she asked, but he ignored her question.

"I hope Andy is none the worse for his experience this afternoon. Please send him my regards." He sketched a little bow, turned on his heel, and left her standing openmouthed.

"So much for rudeness," she muttered in disgust, hoping her face wasn't as red as it felt. Last night he'd certainly been eager enough to go to her house. Why had he changed his mind so suddenly?

The truth came in a blinding flash: if he couldn't have her body, he simply wasn't interested. She shouldn't have been surprised. In fact, she should have been relieved to be rid of a man like that.

Unfortunately, she didn't feel a bit relieved.

Chapter 3

"**D**ora, what do you know about Jared Cain?" Suzanna asked the next morning while they walked back from delivering Dora Hand's gifts of food to the needy people in the poorer section of Dodge. Andy had run a half-block ahead of them with Pistol, the maximum distance Suzanna allowed.

"The gambler? Not much. Keeps to himself most of the time. He's a handsome devil, though, isn't he?" she asked slyly.

" 'Handsome is as handsome does,' my mother always said," Suzanna replied primly.

"Why are you interested then?"

"Because he saved Andy's life yesterday." Briefly, she told Dora the story.

"Good heavens! Seems like our Mr. Cain is something of a hero."

"I'm not too sure. Remember the other night when you and Mr. Kelley walked me home because I'd had some trouble with a customer? Cain was the customer. He wanted to buy my 'services,' and he wouldn't accept my refusal."

"Hmmm." Dora looked sly again. "Maybe he latched onto Andy so he could get in good with you."

"He didn't know Andy was my son until afterwards."

"Of course he'd say that."

"No, that's what Andy said. He told me Cain was very surprised to find out he lived in my house."

"Cain knew where you lived?" Dora asked, not bothering to hide her grin.

"It's a small town," Suzanna argued.

"Do *you* know where *he* lives?"

"Of course not. Don't change the subject."

"He lives at the Western. He probably saw you going down the alley one night and followed you. Anyway, to answer your original question, Jared Cain is from the East—Maryland or Pennsylvania, I'd guess—and from a good family."

"I thought you didn't know anything about him."

"I can tell by his accent. And he's educated. Probably even went to college. He runs an honest game, too, or so Jimmy claims. I figured he must keep a woman, though, since he never flirts with any of the girls."

"Maybe he has a sweetheart back East," Suzanna guessed in the same spirit. "Or maybe she died, and he vowed to be true to her memory."

"Until he saw you, and he knew he couldn't live alone for the rest of his life," Dora finished in the voice she usually reserved for the stage.

"He's changed his mind, then," Suzanna said wryly. "I invited him to supper, and he turned me down."

"He did? Why?"

"He said it wouldn't be a good idea, whatever that means."

"Hmmm," Dora said again, staring at Suzanna thoughtfully.

"Oh, please, no more wild explanations!" Suzanna begged with a laugh.

"No, this is serious. I'm trying to figure out what happened here. Jared Cain wanted to buy you, but when he found out he couldn't, he didn't want you at all. Surely he knows he could've had you for free. A lonely widow is easy pickings for a clever, charming man, especially one as handsome as he is."

"I'm not 'easy pickings,' " Suzanna protested, stung.

"Honey, we're all easy pickings," Dora said. "Look how quick I fell for Jimmy, and heavens knows, he's nothing to look at. Of course a divorced woman on the shady side of thirty can't be too choosy—"

"You could have your pick of men in this town," Suzanna insisted loyally, making Dora smile.

"And if I did, I'd still pick Jimmy. The question is, would you pick Jared Cain?"

"Good morning, ladies," a male voice said, saving Suzanna from answering.

"Good morning, Wyatt," Dora replied, smiling at Dodge City's marshal. "You're out mighty early." The policemen in town usually slept until noon since they worked all night.

"I had court this morning."

"You know Mrs. Prentice, don't you?" Dora said.

"Ma'am," Earp said, tipping his hat.

"Marshal," she replied, noting what an attractive man he was with his neatly trimmed mustache and dapper clothes. Surely, he was as handsome as Jared Cain. Why hadn't she ever felt the least bit disturbed by *his* presence?

"I hear you and the mayor got yourselves an antelope yesterday," Earp said to Dora.

"Yes, although Jimmy and I didn't have much to do with it. Those dogs of his ran the poor thing to ground all by themselves."

"Those dogs are a wonder, all right. I guess General Custer did something right after all."

"Not to hear Jimmy tell it," Dora said. "He claims that when he was Custer's aide, *he* was the one who taught the general everything he knew about training those hounds and breeding them, too."

"Well, no matter who taught who, any dog that can run down an antelope is a dog worth having. Your son's a lucky boy, Miz Prentice."

"Yes, he is," Suzanna replied, surprised Earp knew Andy owned one of the mayor's hounds.

Earp smiled at her expression. "Just about everybody in town saw the two of them out in the plaza yesterday."

"I'm sorry I went hunting," Dora said. "Seems I missed all the excitement."

There was a loud *Woof!* and Pistol and Andy came charging up behind the marshal. "Mama, what's taking you so long?" Andy demanded, skidding to a halt and gazing up adoringly at Earp, one of his idols.

"Mr. Earp was just telling me he saw you and Pistol in the plaza yesterday," Suzanna explained.

"We aren't supposed to go out without Mama anymore," Andy explained to Earp, who nodded solemnly.

"I hope I don't see you out alone then. I'd hate to have to arrest you."

Andy's eyes grew wide for a moment until he noticed Earp's lips twitch. "You're teasing me," he accused. "You don't arrest kids."

Earp glanced at Suzanna. "You'll wish I did if your Mama ever catches you out alone again."

"You're absolutely right, Marshal," Suzanna said.

Andy grinned innocently, promising nothing.

After a few more minutes of idle conversation, Earp bid them good morning and went on about his business. Andy and Pistol ran off again, impatient with the women's slower pace.

"Mr. Earp is such a nice man. It's hard to believe his reputation," Suzanna remarked.

"Bat Masterson says he's the softest-hearted gunfighter he's ever known, and with all the hundreds of people Wyatt's arrested, he's never killed a single man. But you'll never guess what Jimmy told me."

"What?"

"Seems the Texans aren't too pleased with the way Wyatt upholds the law in this town. Jimmy heard that some of them have put up a thousand-dollar bounty for the man who kills Wyatt Earp.''

"Good heavens! Do you think anyone would be foolish enough to stand up to Wyatt Earp?''

"Nobody said they'd have to face him. A man can die from a bullet in the back just the same as a bullet in the front.''

Suzanna shuddered to think what a lawless place Dodge City had become, when a police officer could be murdered simply for doing his duty too well. The sooner she and Andy got away from here, the better.

"Belle, you are my dearest duck,'' Eddie Foy informed the Queen of Song.

"Foy, you are trying to stuff me,'' Belle Lamont replied, and the cowboys roared.

Maisie and Suzanna exchanged a look of infinite weariness. "Fanny'll sing soon,'' Suzanna said encouragingly. "She's doing 'Home Sweet Home' tonight.'' Fanny Garrettson was Dora Hand's best friend from the two years they had worked together in St. Louis before coming to Dodge.

"I like the way Dora does it better,'' Maisie replied.

"You'll have to wait for another night, then.''

"Or maybe I should start going to church. I hear Dora's gonna sing there, too. Pretty soon there won't be no place in town where she *doesn't* sing.''

"Careful, Maisie. People might think you're jealous.''

"I am. If I could sing, I wouldn't have to wear out my feet every night. Can you imagine, I used to think dancing was *fun!*''

"Only two more months until the season ends,'' Suzanna reminded her with a laugh. "You can already see the crowds are smaller than they were a few weeks ago.''

"Which only means Springer'll probably let some of us go.''

"Oh, dear, I hadn't thought of that." Suzanna sighed. "Now I have one more thing to worry about."

Maisie clicked her tongue in disapproval. "Woman like you shouldn't have to worry. You should have a man to take care of you."

Suzanna resisted the urge to point out that Maisie had a man and she was working right alongside Suzanna.

"And speaking of men," Maisie continued, "has Cain made you any more offers lately?"

"Maisie," Suzanna warned.

Maisie grinned, unrepentant. "He saved your kid's life, Suzie. Don't you think you owe him something?"

"I offered to cook him supper."

Maisie giggled suggestively. "If you want him, you'll have to offer him more than food."

"What makes you think I want him?" Suzanna demanded, trying to work up the outrage she knew she should be feeling.

"Oh, I don't know. Maybe the way you keep looking over at his table between every dance."

"I do not!"

" 'Course, he keeps watching you, too, when he thinks you're too busy to notice."

"He does not. . . . Does he?"

"Sure he does," Maisie said smugly. "I wouldn't tease about a thing like that."

Suzanna glanced over at Jared Cain's faro table. His dark head was bent over the layout, his equally dark eyes intent on watching his customers place their bets. Then, as if he felt her gaze on him, he looked up, and their eyes met for a moment before Suzanna turned quickly back to Maisie.

"See what I mean?" Maisie asked. "He's still looking."

"Stop it, Maisie. We're acting like schoolgirls," Suzanna said, mortified.

"You girls don't get paid to warm the benches," Mr. Springer informed them sharply.

They both jumped up guiltily. "Sorry, Mr. Springer," Suzanna muttered, recalling Maisie's prediction that Springer would soon be firing some of the hostesses. She hurried off to find a potential partner.

On the stage, Fanny Garrettson had begun singing 'Home Sweet Home.' Suzanna sought out a cowboy who looked especially homesick. Comforting him would take her mind off whether or not Jared Cain was watching her.

By Friday night, three days after Cain had rescued Andy, Suzanna had begun to feel Cain's presence like a burden. She avoided the gambling tables so conscientiously that Springer had chastened her for not urging her partners to gamble, which was considered part of her job.

"Is that Bat Masterson?" Suzanna's latest partner, a short, chunky fellow, asked her as they wandered amidst the gambling tables.

Suzanna glanced at the trim, good-looking man dealing Spanish monte at one of the tables. "Yes, that's our sheriff," she confirmed.

"Who's the scrawny fellow with him?"

"Doc Holliday," Suzanna replied.

"Shit," the cowboy said, dragging the word out to three syllables. "I figured Doc Holliday'd be a lot bigger. This fellow looks kinda used up."

"He's consumptive, you know. They say he came west for his health."

The cowboy grinned expansively. "He won't get no better hanging around saloons."

"I'll be glad to tell him you said so," Suzanna teased, making him blanch.

"Oh, no, don't do that," the cowboy pleaded. He had no way of knowing Suzanna had never once spoken to Doc Holliday and never planned to. "Let's dance."

They joined a square just as the music began. As usual Eddie Foy stood on the stage calling the steps.

"Allemande right . . . do-si-do your partner . . . all join hands and circle left . . ."

Suzanna's feet were saying 3 A.M., and her face rebelled at any more smiles. Maybe since business was dropping off, Springer would fire her, and she'd have no choice but to go east right away instead of waiting until fall. Oh, well, hadn't she already decided Dodge City was becoming too dangerous a place for Andy?

Bang!

The gunshot exploded through the room, and in an instant, everyone hit the floor amidst shouts and screams. Suzanna dropped down, too, looking for the cloud of powder smoke to tell her from where the shot had come.

"It's outside," someone yelled. "Out in the street."

Another shot splintered the flimsy outside wall of the Comique.

"Oh, God, they'll kill us all!" a woman yelled, and another started sobbing.

"Andy!" Suzanna cried, thinking of her baby all alone. If the gunfire awakened him, he'd be terrified, and—oh, dear heaven, what if the shooters were on a rampage, shooting up the town? What if a bullet smashed into her tiny house and . . . ?

She was on her feet in an instant, running for the door. Another shot exploded into the room, but she didn't care. She had to get to Andy.

From the corner of her eye, she saw someone else up and running, but it didn't matter. Nothing mattered except getting to her baby.

"Suzanna!"

She looked up instinctively as Jared Cain grabbed her and pulled her to the floor. She fought like a wildcat.

"Let me go! Andy's all alone and—"

"He'll really be all alone if his mother gets killed." Cain wrapped an arm around her waist and dragged her behind an overturned table as yet another shot rang out. "Hold still. Ouch! And quit kicking!"

He threw a leg over hers and pressed his chest to hers, to hold her still.

"He'll be scared if he wakes up!" Suzanna cried hysterically, struggling ineffectually against Cain's strength.

"They aren't shooting at *him*, for God's sake. This'll be over in a minute, then you can go to him." He turned her head so their faces were only inches apart. "Suzanna, listen to me. Andy will be fine, but you won't be if you run outside into the middle of a gunfight!"

Another explosion splintered the wall above their heads. Suzanna cried out in terror, and Cain pulled her head to his shoulder. "It's all right," he said, crooning the way she had crooned to comfort Andy after his fright the other day.

Trembling, Suzanna clung to him, desperate for the strength he offered. "Oh, Jared," she whispered, not even certain she had said the words aloud.

But Jared heard them. "It's all right, sweet lady. I'm here," he said against her temple. His breath was soft and warm, his body hard and strong, and she needed someone so badly.

"I'm scared," she said, and the confession encompassed far more than the bullets crashing around them.

"I know," he said, and for some reason Suzanna truly believed he understood the pain and the loneliness and the fear.

She lifted her head so she could see his eyes, and in them she saw all her own vulnerability reflected back at her. "Jared?"

The word held a thousand questions, but he answered none of them. Instead, he pressed his lips to hers, hungrily, urgently. She responded from the depths of her own despair, clutching, clinging, tasting, touching.

For a few wild seconds they were alone in the world, two people who had overcome insurmountable obstacles to find each other. More shots were fired, farther away now, but neither of them heard as their bodies spoke to each other in the language older than words.

"Somebody tried to kill the marshal!" a man shouted.

Suzanna and Jared jerked apart, startled back to reality.

All around them men were scrambling to their feet and shouting questions. Bat Masterson leaped over them as he raced for the door.

Suzanna stared at Cain in horror. What had she done? How could she have kissed a perfect stranger—and kissed him so passionately—in such a public place while death whizzed all around them? How could she have forgotten the danger? How could she have forgotten *Andy*?

She struggled free of Cain's embrace. "I have to get to Andy," she said.

"I'll go with you."

"No!" she cried, more afraid of him than she had been of the bullets. She lunged to her feet and threw herself into the throng of bodies surging toward the door. Vaguely, she heard the shouted conversations around her.

"Who done it?"

"Some Texans, prob'ly."

"Did they get Earp?"

"Ten dollars says they didn't."

Once outside Suzanna broke free of the crowd which was surging toward the river and the toll bridge across which any fugitives would have to flee. She ran in the opposite direction, heedless of her footing in the pitch darkness as she turned down the alley toward the silent little shack where Andy was.

"Andy, Andy!" she called as she reached the door. "Mama's here!" Panic claimed her when she realized she didn't have the key—she'd left her purse at the Comique. Frantically, futilely, she tried the knob. "Andy?"

Tears of frustration burned her eyes. She pressed her

ear to the door, listening for the sounds of weeping from within. It came faintly, but as she strained to hear, she recognized the sound as Pistol's whining.

"What's the matter?" Cain asked, materializing out of the darkness.

"I can't . . . The door's locked," she stammered, surprised to realize she was crying.

"Can you hear him? Is he awake?"

She shook her head, swiping at the tears. "I hear the dog, that's all."

He pushed her gently away from the door and pressed his own ear to the wood. After a few moments, he straightened up. "Seems like he slept through the whole thing."

Suzanna clamped both hands over her mouth to smother the sob that wrenched from her, and once again Cain took her in his arms.

"Please, don't," she begged even as she collapsed against him.

But his touch held no trace of the passion that had flared between them moments ago.

She didn't want to cry on his shoulder, but her need was greater than her resolve. For a few moments she indulged herself in the luxury of human comfort, though she didn't dare surrender completely to her terrors, lest she drown them both in her tears.

She pulled out of his arms, scrubbing ruthlessly at the moisture on her face. "I'm sorry. I . . . I don't usually . . ."

"Nothing to be sorry about. You're a very brave lady."

"Brave?" she echoed incredulously. Surely he at least suspected how many things she feared.

"Yes, brave. A coward would never be able to leave him alone at all."

"I don't have a choice!"

"Yes, you do. You could have stayed in your dugout and starved to death. It takes a lot of courage to go to the Comique every night."

He was right, of course, although she'd never thought of it that way.

"Here." He pressed a handkerchief into her hands.

Gratefully, she wiped her tear-ravaged face. "Thank you. I'll wash it for you," she said when she had composed herself.

"Are you ready to go back?"

"I couldn't work now!" she protested.

"I doubt anyone else could either. You'll want to get your pay, though, won't you? And your key?"

"Oh, yes, I forgot." She glanced uncertainly at the house.

"If you like, I'll stay here until you get back."

"No, I . . . Andy will be fine for a few more minutes. I'm just being foolish."

"It's not foolish for a mother to worry about her child."

She smiled at him in the darkness. "It's foolish to run through a hail of bullets to get to him, though. At least that's what a wise man once told me."

"It's just common sense. Come on. I'm anxious to find out if Wyatt got hurt."

"Oh, dear, I'd forgotten what all the shooting was about in the first place." She fell in step beside him as they walked back up the alley. Oddly, she felt no embarrassment or unease at being alone with him like this, and he seemed to feel none either. Perhaps he realized the kiss they had shared was nothing more than an aberration caused by the unusual circumstances. She certainly hoped so. It would be awfully awkward to explain that she really felt none of the passion she had displayed earlier.

By the time they reached the Comique, the crowd was returning from the toll bridge. In the moonlight, Suzanna could make out several men carrying a burden between them. She quickly realized it was a man stretched out on a plank of some sort.

"Someone's been hurt!" she cried, quickening her pace. Many of the dance-hall girls were clustered in the street, watching the returning procession. Maisie waved to her from the group, and Suzanna hurried over. "Was the marshal shot?"

"No, it was some cowboy," Maisie explained. "Marshal Earp was standing outside the Comique, and this fellow just rode right up to him and started shooting. God in heaven, he could've killed a dozen people inside the theater."

"How did he get shot?"

"Earp fired back at him, of course. Don't know how he hit him in the dark on a running horse, but he did. Say, where'd you get off to, and wasn't that Jared Cain you were with?" Maisie asked, peering into the darkness behind Suzanna.

"I went home to make sure the gunfire didn't wake Andy up."

"He's prob'ly used to hearing shots at night."

"Not so many or so close, or at least that's what I figured, but he didn't wake up."

"And what about Cain?"

"He . . . he just went with me, that's all. Does anybody know who the man was who got shot?" Suzanna asked to change the subject.

"I ain't heard. I reckon everybody'll know by tomorrow morning, though."

When the procession carrying the wounded cowboy had passed, the crowd began to disperse. The dancehall girls and the gamblers returned to the theater. Suzanna realized Jared Cain had left his table—and several thousand dollars—unattended to accompany her to her house. Fortunately, no one had thought to bother any of the gambling tables during the excitement.

When Suzanna had received her wages for the evening, she quickly retrieved her purse and made her way out of the theater. She looked around for Cain, knowing she should thank him for what he had done for her this evening, but he had apparently already left.

Hurrying down the sidewalk, she didn't notice the figure standing in the shadows. "Suzanna?"

She jumped, frightened until she recognized Cain.

"I didn't mean to scare you," he said. She noticed he carried his faro layout bundled under his arm. "I waited to make sure you got home safely."

The ease she'd felt with him before evaporated as she wondered exactly why he was so interested in getting her home safely, but she did remember her manners. "I . . . I never thanked you. Now you've saved my life, too."

"I'm afraid you're giving me more credit than I deserve," he said as they started walking toward the alley.

"I don't think so," Suzanna replied uneasily.

They walked on in silence, and with each step Suzanna grew more aware of her vulnerability. The strength she had admired in Cain only a few minutes ago now seemed ominous. What would happen when they reached her house? Would Cain expect a more tangible expression of her gratitude? How could she possibly prevent him from taking it if she refused . . . and did she even want to refuse?

Shocked by the thought, Suzanna glanced up at him, noting his fine profile and masculine physique. Memories of the kiss they'd shared rushed back, unbidden. Longing tingled through her, and she recalled Dora's assertion that she would be easy prey for a handsome, charming man.

No! she thought frantically. She was still a decent woman, no matter where she worked, no matter what the 'good' people of Dodge City thought. She wouldn't give in to the loneliness, wouldn't compromise her principles even though her very bones ached for the comfort she knew she would find in Jared Cain's arms.

When they turned down the alley, they stepped into complete darkness. Suzanna hefted her purse which contained the small pistol she carried for protection. She'd never actually planned to shoot anyone with it,

only to use it as a threat in case she was accosted.
Could she use it to warn Cain off? Could she point a
gun at a man she knew, a man to whom she owed so
much? The very thought appalled her.

Still, she wasn't about to go to bed with him either.
"Jared?" she said through a constricted throat.

"Yes?"

"I . . ." How on earth did a woman explain such a
thing? In the life Suzanna had led, the subject of sex
was not even discussed with one's husband. Of course,
her life had changed drastically since then. "I can't
invite you in," she finally managed to say as they
reached her house.

Cain stopped dead in his tracks, and even in the
darkness she could feel the anger emanating from him.
Instinctively, she clutched at her purse.

"I'm only walking you home, Suzanna. I have no
intention of asking you for anything else."

Suzanna stared at him in the darkness, the weight
of her gun-laden purse heavy in her hands. She felt an
utter fool. "I . . . I'm sorry. I didn't mean . . . After
what happened, I thought . . . you'd expect . . ."

He sighed wearily, and Suzanna would have given
a lot to see his expression. "I've learned not to take
anything for granted in this world, Suzanna, and
please believe me, even if you were willing, you
shouldn't get involved with me. No woman should."

She had no idea how to answer, and before she could
decide, he said, "You'd better get inside now. I'll wait
to make sure Andy is all right."

She fumbled in her purse for the key, trying not to
think about the gun she had to push aside to get to it.
As she fitted the key in the lock, she could hear Pistol
whining on the other side of the door, eager for her
arrival.

"Don't bark," she commanded, opening the door.
She hurried into the house, dropped her purse on the
table, and went straight into the bedroom to check on
Andy. Finding him asleep, she returned to the front

room. Cain still stood in the doorway, although he remained properly on the other side of the threshold. Pistol sat nearby, keeping a watchful eye.

"Andy's fine. He probably didn't hear a thing," she said, fumbling in the dark for the matches on the table. She struck one and lit the lamp.

When she turned back to Cain, she caught him looking around the room with what she assumed was a critical eye.

"It's awfully small," she said, feeling defensive, "but Andy and I don't need much more room."

"I was just thinking you've made this place into a real home," he said with a wistful smile. "I noticed it when I brought Andy home, too. After being here, the prospect of returning to my hotel room isn't very inviting."

"Oh," she said, resisting an urge to invite him to stay. This was ridiculous! Just a minute ago she was frantic at the thought he might force his way in, and now she suddenly didn't want him to leave. "I . . . uh, thank you for . . . for everything you did tonight."

Obviously uncomfortable with her gratitude, he shifted his feet and reached up to button his coat. "There's no need . . . Oh, drat." The button had come off in his hand. "Another casualty of the evening," he said with a smile, dropping it into his pocket.

"I'll be happy to sew it on for you," Suzanna offered, absurdly glad for the excuse to have him stay for a few more minutes. She really was being ridiculous, but she no longer cared.

"You don't have to . . ." he began, but Suzanna was already ushering him into the house.

"It'll only take a minute, and it's the least I can do. Take off your coat," she said as she ducked into the other room to fetch her sewing basket. When she returned, he had removed the coat and laid it on the table. He stood back in the doorway, although this time he was on the inside. Common sense told her he was trying to catch the slight breeze, but he looked more as if he were simply being wary.

Setting the basket on the table, she pulled out a chair and sat down. She motioned to the other chair. "Have a seat."

"I've been sitting all night," he replied, slipping his hands into his pockets and rocking back on his heels. "It feels good to stretch a little."

Suzanna rummaged in the basket for needle and thread. Conscious that he was watching her every move, she felt awkward and had a little trouble threading the needle. At last she was ready, and she picked up the coat. The fine fabric was smooth to the touch and redolent of Jared Cain. The scent brought memories flooding back, memories of being held against this very jacket. Her hand trembled slightly as she reached into the pocket for the button.

"What brought you to Dodge City?" she asked to fill the uncomfortable silence.

"Money, of course. I've been working the cattle towns for several years, and Dodge City is the biggest of them all."

She positioned the button and began to sew. "You've always been a gambler, then?" she asked, remembering Dora's theory about his past.

"Since I left home, yes." Something in his tone warned her not to pursue the subject.

"You were very good with Andy the other day," she ventured, and was rewarded with a small smile.

"Andy is a fine boy. You must be very proud."

"Not really. Mostly I just feel lucky to have him."

Cain nodded his understanding and a shadow darkened his eyes. "It's a shame his father won't get to see him grow up."

Suzanna had often thought the same thing, but she usually reminded herself that Andy was probably fortunate not to be raised by the man Andrew had become. She pulled the thread through one last time and knotted it. "I know he misses not having a man around," she remarked.

She glanced up at Cain and froze. Once again his eyes held the longing and despair she had seen earlier. "I can't be that man, Suzanna, no matter how much I might want to be."

"No one asked you to," she said, stung.

For a long moment they stared at each other across the small room. Suzanna seethed with outrage, but in all honesty she had to admit her idle words might have seemed like a hint to him. She couldn't even say for sure that they hadn't been.

Finally he said, "Are you finished with my coat?"

"What? Oh, yes," she said, having completely forgotten it. She quickly bit off the thread and set the needle aside. Rising from her chair, she handed the garment to him.

He took it gingerly, being careful not to touch her. "Thank you," he said, slipping it on. He tugged lightly on the button and slipped it through the hole. "You did a nice job."

Nothing any other housewife in the country couldn't have done, she thought, but she said, "You're welcome."

He frowned at the coldness of her tone and for a moment looked as if he would say more. Then, suddenly, he reassumed his blank gambler's expression. "I'd better be going now. Good night."

"Good night," she replied, automatically moving to close the door behind him. He didn't leave until he heard the bolt slide home, and she listened intently until his footsteps faded.

Tears burned her eyes, and she scolded herself for being so weak. After all the things she'd been through tonight, why should she cry because Jared Cain didn't want her? She didn't want him either.

Did she?

* * *

By the next morning, everyone in town was discussing the attempt on Marshal Earp's life. The cowboy had been identified as George Hoyt, and the Dodge City police force had located his name on a list of fugitives wanted by the Texas authorities.

Suzanna heard all this from Dora, whose sources of information were unimpeachable. When Suzanna arrived at work that night, the girls were crowing over a new bit of information.

"Did you hear?" Maisie asked Suzanna the instant she entered the theater.

"Hear what?"

"That fellow what shot at the marshal. He talked this afternoon. Said some rich Texans'd hired him to do the job. Said they promised if he done it, they'd get the warrant against him squashed."

" 'Quashed,' " Polly Evans corrected importantly. "Sam told me all about it. He got it from Earp his own self."

"He's still alive, then?" Suzanna asked. "The cowboy, I mean."

"Yeah, but Doc McCarty don't expect him to last," Polly explained. "Earp got him low down in the back while he was riding away."

"Nobody's taking credit for hiring him, but he's got lots of friends," Maisie continued. "The Texans took up a collection to pay his doctor bills. I guess none of 'em have any love for Earp."

"I sure don't have any love for him anymore either," Eddie Foy announced from the hall. "Look what he did to my suit."

Foy turned to display a bullet hole smack in the middle of the coat.

"Good heavens!" Suzanna exclaimed. "You aren't hurt, are you?"

"I would've been if I'd been wearing the coat," Foy explained, pulling one of his comic faces. "Luckily, it was hanging on a chair backstage when it got ventilated."

Suzanna and the rest of the girls laughed, and Foy

feigned outrage. "I paid eleven dollars for this suit. It's brand-new."

"Too bad there wasn't a reward for killing your suit, Eddie," Maisie teased, making everyone laugh again.

Shaking her head in amusement, Suzanna hurried back to the bar to check her purse with the bartender. She glanced surreptitiously over at Cain's table and missed a step when she saw someone else setting up the faro layout. Cain was nowhere in sight.

She found Sam Goodwin leaning against a wall near the back of the room. "Sam, do you know where Mr. Cain is?"

"Sure, he's in the back room. Some cattlemen wanted a high-stakes poker game. You know he usually plays poker on Saturday night."

Of course she had known. How silly of her to be worried about him. He was nothing to her, after all. She should be glad he wouldn't be in the hall tonight. After last night, she needed some time to regain her equilibrium. Tomorrow, Sunday, was her night off, and by the time she encountered Cain again on Monday, she should be able to face him without a qualm.

She hoped.

Unfortunately, by Sunday morning, Suzanna had come to the disconcerting conclusion that she missed Cain. While she and Andy sat in church, she found her mind wandering from Reverend Wright's sermon to thoughts of the way Jared Cain's graceful hands worked the cards and how he had caressed her so gently.

Sensitive to her inattention, Andy squirmed in his seat and began to kick the bench in front of them. Only when the occupant of that bench, a prune-faced matron, turned and glared, did Suzanna notice Andy's restlessness and quietly reprimand him.

I'm only tired, she excused herself. By the evening service I'll be more awake and able to concentrate.

Just as Reverend Wright had suspected, Dora Hand's performance attracted a record crowd to the Union

Church that evening. Not everyone was delighted, of course. Several matrons pointedly ignored Dora's presence as they glided into the building to find their seats.

"I'm sorry they're so rude," Suzanna whispered to her friend. The two of them were standing outside the church until time for the service to begin.

"Maybe you shouldn't sit with me. They'll be annoyed with you, too."

"Oh, no one ever speaks to me anyway," Suzanna said lightly, effectively concealing her bitterness. "I'm even more of a scarlet woman than you are."

For a moment Dora looked puzzled, but then she recalled Suzanna's 'transgression.' "Surely they don't hold that against you."

"Why wouldn't they?"

"Because they must know you didn't really seduce that horrible man. No one could possibly believe such a story."

"His wife believed it," Suzanna reminded her.

"She *chose* to believe it because it's much more convenient to get rid of your maid than to get rid of your husband."

"Then her friends chose to believe it, too. None of them speak to me anymore, either. But the men are the worst. The way they look at me, as if they thought . . ." She shuddered.

"But they don't really think so. They *couldn't*," Dora insisted.

"Some of them do. The problem is trying to decide which ones are just trying to be kind and which ones are trying to . . . Well, anyway, it's just one more reason not to trust men in general."

"Suzanna," Dora began, but fortunately, Reverend Wright approached them just then, saving Suzanna from a lecture on how not all men were scoundrels.

"Good evening, ladies. We seem to have a full house tonight."

"Which is what you hoped would happen when you

invited Dora to sing in the first place,'' Suzanna reminded the minister cheerfully.

"You're absolutely right, Mrs. Prentice. I just hope they all stay to hear my sermon. Where's that boy of yours?''

Suzanna pointed to where Andy and a few other boys his age were roughhousing in the churchyard.

"I heard about his escapade in the plaza the other day,'' the minister added. "I'm glad he wasn't hurt.''

"So am I,'' Suzanna replied. "I think he understands now why he's not allowed out without me.''

"We're all very grateful to Jared Cain, too,'' Dora added innocently.

"Indeed we are,'' Wright agreed. Suzanna hoped he wouldn't notice her burning cheeks and wonder why she was blushing at the mention of Cain's name. "Well, I guess it's time to ring the bell and get the service started.''

"I'm ready whenever you are,'' Dora said.

When Wright had gone, Suzanna said, "Dora, can we ever have a conversation when you don't mention Jared Cain?''

"Who?'' Dora asked, with false innocence. "You'd better catch Andy. The service is starting.''

Not a moment too soon, Suzanna thought with relief. At least she would have something else to occupy her mind for the next hour or so.

But even Dora Hand's rich alto voice singing the hymns Suzanna had loved since childhood could not completely prevent her thoughts from straying to the mysterious Jared Cain, and she hardly heard a word of the sermon.

Even though she had longed for a full night's sleep all week, she lay awake for hours that night, replaying every conversation she had ever had with the man. By Monday evening, Suzanna felt almost desperate for the sight of him.

Since she'd had more sleep than usual, Suzanna skipped their nap on Monday so Andy fell asleep early, giving Suzanna the opportunity to arrive at the Comique a little before she was due.

She told herself she was only trying to make up for the times she'd been late, but the moment she entered the theater, she looked around for Cain. As she had hoped, he was just setting up his faro layout.

As she hurried over, Cain stiffened visibly. His hands stilled on the cards he was shuffling, then he laid them aside with elaborate care before lifting his head to face her.

"Good evening," she said uncertainly, disconcerted by the blankness of his expression. She had expected more enthusiasm.

"Good evening," he said coldly.

She opened her mouth to speak, but no words came. One look at his dark eyes and nothing seemed appropriate.

"Did you want something?" he asked.

"I . . . No. I mean, I wanted to thank you again—"

"Don't bother. You've been annoyingly grateful."

"I'm sorry!" she snapped, stung.

"Was there something else you wanted?" His fingers flexed impatiently and something flickered deep in his eyes.

"I don't want anything from you, Jared Cain," she replied, remembering to keep her voice low in spite of her irritation. The other girls would love to overhear this conversation. "I was just trying to be friendly."

"I don't want to be 'friendly' with you, Suzanna, and I can't be anything else," he said almost desperately. "Do you understand?"

Suzanna gaped at him, speechless. She wasn't sure she understood what he was trying to say, but she had no trouble at all deciphering the emotion his gambler's reserve could no longer conceal. The flicker in his eyes now burned clearly, and once again she saw all her own vulnerabilities reflected there—the pain, the loneliness, the longing.

"I understand," she whispered, meaning more than he had asked.

He started in surprise, then seemed to get hold of himself. In the next second his eyes were once again the dark mirrors that effectively concealed whatever was inside Jared Cain.

But his withdrawal proved what she had suspected. If her pride had been wounded by Cain's rejection of her—and she wasn't about to admit it could have been anything except her pride—then he had paid a price for wounding it, too. Feeling oddly victorious, Suzanna strolled away.

Jared Cain stared after her. "Damn you to hell," he muttered as he fought down the tide of emotion surging within him. How could he have ever thought he could get involved with Suzanna Prentice and walk away unscathed? One kiss, and he felt as if he had been struck by lightning.

She was a truly dangerous woman because she made him feel. And he knew he was even more dangerous to her.

If only he could explain, make her understand. Surely then she'd stay away from him. Surely then he would never again have to look into her clear blue eyes and imagine things that could never be.

Mechanically, he began to shuffle the cards again. When they were thoroughly mixed, he loaded them into the dealer's box and readied them for the first game. Then he straightened the beads in the casekeeper, the abacus-like contraption on which the players could keep track of which cards had been drawn and thus figure the odds on which ones would be drawn next.

As the operator of a faro bank, Jared Cain was among the most highly respected citizens in the West, and he smiled to think what his family would say if they could see him now. Of course, they would not consider his occupation respectable, nor would they be impressed by the small fortune he had amassed in the five years since he had left home, penniless.

And they would certainly never countenance a relationship with a dance-hall girl, never mind that Suzanna Prentice was as respectable as any of the ladies with whom his mother took tea on Sunday afternoon.

Yes, Jared's family would be scandalized by what he had done with his life, but then, what could they expect of a murderer?

Several hours later, hours during which Jared had consciously avoided glancing up from his faro table lest he see Suzanna Prentice's blue eyes looking at him, Jared announced the last three cards of play and cleared the board. "That's the game, gentlemen," he said, shuffling the cards for the next round.

Most of the players moved on, but the two men Jared had never seen before lingered.

"Say, Cain," one of them said, "how about a game of poker? I hear you're pretty good."

Jared looked the men over with a practiced eye, estimating the size of their bankroll. Both of them were dressed in brown broadcloth suits which had only recently been purchased. From their sun-darkened faces and callused hands, Jared judged them to be workingmen in the process of squandering their wages on a trip to town. He was unimpressed. "I only play for high stakes."

The two strangers exchanged a glance. "Don't worry," the first one said. "We're flush." He reached into his vest pocket and pulled out a wad of bills that changed Jared's opinion instantly.

"All right. Let me get someone to run the board for me. Shall I round up a few more players?"

"Sure," the second stranger said, smiling mirthlessly. "The more the merrier."

Glad for any distraction from thoughts of Suzanna Prentice, Jared swiftly recruited several more players. When they sat down around the table in the back room, they were seven in all.

Ever suspicious, Jared noted that the two strangers took their places on either side of him. The one on his right introduced himself as Smitty. A jovial man with a full beard and big teeth, he put everyone immediately at ease. The one on Jared's left was less congenial. His eyes were close-set, and he had a furtive air about him that put Jared in mind of a weasel. The man called himself Jones. Smith and Jones, Jared thought with amusement. Of course, in Dodge City, a man called himself whatever he pleased, and no one questioned him. Even he no longer used the name with which he had been born.

The play began and for the first hour or so no one won or lost significantly. As the only professional gambler at the table, Jared was particularly aware of the ebb and flow of the chips, but he could detect nothing unusual to indicate the two strangers were cheating.

Then Smitty dealt a hand, and Jared picked up his cards to discover he had four aces. Immediately he realized something was wrong. The odds against being dealt such a hand by chance were astronomical. Therefore he must conclude he had received the cards for a purpose . . . or by mistake.

Had Smitty intended for his partner to receive the hand and botched the job? Or had he given the cards to Jared to bluff him? Only one hand beat four aces—a straight flush. Would Smitty have dared deal his partner such a hand?

The betting began, and gradually the other four players dropped out. Jared and the strangers continued to raise each other until Jared had bet all of his chips.

On his left, Jones shifted in his chair and his elbow struck the glass of whiskey sitting beside him, spilling it across the table.

"Oh, hell," he muttered, pulling a bandanna from his pocket and making a clumsy attempt to check the spill.

Shouted exclamations drew one of the bartenders who made short work of the mess with his wipe cloth.

During the disruption, Jared had watched the dealer carefully from the corner of his eye and saw the man 'milking' the cards, pulling some from the bottom of the deck and placing them on top while everyone's attention was on the spilled drink.

Jared allowed himself a small smile.

"I'll check," the dealer said when the game resumed, seeing no point in raising the bet since Jared was out of chips.

"Mr. Springer," Jared called to the owner of the Comique who was standing nearby, observing. "May I speak with you a moment?" Jared pulled a cheroot out of his pocket and laid it across his cards before he rose from his seat.

Drawing Springer aside, he asked, "May I borrow five hundred dollars?"

Springer frowned. "I saw that Smitty fellow milk the deck a minute ago. They figure to cheat you, Jared."

Jared shook his head solemnly. "You're a cynical man, Ben. I've got a good hand and that fellow wouldn't hustle me. Is my credit good with you or not?"

"Well, it's your money," Springer allowed, obviously wondering if he had misjudged Jared. He instructed the banker to give Jared an additional five hundred dollars in chips.

Jared took his seat again and threw in all the chips. "I raise five hundred."

Surprised but pleased, the two strangers each tossed in five hundred dollars. Jared eyed the pot, estimating it now contained over twenty-five hundred dollars.

Word of Jared's loan quickly spread throughout the hall, and the room began to fill as interested observers drifted in to watch the showdown.

The time had come to draw cards. Jared examined his hand again. With four aces, he could either discard the worthless four of clubs he also held and draw one card or stand pat with a hand that should, in an honest game, easily win.

"I'll take three," he said, tossing away two of his aces along with the four of clubs.

The dealer's eyes opened wide, and he hesitated, the deck in his hand. Jared smiled slightly. "I said three."

Slowly, grudgingly, the man took three cards from the top of the deck and slapped them down on the table. Jared picked them without a flicker of emotion. Two of the cards were the five and ten of spades, either one of which would have completed the straight flush he'd suspected Jones held. If Jared had stood pat, Jones would have drawn the five. If Jared had drawn one card, the ten would have gone to Jones. Either way, Jared's four aces would have lost to Jones's straight flush.

Jared allowed none of his triumph to show on his face. Instead he pretended to study his new hand while Jones asked for one card in a strangled voice and the dealer took three in desperation.

When the showdown came, Jared showed his pair of aces. Smitty tossed his cards aside in disgust, not even bothering to show them, but Jones rose up in his chair, his face red with fury.

"You son of a bitch!" he cried, and before anyone realized what he intended, he reached into his coat, pulled out a pistol, and fired.

Something struck Jared in the chest and sent him toppling backwards with a crash. Gun smoke stung his eyes, blinding him, but he could hear the shouts of men and more shots. Above him someone grappled with Jones for the gun.

Wanting to help, Jared tried to rise, but when he moved his arm, pain lanced through him like a lightning bolt, wrenching a cry from his throat.

"Don't move, Cain. You're hit," someone said, easing him away from the chair which had fallen with him.

Something thumped onto the floor nearby. Jared turned his head to see the man named Jones lying still, his shirtfront stained red and his eyes staring sightlessly at the ceiling.

Who had shot him and when? Everything ran together in Jared's mind, then a man he recognized knelt down beside him.

"How bad am I hit?" Jared gasped, trying to look, but someone had pressed a towel or something to the wound.

"Take it easy. We already sent for the doc."

The pain spread inexorably, radiating outward until his fingers curled against it. He'd been alone so long. He didn't want to die alone. Please, God, he thought, and the vision of a woman with clear blue eyes and honey-colored hair appeared just before the mist closed over him.

Chapter 4

At the sound of the first shot, everyone in the hall dropped to the floor, but this time Suzanna's first thought was not for her son. She looked toward the back room, and sure enough the next shot came from there.

"Jared," she whispered in alarm, not bothering to question the terror she felt.

When the rumor about Mr. Springer lending him five hundred dollars on his poker hand had spread through the hall, Suzanna had been among the first to hear it. She'd been expecting trouble ever since. More than once she'd seen violence erupt at the gambling tables when a lot of money was at stake. Although the customers were required to check their firearms, she knew that most of the gamblers carried hidden guns in case of trouble. Did Jared?

Or had he been the one shot?

After what seemed an eternity, the men near the door of the back room started getting to their feet, which meant the shooting was over. Suzanna was up in an instant and running. She had to fight her way through the men struggling to get a closer look.

"Let me pass, please, excuse me." A few of them instinctively moved aside for a woman and she was able, at last, to break through into the poker room.

She could hardly see for the cloud of powder smoke. "Jared?" she called, looking around frantically.

"Over here, Miz Prentice," Sam called back.

Then she saw the two bodies on the floor, one lying still and alone, the other surrounded by kneeling men.

"Oh, no!" she cried, carefully skirting the dead man. "Jared?" she said softly, going to her knees beside his head. He didn't move, and for one awful moment Suzanna considered the bleak prospect of never again seeing Jared Cain's rare smile. "Is he . . . ?" She couldn't even say the word.

"He's still alive," Sam assured her. "Looks like he passed out, is all. See, he's still breathing."

Suzanna cringed at the sight of the bloody towel someone was holding to Jared's chest, but the unsteady rise and fall of that chest was some comfort. Without thinking, she reached out and brushed the hair back from his forehead. "You're going to be all right," she promised rashly, and she thought she saw his eyelids twitch in response.

"Well, look here," someone was saying. "No wonder that fellow was so mad. See what they had set up."

Suzanna glanced over and saw Doc Holliday examining the cards spread out on the table.

"Those two were in it together, and Cain had it all figured," Holliday told a group of fascinated observers. "See, Cain threw away two aces because he knew the dead man had to draw to finish his flush."

Suzanna couldn't have cared less about the intricacies of the game. "Who started the shooting?" she asked Sam.

"Well, Mr. Cain here won the hand and this fellow"—he indicated the dead man—"jumps up and shoots him. Don't know how he expected to get away with it, what with half the city police force in the room. Jim Masterson plugged him, which was only fitting, him being the owner *and* a deputy marshal."

Suzanna checked Jared's breathing again. "How badly is he hurt?" she asked.

"I ain't no doctor, Miz Prentice, but it's mighty near

his heart, and he's bleeding like a stuck pig . . . begging your pardon."

"Shouldn't somebody get the doctor?" she asked anxiously, since no one seemed to be paying much attention to Jared now that Doc Holliday had begun to explain the motive for the shooting.

"We already sent for him," Sam said with a sympathetic smile. "Gee, Miz Prentice, I didn't know you and Mr. Cain were . . ." He shrugged, unable to think of an appropriate word.

"I . . . We're . . . He saved Andy's life the other day." She faltered, wishing that accounted for the terror coiling in her stomach. There was far more to it than that, of course, feelings she didn't dare name, and this was certainly not the time to examine them.

She leaned over close to Cain's ear. "Jared, can you hear me? It's Suzanna. I'll make sure they take good care of you."

"Suz . . . anna?"

His voice was no more than a whisper.

"Yes, Jared, I'm here," she cried, leaning even closer, watching his lips. "You're going to be fine."

"Suz . . . get the . . ."

"What, Jared? What do you want?"

He lifted his hand, and Suzanna clasped it to her bosom.

"Get the . . . win . . . winnings . . ."

"Winnings?" She looked at Sam in confusion.

"His *winnings*," Sam repeated in delight. "He won the pot. That's why he got shot."

Suzanna stared at Sam in dismay. Of all the things for a man to be concerned about when he was lying on the floor with a bullet in his heart!

"Don't you see, Miz Prentice?" Sam said triumphantly. "If he's worried about his winnings, he can't be too bad off!" Sam leaned down close to Jared's other ear. "I'll take care of 'em, Mr. Cain. Don't you worry. They'll be in Mr. Springer's safe when you're up and around again." Sam lumbered to his feet. "Mr. Springer!"

Suzanna looked back down at Jared. His face was pale, his breathing labored. The hand she held felt clammy, but she clung to Sam's words. If Jared was concerned about his winnings, he couldn't be too far gone. "Jared Cain," she whispered in a choked voice, "I think you're terrible to be worried about money when you're lying here bleeding all over the floor."

His eyelids twitched again, as if he were trying to lift them. Failing that, he pulled his mouth into the semblance of a smile, and Suzanna's heart contracted.

"Oh, Jared," she whispered, clutching his hand more tightly and pressing her lips to his knuckles.

"Well, now, what have we got here?"

Suzanna looked up into the kindly face of Dr. Harry McCarty.

"Give me some room so I can see what's what," he commanded. The men stepped back obediently, and Suzanna reluctantly released Jared's hand, laying it carefully down beside him.

"Suz . . . anna?" Jared croaked.

"She'll be right here," Dr. McCarty said, motioning her away. "I expect she'll want to watch everything I do, too." He winked at Suzanna and shook his head, silently telling her she didn't have to stay. "Now let's see what kind of damage there is."

He lifted the blood-soaked towel to reveal an even more bloody shirt. Suzanna felt the blood rush from her head, and watching Dr. McCarty open the shirt to expose the wound, she fought the nausea rising in her throat, but still she stayed, knowing she couldn't leave until she heard the doctor's verdict. Dr. McCarty examined the wound, checked Jared's pulse, and lifted his eyelid.

"You're a lucky man, Cain. Looks like the bullet missed the heart *and* the lungs. We won't know what kind of damage it did to your shoulder until it's healed, but I'm going to see if I can't get the bullet out before

I sew you back up. That'll give you a better than even chance. Some of you men push a couple of tables together, will you? And get me some lamps.''

"You're going to operate right here?" Suzanna asked in alarm.

The doctor rose to his feet and motioned her away so Jared could not hear what they said. "I don't want to move him all the way to my office. I'm not real sure where the bullet is, and if it moves . . ." He made a helpless gesture, telling Suzanna everything she needed to know. She nodded, blinking at the sting of tears.

"Maybe you'd better wait outside," he suggested.

Suzanna nodded, knowing she could never stand to watch the operation.

Sam Goodwin appeared at her side and escorted her out into the hall. Although the mood was somewhat subdued, it was business as usual, regardless of what had happened in the back room. Eddie Foy and his partner Jim Thompson were clowning on the stage in an attempt to distract everyone from the trouble. The laughter sounded a little forced, but everyone wanted to forget the dead man being carried out on a plank.

No one seemed to know what happened to his partner Smitty, who had disappeared in the confusion.

Sam thoughtfully took Suzanna into Mr. Springer's office where she could have some privacy. She sank down wearily into a chair and began to pray.

"Well, well, who would've thought it?" Polly Evans said from the doorway. "Looks like even Miss Goody Two-Shoes has her price, but I never would've expected her to get mixed up with a gambler. What'll your friends at church say?"

"Polly, that ain't nice," Sam chided. "Mr. Cain saved her little boy's life."

"The way she's carrying on, I'd say he did a lot more for her, too," Polly replied acidly.

"That's enough," Sam snapped, startling both women. Suzanna didn't think she'd ever seen him get annoyed. "You go on now and leave Miz Prentice alone."

Polly stared at him, wide-eyed. "I . . . Sam, I didn't mean . . . I'm sorry . . ."

"Go on, now, git," Sam insisted.

Polly just stared back at him, stricken.

Well, well, who would've thought it, Suzanna mused. Polly Evans was afraid of offending Sam Goodwin.

Polly looked from Sam to Suzanna and back again. "I . . . Will you wait for me tonight?" she asked bleakly.

"Of course he will," Suzanna said, unwilling to witness anyone else's misery. "Both of you can go. I'll be fine, really."

"You sure?" Sam asked uncertainly.

"Yes. In fact, I'd really rather be alone if you don't mind."

"Oh, I don't mind. If you need anything, I'll be nearby," Sam assured her as he hustled Polly out and closed the door.

Suzanna judged the passing of time by the sounds from outside. The show ended and the dancing began. At intervals, Dora Hand and then Maisie checked on her, but she shooed them away, preferring solitude.

Mr. Springer stuck his head in the door once, frowning his disapproval of her idleness, but Dora pulled him away shutting the door firmly behind her. Suzanna could hear Dora scolding him and, mercifully he didn't come back.

When she had prayed herself out, Suzanna once again went over every conversation she had ever had with Jared Cain in an attempt to understand the man and her feelings for him.

She owed him a debt, of course. Two debts, really, her life and Andy's. On the other side of the coin, he'd insulted her and treated her cruelly. His behavior made no sense, especially when she compared his harshness tonight with the tenderness he had shown when she had been so frightened for Andy.

And every time she remembered how he had rejected her offer of friendship, she also recalled the desolation in his eyes. She had suffered loneliness long enough to recognize the same desperate need in another. Why then had he tried to drive her away?

From the music, Suzanna knew approximately an hour had passed when Dr. McCarty entered the office.

"Your Mr. Cain is a lucky man," the doctor said as Suzanna rose anxiously from her chair. "The bullet missed the major blood vessels and the vital organs, and it wasn't lodged too deeply so I was able to get it out without doing too much damage."

"Does that mean he'll be all right?"

The doctor frowned. "He won't die tonight, but I can't really promise much more. As you know, there's always the danger of infection and pneumonia. If he survives, he might have some nerve damage or his shoulder might heal up stiff."

Suzanna hardly heard a word after Dr. McCarty said the awful word 'pneumonia.' Her father had died of it, gasping for every breath until the effort became too much.

"He'll need constant care for the next few days," the doctor was saying. "I can take him to my office, but perhaps . . ." He gave her a questioning look. "Is there someone at his home who could care for him?"

This was the good doctor's discreet way of asking if she and Cain lived together. "No, he just has a room at the Western, and he and I aren't . . . I mean, we hardly know each other."

"Really?" Dr. McCarty said, genuinely surprised. "He began calling for you as soon as the ether started to wear off, and people tend to say what's in their hearts under those circumstances."

"He called for *me*?" Suzanna asked in amazement, weighing this against everything else she knew about Cain.

"Yes, but if you aren't . . . I mean, I'll have him taken to my office and—"

"Wait!" Suzanna said, remembering the desperation she had seen in Cain's eyes tonight. How could she live with herself if she turned him over to strangers after all he'd done for her? "Could I . . . could I take care of him at my house?"

"I didn't mean to make you feel obligated," Dr. McCarty said.

"You didn't. You see, Mr. Cain saved my son's life the other day, and this is the least I can do to repay him." The excuse sounded so perfectly logical, Suzanna herself could almost believe it was her only reason.

"Your son . . . ? Oh, yes, I heard about it. So that was your boy, was it? Well, I can understand why you'd be grateful, but I must warn you, he'll need a lot of care. You wouldn't be able to work for at least a few days."

"I'll manage, I'm sure, but I don't have much nursing experience. Do you think I'll be able to handle it?"

"I'll instruct you, of course, and I'll check on him every day. If there's any problem, you can send for me."

Suzanna nodded, feeling absurdly relieved to have been granted this responsibility. "When can he be moved?"

"I'd suggest doing so immediately, before the ether wears off completely. Perhaps you'd like to go on ahead and make some preparations."

Having instructed Sam to guide the men who would be bringing Jared, Suzanna hurried home. After greeting Pistol and checking on her Andy, who was sleeping soundly as usual, she lit a lamp in the front room and quickly moved the table and chairs out of the way. Then she went into the bedroom to prepare the bed.

"Mama?" Andy questioned, sitting up.

"Yes, sweetheart," she answered, crossing to him.

"What's going on? Why is the light on?" he asked, rubbing his eyes.

"We're having some company. You remember Mr. Cain, the man who helped you the other day?"

Andy nodded groggily.

"Well, he got hurt tonight, and he needs someone to take care of him for a few days, so I said he could stay with us."

"Where will he sleep?" Andy asked logically.

"In my bed."

"But where will you sleep?"

"We'll figure it out later. Now lie back down."

He obeyed, calling Pistol to stay beside him, but they both continued to watch her as she folded back the bedclothes and arranged the pillows.

"Mama, I figured it out."

"Have you?" she asked absently.

"Yeah, you can sleep in my bed, and me and Pistol can sleep on the floor."

"You won't mind sleeping on the floor?" she asked with a secret smile.

"Oh, no, ma'am," he assured her, just as she had known he would. Andy would probably sleep on the floor every night if she'd let him.

"I think you're very nice to offer me your bed," she said, managing to keep a straight face.

Pistol's head came up, his ears cocked to an unfamiliar sound.

"They must be bringing Mr. Cain now," Suzanna said, hearing the commotion in the alley. "Here, put Pistol's rope on him and hold him so he doesn't get in anyone's way. And don't let him bark."

When she threw open the front door, the first person she saw was Mayor Kelley. "Hello, Suzanna. I came as soon as I heard what happened. Is everything ready?"

"Yes," she said, looking past him to where Sam Goodwin and some other man were carrying Jared stretched out on a plank between them. "Be careful he doesn't fall off!"

"We tied him on, Miz Prentice," Sam assured her. "Where do you want him?"

Suzanna directed them, and in a few minutes Jared Cain lay in her bed. He still looked deathly pale, and he hadn't so much as moaned. "Is he all right?" she asked Dr. McCarty, who had followed them in.

"I gave him some laudanum before we put him on the stretcher. He may not wake up for quite a while. I checked his wound, and it hasn't torn open. I'll come by in the morning to change the bandage and show you how to do it. He may have some fever tonight, but it probably won't be bad until tomorrow. I'd suggest you try to get some rest while you can."

Sam and the other man had already gone. Only Mayor Kelley remained. He and Andy had been deep in conversation.

"Mama, Mr. Kelley said he'd take me for a ride tomorrow in his buggy," Andy reported.

"How nice," she said, giving Kelley a questioning look.

"Dora's real worried about you. She said to tell you she'll come over as soon as she's finished at the theater if you need her."

"Thank her for me, but the doctor said Jared will probably sleep most of the night, so I don't expect I'll need her help."

"Well, we'll take Andy off your hands tomorrow for sure. Dora said you'd probably be glad not to have to worry about the boy, too. Besides," Kelley added, squeezing Andy's shoulder, "we like having him around."

"Can Pistol come with us?" Andy asked.

"What?" Kelley said in feigned outrage. "You think I'd be seen in public with a dog?" He snapped his fingers, and the two greyhounds that had been lying just outside Suzanna's front door leaped to attention. Andy burst out laughing. "Come on, Doc. Let's leave these good people alone. Andy, we'll come by for you and Pistol bright and early." He leaned over to Suzanna and added, "We'll keep him all day and all night, too, if necessary."

"Thank you, and thank Dora for me."

"Having Andy will be thanks enough for her," he replied as he closed the door behind himself and Dr. McCarty.

When Suzanna turned around, she saw Andy had wandered back into the bedroom and was staring at the bandaged wound around Cain's chest. "How'd he get hurt?" he asked.

"Someone shot him. It was an accident," she explained hastily, hoping to ward off any further questions.

"Is he gonna die like Papa did?"

Fear tightened in her stomach like a fist. "Not if I can help it. Now let's get your bed fixed."

In a few minutes she had Andy and Pistol settled in a corner of the front room. She carried the lamp into the bedroom and turned the flame low. If Cain woke up, she didn't want to be stumbling around in the dark.

He was still awfully pale. She studied him in the feeble lamplight, thinking how powerful his bare arms and chest looked even in repose. She well remembered the strength of those arms. Surely a man so strong wouldn't die easily, she thought, hoping to comfort herself, and shivered at the thought.

Cain still wore his trousers, although someone had thoughtfully removed his shoes. In spite of the heat, she decided to cover him and pulled up the sheet, adjusting it around his shoulders when she had checked his bandage. Gently, she laid a hand on his forehead. She detected no sign of fever, but he stirred restlessly at her touch.

"Suz . . . Suzanna?"

Her heart leaped. "Yes, Jared, I'm here."

"Wa . . . wa . . ."

She smiled in spite of herself. "Don't worry about your winnings. Sam put them in the safe."

"Water," he croaked.

"Oh!" She hurried into the other room and filled a glass from the bucket. By the time she got back, Jared seemed to be asleep again, but when she dipped her finger in the water and touched it to his lips, he roused.

"Water," he begged.

Carefully, she lifted his head and pressed the glass to his lips. He drank only a few swallows before exhaustion overcame him. She lowered his head to the pillow and set the glass on the crate she used as a bedside table.

She thought he was asleep again when he said, "Suzanna?"

"I'm right here," she assured him.

"Don't leave me."

Tears flooded her eyes. "I won't."

By morning the laudanum had worn off, and Jared was feverish, moaning and muttering disjointed phrases about flushes and aces and drawing three cards.

"What's he talking about, Mama?" Andy asked her for the dozenth time.

"I told you, I don't know," she said in exasperation, looking out the front window in hopes of seeing Dora and Mayor Kelley come to fetch him. "Here they are now," she said with relief.

Andy whooped in delight, covering his mouth repentantly when Suzanna shushed him. The mayor stopped his buggy near Suzanna's door, and he and Dora got out. Andy threw the front door open for them.

"Rough night?" Dora inquired, looking Suzanna over sympathetically.

Suzanna glanced down in dismay at the dress she had slept in for the few hours she had been able to sleep. "Not really. He's got a fever now, though, and his bandage is soaked."

"I saw the doc in town a minute ago," Kelley informed her. "He's on his way."

"I'll stay and help you," Dora said. "Jimmy can take Andy by himself."

"Oh, no, really. I'm sure I'll be fine once Andy's out of my hair."

"I never touched your hair!" Andy protested.

"Of course you didn't," Dora said with a wink at Suzanna. "Let's go before your mama makes up any more lies about you."

"Wow! That sure is a boss buggy team!" Andy cried, running to the wagon and scrambling up onto the seat.

" 'Boss buggy team'? Where'd you hear a thing like that?" Mayor Kelley inquired as he and the women followed him out.

"The newspaper said so," Andy informed him. "Mama read it to me, and anybody can see Old Calamity and Battery Gray are the prettiest horses in town."

"That's God's truth, all right," Kelley agreed, helping Dora onto the seat.

"We'll bring him back after supper and see how you're doing. Andy, how'd you like to spend the night at our house tonight?"

"Could I, Mama?" he asked breathlessly.

"Don't you have to work, Dora?" Suzanna asked.

"I already told Springer neither of us would be in tonight. Please, I'd love having Andy all to myself."

"If you're sure you don't mind," Suzanna said, turning to Andy. "I'll have your things ready for you this evening."

"Give your mama a kiss before we go," Dora said.

Andy leaned across her and puckered obediently. Feeling a strange sense of loss, Suzanna kissed him and said, "Be a good boy."

"I will. Where's Pistol?"

"Right here. Don't worry, he'll follow my buggy. I trained him, remember?" Mayor Kelley said with a laugh.

"Let's go, then!" Andy exclaimed.

Chuckling, Kelley climbed into the buggy and spanked the team into motion. Suzanna waved until they were out of sight. She was glad Andy was in such good hands, of course. She only wished he hadn't been quite so eager to leave her.

A few minutes later Dr. McCarty arrived and gave Suzanna her instructions for changing Jared's bandage and dosing him with laudanum. He also helped her put a piece of oilcloth beneath him to protect the mattress.

"You'll want to sponge him off every hour or so to keep the fever down." Dr. McCarty glanced at Jared's trousers. "You'll have to undress him, of course," he added, reminding her of the bodily functions with which she would have to deal.

Oh, dear, she thought, why didn't I think of this *before* I offered to take care of him? She'd nursed Andrew, but he'd been her husband. Jared Cain was practically a stranger.

"Mrs. Prentice? Are you having second thoughts?"

"Oh, no," she assured him, hoping she sounded more confident than she felt. After all, men's bodies were all the same, weren't they? She wasn't going to see anything she hadn't seen before.

"Would you like me to help you get his clothes off?" Dr. McCarty asked.

"Don't be silly," she replied, thinking she would be far more embarrassed to share the task with him than to do it herself. "There is one thing you can do, though. Would you explain the situation to Mrs. Galland and ask her to have someone bring meals to us for the next few days so I don't have to leave Mr. Cain alone?"

"I'd be glad to. I'm sorry I didn't think of it myself. Anything else you can think of that you'll need?"

"Some fresh water, I suppose. From what you say, I'll be using a lot bathing Mr. Cain, and I can't be running back and forth to the well."

"I'm sure Mrs. Galland can find someone to take care of it. I'll go straight over there on my way back to the office. By the way, have you had any breakfast yet?''

"Uh, no," she answered, thinking she didn't feel much like eating.

"We'll take care of that right away. Can't have you getting sickly on us now, can we?''

When the doctor had gone, Suzanna went back into the bedroom. Hesitating in the doorway for a few moments, she gathered her nerve for what she was about to do, calling herself a ninny and reminding herself she wasn't an innocent virgin but a mature woman with five years of marriage behind her. Taking a man's pants off shouldn't be too difficult.

At least Cain was still out from the recent dose of laudanum. She hastily unbuttoned his trousers and without allowing herself to think about what she was doing, she slipped them over his hips and off his legs, being careful to disturb him as little as possible. Of course he wore underdrawers—what else would she have expected? Unfortunately, they had to come off, too.

Suzanna took a minute to dredge up her courage again, staring down at the blatantly male body lying on her bed. How could she have thought all men were alike? Andrew had been thin and sinewy, his muscles ropy. She would never have called him beautiful in any sense of the word, but without doubt, Jared Cain was beautiful.

The slender gracefulness of his hands had only hinted at the perfection she saw before her now. His arms and chest, lightly furred with the same chestnut hair that crowned his head, were even more imposing in the light of day. His muscular legs matched the power of his upper body, and even his feet were elegant.

Jared Cain would never be mistaken for a farmer. If Suzanna were inclined to be fanciful, she might have guessed him a prince. But she certainly wasn't inclined to be fanciful, not about a man she was going to strip naked.

Swallowing her apprehension, she reached down and swiftly undid the buttons of his underdrawers and, before she could lose her nerve again, began to peel them down his hips.

Except this time when she had to put her hand beneath him to lift, no cloth separated her skin from his. His flesh seemed to scorch her palm, and she called herself a fool, remembering his fever. Of course he felt hot!

Carefully averting her eyes, she finally succeeded in freeing the drawers from the weight of his body. Sliding them down his legs was a simple matter, and without looking at that part of him which she had no business seeing, she flipped the sheet back over him.

She knew she was being silly. She'd have to see him sooner or later, but later was better. After folding his clothes and putting them into the trunk beneath her bed, she went into the front room to prepare a sponge bath for him so he could rest more comfortably.

"No," she heard him mutter. "I'll take three . . . Hot . . ."

Hastily picking up the sacking she intended to use for towels, she carried the basin of water into the bedroom, but when she pushed past the curtain in the doorway she almost dropped the bowl.

"Oh, my," she murmured. Cain had kicked free of the sheet, and now Suzanna knew all men *weren't* the same.

But she had more important things to think about. The way he was thrashing around, he was likely to break open his wound. Setting down the bowl of water and the toweling, she tried to figure out how to soothe him.

"Jared," she tried. "Jared, can you hear me?"

"Mother? I'm so hot."

Mother? Suzanna almost smiled at the thought of a

man like Jared Cain calling for his mother. Delirium did strange things to people.

"Be still, now, and I'll cool you off," she said, lifting the sponge from the water and squeezing out the excess moisture. Gently, she bathed his face, letting some of the water trickle into his mouth.

His thrashing stopped instantly. "Yes," he said, licking the droplets from his lips.

Tucking pieces of sacking around him to catch the drips, Suzanna continued to bathe him, stroking her sponge across his shoulders and down his arms. As soon as he stopped moving, she discreetly draped one of her sacks across his hips, telling herself he would appreciate the gesture. She knew she certainly felt more comfortable with him covered.

"Hot," he muttered from time to time, and since the sound of her voice seemed to quiet him, Suzanna crooned meaningless phrases as she worked.

Yes, she decided, *everything* about Jared Cain was different from her husband. Andrew's body had been hard and angular, but Cain's was amazingly sleek, like satin over steel. Even his palms were smooth, she noticed.

Andrew would have been contemptuous of a man with no calluses, but Suzanna couldn't help thinking how pleasant it would be to be touched by such hands. When Andrew had touched her . . . But then, he hadn't meant to hurt her, not really, it had been the liquor and the bitterness that had made him so angry.

Or so she'd tried to convince herself.

Tentatively, Suzanna laid the sponge on Cain's abdomen. He sucked in automatically, and she smiled to think he was ticklish. His head moved on the pillow, tossing back and forth.

"I said three," he insisted to someone only he could see.

Suzanna chided herself for forgetting that her main task was to ease the man's fever, not make discoveries about his body. Assuming a more businesslike attitude, she moved on to his legs, laving them while she purposefully blocked all other thoughts from her mind.

She didn't need to towel him dry. The heat from his skin combined with the heat in the room evaporated the water almost instantly. That, too, would help cool him, and he seemed to rest more comfortably when she had finished. She wet one of her sacks in the water, folded it into a compress, and laid it on his forehead.

His eyes flickered open, and for a moment he simply stared up at her. She thought perhaps he didn't really see her until he said, "Who are you?"

"I'm Suzanna, Suzanna Prentice."

His eyes narrowed as if he were trying to bring her into focus. "No," he decided at last. "She'd never . . . I'm dreaming." The narrowed eyelids closed completely.

Suzanna smiled. "Yes, she would, Jared Cain." She adjusted the rag across his forehead and laid her fingers along his cheek. Just checking for fever, she told herself, although the prickle of his morning whiskers sent a pleasant tingle up her arm.

She wasn't simply looking for an excuse to touch him. She'd just touched practically every inch of his body, hadn't she? But as if to their own accord, her fingers stroked down his throat to his shoulder, marveling again at the texture of his skin.

Suddenly, she realized what she was doing and snatched her hand away. Good heavens! What had gotten into her? Bathing a man she hardly knew and to whom she was absolutely no relation was scandalous enough. Fondling him was outrageous.

True, Jared Cain was an attractive man, but Suzanna wasn't an innocent romantic who thought love ended with a chaste kiss. She knew all too well what happened between a man and woman in the privacy of their bed, and it was about as far from moonlight and roses as anything could be. She couldn't possibly feel desire for Cain, not knowing what she knew. Why, then, was she so affected by his body?

Suzanna had ample opportunity to consider that question during the next forty-eight hours. Dora brought Andy over for brief visits with his mother, but she continued to keep him for a second night and a third day while Suzanna continued to bathe Jared and tend to his needs. Mrs. Galland sent over gallons of broth, which Suzanna dutifully poured down Jared's throat each time he called for water. She changed his bandages and his sheets and answered him when he cried out.

Familiarity should have overcome whatever awkwardness she had originally felt at having a naked man in her bed, but each time she found him uncovered Suzanna's unease increased.

Dr. McCarty made his usual visit on the third morning and seemed very pleased with Jared's condition. "You're doing an excellent job, Mrs. Prentice. I only wish all my patients could have such good care."

"He doesn't seem much better to me," Suzanna said, frowning at Jared's still form.

"It's the laudanum that makes him so sluggish. His fever is down some today and the wound isn't festering. Perhaps you should try giving him only half the usual dose. If he's more awake, he'll be able to use a bedpan, and that will make your job easier, won't it?" Dr. McCarty inquired cheerfully.

"Y . . . yes," Suzanna agreed, mortified.

"If he manages to make it through without pneumonia, I'd say his chances of complete recovery are very good."

When the doctor had gone, Suzanna gave Jared his laudanum and lay down on Andy's cot for a nap before her patient again awoke, demanding her attention.

Consciousness came slowly. Jared was first aware of the pain, a white-hot burning that throbbed with each beat of his heart. For a long time he lay still, trying to discover the source of the pain, tracing it to its roots so his befuddled mind could sort out what was wrong with him.

Although he hurt in every bone, he at last determined the most agony came from his upper chest, left side. With great effort, he forced his eyelids open. Not surprised to see sunlight—he did most of his sleeping in the daytime—he was confused to realize he did not know where he was.

The room looked vaguely familiar, but it most certainly wasn't *his* room. He thought it over carefully, laboriously sorting through the facts, until he settled on a solution. If he was sick, he was probably at the doctor's office.

But how did he get sick? All he recalled was a poker game and . . . Memories came back in bits and pieces. Four aces, then two, drawing three cards, the showdown, a man rising with a gun in his hand, a flash of powder, and Jared falling . . .

The pieces all fell into place. He'd been shot. He had no idea how badly he'd been hurt, but at least he'd lived through the night. As his head cleared, he was able to localize several more of his discomforts and realized an urgent need to drink and urinate.

He could appreciate the irony of that combination and might even have laughed if he'd had the strength. Instead, he occupied himself with trying to decide how to request the help he needed. Not knowing exactly where he was, he didn't know whom to call. He settled on the most obvious.

"Water," he tried, although the word came out like a croak.

"Coming," a woman's voice said from somewhere to his left.

Turning his head, something that took more effort than he'd felt the need to exert until now, he saw Suzanna Prentice rising from a cot not more than an arm's length away. She didn't even glance at him as she hastened to do his bidding. She disappeared so quickly

behind the curtained doorway, he began to think he
had only imagined her, but just as quickly she returned
carrying a glass of what looked like whiskey. Now Jared
knew he was dreaming.

"Suzanna?" he muttered.

She started and some of the whiskey slopped over
onto her hand. For the first time she looked square into
his face. "Jared? Are you really awake?"

"I doubt it," he replied, waiting for her to disappear
again. He recalled she had been haunting his dreams
quite regularly of late. They'd probably given him
something for the pain, so it was only natural she'd
appear to him while he was drugged.

Strangely enough, she smiled and came closer. "Are
you in much pain? I only gave you half as much laudanum the last time."

Pain? God, yes, he was in pain, but before he could
say so, she reached out and touched his face. Her fingers felt cool against his skin.

"Dr. McCarty was right. Your fever has gone down.
You're sweating, too. That's a good sign. I'll wash you
off in a minute and then you'll feel much better. Oh,
here's your drink," she said, recalling the glass she
held.

She leaned over and lifted his head with her free
hand and pressed the glass to his lips. Her scent engulfed him, musky and female, blocking out even the
smell of the liquor, except it wasn't liquor at all. Beef
broth? When was the last time he'd had broth? he
wondered, swallowing greedily. Drinking only aggra-
vated his other need, but he decided he wouldn't spoil
the dream by mentioning it.

Suzanna smiled again when he had drained the
glass. He enjoyed seeing her smile. Her front teeth
overlapped slightly, and he found he liked to imagine
how they would feel if he ran his tongue over them.

"Do you want some more laudanum before I give
you a bath?"

Pain or no pain, he didn't need to think about that question at all. "No."

"If you change your mind, just let me know." Then she was gone again. Disappointment welled up in him, but although he could no longer see her, he could hear her, or at least he could hear something on the other side of the curtain. Maybe she would come back.

When she did, she carried a large bowl and had several flour sacks draped over her arm. He watched with interest as she set the bowl down someplace beside the bed. He heard water splash, and something cool touched his face.

"Jared, are you really awake? I can't tell."

Water ran into his eye, blurring her image. "I can't either."

For some reason her lips curved again, into her angel's smile. He'd hated seeing her smile at the cowboys in the Comique, but this smile was just for him.

She spread the coolness to his neck and shoulders, and Jared began to notice other things about her. When Suzanna came to work, she was always as neat as a pin, her dress carefully pressed, every hair in place. Today her dress looked as if she'd slept in it, and the bodice clung to her damply. Her honey-colored hair was escaping its pins to hang in tendrils all around her head.

And her face. Purple smudges shadowed her clear blue eyes, as if she hadn't been getting enough sleep lately. But of course she couldn't, not working at the Comique and taking care of a child, too.

"You work too hard," he said.

"You've been keeping me pretty busy," she replied, confusing him again. How could he be keeping her busy? he wondered, and then he remembered this was a dream.

"Oh, in my dreams," he said.

She gave him a puzzled look as she spread the wet coolness across his belly. God, it felt good, but if she didn't stop, he'd likely embarrass himself.

When she had finished with his stomach, she dropped the sponge back in the bowl and peered more closely at his face.

"Jared?"

He didn't know what to say, so he didn't answer.

"You're not really awake," she said, and to his horror, she threw back the sheet. Good God, he was naked! He had barely realized it before she draped one of her flour sacks across his hips, but then she got her sponge again and started on his legs.

Her dainty hand grasped his ankle and lifted, stroking up the calf and behind the knee, and up the thigh, and suddenly the urgency beneath the flour sack changed completely.

And why not? He always had this reaction when he dreamed of Suzanna. Maybe this time she wouldn't turn away. Maybe this time . . .

She'd started on the other leg now. Jared closed his eyes, savoring the sensuous combination of her touch and the cooling water and his own arousal swelling beneath the cloth. The throbbing pain in his shoulder faded into insignificance as a more compelling torment supplanted it.

Suzanna glanced at Jared's face, not surprised to see his eyes were closed again. For a moment there, she'd thought he was finally conscious. Her disappointment had been tinged with relief. She really wasn't looking forward to doing this while he was awake, but she also wanted some assurance that he really was getting better.

Finishing the second leg, she lowered it gently and started to put the sponge back when she noticed the flour sack wasn't exactly where she'd left it.

"Oh!" she cried in surprise and mortification. How on earth . . . ? Her gaze went instantly to Jared's face. His eyes flew open, and she suddenly realized he *was* awake, completely awake, every part of him!

Her cry startled him, and when Jared saw her face, he suddenly realized this wasn't a dream at all. Automatically he made a grab to cover what wasn't covered anymore, but the movement jarred loose every demon in hell, sending agony searing through him and wrenching a groan from his lips.

"Oh, Jared, don't move, lay back. Here, I'll get the laudanum . . ."

Suzanna's hands pressed him back onto the pillow, stroking, soothing. In another moment she brought something to his lips, something foul-smelling and even fouler-tasting, but memory told him to swallow it.

He lay back, gritting his teeth against the pain, but even pain could not wipe away the vision of Suzanna's startled face. He opened his eyes a slit. Through the red haze he could see her expression had changed from horror to concern.

"Suzanna?"

"Yes, what is it?"

Oh, God, what could he say? "Where am I?"

"You're at my house. You got shot the other night. Do you remember?"

"Yes," he said, glancing around. Of course. He recognized the place now. "How did I . . . ?"

"Dr. McCarty took the bullet out right there in the theater, but he said you'd need someone to take care of you for a few days so I told them to bring you here."

This was starting to seem like a dream again. "Why?" he gasped between spasms of pain.

"Because . . ." She hesitated, biting her lip, and he wondered why she would be reluctant to tell him the reason. "Because you saved Andy's life. What else could I do?"

Jared could think of any number of things, but he didn't have the strength to argue.

He drew a shuddering breath, wondering how long it would take for the laudanum to work. At least the pain had taken care of his other problem, but he was still vitally aware of being naked.

"Suzanna?"

"Yes?"

"The . . . sheet . . ."

"Oh!" She hastily pulled it up, covering him to his neck. "The man who shot you is dead. Jim Masterson shot him," she explained without even taking a breath. He knew she was talking to disguise the fact that she was as embarrassed as he. "The other man, his partner, got away. No one's seen him since, but Doc Holliday figured out the trick they tried to pull on you. Everyone seems to think you were very clever to beat them at their own game."

"At the moment, I don't feel very clever."

The ghost of a smile flickered across her face, but she had the grace not to laugh. "No, I don't suppose you do. Mrs. Galland sent over your clothes and things from your room yesterday, and—"

"Yesterday? You mean . . . I've been here two days?"

"Three, or at least today is the third day."

"*Three*? And you've been . . . Good God," he groaned. No wonder she looked tired. But why on earth would she do this for him? Snatching her son from the street had only taken a few seconds of his life. None of this made any sense.

And everything was starting to get fuzzy. The laudanum, he supposed. The pain in his chest began to ease, and as it did, he remembered his original problem which was becoming more urgent.

How could he ask without totally humiliating himself? But if he didn't ask, it would be far worse. "Suzanna?"

"Yes."

"Do you have a . . . a chamber pot or something . . . ?" he stammered, his words slurring from the drug.

"Oh, yes, of course. I have a bedpan the doctor gave me. It's right here."

She would have helped him, but he took the pan from her and motioned her away. Frowning uncertainly, she backed out of the room. The instant the curtain fell into place behind her, Jared lifted the sheet and shoved the pan into place.

Not a moment too soon, he thought, barely aware of the jolt of pain in his shoulder. Not a moment too soon, he thought as his eyes slid shut

In the other room, Suzanna sank down into a chair and waited. For some reason she felt breathless and fluttery. She only wished she could attribute her reaction to the scare Jared had given her with his shoulder. Moving so quickly could have torn it open again and had most certainly caused him a great deal of pain.

She tried not to think about *why* he'd moved so quickly, but the incident was too firmly fixed in her memory to be ignored. She knew she was being a ninny. The man was barely conscious and probably had no control over himself. These things happened. Certainly many more embarrassing things would happen while he was in her care. She would only make the situation more uncomfortable by reacting to it.

She just wished embarrassment was the only emotion she felt.

After what seemed like a long time during which she heard no sound from the other room, Suzanna peeked in. Jared was sound asleep. She sighed, moving quickly. She'd do as much as she could while he was out and try not to think of what on earth she would say to him next time they met face to face.

Chapter 5

When Jared woke up again, the bedpan was gone and so was the sun. He could hear movement on the other side of the curtain, and the sound of Andy's voice muttering in play.

"Mama, when do you think Mr. Cain will wake up?" the boy asked.

"Soon, I'm sure. Put your toys away now. It's time for bed."

"Can I see him before I go to sleep?"

"Just for a minute, but you mustn't bother him. He's still very sick."

The demons in Jared's shoulder began to stir, prodding with their little pitchforks, but he had no intention of calling for more laudanum just yet. Before he allowed himself the oblivion of drugs, he had some decisions to make.

From what he could determine, Suzanna had been caring for him for at least three days. With a flood of humiliation, he remembered what had happened earlier that day. If she'd been taking care of him for three days, she must also have done things for him he preferred not to think about.

And he didn't want to *have* to think about them. He didn't want to be grateful to Suzanna Prentice, of all people. Hadn't he already decided to stay as far away from her as possible?

Yet here he was, in her house, in her very bed, helpless and beholden. But he wouldn't be here for long. The minute she came in, he'd tell her he wanted to be moved someplace—*anyplace*—else.

"Now can I see him?" Andy demanded.

"Let me check on him first. You stay right here."

Jared tensed as he waited for the curtain to part. She slipped in quietly, a shadowy wraith in the dark room.

"I'm awake," he said, startling her.

"How do you feel?" She came closer and laid her cool hand on his forehead.

Like hell, he wanted to say, but he said, "Better."

"Your fever is almost gone. Dr. McCarty is worried about pneumonia, although I didn't think people got pneumonia in the summertime. Can I get you anything? Do you need the bedpan?"

"Yes," he admitted reluctantly, glad he couldn't see her face and even more glad she couldn't see his.

This time she didn't allow him to take it from her. Under the cover of darkness, she slipped it beneath the sheet herself. "I'll get you something to drink," she said, and discreetly withdrew.

That does it, he thought. He would leave here tomorrow if he had to crawl.

"Mama . . . ?" Andy's voice piped plaintively.

"Not yet," she scolded. Jared could hear her pouring liquid and realized he was thirsty again.

"Jared? May I come in?" she asked a few minutes later. He figured she wanted to know if he was finished.

"Yes," he replied, wishing he had the strength to remove the bedpan himself, but she did it so swiftly he almost forgot to be embarrassed. Then she held a glass to his lips. This time it was chicken broth, cooled to room temperature.

When he had finished it, she said, "I guess you heard Andy out there. He'd like to say hello to you. Would you mind? I'll only let him stay a minute."

"No, I don't mind," Jared said, absurdly glad for a

few moments' reprieve from his discussion with Suzanna.

She disappeared through the curtains.

"See, Mama, I told you—"

"Hush, now. Mind your manners."

Jared experienced a poignant rush of memory. How many times had his own mother said the same thing to him in exactly the same tone?

Andy marched into the room, Suzanna at his heels carrying a lamp with the flame turned low which she set beside the bed. The boy wore a nightshirt fashioned from a flour sack, and his face was freshly scrubbed. His innocent grin touched a part of Jared he'd kept carefully secured for a very long time.

"Hello, Mr. Cain. I hope you're feeling better," he said, glancing up at Suzanna for approval.

"I am, thank you," Jared lied, ignoring the pitchforks in his shoulder.

"I been staying with Mr. Kelley and Mrs. Hand. They took me on picnics. We rode in his buggy, and they even took Pistol along. I could've stayed there tonight, too, but Mama said she missed me too much."

Looking at the boy's guileless smile, Jared could easily understand why.

"Maybe when you're better we can all go on a picnic together," Andy continued.

"Maybe we can," Jared said, wishing he dared make such a promise.

Andy peered at him critically. "Your whiskers are getting long."

For the first time, Jared considered his own appearance and carefully lifted a hand to his face. Sure enough, he found three days' growth of beard. "I don't suppose your mother thought to shave me."

"Or would know how if she had," Suzanna replied, giving Andy a disapproving look which he ignored.

"How come you don't have any clothes on?"

"Andy!" Suzanna scolded, but Jared couldn't hold back a smile.

"I've been wondering the same thing myself," he said with a wink. "Your mama hid my pants."

Andy leaned closer. "They're prob'ly in the trunk under the bed. That's where she hides things she doesn't want me to get."

"Andy, say good night to Mr. Cain," Suzanna said, and Jared saw she was blushing.

"Aw, Mama."

"Don't argue."

"Yes, ma'am. Good night, Mr. Cain. I'll see you tomorrow."

"Good night, Andy."

Jared's eyes misted as he watched Suzanna herd Andy out and listened to her putting him to bed. He called himself a blubbering fool, but he couldn't deny the burning sense of loss he experienced when he thought of leaving them both tomorrow.

Which was all the more reason to get away as soon as possible.

By the time Suzanna returned, Jared had regained control of his emotions.

"I would have given you a nightshirt, but I didn't find one in the things Mrs. Galland sent over," she said defensively.

Jared blinked in surprise. Obviously, she'd taken his teasing seriously. "I don't own one."

"Oh," she replied, nonplussed, and her cheeks reddened again. She looked entirely too appealing when she blushed. Jared decided he'd better get down to business.

"Suzanna, I appreciate everything you've done for me—"

"I told you, I owe it to you."

"You certainly don't owe me three days out of your life. You've more than satisfied any obligation to me, and I can't impose on you anymore. First thing in the morning, I'll move back to the hotel and—"

"You can't!" she protested.

"Yes, I can and I will."

"Who'll take care of you?"

"I . . . I'll hire someone," he said, realizing even as he said it that he could just as easily pay her. "Of course, I'll pay you for the time I've been here and—"

"You most certainly will not!" She was genuinely angry now. Jared had forgotten the way her eyes darkened when she was angry. "I didn't take you in for money, and I'm certainly not going to turn you loose now without proper care so you can get sick and die!"

Jared realized he lacked the strength to argue with her. Already he was fading from exhaustion. "I'm imposing," he tried again. "I'm keeping you from your work."

"I'm only too happy for an excuse not to work, and I have some money saved, so you needn't worry that we'll starve. I wouldn't have taken you in if I minded."

"Mama?" Andy asked from the doorway. "Is Mr. Cain going to leave?"

"No, he isn't," she said softly. "Go back to bed, sweetheart."

Jared wished she'd use that gentle tone with him. His head was starting to ache. Andy didn't budge, so Suzanna took him out and tucked him back in his bed. When she didn't return immediately, he thought she might not come back, but to his dismay she returned carrying the basin and towels.

"I don't need a bath right now," he said, feeling an irrational panic.

"Don't be ridiculous. You've sweated right through the sheet."

He had, of course, which made him feel even more a fool.

Without waiting for his consent, she started bathing his face, and it felt so good, he decided not to fight her anymore. Of course, he'd keep his baser feelings in check. He had no intention of suffering any more humiliation than was absolutely necessary.

He glanced up at her face. Her lips were still pressed tightly together and spots of color showed in her cheeks. Her hands weren't as gentle as they had been the other time, which made it easier to maintain his control. He flinched when she jerked the sheet aside, but she covered him with one of the cloths almost instantly.

Jared concentrated on a crack in the ceiling until she'd finished. When she dropped the sponge back in the basin, he released his breath on a long sigh of relief.

"Jared?"

"Yes?"

"If you feel up to it, I'd like to turn you over and do your back and change the sheet."

"Suzanna," he started to protest, but stopped when he noticed she refused to meet his eye. This was as difficult for her as it was for him, perhaps more so.

"I'm sure the sheet is damp and uncomfortable," she continued, still not looking directly at him, "and I can't move you without your help."

She was right about the sheet. His back itched, too. "All right. What do you want me to do?"

"Nothing yet. Let me get the clean sheets."

In a moment she returned with the neatly folded sheets, which she laid at the foot of the bed. "I'll put my hands under your back and lift while you roll over. That should keep most of the strain off your shoulder."

By the time they had executed this maneuver, Jared no longer cared whether he was naked or embarrassed or anything else. The demons in his shoulder were doing a war dance in spiked shoes. He hardly even noticed the blessed relief of Suzanna's ministrations. When she finished washing him, he lay quietly while she fussed with the bedding. How she intended to change the sheets with him lying on them, he had no idea, and enveloped in his cloud of pain, he didn't really care.

"Are you ready to roll back over?" she asked.

He bit back a groan and nodded. Suzanna's hands,

surprisingly strong, did most of the work this time, which was just as well since Jared had all he could do simply to remain conscious. For a long moment the room swam, and he fought nausea as Suzanna gently wiped the perspiration from his face.

"Are you ready for the laudanum now?"

What had he decided about taking more? He couldn't remember. "Yes." He swallowed the bitter brew gratefully.

For several minutes he lay perfectly still as the pain washed over him in waves, but gradually the waves diminished until he no longer felt he would drown.

"Is it better now?"

He nodded slightly, eyes and teeth shut tightly against betraying any weakness. She started doing something else then. At first he couldn't imagine why she had leaned so close to him, but when he peeked out between his slitted eyelids, he realized she was removing the old sheet from the side of the bed nearest the wall. She'd evidently gotten the new sheet under him while he'd been rolled over and was now spreading it out and tucking it into the other side of the bed.

Unfortunately, that side was built flush against the wall, so she had to bend over him to reach it. Or maybe it was fortunate. He couldn't decide. He could smell her again, the warm, womanly scent that was Suzanna's alone. The way she was leaning over, he could admire the supple line of her back, the golden sheen of her hair, the curve of her hips, and the swell of her breasts. If he lifted his hand, he could actually touch her . . .

Oh, God! He groaned aloud as he felt his body quicken in response. She turned to look at his face, thank heaven, though she'd see the other soon enough. "I . . . I'm sorry. It's the laudanum," he explained, sinking gratefully into drugged oblivion.

No matter how hard she tried, Suzanna couldn't seem to fall asleep. Usually, she could drop off at a moment's notice, a consequence of her erratic schedule and the fact that she was always exhausted. Oddly enough, caring for an invalid had been far less taxing than her usual activities, however, so she'd gotten a fair amount of rest in the past few days.

She tried to tell herself that was why she couldn't sleep, but she knew she wasn't being honest. If only there were some way to escape the sound of Jared's breathing, but the house was simply too small. Even though she had dragged Andy's cot out into the front room and put as much distance as possible between herself and Cain, she could still hear every breath he took.

Perhaps she'd been a fool to argue with him when he had insisted he was imposing on her. He was right about her missing work. Every night she stayed home cost her money she and Andy could certainly use when they returned to Georgia. And did she really owe him enough to justify disrupting her entire life to nurse him twenty-four hours a day for a week or even longer?

Suzanna didn't know the answers to any of her questions, but she still felt a profound reluctance to turn Jared Cain out. Even to send him to Dr. McCarty's seemed unthinkable, although after today she should have been happy to be rid of him.

Her face burned in the darkness as she remembered. The first time she'd thought it an aberration, but the second time . . . Suzanna shivered in spite of the heat. A dance-hall girl should have been used to such things: men frequently became aroused when they danced, and like the other girls, she'd learned to ignore it, knowing it was nothing personal. When a man had spent several months following the back end of a cow all the way from Texas, any female would excite him.

Suzanna couldn't seem to keep her perspective where Cain was concerned, though. She couldn't help remembering he had wanted to spend the night with her, having chosen her above all the other women. Considering the way he had lusted after her, his reaction was understandable. It was, in fact, just about the only thing she did understand about him. She could deal with lust. What she couldn't deal with was a man who lusted after her so blatantly yet insisted on leaving her house when he was too weak even to roll himself over in bed.

She wished she could attribute her reaction to injured pride. Her pride had certainly been wounded by his eagerness to leave, but she knew it was more than that. As much as she hated to admit it, she found Jared Cain very attractive, and naturally she'd want him to find her attractive in return. On the other hand, she certainly didn't want to encourage his desire for her since she had no intention of satisfying that desire. The very thought repelled her.

Didn't it?

Of course it did! She couldn't imagine being intimate with a man who wasn't even her husband, letting him kiss her and touch her and . . .

"No!"

The sound of her own voice startled her, and she sat up, staring into the darkness, waiting to see if she had disturbed Andy or Jared. But all she heard was the pounding of her own heart and the rasping of her breath. What was wrong with her? she wondered, noticing that her nipples were erect and throbbing beneath the thin fabric of her nightdress. Her bodily reactions were almost like fear, except she wasn't afraid of anything.

And why should she be? In his present state, Jared Cain was no threat to her, no matter how much he might want to be. Why, when she'd rolled him onto his stomach, he'd been as helpless as a turtle on its shell.

She smiled at the thought until she pictured Jared the way he had looked then, the clean line of his back and shoulders, the gentle rounding of his buttocks . . .

"No," she repeated, more firmly this time, blocking the tantalizing picture from her mind. She flopped down onto her pillow in disgust, but something was happening to her body, something over which she had no control.

Her heart still beat rapidly, and her breasts seemed to strain against the loose material of her nightdress. Even more alarming, she began to ache. It started as a hollow feeling in her stomach, as if she hadn't eaten in a while, and it spread insidiously lower and lower, until it settled between her legs.

Making a disgusted sound, she turned over on her side and pulled her knees to her chest. Maybe she was getting sick. Maybe something was terribly wrong with her.

Or maybe she should let Jared Cain go after all.

When Dr. McCarty came the next morning, Jared was awake and hoping to find an ally in his quest to escape Suzanna's home. In order to speak to the doctor privately, Jared suggested she and Andy take Pistol for a walk since Suzanna hadn't been out of the house in quite a while.

"Why would you want to go back to your hotel room?" Dr. McCarty asked when he had heard Jared's proposal. "You're doing perfectly well here, and you've got a pretty woman taking excellent care of you."

"I'm . . . imposing on Mrs. Prentice," Jared explained lamely, knowing the doctor probably thought he was crazy. "With me here, she can't work, and I know she needs the money."

Dr. McCarty glanced toward the curtained doorway, listening to see if Suzanna and Andy had returned. Hearing nothing he said, "Then pay her yourself. From what I hear about that poker game you won, you can afford it."

"I already offered, and she turned me down."

"Then you don't have to feel guilty. When you're up and around, you can buy something nice for the boy, or both of them for that matter, to show your appreciation.''

Jared sighed in disgust. He wasn't going to get any help from Dr. McCarty. ''Then for God's sake, tell me I can get up so I don't have to use that damn bedpan anymore!''

McCarty's face lit with understanding. ''So that's why you're in a lather. I'm afraid you won't be making any trips to the outhouse for a while, but you can start sitting up today. I'll show Mrs. Prentice how to make a sling for your arm, and we'll start you on solid food which will help build your strength.''

''And tell her to give me my pants,'' Jared added with a disgruntled frown.

Dr. McCarty grinned. ''I think you'd better tell her yourself.''

By noon, Jared was beginning to think he might survive his stay in the Prentice household. The sling Suzanna had fashioned enabled him to sit up with a minimum of discomfort, and he was even able to sleep for a little while without the laudanum. After Suzanna gave him his bath, she helped him put on a pair of his underdrawers. She even got the barber to come over and give him a shave.

''Our dinner just arrived,'' she told him when he had awakened from his second nap of the morning. ''Would you like to try sitting up to eat?''

''I certainly would,'' he replied, admiring the way her calico dress hugged her feminine curves. Her hair shone like spun gold in the afternoon sunlight, and her eyes were as clear and blue as two sapphires. ''Uh, why don't you and Andy eat in here with me for a change?''

She looked a little surprised at the suggestion, but she said, ''Of course. I guess you're getting tired of eating alone.''

When Andy heard the news, he let out a rebel yell, earning a reprimand from his mother but making Jared smile. While Suzanna positioned Jared's tray and arranged a napkin around his neck, Andy dragged the two chairs in from the front room and put them beside the bed.

Suzanna set Andy's place on the seat of one of the chairs, and he knelt in front of it. She took her own plate in her lap. Remembering his manners, Jared waited for his hostess to begin eating, which was fortunate, since she and Andy bowed their heads while she said a brief prayer over the meal.

How long had it been since he'd eaten food that had been blessed? Jared wondered with an unfamiliar pang of homesickness. He would have believed himself incapable of such longing considering how far from idyllic his home life had been, but there it was all the same. Or perhaps he simply longed for something he had never really possessed.

"The doctor didn't think your stomach would be quite up to steak just yet," Suzanna said, explaining the difference between his meal of mashed potatoes with gravy and theirs.

"He's probably right," Jared admitted. "I'm just glad to be eating at all."

"You look better now that you're shaved," Andy informed him around a bite of meat.

"Don't talk with your mouth full," Suzanna cautioned.

Andy swallowed with a loud gulp. "I can't figure out why the razor don't cut your face off, though."

Jared glanced at Suzanna who was trying to hide her amusement. "Your mother must feel the same way, which makes me glad she didn't shave me."

Suzanna looked up, and their eyes met for an instant before they each looked away self-consciously.

"Mr. Kelley and Mrs. Hand are taking me for a ride this afternoon," Andy continued. "They think I might bother you or something."

"They do, do they?" Jared's gaze met Suzanna's again, and lingered.

"Yes," she said, seeming a little flustered. "You'll

want to take a nap, and Andy can't stay quiet very long."

"He didn't bother me this morning."

"We went out when we realized you were asleep."

"Oh." Jared was having a hard time following the conversation. All that had registered was that he and Suzanna would be alone in the house all afternoon.

"I don't mind," Andy was saying. "I have fun with Mr. Kelley. He makes his dogs do tricks for me, and he's teaching me how to get Pistol to do tricks, too. He can roll over. Want to see?"

"Finish your meal first," Suzanna said.

"Yes, ma'am," he said, stuffing in a forkful of food.

Jared picked up a spoonful of potatoes, but they might as well have been sawdust. He could only think about being alone with Suzanna. They did need to talk, to clear the air between them and establish the terms for the rest of his stay here. He just wished those mundane topics could explain the surge of pleasure he felt every time he thought of having Suzanna all to himself.

"Jared, if you're too tired to eat, I'll be glad to feed you," Suzanna said, startling him back to reality.

"No, I'm fine," he said hastily. He couldn't let her feed him on top of everything else.

Andy continued to chatter between mouthfuls while Jared doggedly finished his own meal. When Suzanna removed the tray, Jared slumped wearily back against the pillows, appalled at how exhausted he was from simply feeding himself. Dr. McCarty was right about him not yet being strong enough to go to the outhouse. He'd at least handle the bedpan himself, though, or die trying.

Dora and Mayor Kelley came for Andy a few minutes later. Suzanna hurried Andy outside so they wouldn't disturb Jared, who had dozed off again.

"How's our patient today?" Dora asked.

"He seems a lot better," Suzanna replied.

"Mama made him a swing for his arm, and we got the barber over to shave him and everything," Andy explained.

"A swing?" Mayor Kelley inquired with a grin.

"A *sling*," Suzanna clarified. "Dr. McCarty said he could sit up, and he's eating solid foods."

"Next thing you know, he'll start complaining," Dora said. "Then you'll know he's really getting better."

"I'd be perfectly willing to endure a little complaining under those circumstances," Suzanna said with a smile.

"I'll go in and pay my respects," Kelley offered, but Suzanna shook her head.

"He's sleeping."

"Then I'll wait till we get back." He turned to Andy. "How's Pistol doing with his tricks?"

"I'll show you." Andy and the mayor stepped into the alley where Pistol could perform.

"How are *you* holding up?" Dora asked Suzanna when they were alone.

"Oh, fine. Better than usual, in fact. I get almost a full night's sleep."

"How strange," Dora mused. "I can't remember what that feels like."

"It feels wonderful, take my word," Suzanna assured her.

"You still look a little strained," Dora noted. "Are you worried about him?"

"Not really. Dr. McCarty says he'll be fine. It's just . . ."

"Just what?"

Suzanna hesitated, uncertain about sharing her concerns with Dora, uncertain even about how to put them into words. "I . . . it's difficult taking care of him now that he's awake."

For a moment Dora looked puzzled, but comprehension soon lightened her eyes. "Difficult or embarrassing?"

"Both."

"For you or him?" Dora asked archly.

Suzanna smiled in spite of her chagrin. "Both."

"Well, well, well. If you're too embarrassed, I wouldn't mind giving Mr. Cain his bath. I'll bet he's even more delicious with his clothes off then he is with them on."

"Dora!" Suzanna scolded.

"Is he?"

"He's . . . very attractive," she admitted, her cheeks burning.

"And you're feeling attracted?"

"Of course not!" she lied, glancing nervously at where Andy and the mayor had disappeared around the corner.

"Then that no-good husband of yours did more damage than I thought."

"Dora, leave Andrew out of this," Suzanna warned.

"I wish I could. I wish *you* could. Not all men are like Andrew."

"Jared Cain is a gambler, Dora, and nobody knows anything about him."

"You know he doesn't drink," Dora pointed out, "so he won't abuse you when he's drunk."

"Dora!"

"I'm sorry, dear, but you're too young to spend the rest of your life alone just because you made a mistake in your first choice."

"Andrew was a good husband," Suzanna said dutifully, knowing her lack of conviction made the words sound feeble. When had she stopped respecting Andrew? Long before the first time he'd threatened her, certainly.

"You don't have to convince *me* how good a husband he was," Dora pointed out. "Anyway, Andrew's dead, no matter what kind of a man he was, and you're very much alive, and Andy needs a father. At least give this Cain fellow a chance."

"Dora, the man offered to *buy* me, for heaven's sake!" Suzanna whispered, scandalized.

"Then you don't have to worry about whether he wants you or not, do you?"

Suzanna thought of the more recent indications of Jared Cain's desire and blushed again. "I'm not interested in . . . in *that*."

"What *do* you want, then?"

"I . . . I don't know."

"A man to take care of you?"

"No! I can take care of myself and Andy both."

Dora nodded wisely. "Well, if you don't want sex and you don't want somebody to feed you, then you want somebody to love you, somebody to turn to in the night when you wake up in the dark and . . . Oh, honey, I know all about the loneliness."

Dora was right, loneliness must be at least partly to blame for her reaction to Jared Cain. But Suzanna also knew loneliness alone couldn't account for the strange aching and the way she couldn't seem to banish visions of his naked body from her mind. She wasn't going to admit that to Dora, though.

"I'm not going to give myself to a man just so I won't wake up alone."

"You'd be a fool if you did, and I don't think you're a fool, Suzanna."

"Of course she's not a fool," Mayor Kelley said, coming around the corner with Andy and Pistol in tow. "Whatever are you talking about?"

"Nothing," Dora replied innocently. "You fellows about ready for our ride?"

"I am!" Andy exclaimed. "C'mon, Pistol!"

"Kiss your mother first," Dora insisted.

Andy made a sharp reversal and charged back at Suzanna, pausing just long enough to catch the kiss she pressed to his cheek. "Be a good boy," she called.

"Take good care of our invalid now," Mayor Kelley said with a smile, "and tell him he'd better be awake

when we get back. I've been dying to hear his version
of that poker game.''

Dora leaned close to her ear. ''And give him a kiss
for me.''

Before Suzanna could express her outrage, Dora was
following the others to the waiting buggy.

''Give him a kiss, indeed,'' Suzanna muttered, wav-
ing good-bye. Entering the house quietly, so as not to
disturb the patient, she peeked into the bedroom to
make certain he was sleeping soundly and noticed he
was still propped up.

On tiptoe, she stole into the room and gently tried
to remove one of the pillows from behind his head so
he could lay flat.

''Suzanna?''

''I'm sorry. I didn't mean to wake you,'' she said,
pulling the pillow free. ''There, now you'll be more
comfortable.''

''I didn't mean to fall asleep. I want to talk to you.''

''About what?'' she asked with forced cheerfulness.
Suzanna didn't think she wanted to talk to him just
yet, certainly not about anything serious, and his expression was very serious.

''About . . . I don't want to be a burden to you.''

''Too late,'' she replied, maintaining her cheerful
pose.

''You know what I mean. Not only are you missing
work, but you're feeding me and paying the doctor
and—

''I'm not paying the doctor. He heard about the
poker game and said your credit was good.''

Jared winced, and Suzanna instantly regretted her
attempt at humor.

''I'm sorry. I don't suppose you think the poker
game is a joking matter''

''What I'm trying to say is, I want you to at least let
me pay the expenses of taking care of me.''

''Of course,'' she agreed, seeing a way to put him
at ease and end the argument once and for all. ''As

soon as you're better, we'll figure out how much you owe me.''

She could tell from his expression he'd been expecting a fight. ''Well, all right,'' he agreed after thinking it over for a moment. ''And there's also no reason you can't go back to work now. I'll be up and around in another day or so, and I'm not going to take any more laudanum, so I'll be in my right mind.''

''I told you before, I'm only too glad for an excuse not to go to work,'' Suzanna said, even though she knew she should have been anxious to start earning money again.

''If you're gone too long, Springer might not be willing to give you your job back.''

''I'm sure he'll take me back,'' she said with more conviction than she felt.

''Suzanna, there's no reason for you to stay here with me night after night anymore. Think about it this way: for once you'll have somebody to stay with Andy while you work.''

''Then I'd be worried about both of you!''

''Don't be ridiculous. The only thing wrong with me is that my arm is in a sling.''

''You can't even get out of bed,'' she reminded him, taking perverse pleasure from his disgruntled frown.

''Dr. McCarty said I could get up tomorrow. Besides, if anything happens, I can send Andy over to the Western for help.''

Suzanna knew he was right, but for some reason she couldn't bring herself to agree with his plan. She told herself she had just grown accustomed to not going to the Comique every night, and taking care of Jared was a convenient excuse. Unfortunately, she knew perfectly well that wasn't the real reason.

''I'll see how you do tonight without the laudanum, then talk to the doctor tomorrow,'' she said, reluctant to promise more.

''Suzanna, I'm a grown man,'' he reminded her in exasperation.

"Then act like one!" she snapped, unaccountably annoyed. "You were shot, for heaven's sake, and you might've died. I worked awfully hard to make sure you didn't, and now you want to—"

"All right, all right," he said, absently rubbing his temple as if she were giving him a headache.

Instantly contrite, she touched his cheek. "I'm sorry. I'm just worried about you." His skin felt smooth beneath her touch, and she let her fingers slide along his jaw for a second until she realized what she was doing and snatched her hand away. His eyes widened in surprise. "I . . . Can I get you anything? Are you thirsty?"

"A little water." Did his voice sound husky? No, she was only being fanciful. She hurried to get the water.

When she returned, she found him sitting up on the edge of the bed and looking positively wanton clad in only his underdrawers. "What are you doing?" she demanded in alarm.

"Showing you I'm not an invalid," he said, snatching the glass from her hand and taking a long gulp.

Except for the white bandage and the sling, he could not have resembled an invalid less. With his broad shoulders and powerful arms and legs, he looked exactly like what he was: a strong, vital male.

Her chest felt as if a giant vise were squeezing it, and she could barely draw a breath.

Jared plunked the half-empty glass down on the crate-table beside the bed and gave a disgusted sigh. When he looked up, his chocolate eyes were surprisingly vulnerable. "Suzanna, I don't want to fight with you."

"I don't want to fight with you either," she said, instinctively reaching for him. His freshly shaven cheeks were warm to her hands, and she felt the familiar ache in the pit of her stomach.

"It's just . . . Don't you know . . . ?" His good hand came up and encircled her waist, drawing her closer. "You're so beautiful," he murmured, and something inside her seemed to melt.

She slipped her arms around his neck as he pulled her between his thighs and pressed his face against her breasts.

"God, you smell so good," he said, his breath hot through the thin fabric. Struggling with the sling, he clutched at her waist with his other hand, running his palm up her side until it grazed the underside of her breast.

Her heart fluttered like a trapped bird, and the ache inside her became a need. He lifted his face, his hands urgent.

"Suzanna . . ."

She could not refuse. His mouth was hungry, demanding everything. He pulled her close and closer still, falling backwards on the bed and carrying her with him.

Warning bells went off in her head, and in that instant she lost her balance and fell against him.

"*Oww!*"

Suzanna broke away, rolling free as he clutched at his shoulder and moaned. "Oh, Jared, what . . . ? Are you hurt? Is it bleeding? Do you want some laudanum?"

"No, dammit, leave me alone!" he snapped through gritted teeth.

Suzanna sat up, watching helplessly while he grimaced in pain. As Jared's agony subsided, Suzanna's own breath slowed to normal and her heart ceased in its effort to pound its way out of her chest. At last he lay still, his body limp and exhausted, and Suzanna breathed a sigh of relief. "Jared, I'm sorry."

His eyes flew open, and to her surprise, they were filled with rage. "Now do you see why I shouldn't stay here? Do you know what almost happened?"

She most certainly did, but she didn't find it nearly as alarming as she should have. In fact, she felt almost annoyed by his chivalry. "You don't have to worry about my virtue. A dance-hall girl doesn't have any."

"But *you* do, don't you? And you guard it very carefully."

She had, of course, until this moment. Now she suddenly found herself lying on a bed with a nearly naked man whom she didn't feel the least bit guilty about having kissed. But enough was enough. Carefully, so as not to jar Jared, she levered herself off the bed.

Straightening her clothes self-consciously, she said, "You didn't exactly force me."

"Suzanna," he said in the impatient tone she was beginning to recognize, "I'm not the kind of man a woman like you should get involved with. There are things about me you don't know, and even the things you do know are bad enough. I'm a gambler, Suzanna, a man without a home or a future. You should be married to a storekeeper or a farmer, someone who'll give you the kind of life you deserve."

"I *was* married to a farmer, and I hope I never deserve that kind of life again!" she informed him bitterly.

She'd shocked him, and she'd even shocked herself a bit. She made it a point to keep her private hurts private. "And another thing," she continued before he could reply, "you needn't worry about seducing me. I forgot myself for a minute, but it won't happen again, I promise you. Since you can hardly hope to force me with only one good arm, I think my virtue is perfectly safe, don't you?"

He just glared at her, his breath coming in quick, angry gasps.

She looked at the way he was sprawled across the bed, his feet still on the floor.

"Do you need some help getting back into bed?"

"No, thank you very much." Gingerly, he pushed up on his good elbow and began to laboriously maneuver himself around. Suzanna knew an almost overwhelming urge to help, but she curled her hands into fists and resisted.

When he had again collapsed against the pillow, she said, "I'm going to run a few errands while you rest."

"Fine," he said, panting, not even looking at her.

Feeling absurdly slighted, she left in a huff.

The town was quiet in the early afternoon heat, so Suzanna accomplished her shopping quickly. By the time she was heading back to her house, she had begun to feel foolish for the way she had carried on with Jared. He was right, of course—she had no business getting involved with a man like him. Hadn't she said the very same thing to Dora just a little while ago? Unfortunately, saying it herself and hearing it from him were two different things.

She'd also told Dora she wasn't interested in sex, yet she'd fallen straight into Jared's arms at the first opportunity and thoroughly enjoyed every one of his kisses. Of course she didn't want anything *more* than his kisses. She knew enough to know she didn't desire further intimacies with Jared Cain or any other man.

Which made Jared's suggestion of another farmer-husband a little impractical, she thought with amusement as she turned the corner of the alley to her house.

When she opened the door, she was surprised to hear voices coming from the other room. Had Mayor Kelley come back already? she wondered, remembering his promise to visit.

"Jared?" She sniffed the air with disapproval. Cigars! How would she ever get the smell out?

"We have a visitor," he replied, more cheerful than she had ever heard him.

She set her purchases down on the table and hastily drew back the doorway curtain. She almost gasped aloud to see Doc Holliday's emaciated form rising from the chair beside Jared's bed.

"Suzanna, you know John Holliday, don't you?"

"We've . . . never actually met," she said, remembering her conviction that she would never even have an opportunity to do so.

Jared quickly made the introductions. Holliday bowed

from the waist like a proper Southern gentleman although Suzanna caught a whiff of whiskey. People said Holliday wasn't even civil unless he was intoxicated, so Suzanna assumed he must be thoroughly drunk. "You're from Georgia, aren't you?" he asked.

"Why, yes, how did you know?"

He smiled slightly, although it did not quite reach his pale blue eyes. "From your speech. One Georgian knows another instantly."

Hearing his accent, she realized he was correct. "Where are you from?"

"Born in Griffin, but during the war we moved to Valdosta, a tiny place near the Florida border. And you?"

"Savannah, south of there. We had a farm."

He nodded absently, coughing, and studied her face intently. The silence stretched while Suzanna tried to think of something to say. His eyes took on a vacant look, as if he were no longer seeing her at all, and for one awful moment she thought he might be even sicker or drunker than she had thought. "Dr. Holliday?"

He shook his head as if to clear it and smiled his slight smile again. "Excuse me for staring, Mrs. Prentice, but you put me in mind of someone." His smile became self-mocking. "Golden-haired ladies with Georgia accents always make me homesick. Forgive me for making you uncomfortable."

"Doc was just filling me in on what happened the night I was shot," Jared explained, his own good breeding compelling him to smooth over the awkward moment.

"Yes, I thought Jared should know he earned the respect of every gambling man in Dodge that night."

"I'm sure that will make his shoulder hurt a lot less," Suzanna said wryly.

Holliday's pale eyes lit with appreciation. "As you say, madam," he conceded.

"May I offer you something, Dr. Holliday?"

"No, thank you. I should be leaving so Jared can get some rest. A pleasure meeting you. Jared, take care.

We're looking forward to having you back with us at the Comique.''

He didn't wait for Suzanna to show him out. She stared after him, bemused.

"You must remind him of his beloved."

Suzanna looked at Jared in surprise. "I don't look anything like Kate Elder," she informed him, naming the woman with whom Dr. Holliday shared a residence whenever they weren't quarreling too much.

"Neither does his beloved," Jared replied with a knowing grin. "Everyone knows he broke his engagement to a girl back in Georgia when he found out he was consumptive. The young lady still writes to him faithfully. They say she never married."

"He can't be too heartbroken if he's taken up with Kate Elder," she said with a skeptical frown.

Jared shrugged. "Letters can only give a man so much comfort. I suppose he selected Big Nose Kate as a paramour because she was as different from his fiancée as any woman could be."

In her mind's eye Suzanna considered the woman known as Big Nose Kate. Tall, big-boned, and buxom, the brunette was the complete antithesis of Suzanna. If Suzanna did indeed resemble Holliday's long-lost sweetheart, he had most certainly chosen the one woman least likely to put him in mind of her. Of course, Kate Elder was a prostitute, so not even her character would cause Holliday any unpleasant memories.

"I've heard they fight like cats and dogs," Suzanna remarked. "Some of the girls at the Comique live in Tin Pot Alley, too, and they say the two of them have even fired shots at each other."

"I would've have expected you to live over there, too, farther away from the cribs," Jared said, referring to the tents and hovels where the cheapest prostitutes plied their trade down by the river. Tin Pot Alley was the street behind Front Street on the north side of town, the so-called respectable section. "At least on the North Side men can't shoot off guns at all hours of the day and night." The carrying of firearms was prohibited north of the railroad tracks.

"Since I had to leave Andy alone, I wanted him as close as possible. If anything happens, I can be here in two minutes."

Jared nodded. "Like the night the cowboy tried to kill Marshal Earp?"

Feeling her face burn at the memory of her foolhardy attempt to rescue Andy that night, Suzanna refused to acknowledge her embarrassment. "If there's a fire or . . . something."

"Oh."

They stared at each other across the small room, and Suzanna realized she had forgotten to be awkward with him, as she had expected to be after their kiss. From the expression on his face, he might have been realizing the same thing. "How are you feeling?" she asked to change the subject.

"Tired. I'd just fallen asleep when Doc came knocking at the door."

"You smoked cigars in my house," she said, trying to sound outraged.

He grinned unrepentantly. "I knew I should have refused, but I hadn't had a smoke in so long, I had it lit before I could think about it.'

"I'll never get that awful smell out," she complained, fanning the air with her hand. "I suppose he gave you liquor, too."

"You'll be happy to know I resisted the temptation, although the prospect of numbing this shoulder of mine was very enticing."

Suzanna frowned, remembering what Dora had said about Jared not drinking. She hadn't questioned the remark at the time, but now she realized she had never seen him take a drink, not even when he was working at the Comique. Dr. McCarty had suggested Jared might take some whiskey for the pain if he didn't want to use the laudanum anymore, and alcohol *was* the most commonly used painkiller in the world. Although the thought of a man drinking in her house made her blood run cold, she was probably being cruel not to offer Jared the opportunity to ease his suffering. "I don't approve of alcohol, of course, but if you feel you need some, for your shoulder, I mean . . ."

Jared shook his head. "If I'd wanted a drink, I would have taken it from Doc. I'm not exactly a prohibitionist, but I make it a rule never to imbibe. Liquor robs a man of his judgment and his control."

Suzanna nodded, understanding far more than he guessed. Unpleasant memories made her shudder slightly before she mentally pushed them away. "Well, you'd better try to get some rest before the mayor brings Andy back. Mr. Kelley wants to visit you, too."

Later, while Jared slept, Suzanna considered what he had said about alcohol making a man lose control of his judgment. Of course a gambler would need to keep his wits about him, but Jared wasn't going to be doing any gambling for a while. She wondered why he would need to worry about such things here until she recalled the scene in the bedroom this afternoon. Even cold sober, he had almost lost control with her, and she with him.

She had best keep alcohol as far away from Jared Cain as possible.

When Dora and Mayor Kelley brought Andy home, they also brought a hamper of food they had obtained at the Western, which provided supper for all of them. Kelley pulled the table into the bedroom so he and Jared could sit on the bed while the two women used the chairs and Andy sat on the bedside crate. Even though they were elbow to elbow in the stifling room, no one seemed to mind.

Suzanna worried that the excitement might be too much for Jared, but on the contrary, he seemed invigorated by it. He had even struggled into pants and a shirt for the occasion, not asking her for a bit of help.

Although she knew she should be glad to see him

looking better, the knowledge that he was indeed improving irritated her. The others talked and laughed so much, however, that no one noticed her mood.

"I can't imagine how you figured out what those two men were doing," Dora said after Jared had explained the poker game to Dog Kelley.

"Me neither," Andy piped between bites of fried chicken, making everyone laugh.

"You have to know how to play the game first," Kelley pointed out.

"Maybe Mr. Cain'll teach me," Andy said, giving Jared a questioning look.

"You're a little young for poker," Jared said, glancing at Suzanna, who appeared appalled at the very thought.

"I'm afraid you have to learn how to count before you can play cards," Suzanna said, hoping she didn't sound as cross as she felt, although why she should be so irritated with Jared's friendly bantering, she had no idea.

"Your mama's right," Kelley said with a grin. "I can't think of a better way to learn than by counting the spots on the back of a card, either."

"Jimmy," Dora scolded, "I doubt Suzanna is amused by your humor."

Suzanna managed a tolerant smile. "If Jared can teach a four-year-old boy to count, I don't care how he does it."

Jared winked at Andy. "We'll have our first lesson after supper."

"Oh, boy!" Andy whooped. After that he was too excited to eat another bite, so he crawled under the table and went into the front room to play with Pistol.

"I suppose we'd better be going," Dora said a few minutes later. "I have to be at the Comique soon, and Jimmy likes to be at the Alhambra when the crowd arrives."

Jared glanced thoughtfully at Suzanna. "I've been trying to tell Suzanna she doesn't need to stay home and take care of me anymore, but for some reason she doesn't believe me."

"Maybe she doesn't *want* to believe you," Dora said

slyly. "If I had a choice between going to the Comique and staying home with a handsome man, I know what I'd choose."

Suzanna kicked Dora under the table, but Dora didn't seem to notice. Mercifully, Jared acquired a sudden interest in his food so he didn't see Suzanna's burning face, but Mayor Kelley did. His heavy-lidded eyes grew wide with understanding.

"I'll probably go back to work tomorrow," Suzanna allowed grudgingly, hating her own reluctance because it seemed to prove Dora's theory. "Saturday night is always my busiest night, and I shouldn't miss it."

"Springer has been asking about you," Dora said, obviously disapproving of Suzanna's decision. "Should I tell him you're coming back?"

"No," she replied too quickly. "I mean, I want to see how Jared does tonight first. It'll be his first night without the laudanum."

"He seems to be doing just fine to me," Kelley said to Suzanna's disgust. "With Jared here, you won't have to worry about leaving Andy, either."

Dora seemed to sense Suzanna's discomfort and rose from her chair. "I'm sure Suzanna can make her own decisions without any help from us. Let's get this cleared away before we go," she said, starting to repack the hamper they had brought.

When Suzanna had bid them good-bye at the door, she went to the bedroom doorway where she could hear Andy and Jared deep in conversation. Peeking through the curtain, she found Andy sitting cross-legged at the foot of Jared's bed, staring intently at the cards Jared had spread out on the quilt. Jared had removed his shirt in deference to the heat, and sat at the head of the bed with his own legs crossed.

"See, this card has two hearts on it," Jared was saying. "Count them with me. One, two. And this number in the corner is a two. How many hearts are on this card?"

"I don't know," Andy said.

"Count them."

"One, two, three. *Three!*"

Suzanna gaped. She'd had no idea Andy knew how to count.

"Good, and this one."

"One, two, three, four. Four! That's how old I am!"

Jared reached out and ruffled Andy's flaxen hair affectionately. "That's right, partner. Can you count higher than four?"

"I can count my fingers, all the way to ten."

Jared smiled, a grin full of delight and mischief. The sight almost took her breath. "Then you know everything you need to know. Count this card."

With wonder, Suzanna watched the gentle way Jared led Andy through the entire suit, his dark eyes alight with genuine affection as the boy counted and laughed and counted some more.

"That's it," he pronounced when Andy had counted to ten. "We'll show your mama, won't we?"

"I love you, Jared," Andy exclaimed, launching himself into Jared's arms.

Suzanna almost cried out in protest, as appalled to hear her son express his love for this virtual stranger as she was fearful the boy would hurt Jared's wound. But Jared caught him with his good arm and hugged him close, and for once she could easily read Cain's every emotion. Joy and longing and love returned, a sight that tore her heart.

Suzanna placed a hand over the pain and let the curtain fall shut. No, it can't be, she told herself. But it could be and it was. She'd tried to deny it, tried to pretend it was something else, tried to tell herself Jared Cain wasn't worthy, but she couldn't pretend any longer. Seeing him with Andy proved to her Jared was everything she'd wanted in a man and never dreamed of finding: he was kind and generous and loving and funny and passionate and, God help her, she was hopelessly in love with him.

Chapter 6

❝**C**an Jared live with us from now on?❞ Andy asked as Suzanna was tucking him into his makeshift bed a little while later.

"You should call him Mr. Cain," she replied evasively.

"He told me to call him Jared. Can he stay? I don't mind sleeping on the floor."

Looking down at her son in dismay, Suzanna tried to think of a way to explain things to Andy. Painfully aware that Jared could hear every word she said, she swallowed self-consciously. "Mr. Cain is only staying here because he's too weak to take care of himself. It really wouldn't be proper for him to stay with us once he's well."

"Why not?"

"It . . . it just wouldn't," she hedged. "Now go to sleep." She bent down, kissed his forehead, then rose from where she had knelt beside him.

She blew out the lamp and realized with a slight sense of panic that she really had no place to go now. She could sit in this room in the dark with Andy while he tried to fall asleep, sit outside where she might be accosted by a wandering drunk, or go into the other room with Jared.

Her stomach did a rebellious little flip at the mere thought, but she called herself a fool. What did she have to be afraid of? Cain had no inkling she had realized she was in love with him. If he was awake—and she had every reason to believe he was—she should at least be hospitable and visit with him until it was her own bedtime.

Oh, dear, she thought as she moved toward the bedroom doorway, why hadn't she taken Jared's advice and gone to work tonight?

"Jared? May I come in?"

"Of course."

He'd been lying down, although he still wore his trousers, she saw with relief.

"Don't get up," she said when he started to push himself into a sitting position, but he ignored her. She busied herself arranging one of the chairs so she wouldn't have to watch the play of muscles across his bare shoulders as he moved.

"I was trying to fall asleep, but I guess I slept too much today already."

Suzanna sat down in the chair and composed her expression into polite concern, keeping her gaze fixed on his face so she wouldn't be disturbed by the sight of his bare chest. "Is your shoulder bothering you?"

"Some, but I can stand it. I have no intentions of taking any more laudanum."

Suzanna wondered if *she* should take some instead, but quickly discarded the ridiculous thought. "I hope our little party didn't wear you out too much."

"Not at all. I'm glad you finally got to see your friends. You must be getting cabin fever being cooped up with me all this time."

"I'm used to staying home. That's what I mostly did before . . ." She caught herself, not wanting to discuss her previous life.

"Oh, yes, you lived on a farm. I'd forgotten. Were you raised on a farm, too?"

"Yes, back in Georgia," she admitted reluctantly.

"What brought you to Kansas?"

"Land." Suzanna shifted uncomfortably in her chair,

unnerved by the gentle interest in his eyes and in his voice.

"Didn't you already have land in Georgia?"

"We were only tenant farmers. When Andrew, my husband, heard he could homestead a hundred and sixty acres here, he thought it was the chance of a lifetime."

"But you didn't."

Suzanna stared at him, surprised at his perception. "No one told us how barren Kansas is, how it didn't have any trees and how we'd have to live in a hole in the ground and . . ." She caught herself again, knowing she shouldn't reveal her bitterness to Cain.

"Andy said you lived in a cave." Jared's eyes were soft and full of sympathy, and her resolve to remain silent slipped away.

"He liked the bugs and even the snakes, although he'd cry when the rain made mud puddles in his bed."

"You must have hated living like that, with all the dirt and the vermin."

"And the wind." She shuddered. "The wind never stops, all day and all night, and sometimes it's the only sound you can hear. Last spring they sent three women back East because they'd gone crazy from it. It happens every year."

She glanced away, embarrassed for having said too much. A few moments of silence ticked away before he said, "How did your husband die?"

Ordinarily, Suzanna would have hesitated to share this story with anyone, but the tender interest in Jared's eyes overcame her reticence. "He froze to death, out on the prairie. We'd borrowed money to come West and stake our claim, so times were hard. They pay cash for buffalo bones, so Andrew was collecting them to sell in town, and he . . . he must've fallen asleep or something. . . . He fell out of the wagon and froze to death."

"How awful. I'm very sorry."

Suzanna didn't want his sympathy, so she looked

away again, studying the wall with intense interest and berating herself for burdening Jared Cain with her troubles. At least she hadn't told him everything, about how Andrew had fallen out of the wagon because he'd been too drunk to sit upright and how he'd lain there in a drunken stupor until the cold claimed him.

"Suzanna?"

She started guiltily.

"I'm sorry to stir up painful memories. By rights you should still be in mourning."

"Dance-hall girls aren't allowed to mourn," she said with her professional smile.

"You aren't really a dance-hall girl," he said. "You don't belong at the Comique any more than Andy would."

He pronounced the name of the theater "Com-meek," not "Commie-kew," the way almost everyone in Dodge did, everyone except the educated few. Although she'd noticed it before, she found it irritating tonight since it symbolized for her the vast gulf separating a man of good family—even if he was a gambler—and the widow of a penniless farmer. "Where *do* I belong, then?"

Reading the challenge in her question, he smiled slightly. "Don't worry, I'm not going to say you belong on a farm." His eyes narrowed thoughtfully. "You belong in a big house with tall white pillars and a wide green lawn and a rose garden. You should wear silk dresses and have servants bringing you tea on a silver tray."

She stared at him incredulously until she realized he was looking past her, as if he were seeing something far beyond her tiny house in Dodge City. Of course. He was describing the home from which he had come and the women he had known.

The kind of woman she could never be, she told herself ruthlessly, ignoring the wrench of anguish. All this time she'd been worried that Jared wasn't the right man for her, but now it seemed she might not be the right woman for him. She managed a brittle laugh. "You've got me confused with somebody else."

His fine eyebrows lifted, and he smiled sardonically. "I don't think so."

She looked down at her hands. No longer reddened from the grinding chores of farm work, they still bore the telltale burn scars and calluses from her previous life. No one in his right mind would ever mistake her for a fine lady. "You're starting to talk nonsense," she chided with forced lightness. "I think it's time you went to bed."

"You're probably right," he agreed, but when she stood to blow out the lamp he stopped her.

"Wait a minute. You're not going to go into the other room and sit there in the dark, are you?"

"I'll just go on to bed. I don't want to disturb you."

"You can't be tired yet. Why don't you leave the lamp on and stay in here? It won't bother me."

"Are you sure? I mean, I do have some mending, but I don't want to keep you awake."

"I'm used to sleeping in broad daylight," he reminded her. "A little lamplight won't bother me."

She started to fetch her sewing basket from the front room, but when she saw he was struggling to rearrange his pillows, she automatically went to help him. Then she realized with alarm he would probably want to undress, too. The night was far too hot for trousers. His chest glistened from the heat already.

As a conscientious nurse, she should be more concerned with her patient's comfort than with her own sensibilities, though, and she'd been neglecting his comfort. Dutifully, she asked, "Would you like a bath before you go to bed?"

"No!" he replied so quickly she knew she'd been right to be reluctant. "But I wouldn't mind washing up a bit. Could you bring me—"

"Of course." She was back in a few moments, then she left discreetly until he was finished. When she returned with her sewing basket, Jared lay quietly. He'd removed his trousers and drawn the sheet up to his waist, and she could see he was half-asleep already.

She felt a ridiculous urge to tuck him in the way she always tucked Andy in and recognized it for what it was: a simple longing to touch him. Sitting down quickly, she rummaged in her basket for needle and thread and found one of Andy's torn shirts. Although her fingers were occupied, her mind kept wandering. The sound of Jared's regular breathing reminded her she could watch him undetected, and her hands stilled as she lifted her gaze.

He'd removed his sling, revealing the broad expanse of his chest with its covering of chestnut hair. The sheet covered the lower half of his body, but Suzanna knew every inch of his muscled legs and lean hips. He was, without doubt, the finest-looking man she had ever seen. A familiar ache started in her stomach and spread outward until her whole body throbbed. For the first time she recognized the longing for what it was: pure, unadulterated desire.

Not desire for sex, of course. No woman would want *that*, but she did want what went with it, the holding and the kissing and the closeness. And the loving. Oh, yes, she dearly wanted someone to love her, and she wanted that someone to be Jared Cain.

Why did he have to be so handsome? And why did he have to be so gentle with Andy? And why did he have to be who he was? Even if he wanted to be with her . . . which he didn't, as he'd made perfectly clear.

Tears of frustration burned her eyes. She threw her mending back in the basket, jumped up, blew out the lamp and hurried into the other room. What was wrong with her? Was she losing her mind? She wrapped her arms around her middle to ease the pain.

She thought of the women who'd had to be taken back East. Perhaps she'd been wrong about what had driven them insane. Perhaps it had been loneliness instead, loneliness and longing for what they could never have.

* * *

The next morning Suzanna awoke with a start, sitting bolt upright on the cot at the sound of her front door closing. "Who . . . Jared?"

He was leaning against the wall by the door looking pale and very near collapse. In an instant she was beside him. "What on earth are you doing up?"

"I went . . . to the . . . outhouse," he informed her through bloodless lips.

"Good heavens! Whatever possessed you! What if you'd fainted or fallen or—" Realizing her tirade wasn't doing any good, she stopped. "Here, put your arm over my shoulder, and I'll help you back to bed."

He'd gotten himself dressed, too, she noticed irrelevantly. She supposed he wouldn't think of going out, even to the outhouse, without being properly clothed.

"Mama? What's going on?" Andy inquired sleepily.

"Nothing, dear, go back to sleep," she said, struggling to bear Jared's weight into the bedroom. After what seemed an eternity, she lowered him onto the bed and helped him stretch out. He relaxed with a weary sigh.

"Jared, that was a fool thing to do! You could've hurt yourself. You could've fallen down or . . ." She stopped when she saw he was smiling.

"I made it, didn't I?" he asked, the twinkle in his eyes belying the paleness of his face.

"Only by the grace of God," she replied angrily, planting her hands firmly on her hips. "When I think what could've happened—"

"I'm fine," he insisted, "or I will be in a minute or two. And when I am," he added with a sly grin, "you'd better have some clothes on, Mrs. Prentice."

Suzanna glanced down at her flimsy nightdress which must be nearly transparent in the morning light. "Oh!" she cried and darted through the curtains into the other room.

By the end of that day, Suzanna had decided Jared Cain was the most infuriating man she had ever met.

First of all, he'd charmed Andy until the poor boy was besotted with him. While Jared was teaching Andy a simple version of solitaire, she'd heard the child ask Jared to live with them even after he got well.

"I thought your mama told you that wouldn't be proper," Jared said.

"She did, but I don't see why not. Why wouldn't it be, Jared?"

"You'll have to ask your mother," Jared had replied infuriatingly.

Later in the day Jared had asked him, "Did you like living on a farm?"

"I liked the animals. I was supposed to get a pony when I got bigger, but now Mama says we don't have anyplace to keep one. Did you have a pony when you was little?"

"Oh, yes, I had several. I got my first one when I was about your age, but that was because the farm where I lived raised horses instead of crops."

"You mean horses grow out of the ground like corn does?" Andy asked in amazement.

Jared's rich laughter raised goose bumps on Suzanna's arms. "No, I mean instead of corn we grew grass in our fields for the horses to eat. The horses had baby horses, and that's how we raised them."

"Oh. Our cow had a calf, but we sold it when we moved to town."

"It's the same basic principle."

"What's a principle?"

Suzanna had listened with growing dismay as Jared patiently explained and continued to answer every one of Andy's myriad questions. How dare he be such a fine man? How dare he make her love him more by being kind to her son?

And how dare he torture her by flirting?

"You're lucky to have such a pretty mama," he'd said to Andy when they'd retired to the bedroom right after breakfast.

"You saw her in her nightdress. Boys ain't supposed

to look at girls when they ain't dressed. Is that why she says it wouldn't be proper for you to live here, 'cause you might see her undressed?''

"I'm sure that's one of her concerns," Jared had replied with maddening coolness.

Of course, such an exchange couldn't be called flirting in the usual sense, but Cain knew perfectly well she could hear every provocative word he said, and he said quite a few in the course of the day.

And the way he looked at her, making her blush and then turning away as if *he* were the one embarrassed. By eight o'clock, Suzanna was actually eager to go back to work at the Comique.

"Are you sure you'll be all right?" she asked Jared for the third time in an hour. "I didn't promise to come in tonight, so they won't miss me."

"We'll be fine, won't we Andy?" Jared replied, and Andy nodded his vigorous consent. "I'll keep him up late so he'll let you sleep in the morning, too."

"But tomorrow is Sunday. We don't want to miss church," she protested.

"You go to church after working all night?" Jared asked in amazement.

"Of course. Having to work late doesn't excuse a person from breaking one of the commandments."

"You'll be awfully tired since you didn't take a nap this afternoon."

"I've been tired before. Andy, give me a kiss before I go."

Andy jumped into her arms and gave her a wet smack on the cheek. "I love you, Mama."

"I love you, too. Be good for Mr. Cain and go right to bed."

"I will," he promised, but the gleam in his eye warned her he had not intention of doing so.

"Don't keep him up too late, or I'll never get him up for church," she warned Jared.

Jared grinned. "We'll be good, Mama."

Pursing her lips so she wouldn't smile back at him,

she hurried out before he could say anything else she might find charming or delightful. Why on earth had she talked him into staying at her house in the first place?

That night at the Comique was one of the longest Suzanna had ever lived through. Springer actually seemed pleased to have her back, but the girls bombarded her with questions about Jared, questions she didn't want to answer, like how long he'd be staying and what he was like. Even Dora's singing, which she normally enjoyed, unsettled her, especially when she sang of lovers parting and broken hearts.

For the first time since Suzanna had started at the Comique, she was unable to block out thoughts of Andy while she worked. Since this was also the first evening he had truly been safe, she recognized the irony of the situation and blamed it on Jared Cain and his unsettling presence.

When at last the long night was over and she had collected her pay from Springer, Suzanna hurried down the dark alley with a renewed sense of alarm. Why was the light on in the bedroom? she wondered anxiously as she fumbled with the lock, only to discover the door was open.

Lamplight filtering through the curtain illuminated the pallet where Andy slept peacefully. Pistol didn't even feel he needed to get up from his spot beside the boy and greeted her only with a wag of his tail. "Jared?" she called softly, moving toward the curtain and pushing it aside.

"Welcome home," he said, smiling as if nothing in the world were wrong. He was sitting up in bed, the sheet pulled to his waist, his chest bare. At least his sling covered most of it.

"What are you doing awake at this hour?" she asked, plunking her purse down on the bedside table.

"Please don't be mad, Mama," he said, doing a credible imitation of Andy's voice and making her smile in spite of herself.

"I'm not mad," she insisted, "but you need your rest."

"I was sleeping very well, thank you, but I rolled over the wrong way and woke myself up a little while ago," he explained. "Since then I've been reading." He gestured to a book lying on the bed beside him.

"The Bible?" she asked in amazement.

"Your library is rather limited," he reminded her.

"Oh, yes, of course."

"You look tired."

"I am," she admitted, sinking down into the chair which still sat beside the bed. Absently, she unlaced the rugged boots she wore to protect her feet, slipped them off and flexed her toes gingerly.

Jared watched sympathetically. "I don't suppose I ever thought about how hard your job really is—a lot harder than sitting at a card table every night."

"The pay is good," she reminded him.

"But, as I mentioned before, the Comique isn't a very nice place for a lady to work. I'm surprised you didn't ask the church for help after your husband died. Reverend Wright would have been glad to—"

"He was," she said bitterly.

Jared frowned. "He was what?"

"Willing to help. He helped me find a 'respectable' job. I cleaned house for a 'good Christian family' for a few weeks until . . . Well, it didn't work out."

"Why not? What happened?"

Suzanna hesitated. Did she dare tell him? What would he think of her? Would he assume she was innocent, or would he start looking at her the way so many men in town did, as if she were no better than the women who sold their bodies in tents by the river? She could ignore those men, but she loved Jared. How could she bear his contempt? On the other hand, if he held her in contempt, he would no longer be the man she'd fallen in love with.

"I worked for this family until one night . . . the

husband sneaked into my room and tried to . . . He attacked me.''

"Good God!"

"And when I screamed and woke up his wife, he claimed I'd lured him in and tried to seduce him, and of course she believed him because what else could she do?''

"She could have thrown the bastard out!" Jared said, every bit as outraged as she could have wished. Her heart swelled.

"If she'd thrown him out, she would have been as alone and unprotected as I was. Far better to ruin the reputation of a poor nobody like me than to lose her husband. After that, of course, no other women wanted me in their houses, either, so . . ." She shrugged.

"So with your reputation already ruined, you had nothing to lose by going to the Comique," Jared finished for her.

"Exactly."

His dark eyes were tortured. "I'm sorry, Suzanna."

"It wasn't your fault."

"No, but someone owes you an apology. I once said you were a brave lady, but I didn't know how brave until this moment.''

He believed her! Suzanna blinked against the sting of tears. For one wild second she considered throwing herself into his arms for the comfort no one had ever given her, but she resisted the impulse. She would settle for simply knowing he trusted her.

"What time did you finally get Andy to sleep?" she asked to change the subject.

"Well before midnight, I'm sure. We played cards until his eyes started to cross.''

"I'm not sure I approve of the way you're corrupting my son, Mr. Cain,'' Suzanna said with feigned disapproval.

He grinned unrepentantly. "I'd be happy to concentrate my efforts on corrupting his mother instead if I thought I'd have any success."

Her cheeks warmed, but she wasn't as embarrassed as she should have been. "If all the cowboys in Texas haven't been able to corrupt me, I doubt one Yankee gambler stands a chance."

Jared sighed dramatically. "That's what I was afraid of."

With a start, Suzanna realized she and Jared were flirting! Disconcerted, she jumped to her feet. "I guess I'd better be getting to bed."

"It *is* late." He watched her pick up her shoes and her purse. "I feel guilty for making you sleep on the cot."

She gave him a hopeful smile. "Are you offering to take it yourself and give me the bed?"

He pretended to consider. "No, but I'd be perfectly willing to *share* the bed."

Suzanna gasped. "Jared Cain, you're a wicked man," she informed him, hurrying toward the curtained doorway.

"So I've been told," he called after her.

When the curtain had fallen shut behind her, Suzanna dropped the things she was carrying and covered her burning cheeks with her hands. Jared Cain *was* a wicked man, and it was a good thing he didn't know how very tempting his offer was.

On the other side of the curtain, Jared waited while Suzanna lit the lamp in the other room, then blew out his own. If he lay very still and held his breath, he could hear the rustle of her clothing as she undressed. The shadows on the fabric separating them were indistinct, but Jared needed no help in picturing what Suzanna looked like.

As clearly as if she stood before him, he could see her milk-white skin, her small, upturned breasts with their pink tips, her narrow waist and flat belly, and the golden curls at the apex of her long, shapely legs. With equal clarity, he recalled the sweetness of her kiss, and by the time the light went out in the next room, his damp body pulsed with desire.

He was crazy to torture himself this way, especially when he could never take Suzanna Prentice even if she were willing. She'd already known far too much tragedy in her life. The last thing she needed was to become involved with a hunted man. Still, he couldn't deny how wonderful it felt to want someone again.

Jared lay awake for long minutes until the throbbing in his shoulder once again became greater than the throbbing down below. With a sigh, he surrendered once again to sleep.

"No!"

Suzanna awoke instantly at the cry, thinking Andy must be having a nightmare, but in the predawn light she could see he still slept soundly.

"No, Father . . . *Don't touch her!*"

"Jared?" Suzanna jumped off the cot and hurried into the bedroom where she found Jared tossing restlessly in the throes of a nightmare. He'd removed his sling, and she feared he might tear open his wound.

"Jared, wake up," she said, shaking him gently. "Jared, it's just a dream."

His eyes flew open and his whole body went rigid. Rage twisted his face, and he grabbed her arms in a bruising grip.

"Jared, wake up! It's me, Suzanna!"

For one awful second, she thought he wouldn't recognize her. "Suzanna?"

"Yes, Jared, you were dreaming." She touched his cheek. "It's all right now."

"Oh, God," he murmured, pulling her to him in desperation. His breath came in ragged gasps, and his heart thundered beneath her breasts. She slipped her arms around his neck, being careful not to hurt his wound.

"It's all right, Jared. You're awake now."

Minutes passed. His breathing slowed and his hold on her gentled into a caress. "Suzanna?"

"Yes, I'm right here," she whispered against his cheek.

He sighed, as if in relief, and his hands began to move over her back, lightly at first, then more possessively, warming her through the thin barrier of her nightdress. She savored his touch, reveling in his nearness and his strength, and after a while she lost track of who was comforting whom. How long had it been since someone had held her tenderly and whispered her name? She inhaled his scent, as potent as incense to her starved senses. The skin she had bathed in fever now burned with a different heat, a heat that radiated to her and through her, igniting a need she was only beginning to understand.

His mouth found hers, hot and demanding, and he parted her lips with his tongue, plunging in with a force that sent a spasm of desire shuddering through her.

This was crazy! She should stop him, she knew she should, but it felt so good to have the man she loved hold her and kiss her. Just a little while longer. What could it hurt?

He lifted her hips until she lay on top of him. She wanted to warn him to be careful of his shoulder, but he wouldn't let her go long enough to even breathe. The strength of his desire strained against her belly, against the ache that had tortured her for days, and she realized this was what she had been wanting all along.

His hands molded her to him, stroking and cupping all the rounded places, hips and breasts and buttocks, until she burned from wanting more. Then flesh touched flesh as he lifted her nightdress and caressed the backs of her legs. The most delicious shivers raced over her, and she moved instinctively, pressing her hips to his, seeking the closeness for which she yearned.

In an instant she was on her back, and Jared lifted her nightdress to her neck. Before she could register her shock, his hands were on her, touching every-where. He stroked her nipples into tingling nubs, skimmed down her quivering belly, and grazed the mound of curls he encountered there.

"Jared," she said, knowing she should stop him, but the word was more plea than protest.

His fingers continued their quest, teasing and tor-menting, easing her thighs apart until he touched the spot that was moist and aching for him.

She cried out in surprise as sensation streaked through her, but before she could think, Jared had cap-tured a nipple in his mouth. All thoughts of protest evaporated in the heat of his passion, and her body melted in surrender. His fingers probed, and she gasped for breath. Blood roared in her ears, and she knew she wanted Jared, wanted him so badly she would die if she did not have him.

Clutching at his back, she called his name or thought she did. He rose up over her, naked and magnificent in the predawn light. Bracing for the pain, willing to suffer anything to have him inside her, she opened to him.

But there was no pain. He claimed her gently, surely, sheathing himself in her body with a groan of pure ec-stasy that sent answering echoes thrumming through her.

His eyes were black and fierce, yet full of awe. "Beautiful," he whispered reverently.

Yes! her heart cried in response, so beautiful she could hardly bear it. She'd never dreamed it could be like this, sweet and exciting and tender and thrilling, all at once. She looked up into his wonderful face, and her heart overflowed. "Jared, I love you."

His eyes burned with black fire. "Oh, God, Suzanna, I love you, too."

He claimed her mouth in a kiss that seared her soul, and when he moved inside her, she soared into the mysterious realm of desire. Overwhelmed by a driving need for union, she met his thrusts instinctively. Ten-tative at first, she grew more bold as passion wrought more passion. Why had she never felt this way before? How could she have lived so long and never known the joy her body could experience?

And with each second the pleasure increased, building and tightening. Suzanna writhed with need, wanting something she didn't understand. She clung to Jared, desperate for what he alone could give. The pressure built with each plunge, higher and higher until she thought she might explode, and then she did, shattering into a million blazing stars that streaked out and out into infinity only to settle gently back into her heart.

Jared convulsed within her, moaning her name against her breast, and she clung to him, absorbing his spasms until at last he shuddered and was still. They lay together, bodies still joined, for long minutes. She cradled his head, stroking his hair until their breathing returned to normal. Suzanna wanted to stay like this forever, never to be separated from him again, but soon his weight became a burden and reality intruded. Slowly, carefully, he slid off her, but he pulled her with him until they lay side by side, facing each other.

In a way, this was almost better because she could enjoy the adoration in his eyes without any distractions. He kissed her nose and then her chin and then her lips, lingering to savor her mouth. His leg tangled with hers and his hand idly caressed her bare hip. She knew she should pull her nightdress down and cover herself, but the feel of her naked flesh pressed against Jared's was just too wonderful and new.

"You're a remarkable woman, Suzanna."

Suzanna certainly felt remarkable. She wanted to ask him what had happened between them, why this had been so different from anything else she had ever experienced, but decent women simply didn't discuss such things, so Suzanna had no words to voice the questions burning in her mind.

Still, she couldn't let this feeling of intimacy end. She knew Jared's body now, and she had grown greedy. She wanted to know everything else about him, too.

Stroking his face, she smoothed back the hair perspiration had stuck to his forehead. "I don't know anything about you at all, Jared. Where are you from?"

For a second a shadow seemed to pass across his face, but it was gone so quickly she decided she must have imagined it. His eyes took on the playful expression she had come to love. "I'm from Maryland, and many people in Maryland would resent being called 'Yankees,' so I'll thank you to watch yourself in the future."

"Oh, I certainly will," she promised, feeling almost giddy at his teasing, "You lived on a plantation and raised horses, and roses, too."

"How did you know?"

"You told Andy about it."

"Not about the roses."

"I guessed about the roses," she said, recalling what he'd said to her last night about rose gardens.

"You guessed right. Rosewood had dozens of rosebushes. My mother raised every color known to man and created some new ones, too."

"Rosewood. What a beautiful name."

"It was a beautiful place."

Suzanna smiled impishly. "With white pillars and a green lawn and thoroughbred horses growing in the fields."

He smacked her playfully on her bare bottom, and when she tried to get revenge, he wrestled her down, pinning her to the bed with his weight.

"Be careful of your shoulder," she said in alarm.

"Now's a fine time to think of my shoulder," he reminded her, nuzzling the curve of her breast and sending delightful shivers dancing over her.

"I did think of it before, but . . ."

"But what?" he challenged, lifting his head so he could see her expression.

"You wouldn't stop kissing me, so I couldn't say anything."

He collapsed on top of her, his body shaking in silent laughter. After a minute or two he managed to compose himself, and when he lifted his head again, his dark eyes were filled with joy. ''You really are a remarkable woman, Suzanna.''

''I try to be,'' she replied, feeling reckless and wild. ''Oh, Jared!'' She took his face in her hands and pulled his mouth to hers, the first time in her life she had ever initiated a kiss.

He rewarded her for her boldness with a long, lingering exploration of her mouth that left them both breathless.

''That's enough,'' Jared gasped when he pulled away. ''If you aren't careful, I'll forget you've hardly slept in the past twenty-four hours and make love to you all over again.''

She laughed in delight. ''Don't tease me. I know you can't . . . I mean . . .'' she stammered, suddenly mortified when she realized what they were discussing.

''You don't think I can?'' he challenged, grabbing her hand and guiding it downward until she was more than certain that he could.

''Jared!'' she cried, totally shocked, as she jerked her hand away.

''Shhh, you'll wake Andy up.''

Suzanna instantly clamped her mouth shut, making Jared chuckle.

''That'll teach you to make fun of me,'' he said. ''Now come here and go to sleep before I change my mind.'' He settled himself while Suzanna modestly adjusted her nightdress back to its proper position. Then he pulled her onto his good shoulder where she snuggled contentedly.

She was too overwrought for sleep, though, and her conscience began to stir as the reality of the situation began to dawn. She had just made love with a man to whom she wasn't married. Guilt burgeoned, black and ugly, and rightly so. After all, she'd sinned abominably, violating the one commandment she had never before had the slightest temptation to break. She thought of her own self-righteousness in feeling superior to women too weak to remain chaste. Even as much as she loved Dora, she'd never been able to understand how she could live in sin with Mayor Kelley.

Now, of course, Suzanna understood perfectly. Now, finally, she had done the deed of which the good people of Dodge had accused her months ago. By the world's standards, and by her own standards, too, she was a fallen woman.

But as strongly as her reason condemned her, her heart urged mercy. How could anything so wonderful be completely evil? She loved Jared, and he had said he loved her, too. Love didn't make it right to do what they had just done, of course, but they could be married immediately, and then everything would be all right. As for their sin, God wasn't like the people who had condemned her forever for one indiscretion, even when she was innocent. God understood the weakness of human flesh, and she knew He'd forgive her and Jared for consummating their union a little prematurely.

Yes, when they were married, everything would be fine.

Taking comfort in the thought, Suzanna could deal with the prickling of her conscience, tamp down her burgeoning guilt, and concentrate on her newfound happiness.

"I'm awfully glad you had a bad dream," she said, idly tracing the flat nipple she found nestled amongst the curly chestnut hair just below the bandage on his chest.

His breath caught, and Suzanna smiled, reveling in her newly discovered power to excite him. "Do you remember what you were dreaming about?"

"No," he said, his voice strained as her fingers continued their exploration of his chest.

"You called out to your father."

"Did I?"

"Yes. I got the feeling you were angry at him."

Jared drew an unsteady breath, and Suzanna allowed her fingers to stray toward his navel. "We didn't get along very well," he said.

"Is he still alive?"

"No." He grabbed her hand and moved it firmly

back up to his chest. "Suzanna," he said sternly, "I think you'd better try to get some sleep. Andy will be awake soon."

"Mmmm, yes . . ." she murmured, then thought of the boy walking in to find them together. Oh dear! He'd ask so many embarrassing questions. What on earth would she tell him? She should probably go back to her cot, but the mere thought of leaving Jared's side was more than she could bear. No, she'd face Andy and answer all his questions. Besides, if she and Jared were going to be married, Andy would find them together every morning from now on, she thought with a smile.

She pressed a kiss to Jared's jaw and snuggled into a more comfortable position. Beneath her palm, his heart beat quickly enough to tell her he was still affected by her nearness. "I love you, Jared," she whispered just before sleep finally claimed her.

Jared's heart wrenched in agony as the black memories closed over him. Sweet Jesus, he had dragged Suzanna straight into his own private nightmare. How could he have forgotten who he was? How could he have violated every principle he'd ever held sacred and hurt the woman to whom he owed so much? And whom he *loved* so much, for God's sake?

Oh, yes, he loved her. He loved her beautiful face and her passionate body, but more, he loved her pride and her stubbornness and her gentleness and her sweetness. In her arms, for a few blissful moments he'd found the only happiness he had known in the five years since the night he'd taken another human life and forfeited any possible right to a woman like Suzanna Prentice.

Suzanna stirred, wrapping her arm more tightly around him as if she could sense his thoughts. Jared pulled her closer, savoring the feel of her body next to his and vitally aware he had no right even to touch her hand.

He watched with unseeing eyes as the rising sun traced ever-lengthening streaks across the ceiling. Beside him lay the woman he loved, the woman who had brought him more joy than he'd thought it possible for

one person to know. He would have sold his immortal
soul for the chance to stay with her, to share her life
and know the love she offered.

But it was too late for such bargains. He'd already
bartered away his future, and to stay with Suzanna
would cause her ruin, too. Hers and *Andy*'s, he corrected, thinking with renewed anguish of the boy he
had come to cherish like a son. If Jared were selfish
enough to stay with them, he'd be risking the future
of two people he loved more than life itself.

But was that his choice to make? Shouldn't he let
Suzanna make the decision herself? After all, she'd told
him the story of her disgrace. She'd trusted him;
surely, he could trust her, too.

Except that Suzanna had been innocent. She'd been
the victim of injustice, but Jared couldn't make such a
claim. No, he was unquestionably guilty of the most
heinous crime of all, and he could easily picture her
reaction to the news: horror, disgust, perhaps even hatred. How could he bear it?

No, he would have to leave them. He had no choice.
They would feel betrayed, of course. They would think
him a heartless monster who had used them and then
discarded them, and they would despise him. Jared
cringed at the thought, wondering how on earth he
could survive knowing what he had done to them. But
as agonizing as such a prospect was, it was far prefer-
able to having Suzanna one day learn the truth about
him and be publicly disgraced, her life ruined. It would
actually be kind of him to cause her a little pain now
and spare her the greater suffering.

Kind? He almost laughed aloud at the thought. Suzanna certainly wouldn't think him kind. How could he
bear to look her in the eye and see her pain? But perhaps she didn't love him as much as he loved her.
They hardly knew each other, after all. In any case,
once he showed her what a bastard he was, she
wouldn't love him anymore. And she was strong.

She'd borne far worse tragedies. She could surely survive a broken heart.

But would he?

The church bells woke her. At first she couldn't figure out what was wrong beyond the fact that she had overslept. Then she realized she was in her bed, alone. Memories of what had happened in this bed several hours earlier came flooding back, bringing with them a surge of the joy she had known then. Smiling, she rose to a sitting position, smoothing her tousled hair and wondering where Jared had gone.

"Jared, what are you doing?" she heard Andy ask in the other room.

"I'm packing."

Packing?

Suzanna sprang out of bed and across the room. Flinging the curtain aside, she saw Jared, fully clothed, his arm in a sling, stuffing things into his carpetbag with his free hand.

"Jared?" she asked in alarm.

His head came up with a guilty jerk, but he did not look at her. Instead he continued his stuffing.

"Jared, why are you packing your clothes?"

With elaborate care, he tucked all the straggling ends of garments into the bag. When he finally turned to face her, his face bore that horrible blank expression he wore when he played cards. "I think it's time I moved back to my room at the hotel, don't you? My shoulder is almost completely healed, and my presence here is crowding you."

"We don't mind being crowded, do we, Mama?" Andy asked. She was vaguely aware of him coming to her and catching hold of her nightdress, but she couldn't seem to take her eyes off Jared. Maybe this was a dream, a nightmare, and she'd wake up soon, trembling and terrified, only to find Jared's arms wrapped comfortingly around her.

"You can't go," she stammered, hoping the sound

of her own voice would wake her, but it only convinced her this scene was real, too real. "You're still too weak to take care of yourself."

He lifted his eyebrows in mild surprise. "I think last night proved I've recovered my strength."

Stung by his callousness, Suzanna gaped, her face burning.

Andy tugged on her nightdress. "Make him stay, Mama. Tell him we want him to stay."

Ignoring them both, Jared returned to his task, carefully buckling the bag closed.

Suzanna tried desperately to shake off the last vestiges of sleep and make some sense out of all this. She simply couldn't figure out why the man who had made love to her and professed love to her only a few hours ago would be leaving her.

Unless . . .

"Jared, you don't have to go." She grabbed his arm to stop him when he would have picked up his bag. "If you're worried about my reputation, you're wasting your time. I don't have one, remember?" she said with a forced laugh. "And we can be married right away—"

"*Married?*" he said in disgust, shaking off her hand. "Are you crazy? A gambler doesn't have any use for a wife." He glanced coldly at Andy. "Or a family, either." He picked up the bag and turned toward the door.

"Jared, stop!" she cried, fighting panic. "You can't leave like this, not after what happened!"

His dark eyes held not the slightest flicker of emotion. "As soon as you figure out what I owe you for your services, let me know."

"My *services!*" she repeated incredulously. "My *services* aren't for sale, Jared Cain! You said you *loved* me!"

"A gentleman always does."

Suzanna stared at him in mute horror. This couldn't really be happening. Jared couldn't have been lying to her. But it was, and he had. She could see it in his eyes. He'd never cared for her at all, and now that he'd gotten what he wanted from her, he was leaving. She felt stunned, as if she'd received a mortal blow and was only waiting for the oblivion of death.

As if from far away, she heard Andy calling Jared's name, begging him not to go.

"Please, Jared, please!" Andy grabbed the handle of the carpetbag and tried to wrest it from him. Pistol jumped up from where he had been observing the proceedings and barked sharply.

"Remember what your mother told you," Jared said coldly. "It wouldn't be proper for me to live with you."

Not proper? Suzanna felt an hysterical urge to laugh. Jared Cain had used her like a harlot and now he was trying to convince her son he was worried about propriety! But through the haze of agony and her own humiliation, Suzanna realized she couldn't just stand there and let Andy humiliate himself, too.

Calling on the reserves of pride that had sustained her when she'd had to grieve for a husband she no longer loved, when she'd had to sell even Andy's cradle to pay her husband's debts, when she'd scrubbed another woman's floors to put food in her son's mouth, and when people had believed her a slut and turned away from her, she stepped forward and pried the boy's fingers loose from Cain's bag. "Stop it, Andy," she said, somehow imitating Cain's calm. "We don't want Mr. Cain here if he doesn't want to stay."

"Yes, we do!" Andy insisted, tears coursing down his cheeks. Blinking to hide her own tears, she picked him up and hugged him to her, muffling his sobs.

She lifted her gaze to Cain's, looking him squarely in the eye. "*I* don't want him here. Get out!"

For an instant Cain's perfect reserve cracked, and she saw a flicker of what might have been guilt, but it disappeared too quickly for her to be sure. "Goodbye," he said and then he was gone, closing the door softly behind him.

Suzanna stared blindly at the door as the agony

washed over her in sickening waves, hugging her son to her in a futile attempt to lessen the pain.

"Mama, why'd he have to go?" Andy sobbed. "You could've made him stay if you wanted!"

Andy's accusation was like a knife in her heart, but she hugged him more fiercely. "No, I couldn't, sweetheart. I told him to stay. Didn't you hear me?"

"I don't want him to leave, Mama! Make him come back!" Beside them Pistol whined and nudged her leg, wanting comfort, too.

On leaden legs, with the dog at her heels, Suzanna carried her son into the bedroom and sank down on the bed with him. Rocking him back and forth, she crooned meaningless sounds in a futile attempt to comfort them both, but soon the sounds became sobs as her own grief overwhelmed her.

This couldn't be happening, she thought again. Where was the man who had loved her in the dawn's golden glow? Where was the man who had spoken of his childhood home and teased her and kissed her and laughed at her outrageous remarks? Where was the man whose body had brought hers unspeakable joy?

And who was the cold stranger who had offered to pay her for what she could only have given out of love?

Suzanna had never known such pain, not when her parents had died, not when they'd brought her Andrew's frozen body, not when her Christian friends had turned their backs on her. None of those things had hurt this much because at least then she'd still had her pride. Jared Cain had made her a fool, a weak, stupid, lovesick fool. How could she ever hold her head up again?

A long time later Suzanna and Andy lay side by side in the bed she and Jared had shared just a short time ago. Andy had finally stopped crying, although Suzanna hadn't really noticed. He touched her face.

"Mama? Please don't cry anymore."

His sweet request sent her into new spasms of grief, but she quickly regained her control, knowing she was frightening her son.

"I don't like Jared anymore," he announced when she'd dried her eyes with the corner of the bedsheet. "Why was he so mean today?"

"I don't know," Suzanna said brokenly. "I guess he isn't a nice person."

"He seemed nice."

"Yes, he did, but maybe he was only being polite so we'd take good care of him," she said lamely, wishing her excuses didn't also explain the time she and Jared had spent together in this bed.

"Yeah, maybe," Andy allowed. "I'm not gonna cry anymore, though. Only babies cry."

Only babies and heartbroken women, Suzanna thought, but she smiled through her misery and kissed her son's damp cheeks. In the distance they could hear the church bells ringing again, a joyous sound offering hope and promise.

Although she wanted nothing more than to hide away and lick her wounds, her pride rebelled at such a thought. She couldn't let Cain know how much he'd hurt her, and she had Andy to think of, too. He shouldn't have to suffer for her weakness. No one except she and Jared Cain knew how thoroughly she had humiliated herself, and she certainly had no intention of letting him think he'd broken her spirit.

Wasn't she the same Suzanna Prentice who had walked boldly into church the Sunday after being accused of seducing her employer, the same Suzanna Prentice who had stared her accusers in the eye and made them flinch? Was she going to let one lousy, Yankee—yes, *Yankee*—gambler steal her self-respect?

Ignoring the dull ache of her battered heart, Suzanna forced herself to smile at her son.

"Listen, Andy. Can you hear the bells?"

He nodded.

"If we hurry, I'll bet we can make it to church."

Chapter 7

Every time Suzanna walked into the Comique, she swore she wouldn't look over at the faro table to see if Cain was there, and every time she walked into the Comique, she looked. Except Cain wasn't there, not on Monday or Tuesday or Wednesday. She told herself she didn't care. She told herself she hoped he'd left town so she'd never have to set eyes on him again.

Coming to work on Monday had been the most difficult obstacle to pass. Luckily, the girls at the Comique had enough experience with men to accept her explanation without question. "As soon as he was strong enough to walk, he walked out the door without so much as a 'Thank you very kindly,'" she told them.

They'd given her their sympathy and their I-told-you-so's and let the matter drop. Suzanna had arranged her furniture back the way it had been before Cain entered her life and pretended everything else was back to normal, too. If she fell asleep with tears on her face and her dreams were still haunted by a dark-haired man, no one else need know.

She'd managed to fool everyone except Dora, who'd listened to her explanations in tight-lipped silence and was the only one who seemed to notice how Suzanna's glance frequently strayed to the faro table where Jared Cain no longer sat.

By Thursday night the girls at the theater had a crisis

to occupy them, and Suzanna was grateful for the distraction.

"Can you believe it?" Maisie demanded. "We're the ones who keep this town going. If it wasn't for the money the saloons and the dance-halls bring in, Dodge City would be just a big patch of tumbleweeds. Now they're trying to put us out of business."

"It ain't as bad as it seems," one of the girls said. She called herself Annie Ladue, and she took great pains to let everyone know Sheriff Masterson had taken a personal interest in her. "Bat says nothing's going to change."

"Nothing's going to change?" Polly echoed incredulously. "The city council made it against the law to gamble in the city. How long do you think the Comique can stay in business?"

"Quite a while," Suzanna informed them all, repeating what the mayor had told her and Dora about the new law earlier that evening. "The law isn't intended to stop gambling *or* prostitution," she explained, naming the two activities forbidden by the new ordinance. "It's intended to bring money to the city from the fines the gamblers and the madams will pay when they get arrested for breaking the law."

"If that isn't the crookedest thing I ever heard," Maisie sputtered. "The saloons and the brothels already pay a license fee. How much money does the city want, for God's sake?"

"I'll tell you one thing," Polly said. "Them madams'll never stand for it. I heard they was getting together and hiring themselves a lawyer to fight this thing."

Suzanna smiled at the thought of prostitutes hiring legal counsel to protest a duly passed city ordinance, but apparently no one else found the idea amusing. A heated discussion followed in which Annie Ladue kept trying to tell everyone what Bat said, and everyone else kept trying to shout her down.

Finally, Springer came over to inform them it was

time to start talking to the customers instead of each other.

"Mr. Springer, will the new ordinance affect us?" Suzanna asked, half-hoping he would tell her he'd have to let the lot of them go. For the past several days the idea of leaving for Georgia immediately had grown increasingly attractive.

"Not likely. Them damn politicians just figured out a way to put more of my money in their own pockets is all. Now get your bustles out onto the floor, you lazy bitches."

As usual, Suzanna sought out the loneliest-looking cowboy she could find and coaxed him to talk about his home. Concentrating on someone else's misery was the best way to forget her own.

A few hours later, when Dora's stint at the Alhambra was finished, Mayor Kelley escorted her into the theater for her performance there. Suzanna waved a greeting, but instead of simply returning it, Dora left Kelley and made her way across the floor toward her.

Alarmed by her friend's solemn expression, Suzanna hurried to meet her. "Is something wrong? Andy . . . ?"

But Dora was shaking her head. "Not Andy. I saw a friend of yours tonight."

Suzanna knew instantly who she meant. "Jared Cain's no friend of mine," she replied, feigning outrage to cover the twisting agony she felt at the mention of his name.

"Suzanna, I . . ." She glanced around, aware of the possibility of being overheard in the crowded room. "Come in here." She took Suzanna's arm and led her into the privacy of Springer's empty office.

"Jared is working at the Alhambra now," Dora said, and hastened on when she saw Suzanna's pained surprise. "I know how you feel, honey, and I gave Jimmy a piece of my mind when I found out. You never told me exactly what happened between the two of you, but any fool can see he hurt you badly, so when he came up to me tonight, I treated him real cold until he asked me how you were."

"He what?" Suzanna asked, no longer needing to feign her outrage. "He's got no right to—"

"He probably doesn't, but he did anyway, and honey, let me tell you, I've seen a lot of misery in my time, and Jared Cain has got a double dose of it."

"I suppose he tried to borrow your hankie to dry his tears," Suzanna asked acidly, fighting the sting of her own.

"I didn't say he cried on my shoulder, and I doubt anybody else would've noticed how unhappy he is. He's pretty good at hiding his real feelings, but I'm an actress, and I can tell when somebody's putting on a show."

Suzanna bit her tongue to keep from asking for details. Let Dora think what she wanted, but Suzanna would be damned before she'd give her any reason to think she cared a fig for Jared Cain.

"Jimmy told me he's been laying in his hotel room until he could go without the sling. Nobody wants to play cards with a man who's got such a convenient place to stash an ace. Anyway, he came to Jimmy this afternoon and asked for a job. Jimmy told me he didn't want to hurt your feelings, but he also couldn't turn away the best faro dealer in town. Besides, Jimmy figured you'd be glad not to have him at the Comique anymore."

Suzanna grudgingly admitted this was true. "You said he asked about me," she reminded Dora.

"He wanted to know if you were working and how Andy was. He even asked if you were 'well.' I figured he was worried you might be pining away for him."

"Of all the gall!"

"Believe me, I don't think the knowledge would've given him any pleasure. In fact, he looked like he'd been doing some pining himself. Oh, I know he was shot, but he looks worse than he did the last time I saw him at your place, like he hasn't been sleeping or eating much.''

Suzanna should have taken pleasure in hearing this news, but perversely, she felt concern. ''Is he still seeing the doctor? You don't suppose he's got pneumonia and—''

''I think he's got whatever you've got and that you caught it from each other, but I'm not trying to meddle. I'm just going to deliver a message. He sends his sincere gratitude for all you did to save his life, and he also sends this.''

Dora pulled a small pouch from her pocket and dropped it into Suzanna's hand with a clink.

''Good heavens!'' she said in dismay, hefting the coin-filled pouch. It must contain a fortune!

''He said he wanted to pay you for the time you missed work, too.''

''I don't want his money!'' Suzanna cried, trying to give the pouch back to Dora, but Dora stepped back, refusing to take it.

''I told him you'd be angry, but I guess he already knew that which is why he gave it to me instead of giving it to you himself. If you don't want it, I suggest you return it.''

''I can't,'' Suzanna insisted. ''I never want to see that man again. Please, Dora.''

''Absolutely not. I've already gotten more involved in this than I wanted to. Besides, you deserve the money, Suzanna. He might only be trying to ease his conscience, but think of what you can do for Andy with it.''

Dora was right, of course, but then Dora didn't know exactly what the payment was for, so she didn't know Suzanna couldn't possibly keep it.

''Like I said, you never told me what happened between you two,'' Dora continued, ''but I can pretty much guess. Before you give up on him completely, though, at least see him one more time, and when you do see him, look real close. If he's as unhappy as you are, maybe whatever split you two apart was a misunderstanding.''

''Believe me, there was no misunderstanding at all. He made his feelings very clear.''

''Then maybe he misunderstood yours,'' Dora suggested. ''At least give him one more chance.''

''Dora, I never took you for a romantic,'' Suzanna scolded, wishing her friend were right and her troubles could be cleared up simply be seeing Jared again.

''Don't tell me you haven't heard the stories about me leaving Boston because of a broken heart,'' she countered.

''You aren't even *from* Boston,'' Suzanna reminded her.

''Not so loud! You'll ruin my reputation,'' Dora teased but grew instantly serious again. ''At least see him again before you give up on him. That's all I ask.''

''I don't think I can,'' Suzanna admitted, ''at least not on purpose.''

''Well, it'll have to be on purpose since he seems dead set on avoiding you, too. If you don't want to be alone with him, you can always take Andy with you as a chaperone.''

''I don't know. Andy was awfully hurt when Jared left. Seeing him again might upset him.''

''It might upset Jared, too. From what I saw, he thinks the world of the boy. I doubt he'd be able to hide his feelings as well if Andy was there.''

''Is this some kind of tea party?'' Springer asked from the doorway.

Both women jumped in surprise, and Suzanna guiltily stuffed the pouch of coins into her pocket.

''I had something to tell Suzanna,'' Dora explained without the slightest hint of apology.

Suzanna didn't feel she could be quite so bold. ''I'm sorry, Mr. Springer. I'll get right back to work.'' She hurried out, more troubled than she cared to admit over what Dora had told her. The pouch of coins weighed heavily in her pocket, distracting her from her duties as a hostess. Later, when Springer counted out her earnings for the evening he frowned and remarked on her lower-than-average earnings, but by then Suzanna was much too distracted to notice.

Once she had reached the sanctuary of her own home and had checked on Andy, Suzanna emptied the pouch onto the table in her front room and counted the coins. The amount astonished her. Even generously estimating what she had spent on food and how much she would have made on the nights she'd stayed home to care for Jared, there was several hundred dollars too much.

Payment for her services, she thought bitterly. Or, if Dora was right, payment to ease Jared's conscience. Absently, she stacked the coins into neat piles as she tried to decide what to do with them. She didn't want Jared's money, of that she was certain, but on the other hand, Dora was right about how she deserved the money and about what she could do for Andy with it. They'd need every penny they could scrape together to make a new life for themselves back in Georgia, and although her nest egg was growing nicely, this money would make a nice addition.

Heaven knew she'd earned it. She'd probably saved Jared's life, taking care of him day and night as if he'd been her husband. Ten times this amount would never make up for the hurt and humiliation she'd suffered, either.

On the other hand, did she want him to think he could buy himself a clear conscience? Did she want him to think he had paid her for *everything* she'd done for him? Certainly not! She ought to take this money and throw it right in his face!

But in order to do that, she'd have to actually see his face, and she also couldn't forget what Dora had said about how unhappy he'd looked tonight. Was it possible he regretted the way he had treated her? Was it possible he'd felt a fraction of the agony she'd known the past few days? And if he had, did she want to know?

"Do you think he'll be surprised?" Andy asked for at least the tenth time since they had started getting dressed.

"Of course he will," Suzanna assured him, nervously smoothing the skirt of her Sunday dress and resisting the urge to re-pin her hair one more time. Carefully she set her hat on her head and slid the long hatpin in to anchor it securely.

"You look pretty, Mama," Andy said, watching impatiently. "Jared said you're pretty. Did I tell you?"

"Yes, dear," she replied, ignoring the twinge in her heart. "Have you got Pistol's rope?"

"Yes, ma'am," he replied in a long-suffering tone, holding it up to show he'd already put it around the dog's neck. "Can we go now?"

Suzanna glanced in the mirror one last time, wishing the circles under her eyes weren't quiet so dark. Ruthlessly, she pinched her cheeks, hoping to coax some color into them, but nothing could erase the panic she saw glittering in her eyes. What had possessed her to do this?

"Mama," Andy whined, and Pistol scratched urgently at the door.

"Coming," she replied breathlessly, placing one hand over her churning stomach and reaching for her purse with the other. Weighed down with Jared's money, it felt unnaturally heavy, and she clutched it tightly so it wouldn't jingle as she walked.

She opened the door and allowed Andy and the dog to go out ahead of her. They were halfway up the alley by the time she had the door locked. Although she wasn't in a hurry, she quickened her pace to catch up with them.

"I'll bet we're too late," Andy complained, struggling to hold the excited dog as he waited for her.

"Mrs. Galland told me he never leaves his room before twelve-thirty, and we haven't even heard the whistle for the noon train yet."

"Can't you walk faster?" Andy said, reminding her he knew nothing about time.

This whole idea was crazy, she told herself when they reached the front of the Western Hotel and started up onto the porch. She'd only suggested to Andy that they visit Cain because she'd been certain he wouldn't want to. Instead, the boy had literally jumped at the idea, doing a little jig with Pistol at the prospect of seeing his friend again.

Andy had apparently forgotten the ugly scene the morning Cain had left, but Suzanna certainly hadn't. She'd been hoping Andy would give her an excuse not to do what Dora had suggested, and instead he'd made it impossible for her not to go. She just prayed Cain wouldn't be mean to Andy. She could endure anything but that.

Dr. Samuel Galland himself was behind the hotel desk, and he looked up expectantly from the newspaper he was reading. "Good morning, Mrs. Prentice. What can I do for you?"

"We came to visit Mr. Cain," Andy announced more loudly than Suzanna would have wished.

Dr. Galland's distinguished mustache twitched suspiciously, but he managed to maintain his dignity as he gave Suzanna a questioning look.

"We aren't going to visit him exactly," Suzanna explained quickly, painfully aware of how improper it would be for a lady to enter a man's hotel room. "We're just returning something he left at my house."

Dr. Galland nodded, not bothering to hold back his smile any longer. "Room seventeen."

Suzanna turned, hoping she wasn't actually blushing.

"I can't count to seventeen," Andy complained, wrestling with Pistol's rope as the dog tried to pull him down the long hallway.

"It's a one and a seven," Suzanna explained, her

heart pounding ominously as the numbers on the doors she passed got closer to seventeen. "The next one. Right here."

They stopped. Suzanna's breath caught painfully in her chest and for a moment she actually considered fleeing, but Andy was already knocking on the door.

What was she doing? What had she been thinking to come here at all? What if he laughed in her face? Frantically, she fought for control of her careening emotions and sternly reminded herself she had only come to give Jared Cain back his money. If he laughed, she'd be haughty and spill the coins on the floor at his feet. If he were coldly contemptuous, she'd fling them in his face. And if Dora was right . . .

But something was wrong. He hadn't answered the knock. She should have been relieved. If he wasn't there, she wouldn't have to see him at all. Andy would forget, and they could put the whole thing behind them.

Except suddenly, Suzanna didn't want to put it behind her. She wanted to know, once and for all. "Andy, knock again, louder."

Jared woke instantly at the second knock, his mind clear, ready to deal with danger. He was already reaching instinctively for his gun when he called, "Who's there?"

"It's me, Andy."

Andy? The child's voice set loose an avalanche of emotion, joy and pain and loss and, God in heaven, *terror*. Why would Andy be here unless something had happened to Suzanna!

"Just a minute," he called, hastily jerking on his pants. He'd only managed one button when he threw the door open. He saw Andy first because he was looking down, Andy and his faithful dog, both of them grinning up at him. Behind them he saw her skirt, and his gaze flew up to find her face, her beautiful angel's face.

Her sapphire eyes were wary, her sweet mouth

pursed, but he hardly noticed her expression. As if he'd been dying of thirst, he felt her presence like a sparkling waterfall, drenching the arid wastes of his soul. For one glorious moment, he drank in the sight of her.

"You must've been sleeping," Andy said, shocking Jared back to reality.

Hastily, he finished buttoning his pants. "Please excuse my appearance," he muttered, remembering too late he shouldn't be pleased at all to see Suzanna Prentice on his doorstep. He summoned up a measure of his usual control. "I wasn't expecting company."

Suzanna looked him over from head to toe, savoring his discomfort and congratulating herself for having come. "We've seen you looking worse," she said with a small smile. Thank heaven she'd decided to catch him unawares. He'd had no time to conceal his joy, the same joy she felt at seeing him, in spite of all the hurt he'd caused her. Whatever his reasons for leaving her, he still cared. She would have bet her life on it.

Jared studied her face, and what he saw alarmed him. Her wariness had disappeared. Her eyes were clear and shone with what he could only describe as confidence. Before he could do more than register that fact she said, "Your wound seems to be healing very well."

He glanced down at his bare chest. Dr. McCarty had told him to leave the bandage off as much as possible, so the angry red scar was clearly visible. For some absurd reason, he felt self-conscious under Suzanna's unwavering gaze, and he reached for his shirt.

"The doctor says I'm as good as new," he said, shrugging into the garment. "I don't have to use the sling anymore."

"Can you walk?" Andy asked. " 'Cause if you can, maybe you can go shopping with us. We're gonna meet the train first, though."

"Andy," Suzanna scolded gently. "I told you, we're only going to stay for a minute. I'm sure Mr. Cain has plans of his own."

God, how could he have forgotten how beautiful she was? Or how lovely her voice was, sweet and pure like the ring of fine crystal?

"You don't have no plans, do you, Jared?" Andy asked.

Somehow Jared managed not to return the boy's hopeful smile. "As a matter of fact, I have to go to the barber shop for a bath and a shave before I'm fit to be seen with anyone."

"We're sorry we woke you," Suzanna said, not looking sorry at all, "but we wanted to be sure to catch you. Mrs. Hand gave me your . . . your message last night." He caught a glimpse of anger, but it disappeared almost instantly. "I'm afraid you were entirely too generous. I took out what I thought was a fair amount, and I'm returning the rest."

Before he could protest, she was handing him the sack he'd given to Dora Hand last night. "I wanted you to have it," he said lamely, thinking he'd really wanted to give her more than that. Everything he owned, every cent he possessed wouldn't be enough. "You saved my life," he said.

"I doubt I really saved your life," she replied, that strange confidence still gleaming in her eyes. She thrust the pouch into his hands. "Besides, I'm afraid you might need this money to pay your fine when you get arrested under the new law."

She smiled slightly, and his heart lurched painfully in his chest.

"Andy, we'd better be going now."

"I know!" Andy said ingenuously. "We can go to the barber shop with him and wait until he's ready. Then he can go shopping with us."

"I'm afraid ladies aren't allowed in the barber shop," Jared said, resisting the almost overwhelming urge to suggest an alternate plan that would bring him together with Suzanna. What had happened to his resolve? His iron will? His gambler's coolness?

"Oh," Andy said, his disappointment twisting

Jared's heart. But his expression lightened again at once as a new thought occurred to him. "I'm not a lady," he reminded Jared triumphantly. "I could go with you."

"Andy, it's rude to invite yourself," Suzanna chided, but Jared stopped her.

"He's right. Have you ever been to a barber shop, Andy?" Jared asked before he could think of a reason not to. It was a perfect idea. He could make Andy happy and be sure of seeing Suzanna again, just briefly, not long enough to do any harm, but still see her.

"No, neither me or Pistol's ever been to a barber shop," Andy replied.

"Then why don't you come with me? Afterwards, we could have breakfast at the Dodge House."

"I already had breakfast," Andy said with a worried frown, concerned this detail would ruin the plan.

"I meant dinner. I forgot what time it was."

"All right!"

"Andy, you didn't ask permission," Suzanna reminded him, and Jared knew an irrational fear that she would refuse to let him go.

"I'll take good care of him," Jared promised, as eager as Andy now.

Suzanna's eyes lifted to his, and he saw her hesitate. She had every right to refuse. Why should she trust her son to a man like him? Why was she even considering this at all? He had no idea, but after another minute her doubtful expression faded. "When will you bring him back?"

"Whenever you say. After we eat, I could take him to Johnson's Saloon to see the Indian relics from the battle of Adobe Wells. I think I could keep him busy until suppertime, and then . . ." Jared caught himself just in time. He'd been about to invite Suzanna to join them for supper, but that was certainly out of the question. "Then I'll bring him back to you."

Suzanna glanced down at Andy, who was jumping

ıp and down, tugging at her skirt. "Please, Mama, please!"

"All right," she said, "but you have to promise to be good for Mr. Cain. No whining, and eat everything on your plate, and drink your milk."

"Yes, ma'am, I promise!"

Jared felt an unreasonable joy, although he had no idea why the prospect of playing nursemaid to a four-year-old boy should please him so inordinately.

"Give me a kiss, then."

Jared's heart lurched again, then he realized she was talking to the boy. He watched enviously as she leaned down and touched her lips to Andy's, admiring the way her prim dress hugged her breasts. Awareness tingled through him, but he knew how to control his responses. He'd better, he thought wryly, considering how few clothes he had on at the moment.

When she straightened, she turned to Jared again, and his breath caught at the directness of her gaze.

"If you get tired of him, you can bring him home earlier. I have some shopping to do, but then I'll be home the rest of the afternoon."

Yes, he thought, sleeping. A vision of her lying in bed the way she had been the other time he'd brought Andy home sent another jolt through his system, and his mouth went dry. "I'm sure we'll have a fine time together, won't we, partner?" Jared said, knowing he didn't dare bring Andy back until he was certain Suzanna was up and dressed, but at least he'd see her again. One more time to last him the rest of his life.

"We sure will," Andy replied, pulling Pistol across the threshold into Jared's room.

Suzanna stared after him for a moment, smiled uncertainly, and said, "Well, good-bye." She made no move to leave, however. For an instant, Jared entertained the fantasy that she didn't want to be parted from him, but he knew she was probably only having second thoughts about trusting him with the boy.

"See you later," he said, making it a promise.

"Yes, later," she replied thoughtfully, and finally turned away.

He stood there in the doorway, watching, until she disappeared into the lobby.

"Jared, hurry up!" Andy urged. "We're gonna have so much fun!"

For the first time since that awful morning when he'd left Suzanna's house, Jared smiled.

If possible, Suzanna primped even more for her second meeting with Jared. The first time she'd only been concerned about her pride. This time she was concerned about her future.

Dora had been right, Suzanna thought, hugging the knowledge to her like a precious treasure. Jared did look miserable and not because he'd just woken up and not because he wasn't recovered from getting shot. It was something in his eyes, the tortured loneliness she'd seen before, but multiplied a hundredfold. And he'd been so glad to see her! Oh, he'd tried to hide it, but she'd seen it just the same.

He still cared for Andy, too. Imagine him wanting to take charge of a four-year-old boy for the afternoon! So much for his claim that he didn't want to be saddled with a family. He'd been almost as disappointed as Andy when he thought she might refuse.

Outside she heard voices, a man and a boy talking excitedly. Her heart began to race in anticipation, but she drew several deep breaths so that when she opened the door to them she at least appeared calm.

"I guess I don't have to ask if you had a good time," she said as Andy and Pistol rushed inside. Below his short pants, Andy's knees were black, and his shirt was stained with what appeared to be tea.

"Sarsaparilla," Jared explained from where he hovered tentatively in the doorway, hat in hand.

"It tasted so good, and it was *cold* from sitting in ice, and they let me sit up on the bar to drink it," Andy informed her happily. "They had bows and arrows and feathers and bullets, all left over from 'Dobe Wells."

Suzanna knew Andy had no idea of the historic significance of the battle of Adobe Wells, the last big Indian battle before the Comanche were finally subdued. She also knew the Indian paraphernalia on display in Johnson's Saloon would be fascinating to him nevertheless.

"What did you do after you spilled sarsaparilla on your shirt?" she asked with amusement.

Andy turned to Jared with a triumphant grin. "See, I told you she wouldn't be mad."

Jared covered a smile and exchanged a glance with Suzanna that set her heart racing again.

"Jared took me for a ride. Did you know he's got his very own horse over at the livery?"

"A ride?" she asked, feeling a prickle of alarm. Her baby on a horse?

"I put him up in front of me," Jared explained. "We just went to the edge of town and let Pistol have a little practice fetching sticks."

"Oh," she said, noticing how much better Jared looked, and not just because he'd shaved and dressed. Although he seemed a little uncertain of his reception, the haunted expression had vanished from his eyes.

"Then we went to the store, and Jared bought me a peppermint stick and a deck of cards so I can practice my counting even when he's not around. See," he said holding out the pack for her inspection.

"I hope you don't mind," Jared said.

"No, not at all," she replied, thinking how handsome he looked when he was a little unsure of himself.

"I even got to take a bath with Jared at the barber shop," Andy continued, "and the barber put tonic on my hair. Smell." He stuck his head under her nose, and she sniffed obediently. The faint scent of hair oil was overpowered by the odor of dirty little boy.

"It's too bad you got your bath *before* all your adventures, because now you need another one."

"Aw, Mama!"

"I can't take you to eat supper looking like a raga-muffin," she said, ruffling his hair.

"She's right, partner," Jared said, earning a black look from Andy. "I'm sorry. I should have cleaned him up before I brought him home."

"That's all right. I have some water heating outside. I'll have him fixed up in no time."

Jared fidgeted with his hat brim looking as if he felt he should take his leave. Suzanna would have done anything to keep him longer, because the longer she could study him, the better opportunity she would have to gauge his real feelings for her. Unfortunately, she had already made the first move by going to his hotel room today. If there was to be a second move, it had to be Jared's.

"Andy, have you thanked Jared?"

"Not yet. We was thinking . . ." He caught himself and glanced sheepishly at Jared.

Some silent communication passed between them. "What did you think, Andy?" Suzanna prompted.

Andy cast Jared an appealing look.

"Andy and I thought, that is, if you'd like . . . I was hoping you'd both join me for supper at the Western."

Suzanna blinked in surprise, uncertain whether she was happy or terrified at the prospect. She did want to spend time with him, but she didn't want to give him the impression she was willing to do more than that.

As if sensing her doubts, he said, "I just want to buy your supper, Suzanna. That's all."

Was he telling the truth? Suzanna wished she could see beyond his gambler's poise and know what was really in his mind and in his heart. Of course, she didn't have to worry about tonight. Andy would be with them, so nothing untoward could happen. "I . . . That would be very nice," she said. "You'll have to wait while I get Andy cleaned up, though."

"Of course. Here, I'll get the tub down for you."

Suzanna couldn't believe how easily the three of

them fell into their former relationship. The time Andy and Jared had spent together had brought them closer even than they'd been when Jared was teaching Andy to play cards.

Of course, Suzanna and Jared had never really let down their guards except for the brief time they'd spent making love, but Jared adopted the same friendly, almost formal attitude he'd had toward her prior to that interlude.

For her part, Suzanna decided to match his reserve. Her instincts told her he still loved her, but still he'd hurt her terribly. She wanted to believe he had some perfectly logical explanation for walking out, but until he told her what it was, she would be careful.

In remarkably short order, they had Andy presentable again, and the three of them walked down the alley to the Western Hotel. If Mrs. Galland was surprised to see them together, she gave no indication as she took their order for antelope steak.

Andy chattered excitedly, exclaiming over everything and recalling incidents from earlier in the day he had forgotten to share with his mother during his bath. Ordinarily, Suzanna would have chastened him for his bad manners, but she was grateful for the distraction he provided. She had been afraid she'd be too nervous to eat, but with Andy to act as a buffer, she hardly felt the tension at all.

"Andy, ask your mother if she'd like some more coffee," Jared would say.

"Andy, ask Jared how he got a job at the Alhambra," Suzanna would say.

They spoke to each other through Andy all during dinner. The boy didn't seem to mind, although Suzanna caught him giving her a puzzled look from time to time. Everything worked beautifully until late in the meal when Andy said, "I still don't understand why Jared can't live with us like before."

Suzanna didn't either, of course. She hated the heat she felt in her face, but she was gratified to notice

Jared's face had reddened also. If he was embarrassed, Suzanna had no intention of making things easy for him.

"Jared doesn't *want* to live with us," she told Andy.

"Yes, he does. He told me, didn't you, Jared?" Andy insisted.

Shocked, Suzanna looked to Jared for confirmation, but suddenly, he was intent on paying the bill, digging in his pocket for the proper coins.

"It's getting late," he said. "We'd better be going."

Andy wouldn't be put off so easily, however. As soon as they were in the alley, he said, "You told me you liked living with us."

"I also explained why I can't," Jared replied, carefully to avoid looking in Suzanna's direction.

Unable to resist the opportunity to make Jared feel more uncomfortable, Suzanna said, "Andy, you shouldn't pester Jared. If he doesn't want us, I'm sure he has a good reason."

Jared made an odd, choking sound, but Suzanna didn't deign to glance in his direction. She hoped she'd struck a nerve, but before she could dwell on her triumph, Andy started in again.

"I want him to live with us, Mama," he whined. "Please tell him he can!"

Her mother's instinct recognized the unmistakable irrationality of an overly tired child. Oh, dear, how could she have let this happen? She'd been concentrating too hard on Jared, that's how, she scolded herself, using Andy and letting him get all wound up. Tears were already glistening in his eyes. She stopped and scooped him up in her arms.

"Shhh, it's all right. You're just tired."

"I am not!" he insisted, struggling frantically. "I don't want you, I want Jared!"

"Hold still!" she cried, losing her grip on him, but before he could fall, Jared plucked him out of her arms.

"Settle down, partner," Jared commanded, and

Andy instantly began to wail, wrapping his arms around Jared's neck and clinging for dear life.

Stricken by her son's rejection, Suzanna almost missed the naked agony on Jared's face as he hugged the boy to him. "There now, don't cry," he murmured, patting the small back awkwardly.

She wasn't sure how long they stood like that, Andy crying, Jared holding him, and Suzanna staring in wonder at the evidence of Jared's pain. Resisting an absurd desire to comfort him—he *deserved* to suffer, didn't he?—she eventually gathered her wits enough to say, "He's tired. When a child gets like that, the only thing you can do is try to get him to sleep."

Jared nodded, and moved on down the alley toward her house. She hurried ahead, opening the door for them and standing aside so Jared could take Andy into the bedroom. With Jared's help, she got Andy undressed and into his nightshirt. By then the boy was sobbing hysterically, and nothing Suzanna could do would satisfy him. He only wanted Jared.

At last Jared sat down on the cot with him, rubbing his back until his sobs subsided and he fell into an uneasy sleep. Suzanna watched from the doorway, leaning there and hugging herself against the dual pain of having lost Jared and knowing her son was suffering as much as she. She only wished she wasn't certain Jared was equally miserable. It simply didn't make sense.

Although Andy still whimpered occasionally, Suzanna knew he was asleep, but she suspected Jared didn't since he continued to massage the little back.

"You can stop now. He's sleeping," she said.

Jared looked up in surprise, as if he'd forgotten she was there. His dark eyes were bleak. "I never should have taken him today."

"Don't blame yourself. I should have noticed how tired he was and just had a simple meal here at home and put him to bed."

Jared drew a deep breath and let it out in a shaky

sigh. His hand had stilled on Andy's back, but he hadn't removed it, as if he couldn't quite bring himself to break the contact. "No, I meant I shouldn't have gotten his hopes up. I had this crazy idea that maybe . . ." He hesitated, looking away.

"Maybe what?"

When his dark eyes lifted to hers again, she actually flinched at the depths of his despair. "I thought maybe we could be friends."

"*Friends?*" she echoed angrily. Andy stirred restlessly, and she lowered her voice. "Is that how you treat your friends? Seduce them and walk out and then try to pay them for their 'services'?"

He closed his eyes for a moment, and when he opened them again, he had managed to conceal whatever emotions he was feeling. "Suzanna, you were wrong when you told Andy I didn't want to be with you, but you were right when you said I must have a good reason. I do."

"I know what it is, too," she said bitterly. "You don't want a wife and family tying you down."

"No, that's not it," he said, desperation in his voice. "I'm not the man you think I am. There are things in my past that . . . Well, let's just say I know what your life has been like up till now, and if you get involved with me, your future is likely to be even worse. I don't want that for you or for Andy either. I want you to be happy, Suzanna, but if I stay with you, you won't be."

Suzanna didn't know whether to laugh or to cry. "This whole thing sounds like a scene out of a penny-dreadful novel. If you're trying to convince me I'd be better off without you, you're too late. I figured that out days ago. There have even been times when I wished the man who shot you had a better aim!"

Jared rose slowly to his feet, his eyes glittering with suppressed emotions. "There have been times when I wished the same thing."

Stunned, Suzanna could think of no reply. The silence throbbed between them for several seconds before he said, "If you're ready to go to work, I'll walk you over."

"No!" she cried, unwilling to spend another moment with him. "I mean, no, I have to change my clothes first. Don't wait for me."

She backed out of the bedroom and hurried to the door, opening it so he would know she intended him to leave. He didn't come out of the bedroom immediately, and she guessed he was saying his private good-byes to Andy. When he finally came through the curtain, his expression was completely blank.

He paused at the front door, looking down at her. She tried to match his calmness but knew he could probably sense her fury and her pain.

"Suzanna, I've been cruel and selfish. I don't expect you to forgive me, but please understand I never meant to hurt you or Andy either."

Her mouth dropped open in outrage. "I certainly hope you never hurt us on *purpose*. I doubt we'd survive!"

Pain flickered in his eyes, but only for a moment. "Good-bye, Suzanna."

She slammed the door behind him, striking it with her fist and collapsing against it, holding her tears in check until the sound of his footsteps faded. This time her grief was worse because she'd allowed herself to hope he'd come back and because she knew he cared about them and because she couldn't understand why it wasn't enough.

Jared shuffled the cards and placed them back into the dealing box for the next game while his lookout, the man paid to watch the customers and make sure they didn't try anything sneaky, paid off the bets. Jared had never worked with a lookout at the Comique, but he found he needed one lately since his attention often strayed from the game.

He'd be fine as soon as Dora Hand's performance was over, he reminded himself. It was her love songs that disturbed him, and she seemed compelled to sing "Oh, Susanna" at least once each evening. The first time Jared had thought it an unfortunate coincidence until he'd seen Dora watching for his reaction.

He'd be damned if he'd oblige her, but he couldn't seem to control his mind as well as he controlled his expression. If Dora intended to distract him, she succeeded admirably.

"Get your money down, gentlemen," he said. When the bets were in place he pulled the first card out of the box, the 'soda,' which counted for nothing. The next card would be a loser and the third a winner. He called the numbers out and waited while the lookout cleared the bets for the next round.

Dora was warbling a request to be carried back to Old Virginny in her New England accent, and Jared allowed himself a small smile at the irony. He drew the next two cards, called them out, and waited for his lookout to clear the bets again.

Of course, Virginia wasn't too far from his own home. Odd how the memory of it no longer brought the usual painful longing. He supposed the anguish of losing Suzanna had made other losses insignificant and wondered dismally whether five years would have to pass before he could think of *her* without suffering the agonies of hell. In the week since he'd last spoken to her, the pain had only increased.

He pulled two more cards and called them out.

"Oh, hell!" one of the players said, gathering what remained of his chips and rising abruptly from the table. He was a good-looking young Texan whom Jared had seen hanging around the saloon a lot the past few nights. Rumor said he was the only son of one of the wealthiest ranchers in Texas, a Quaker by the name of Miflin Kennedy. The boy didn't look much like a Quaker, though, or act like one either. Small and slight of build, his coloring showed his Mexican mother's Latin heritage and the fiery temper that went along with it.

"Where you going, Spike?" one of his companions asked as Kennedy stalked away."

"I'm gonna listen to Miss Hand sing. Can't lose no money doing that," he replied, tossing Jared a black look over his shoulder.

Good riddance, thought Jared as he pulled the next two cards. The boy was trouble. Rich, spoiled boys always were, and Spike Kennedy was the worst of the lot.

"Sing 'The Yellow Rose of Texas,' " Kennedy shouted when Dora finished her song.

Jared frowned. The kid was drunk. Jared glanced around and was relieved to see Dog Kelley watching. Kelley wouldn't let things get out of hand, Jared thought, finishing up the game.

"Thank you, gentlemen. Get your bets down."

On the makeshift stage at the far end of the room, Dora began a rousing rendition of "The Yellow Rose of Texas." Texans all over the room began to clap and stomp their feet. Rebel yells split the air, drowning out the piano. Dora raised her voice, using the training she had received as an opera singer and inspiring the Texans to even more hilarity.

Spike Kennedy grabbed a half-filled bottle of whiskey off the bar, took a healthy gulp, and flung the bottle against the wall where it exploded into a spray of liquor and glass. "Yee-haa!" he yelled and bounded up onto the stage.

Dora tried to ignore him. He grabbed for her, and she dodged, but he wasn't so drunk that he couldn't catch her in the small space.

"How about a kiss?" he howled as Dora struggled.

Jared was already running for the stage when Kelley jumped up and grabbed Kennedy by the scruff of the neck. Surprised, Kennedy lost his hold of Dora who stumbled free as Kelley hauled back and punched Kennedy square in the face.

Blood spouted from his nose and his knees buckled, but Kelley didn't let him fall. Instead, he caught hold of the seat of his pants with his other hand and headed for the door, half-carrying, half-dragging his semiconscious burden.

The crowd roared, and Jared reached beneath his coat for the pistol he kept concealed there, but the crowd's anger seemed directed against Kennedy for daring to accost Dora Hand.

"Get him out of here," someone yelled, and the others shouted their agreement.

When Kelley reached the swinging doors, he didn't even hesitate. Plowing on through, he heaved and tossed Kennedy out into the street. "That's what we do with all the garbage, Kennedy. Don't come back if you know what's good for you."

The crowd cheered its approval, but Jared noticed one or two men sidling out quickly, the ones who had been gambling with Kennedy at his table. Jared only hoped they'd make sure their friend got out of Dodge before he sobered up enough to start thinking about revenge.

Seeing Kelley needed no help, Jared hurried to the stage where Dora still stood, slumped against the wall, her hand to her throat.

"Are you all right? Did he hurt you?"

"Oh, no," she assured him, straightening and smoothing her dress. "I'm just a little startled. It's been a while since I had such an enthusiastic admirer."

Kelley appeared at Jared's elbow, still flushed from his exertion. "You all right, honey?"

"I'm fine, but do you know who you just threw into the street? That was Spike Kennedy. His father used to be partners with Captain King," she said, naming the biggest rancher in Texas.

"I don't care if he's the king of England," Kelley said. "Nobody lays a hand on you."

"He's trouble, Jimmy."

"She's right, Dog," Jared said. "That boy is as mean as a snake and twice as slippery. You'd better have somebody with you when you leave tonight. I wouldn't put it past him to ambush you.''

Kelley laughed derisively. ''Let him try.''

''Jimmy, don't be foolish. Jared is right.'' She gave Jared a beseeching look.

''I'll make sure he doesn't leave here alone tonight,'' he promised her.

''Or for the next few nights, until we're sure he and his friends have left town,'' Dora said, clutching at Kelley's arm.

''For God's sake, Dora, I don't need a nursemaid.''

''Being brave won't stop a bullet in the back,'' Jared pointed out. Dora shuddered.

''All right, I'll do it for you,'' Kelley said.

''And I'll escort Dora over to the Comique when she's ready,'' Jared added.

Kelley swore. Dora smiled indulgently and patted his arm. ''Just for a few days, until Kennedy goes back to Texas.''

Only when Jared and Dora had left the Alhambra a few minutes later did Jared realize his mistake. The woman who had tormented him with ''Oh, Susanna'' wasn't about to miss an opportunity like this.

''How have you been lately, Jared?''

''My wound has healed very nicely, thank you,'' he replied warily, alerted by her overly solicitous tone.

''Are you sleeping well? You look a little pale.''

''It comes from working all night and sleeping all day. We all look pale.''

''Suzanna's even paler than usual. I'm worried about her.''

Guilt stabbed through him, but he reminded himself she was probably just trying to get his goat. ''Are you?''

''Yes, I don't think she ever sleeps anymore, and she's lost weight.''

One look at Dora's face, and Jared knew she was telling the truth. Fear clutched at his vitals. ''Do you think she's ill?''

"Not really. Heartsick would be my guess, and we both know who's responsible."

"I don't expect you to believe me, but I didn't mean to hurt her. I never would have let her take care of me in the first place if I'd known, and as soon as I realized where I was, I tried to leave, but she wouldn't let me."

"Suzanna's a stubborn woman all right. The only thing I can't understand is why you left her. Surely you know how she feels about you. Even if you don't feel the same, I'd think you'd stay just to have a woman in your bed for a change."

Rage welled up in him, and he held his temper with difficulty. "If you are truly Suzanna's friend, you know she isn't that kind of woman," he said stiffly.

Dora stared up at him in amazement. "My goodness," she said after a moment. "I suppose I'm lucky you're a gentleman or you'd be telling me to mind my own business, too."

"I may do it anyway."

Dora sighed in disgust. "I just don't see why you both have to be unhappy apart when—"

"Dora," he said in warning.

She sighed again, this time in defeat. "I'm sorry. I'll try to behave myself."

They had reached the front door of the Comique.

"Are you coming in?" she asked.

"I don't think it would be wise."

"She knows you watch her walking home every night."

"It isn't safe for a woman to walk home alone at that time of night," he said defensively, glad the darkness hid his heated face.

"Jimmy and I are almost always with her."

"I watch in case you aren't."

"If you don't love her, why do you care?"

He couldn't possibly answer that question. "Good night, Dora."

She smiled slyly. "You're going to be with Jimmy later when he comes to get me, aren't you?"

Jared's nerves prickled in warning. "Don't try to throw us together, Dora. She won't thank you."

"Are you sure?"

Knowing he had to end this conversation, Jared started to turn away, but Dora caught his arm.

"Oh, Jared, I'm sorry. I'm a meddling fool, but I can't resist trying to help the people I care about. I'm a lot older than you, and I know how hard it is to find someone as fine as Suzanna. Do you have any idea what you're throwing away?"

God, yes, he wanted to say, but he called on all his reserves of strength and said, "It's for Suzanna's own good. Do you think I'd leave her for any other reason?"

Dora snorted in disgust. "Does Suzanna agree it's for her own good? Is that why she's withering up like an old woman? Is that why Andy cries for you at night?"

"Stop it!"

"I would if I thought you didn't want her. Jared, please, listen to me. Life is too short to worry about all the things that were important to you back East. If you've got another wife or—"

"I don't!"

"Or whatever your reason, it isn't important, or at least not as important as making you and Suzanna and Andy happy. Forget honor and everything else about the past. Take what life is offering you right now."

"Even if it hurts the people I love most in the world?" he asked bitterly.

Dora took his hands in hers. "Jared, you have to ask yourself what would hurt them more, having you or not having you. When you know the answer, you'll know what to do."

Chapter 8

❦

"You'll never guess who just walked me over from the Alhambra," Dora said with her sly smile.

Suzanna felt the familiar sinking sensation she always got at the mention of Jared Cain. "Mayor Kelley?" she tried, hoping she was right.

"No, we had some trouble over at the Alhambra tonight and—"

"Was anyone hurt?" Suzanna asked anxiously, hating herself for instantly thinking of Jared.

"A cowboy had his pride severely wounded, but no one else was injured. That boy, Spike Kennedy, started acting up. You know the one I mean, don't you?"

"The one who was in here last night wanting you to dance with him?"

Dora nodded and rolled her eyes. "I'm probably old enough to be his mother, too, more's the pity. Well, tonight he got a snootful and jumped up on the stage and tried to kiss me."

"Oh, no!"

"Oh, yes! As you can imagine, Jimmy didn't approve of such conduct. I think he may have broken the poor boy's nose, and then he threw him out into the street."

"How awful! Spike Kennedy's not one to take treatment like that, either."

"Exactly what I told Jimmy, and Jared agreed with me."

"Jared?" Suzanna echoed with renewed apprehension.

"Yes, Jared rushed to my rescue, too. We both managed to convince Jimmy he'd better be careful for the next few days until Kennedy and his friends leave town, so Jared walked me over here tonight, and he'll be coming with Jimmy later."

"Thank you for warning me. I'll be careful to avoid him."

"After I went to so much trouble to arrange this?" Dora said in feigned outrage. "Honestly, Suzanna, sometimes I wonder about you."

Suzanna smiled in spite of herself. "I wish you'd find someone else's life to straighten out. How about Polly and Sam? She must be leading him a merry chase. Have you seen him tonight?"

"Yes, he looks like a hound dog who lost his bone, but I don't want to help them because I don't think Polly's the right girl for him. Now you and Jared—"

"Dora, you're going to get in trouble if you don't stop meddling in other people's lives," Suzanna warned, only half-jokingly.

"Trouble comes no matter what you do," Dora replied. "I'd better get backstage. I think I'm supposed to sing after this skit, and you'd better get to work."

"I'm trying to hide," Suzanna admitted. "Too many soldiers in here tonight."

Dora nodded her understanding. The residents of Fort Dodge were a rowdy bunch and not nearly as easy to fend off as the Texas cowboys. "Looks like they're more interested in gambling than dancing, though."

"So far, anyway."

When Dora had gone, Suzanna took a fortifying breath and waded out onto the floor in search of a likely-looking partner. She'd just located a lonesome cowboy when someone started shouting down by the faro table.

"You son of a bitch! You're cheating!"

Craning her neck, Suzanna could see a soldier had

grabbed the new faro dealer by the lapels and dragged him across the table, scattering cards and chips everywhere.

"You're crazy!" the dealer yelled back, struggling to get free.

Sam Goodwin lumbered past her, ready to quell the disturbance, but several other soldiers started yelling and surrounded the hapless dealer, intent on violence.

Boom!

Suzanna was already halfway to the floor when she realized the shotgun blast had been fired by Springer to restore order. Instantly, the shouting and all other sound in the room ceased. "What in the hell's going on here?" he demanded.

The soldier holding the dealer released him slowly, allowing him to slide back to his own side of the table. "This tinhorn cheated. He's pulled out three pairs in this game. That don't happen unless somebody planned it." The other soldiers murmured their agreement.

From watching her partners play during her months in the dance hall, Suzanna had learned that when the two cards drawn in a play were the same, the dealer won half the bets placed. Even in her ignorance, she realized the odds against drawing three pairs in one game were great.

"You saying I run a crooked house?" Springer wanted to know.

The soldiers looked at the shotgun. Only one barrel had been fired. Behind Springer, the bartenders had formed a ragged line. Each of them held a Winchester.

The soldier who had started the fracas raised his hands to show he didn't want any trouble. "I'm saying you oughta be careful who you hire to run your faro bank."

"And you oughta be careful who you accuse of cheating. All of you, get out. I don't want to see a single blue coat in this place. Move!"

Grudgingly, the soldiers picked up their chips and

began shuffling toward the banker to cash them in. Those without chips headed straight for the door, muttering among themselves ominously. For a few moments Suzanna feared they might decide to turn on Springer and overpower him, but apparently the threat of his shotgun was enough to deter them.

When the last blue coat had disappeared through the door, Springer said, "Let's have some music."

Obediently, the orchestra struck up a rousing march while the actors on the stage abandoned their skit to make way for Dora who sang the ever-popular "Reuben and Rachel." Soon the crowd had livened up again, and everyone forgot the trouble with the soldiers.

Every now and then, Suzanna glanced over at the faro table, and she noticed the remaining patrons avoided it, choosing instead to play chuck-a-luck or keno. Finally, Springer called the dealer into his office and closed the door. She'd never liked the new dealer, who struck her as an oily character, but she'd supposed her dislike had come from his having taken Jared's place. Now she realized she'd judged him correctly. Near the end of the evening, she noticed the faro layout was gone. Apparently so was the dealer.

When the dance hall closed, Suzanna was first in line to draw her pay for the evening. As soon as she had it, she hurried out of the theater, not even looking around for fear she might see Dora trying to catch her eye. She had absolutely no intention of walking home with Dora and the mayor if Jared Cain was going to be with them. She'd walked home alone many times in the past and could do so again.

The next evening when they met at church, Dora chided her, but Suzanna refused to relent. There was no use rubbing salt in her wounds by subjecting herself to his company.

When Suzanna returned to work on Monday, the other girls were discussing the new faro dealer Springer had hired that morning.

''He's a drunk,'' Maisie said knowingly.

''I don't care,'' Polly said, ''so long as he don't cheat the customers. That other fellow took an awful chance.''

''Mayor Kelley is worried,'' Suzanna added, having discussed the matter with him earlier in the day. ''He's afraid the army will take some sort of revenge because their men were cheated.''

''Springer's a fool,'' Maisie said. ''He should've given those boys their money back.''

''If he did, he'd have to pay off everybody who ever lost money in this place, and he'd go out of business,'' Suzanna pointed out.

Annie Ladue fluttered her eyelashes and smiled importantly. ''Bat says we don't have anything to worry about. If the army was coming, they would've come yesterday.''

''I suppose 'Bat' was sitting up all night waiting for them,'' Maisie said snidely.

''The police force was ready for them, if that's what you mean,'' Annie replied, sticking her pert nose in the air. ''The army would never take on Bat Masterson anyway.''

''Bat Masterson isn't the law in this town, Wyatt Earp is,'' Polly reminded her.

''Bat is the law in the county, and Dodge City is in Ford County,'' Annie insisted.

''No matter who's in charge, I hope they're right about the army not coming back,'' Suzanna said. ''Those boys were awfully mad. If you see any soldiers come in, I'd suggest you find some cover.''

''Good advice,'' Maisie agreed.

Unfortunately, they didn't see the soldiers at all. The music in the Comique drowned out the sound of marching feet as the soldiers entered the town under cover of darkness and surrounded the hall. The first hint of danger was the blast of gunfire that splintered the walls and sent everyone inside diving for the floor.

Women screamed and men shouted. Suzanna huddled in a corner and covered her head, praying desperately that someone would look after Andy if she were killed. She thought of Jared and the way he had held her and kept her safe the last time death had ricocheted through the Comique. Oh, Lord, she loved them both so much. What if she never got to see them again?

Trembling with terror, her heart pounding in her throat, Suzanna hugged the floor and waited, expecting to feel the hot sting of lead piercing her flesh at any moment. The seconds ticked by with agonizing slowness, but nothing happened.

Everyone lay still for what seemed a long time, but after the first blast, no other shots were fired. Then someone from outside called, "Springer, we just wanted to let you know what happens when you cheat the army!"

In the silence that followed, they could hear the troops marching away toward the bridge. On the other side of the room, Springer jumped up and began to swear. "I fired that son of a bitch!" he kept telling anyone who would listen, but no seemed particularly interested. Gradually, people began to get up, crawling out from under tables and brushing themselves off.

Suzanna pushed herself up off the floor and looked around, too stunned to quite comprehend that she was safe.

"*We* didn't cheat them!" one of the cowboys insisted. "Why'd they try to kill us?" This started an argument that grew progressively louder. Someone tried to point out that the bullet holes, all in a straight line across the front wall of the theater, were at least ten feet off the ground, well above the heads of the patrons, but nobody seemed interested in listening to him.

"They tried to kill us all just because they was mad at Springer!" someone else insisted, and just about everyone took up the cry. By the time Marshal Earp and the other members of the Dodge City police force arrived, they could hardly manage to get a coherent account of what had happened.

People from all over town had come running, and soon the theater and the street outside were jammed with curiosity seekers. Still somewhat numb, Suzanna hurried to retrieve her purse from behind the bar and was trying to work her way to the door so she could run home and check on Andy when she heard someone calling her.

"Suzanna!"

She stared in disbelief at the sight of Jared forcing his way through the press. What was he doing here?

"Suzanna!"

Should she answer? Before she could decide, he found her and started for her, literally shoving people out of the way in his haste.

"Thank God!" he said in the instant before he took her in his arms.

He crushed her to his chest, burying his face in her hair and whispering her name over and over. Beneath her ear, his heart pounded and his breath came in ragged gasps. He must have run all the way across the plaza.

"Thank God, thank God. You're not hurt, are you?" he asked, pushing her away a little so he could see her face.

Suzanna stared up at him, still not quite able to believe he was here. Nothing seemed real. "No, they fired over our heads."

"Thank God," he repeated, hugging her fiercely again. This time she hugged him back. "They said the army had shot up the theater. They said dozens of people had been hit. I thought I'd go crazy until I found you. Are you sure you're all right?"

She nodded against his chest. One of them was trembling, or maybe both of them were. She couldn't be sure. Reaction, she supposed. Being fired upon by a troop of soldiers was a harrowing experience, but being held by Jared was equally harrowing. Was he really here or was she in shock?

"Come on, let's get you home. Andy must surely be awake."

Andy! The thought of her son jarred her out of her fog, and she let him lead her from the building. They made slow progress against the flood of people attempting to enter, but Jared got them out somehow. They hurried down the darkened street and deserted alley, Jared's firm hand steadying her against the uncertain footing. Suzanna found her key and opened the door.

Pistol greeted her, whining and sniffing suspiciously at Jared. In the other room she heard Andy whimpering.

"Mama?"

"Yes, dear, I'm here," she called, rushing in to comfort him.

"I heard a noise," he said as she took him in her arms.

"I know, but everything's all right now. Mama's here and you can go back to sleep."

In the front room, Jared lit the lamp and the light filtered through the curtain. She waited apprehensively for Andy to ask who was out there, but he didn't seem to notice. In another minute he was asleep again. She lay him down carefully and waited until she was sure he wouldn't awaken again.

Only then did she realize the awkwardness of the situation. Jared Cain was in her parlor. For the past ten days they had studiously avoided each other. Suzanna had even begun to think she might survive the pain of losing him, and tonight he'd come rushing back into her life with a force of a cyclone, claiming a concern for her safety that he had no right to feel.

What was he doing here? Did he think he could walk into her house as if nothing had ever happened? Did he think she was a fool? All the fury she had stored up for the last ten days boiled up inside her, ready to spill over and scald Jared Cain. She shoved the curtain aside angrily.

Jared was sitting at the table. He rose instantly. "Is he all right?"

"Yes," she snapped.

"How about you? Are you going to be all right?"

His genuine concern disconcerted her for an instant, but she held fast to her anger. "What do you care?"

He flinched as if she'd struck him. "I care very much."

"Oh, yes, you care so much you walked out on us, and you weren't even man enough to tell us why."

The challenge hung between them for several seconds, and Jared drew himself up straighter. "Do you want to know the reason?" he asked.

Fear prickled her nerve endings. Did she really want to know? "Yes, I do. I want to know the *real* reason, the truth for a change." Then she could put Jared Cain out of her life once and for all.

"I'm a wanted man, Suzanna."

At first the words didn't register. Jared, wanted? That was absurd. "For what?"

"For murder."

She cried out in surprise and instantly covered her lips. *Murder?* How? And when? And why? The questions tumbled over themselves in her mind, but Jared didn't wait for her to ask.

"I killed a man, a long time ago. I changed my name and went far away. Ever since I've been careful not to make friends because friends have a way of finding out your secrets, and I've especially avoided women."

"You didn't avoid me!" she reminded him bitterly. "You even offered me money to—"

"Only because I didn't know you, Suzanna." He took a step toward her and held out his hand beseechingly. "I thought you were just one of the other women, someone who'd make the loneliness a little less horrible for a few hours, but when I saw you here, with Andy, I realized I was wrong. I knew you were the kind of woman who was most dangerous—someone I could really care for. Then, when I was shot, I didn't want to stay with you because by that time I'd fallen in love with you."

"Oh, Jared," she cried, running to him, but he caught her before she could embrace him.

"Don't you understand what I've just told you? I'm a killer. If you're with me when they catch me, you'll be disgraced."

She stared up at him incredulously. "Jared, I'm already disgraced. I'm a dance-hall girl. I'm a 'seductress.' Decent women won't even acknowledge me on the street. What more harm can you do me?"

He had no answer.

"Jared, listen to me. I love you, and Andy loves you. We've been miserable since you left us. Andy asks for you every night, and I cry myself to sleep for missing you." His hands tightened on her arms, and his beautiful eyes filled with despair. "If you left us because you didn't want to hurt us, then you have to understand you're hurting us much more by staying away. Do you really love me, Jared?"

"Yes, oh, yes."

"Do you want to be with me?"

His face twisted with longing, but he said, "I'm a murderer, Suzanna. You deserve someone better."

"A murderer!" she scoffed, unable to believe it. "You couldn't *murder* anyone, not shoot a man down in cold blood. If you killed someone, it must have been an accident or self-defense."

His expression hardened against her declarations, but she couldn't stop, not now. "It was in a saloon, wasn't it? You were playing cards and a man drew on you, just like when you were shot at the Comique. It was self-defense, wasn't it?"

He stiffened, his hands like talons on her arms. "It wasn't like that, but it was an accident. I was defending someone else."

"I knew it! Jared, don't you see? You didn't have to run away. Even if you stood trial—"

"I can't stand trial, because if I tell what really happened, I'll hurt some innocent people. That's why I ran in the first place, and now I'll hurt you, too."

"Only if you leave us!" She grabbed his lapels, wishing she could shake some sense into him. "They might never catch you. Have you thought of that? You said it's been a long time already. Maybe they aren't even looking anymore. Maybe you'll leave me and Andy for no good reason, and we'll all three of us be alone and for what? Oh, Jared, don't you see? Nothing can hurt us as much as losing you!"

He wanted to believe her. She could see it in his eyes, so she used the only weapon remaining to her. She slipped her arms around his neck and pressed her mouth to his. His resistance lasted only an instant, then he pulled her to him with an agonized groan.

She opened to his possession, and he claimed her with his tongue, pressing her to his heart. For long minutes they kissed, rekindling the passion that had raged between them before. At last, breathless and gasping, they pulled apart. He touched her face, and she saw that his eyes were still shadowed.

"I can't marry you, Suzanna. If they find me, I don't want you tied to me in any way."

"Then I'll be your mistress."

"Suzanna!" he said, shocked. "You can't live in sin with me."

A few days ago, Suzanna would have recoiled at the thought, but it no longer seemed shocking. Marriage and propriety seemed irrelevant when she envisioned the lonely years without him. Besides, she figured she could change his mind about marriage in time. "I can if you're willing."

"What will people say?"

"The same things they say about Doc Holliday and Kate Elder: what can you expect from a gambler and a dance-hall girl? Bat Masterson is sharing a room with Annie Ladue, and Wyatt Earp—''

"You aren't like those other women, Suzanna. You may not care what other people think, but how will you live with *yourself*?"

Her bold smile faded. He was right, of course. Tomorrow her bravado would fade, and she'd have to deal with the guilt. But would the guilt be worse than the loneliness or would waking up in Jared's arms be worth any shame she had to endure? Considered in those terms, the choice was really no choice at all.

"Jared, I love you, and I want to live with you. Heaven knows I've never gotten any particular rewards for being good up till now, so I guess I'm willing to take my chances at being bad."

He shook his head in despair. "If I'm caught, it won't make any difference whether we're married or not. You'll still be disgraced."

"I already told you, I don't care if I'm disgraced," she said, frantically trying to think of an argument to convince him. "And you're wrong. Everyone in town knows we just met. If you were . . . arrested," she went on, almost choking on the word, "no one here would hold it against me."

"But you'd carry my name wherever you went."

"Not if we weren't married," she pointed out triumphantly, "and as long as we're together, I don't care if we're married or not."

She tried to kiss him, but he held her off. "There's one more thing you haven't thought of. What if you have a child?"

A child, Jared's child. The thought was too beautiful to contemplate, a dream that could never come true. "I can't have any more children, Jared. After Andy was born, I was real sick. It's been four years, and I never had another baby. The midwife said . . ." She shrugged, her throat clogged with tears.

"My poor darling," he said drawing her to him in a tender embrace. For a while they clung to each other, two lost souls who had found comfort at last. He pressed a kiss to her forehead. "Do you want to go back to the Comique tonight?"

She shook her head against his shoulder. "Does Mr. Kelley expect you back?"

"I doubt it."

In the silence, Suzanna noticed his breath came a little unsteadily.

"Suzanna, do you want me to go?"

She pulled back and looked up into his face. "I thought we settled that."

His eyes were still tortured. "Are you sure? I don't want you to be sorry later."

"I'll only be sorry if you go."

He groaned and lowered his mouth to hers. The kiss went on and on, then his arms came down and picked her up and she was floating. For a moment everything was like a dream until they reached the doorway and they didn't fit through.

Jared muttered something that sounded like a curse, and Suzanna giggled. So much for romance. He set her on her feet, his arms still around her, and walked her into the bedroom, but in the faint light she caught sight of Andy still sleeping peacefully on his cot, his dog curled up beside him.

"Oh, dear, I forgot," she said, looking up at Jared apologetically.

Jared smiled. "If you can lift him, I'll carry his bed into the other room."

Suzanna lifted the boy carefully, soothing him when he murmured a protest. As soon as Jared had the cot set up in the front room, she put him back down. He hadn't even wakened.

Jared picked up the lamp and carried it into the bedroom, holding the curtain open in silent invitation. Suddenly Suzanna felt shy. The first time they had made love had been spontaneous, with no time for second thoughts or embarrassment.

He frowned at her hesitation. "If you've changed your mind—"

"No," she said quickly, moving toward him. "I'll never change my mind."

He stepped back and set the lamp on the crate beside the bed. For a minute they just looked at each other, then Jared shrugged out of his suit coat and hung it on a peg beside Suzanna's Sunday dress.

When Jared began to unbutton his shirt, Suzanna quickly sat down on the bed and unlaced her boots. From the corner of her eye, she saw him strip off his shirt, revealing the broad chest that had haunted her dreams. She shivered slightly and tugged off her boots.

"Here, let me," he said, kneeling before her and reaching underneath her skirt to remove her stockings. Suzanna's breath caught at the sight of his naked torso so close. His skin looked golden in the lamplight, the hair on his chest glinting red. "I wanted to do this the other night when I watched you taking off your shoes."

His fingers gently stroked her calves as they peeled down first one stocking and then the other. Gooseflesh rose on her thighs, and Suzanna felt the familiar aching emptiness. He took one of her feet in his hands and began to massage out the soreness. Sensation streaked up her leg, and Suzanna moaned involuntarily.

"Does this feel good?" he asked, and she nodded, unwilling to trust her tongue.

His fingers worked diligently until her foot tingled with relief. Then he went to work on the other one.

"The other night when you came in here, I wanted to take off your stockings and touch your legs and your feet, and then I wanted to take off your dress and your petticoats and your corset and your chemise, slowly, one by one, like unwrapping a present, until there was nothing but you, beautiful, beautiful Suzanna."

If his touch was heaven, his words were magic, weaving a sensual spell around her. Of their own accord, her fingers began to work the buttons of her dress. When it was open to the waist, he reached up and helped her slide it off her shoulders.

He took her hand, and they both rose to their feet. Working together, they unfastened her petticoat and let it fall to the floor, carrying her dress with it. While Suzanna fumbled with the fasteners of her corset, Jared caressed her shoulders and pressed a string of kisses across the swell of white flesh above her bodice.

Suzanna's breath became more constricted, even after the corset fell away and she should have been able to breathe freely. Jared quickly disposed of the ties on her chemise and spread it open.

Her nipples hardened instantly, and she resisted an urge to cover herself.

"You're so lovely," he whispered, easing her down onto the bed. His palms closed over her breasts, kneading and sending a surge of desire downward where it flooded her loins.

"Why does it feel so good when you touch me?" she wondered aloud.

"Does it? I'm glad," he said, his lips against her throat. "It feels good when you touch me, too."

Taking his cue, she lifted her hands, placing them tentatively on his bare back. His flesh was hot and silken, slick from the heat.

"Don't be shy," he said through a smile. "You weren't shy the other night."

"I . . . it was dark the other night," she said, glancing hopefully at the lamp.

"I want to see you, Suzanna. I *need* to see you."

"Oh, dear," she said in dismay, making him chuckle.

"What's this, maidenly modesty?" he scoffed, gently pulling her chemise down her arms and easing it from beneath her hips. "Where's the golden-haired vixen who stole into my bed in the dark of night and—"

"I didn't steal into your bed," she insisted. "You were having a nightmare."

"—and pressed her luscious body against mine until I couldn't even remember my name and—"

"Jared, I did no such thing!"

"—and took advantage of my weakened condition and seduced me."

"Jared!" she protested, but the word ended in a surprised squeak as he slipped her underdrawers down and pulled them from her legs, leaving her completely naked. "Oh, my!" she whispered, wishing she had more hands and not knowing what to cover first.

But Jared wouldn't allow her to cover anything. He captured her wrists and pinned them firmly to the bed. Then he looked at her, examining every inch, until the heat of her embarrassment became something else entirely.

"My God, you must be the most beautiful woman alive," he said, his dark eyes filled with love and wonder when he met her gaze again. "Don't move," he commanded, rising quickly and stripping off the rest of his clothes.

Suzanna forgot her own nudity in the face of his. She knew his body intimately, yet it was like seeing him for the first time. His bold virility, his blatant arousal, sent her blood racing. Desire washed over her in a silken wave.

"Jared," she said, holding out her arms. He came to her, lowering himself slowly until he covered her, caressing her with his body as well as his hands.

"Suzanna, I love you."

"I love you, too. Don't ever leave me again."

A shadow flickered in his eyes. "Never willingly."

She didn't want to think of that now, so she pulled his mouth to hers, banishing everything unpleasant from both their minds.

When Jared had thoroughly ravished her mouth, he explored her throat and then her breasts, teasing them to throbbing peaks then soothing them in the moist haven of his mouth. Soon she was writhing with the heavenly sensations and he moved down to nip her belly. At his urging, she opened her thighs, and he grazed them with his fingertips, sending shivers vibrating up and up. Then he probed her secret places until she dewed from want and the fragrance of her desire rose around them like incense.

She called him to her, and he entered her, hard and heavy with the love he bore her. She took him with a cry of joy.

"Look at me, Suzanna."

Obediently, she opened her eyes to see her own rapture reflected on his face. "Oh, Jared, I love you so much."

He cupped her cheek adoringly. "I'll try to make you happy, Suzanna."

She smiled. "I couldn't be any happier."

But she was wrong, as Jared proved. With his hands and lips he worshipped her body, breathing endearments as he moved within her. Want and need fused in white-hot desire that turned Suzanna's blood to liquid fire and melted all her bones until she became a quivering mass of sensation.

Above her Jared drove into her as if he willed their bodies to become one. She met his strokes with feverish urgency, his goal becoming hers. Wrapping her legs around him, she clung with hands and lips, striving with him in the impossible quest that seemed more possible with each pounding heartbeat.

Her lips formed his name, but could utter only a moan of pleasure, pleasure that surged and spiraled and surged again, taking her higher and higher until she saw stars dancing behind her eyelids. Just when she thought she could bear it no more, her body convulsed, shuddering again and again in spasms of bliss. She cried out her joy, and Jared captured the sound with his lips, pressing his mouth to hers as he quaked with his own release.

Afterwards they lay together, trembling and breathless from the force of their union.

"I've never felt like that before," Suzanna said, still

awed and somewhat overwhelmed. "What did you do to me?"

Jared's beautiful mouth quirked in a grin. "The same thing you did to me, my love."

But Suzanna wasn't satisfied with such a glib answer. Long after Jared had put out the light and they had snuggled down to sleep, she continued to wonder.

"Are you awake?" she asked after a while.

"A little bit," he replied drowsily.

Suzanna hesitated, uncertain how to phrase her question.

"Is something wrong?" he asked when she didn't speak.

"No, I . . . I've just been wondering something."

"What?" he prompted, sounding fully awake now.

Glad the darkness hid her face, Suzanna said, "You must have known lots of women."

She could almost feel him trying to figure out what she was really asking. "What do you mean, 'known'?"

Oh, why had she brought up the subject? "I mean, surely I'm not the first woman in your life."

He turned toward her, even though he couldn't possibly make out her expression in the blackness. "I told you I especially avoided women since . . . since the trouble. Women have this annoying habit of wanting to know every little thing about a man." She could hear the hint of teasing in his voice and felt bolder.

"There must have been someone," she prompted.

He drew a deep breath and let it out slowly. "There was one. Her name was Claire. We met in a saloon where I was gambling. I was lonely, and she was available."

"Did you love her?"

He touched her face, caressing her cheek. "No, I didn't love her, and she didn't love me, or at least she didn't act heartbroken when I told her I couldn't see her anymore."

"But you were lovers."

"Yes, we were lovers."

"Was it . . . ?" Suzanna caught herself just in time.

"What? You can ask me anything, Suzanna."

Suzanna bit her lip, knowing she couldn't ask *this*. In the first place, she didn't know the words to use, and in the second place, she wasn't even sure she wanted to know.

His fingers played along her cheek. "Are you blushing?" he teased.

Suzanna shook her head, but he knew she was lying.

"Is this about sex?"

Suzanna's face was scalding now. Surely he could feel the heat.

"Do you want to know how you compare with Claire?" he asked in amazement.

Not exactly, she thought, but close enough. She nodded against his hand.

"Well, now, let me think about this," he said, far too amused for Suzanna's peace of mind.

"Jared," she warned, but he ignored her.

"You have to understand, Claire was far more experienced than I. She educated me in the ways of pleasing a woman—for entirely selfish reasons, of course—but I must confess that pleasing her was never as rewarding as pleasing you."

Suzanna held her breath, but he didn't continue. "What do you mean?" she asked reluctantly.

His fingers trailed down her cheek to tantalize her throat. "I mean you're more woman than Claire ever dreamed of being. You make me crazy, Suzanna. I've been thinking about you constantly since the first time I saw you, and since we made love, I've been obsessed. I can't sleep for dreaming about you, and when I'm awake I can't get you out of my mind. And when we make love . . ." He sighed rapturously.

"It's not always like that for you, then?" she asked, abandoning her modesty.

"Oh, no," he assured her. "Never. Only with you."

Relieved and elated and inordinately pleased, she

threw her arms around him, hugging him close. He hugged her back, but she could sense he was holding back.

"Suzanna?" he said after a moment.

"Yes?"

"How about you and . . . ? Never mind," he added hastily. "I don't have any right to pry."

"Me and Andrew?" she guessed.

"You don't have to tell me anything. I don't have any right to be jealous of a dead man. It's just that I can't stand the thought of you with another man, not even your husband."

"You don't *need* to be jealous of anyone," she assured him. "Andrew and I were children when we married. I was seventeen, and he was nineteen. We thought we were in love, but it wasn't like what I feel for you." In fact, she thought, *nothing* about her relationship with Andrew was anything like her relationship with Jared. Sex with her husband had been an onerous duty even before things got bad, but she wouldn't tell Jared that, and she certainly wouldn't tell him about Andrew's drinking.

He was silent a moment, absorbing her words. "And what exactly do you feel for me?" he asked.

Suzanna wasn't certain she could answer such a question. "I love you, but it's more than that. You make me feel things, wonderful things, and I'm so happy when we're together. I even liked having you here when you were unconscious. I liked to look at you and—" She caught herself, mortified. What was she saying?

"You liked to look at me?" The humor was back in his voice. "What did you look at, Suzanna?"

"Nothing," she murmured, but he wasn't going to give up.

"Did you like to touch me, too? Did you give me baths?"

"I had to lower your fever!"

"But you didn't mind, did you? You liked touching

me. Where did you touch me, Suzanna?'' he teased, taking her hand and bringing it to his chest. ''Here? And here?''

He moved her hand to his belly, lower and lower. ''And here?'' He wrapped her fingers around the hot, hard shaft.

Suzanna gasped. ''Jared!''

''I don't mind,'' he continued innocently. ''You can touch me anywhere you want, so long as you let me touch you back.''

He slid his hand between her thighs, and she gasped again. ''Jared, what are you doing?''

''Wait and see,'' he suggested, catching her bottom lip between his teeth and nipping gently.

Suzanna's blood began to race. He couldn't mean—not really! But he did.

And he showed her, lifting her to the stars and back again and again, until she was too sated to move and he fell asleep cradled against her breast.

''Mama?''

Suzanna awoke instinctively in response to Andy's call. Momentarily disoriented, at first she couldn't figure out why she couldn't move. Then she found Jared's arm around her waist, weighing her down, and felt his warm breath against her shoulder.

Oh, dear! What would Andy think when he found them in bed together?

''Mama? Where are you?''

''I'm in here,'' she called. Behind her, Jared awoke with a surprised grunt. Thank heavens she'd at least thought to put her nightdress on at some point last night. Jared, of course, was naked, but she snatched the sheet up over them both.

''Mama, why is my bed in the—*Jared!*'' Andy shrieked, throwing himself on the bed and scrambling over Suzanna to get to him.

''Hey partner, not so loud. You'll wake the neighbors." Jared caught the small body and allowed Andy to straddle his chest.

"Jared! Why're you here? Are you back to stay? Are you going to live with us again?"

Jared glanced at Suzanna who nodded. "Yes, I'm going to live with you and your mama."

Andy whooped his delight, and Pistol barked, trying to jump up on the bed to join the fun.

"Down," Suzanna commanded, pushing the dog away only to have him stick his wet nose in her face. "Pistol!" she cried, ducking to avoid the dog's tongue.

Jared and Andy laughed. The sound was like a symphony of joy to Suzanna's heart, and she laughed, too. Soon the three of them were tumbling together on the bed, wrestling and hugging, until Andy lay between them.

"You don't have to sleep with Mama," Andy informed Jared. "I said you could have my bed. Don't you remember?"

Jared bit back a smile and pretended not to notice Suzanna's blush. "Your mama doesn't want you sleeping on the floor anymore, so I said I'd sleep with her."

"This bed's awful crowded for two people," Andy pointed out.

Jared coughed, covering his mouth with both hands for a few seconds while Suzanna squirmed with embarrassment. "I don't mind," Jared managed at last. "Your mama is fun to snuggle."

Andy grinned. "I know. She's soft, and she smells good, too."

Jared grinned wickedly, but before he could say anything outrageous, Suzanna jumped up. "Let's get washed and dressed. I'm starving."

"Can I go to the barber shop with Jared?" Andy asked.

"Sure you can, partner," Jared said, but Suzanna shook her head.

"You'd better lay down the law now or you'll have

him tagging along with you every morning," she warned.

Jared considered Andy's stricken expression and smiled. "I like having him tag along. Now get your pants on, young man. You can't go traipsing across the plaza in your nightshirt.

"And you get your pants on, old man," Andy mimicked. "You can't go across the plaza buck-naked!"

"Andy!" Suzanna scolded, but Jared roared with laughter. She could see she'd have her hands full disciplining Andy with Jared around to spoil him. She and Jared would have to get a few things straight before their relationship went much further. The thought of once again having someone with whom to share such things warmed her, and while she helped Andy get dressed, he wanted to know why she was humming. She couldn't explain.

"All things considered," Dora remarked as she and Suzanna walked back from visiting Dodge City's poor and needy two mornings later, "I guess I can't complain about the army's way of extracting revenge if it got you and Jared together, although I probably had ten years taken off my life the other night,"

"I think my life was shortened a little, too. I can't remember ever being so scared. All I could think of was who would take care of Andy if anything happened to me." Suzanna shuddered at the memory.

"So tell me everything," Dora urged.

"There isn't much to tell. You already know Jared came for me when the soldiers fired on the theater. When we got back to my house, he finally confessed that he loved me and he didn't really want to leave me."

"Didn't he at least tell you *why* he left? Surely he made up some reasonable-sounding lie. Men are usually good at that, and I expect a man of Jared Cain's intelligence came up with something remarkable."

"He . . . he got into some trouble a long time ago,"

Suzanna improvised. She couldn't tell Dora the truth, of course, but she knew her friend wouldn't be satisfied until she'd heard enough to know Suzanna hadn't just been taken in by a clever bounder. "He had some silly idea he'd disgrace me."

"Are you serious?" Dora asked in amazement. "That's all it was?"

Suzanna nodded.

"Men! Sometimes I think they're all crazy. Obviously, you convinced him he was wrong."

"I just reminded him I was already disgraced, so anything he did couldn't possibly matter."

Dora frowned thoughtfully. "Are you really happy he's come back?"

"Oh, yes," Suzanna assured her. "It's only been two days, of course, but I can't remember ever being so happy, and Andy adores him. Jared spoils him terribly, but he's learning he can't give him everything he wants, even though he'd like to."

"And has Jared told you his life history yet? Was I right about him? Is he from Pennsylvania?"

"Maryland—a place called Rosewood where they raised horses. When he first told me about it, I thought it had been lost in the war, but apparently his mother still lives there, and he has a sister, too. I get the feeling Jared would love to go home, but he's afraid the trouble he got himself into will disgrace them, too."

"Good heavens. I'll never understand men and their ridiculous sense of honor. Doesn't he know his mother would probably sell her immortal soul just to set eyes on him again?"

"I tried to tell him the same thing, but he didn't want to talk about it."

"Have you thought about contacting her yourself?"

"What!" Suzanna thought she'd seen the limits of Dora's meddling in the way she'd insisted on helping her and Jared get back together, but Dora was obviously capable of being even more aggressive in helping her friends.

"You could write her a letter," Dora suggested. "Just tell her he's well and happy and put her poor mind at ease."

"I couldn't do a thing like that. Jared would be furious, and I wouldn't blame him one bit. Besides, how could I write a letter? I don't know where she lives."

"She lives in Rosewood, Maryland," Dora reminded her.

"Or what her name is. Jared changed his name to protect his family."

Dora snorted in disgust. "Address it to the lady of the house. Honestly, Suzanna, don't you have any imagination at all?"

"I have enough to imagine what Jared would do to me if I wrote to his mother behind his back," Suzanna replied dryly. "Not everyone can get away with meddling the way you do."

Dora opened her mouth to reply, then she caught sight of Mayor Kelley hurrying toward them, two greyhounds trotting loyally at his heels. The expression on his face warned them of trouble.

"What's wrong?" Dora asked when he reached them.

"That boy died this morning," he said. "George Hoyt, the one who shot Earp."

Suzanna murmured her dismay.

"Oh, dear," Dora said, even more distressed. She'd been visiting Hoyt almost daily. "He seemed a little better yesterday."

"He woke up and looked around. The doc said he thought he recognized him, and he even smiled a little, then he closed his eyes and died."

Tears came to Dora's eyes, and Suzanna squeezed her friend's arm comfortably. "At least his suffering is over," Suzanna pointed out. "He's been in agony for almost a month now, and since the heat made his wound fester—"

"I know," Dora said, dabbing at her eyes with a handkerchief. "It's just such a shame."

"The man was an assassin, Dora," Kelley reminded her. "He confessed he'd been hired to murder Earp in cold blood."

"Then he should have named the men who hired him so they could suffer, too."

"He probably thought he'd get better," Suzanna suggested, "and he didn't need to make any more enemies."

"You're probably right," Dora said, tucking her handkerchief back in her pocket and putting on a brave face. "What are the funeral arrangements, Jimmy?"

"You don't have to trouble yourself. The Texans took up a collection for him, and I think Reverend Wright will say a few words over him."

"Just so he doesn't have to be buried a pauper."

Jared and Andy called a greeting from the other side of the Plaza and hurried over to meet them, so Dora covered her grief with a smile, not wanting the child to see her crying.

"Jared wouldn't buy me any candy," Andy complained to the mayor when they reached the sidewalk.

"Would you like me to have Marshal Earp arrest him?" Kelley asked somberly.

"Don't arrest *me*," Jared protested. "His mother is the one who said no candy."

Kelley frowned. "Well, I can't ask Earp to arrest Suzanna. He's scared of women, you know."

"He is not!" Andy said with a laugh. "You're teasing."

"And you're too smart for your own good," Suzanna said. "You can't have candy now because you'll spoil your dinner."

"I like being spoiled," Andy insisted, having figured out from overheard conversations that the word meant all the finer things of life.

"Well, so long as I'm your mother, you aren't going to be," Suzanna replied.

"Is something wrong?" Jared asked, having noticed Dora's tense smile.

"George Hoyt died this morning," Kelley explained.

Jared frowned and shook his head. "Poor fellow. He took a while, didn't he?"

"Nearly a month," Kelley said.

Suzanna caught Jared's eye and knew he was also recalling the night Hoyt's gunfire had pierced the walls of the Comique and how she had sought comfort in Jared's arms.

"Who's George Hoyt?" Andy wanted to know.

"The man who tried to shoot Marshal Earp," Jared explained.

"Do you know when the funeral will be?" Suzanna asked.

"Probably tomorrow with this heat," Kelley guessed.

Suzanna turned to Dora. "Would you like me to go with you?"

Before Dora could answer, Kelley said, "I'll go with her."

Dora shook her head. "I don't think it would be a good idea for the mayor to be seen grieving for a man who tried to kill his marshal. Yes, Suzanna, I would dearly love your company. I don't expect many other people will come, but even Marshal Earp will understand if two softhearted women see a poor cowboy laid to rest."

After a few more minutes, Suzanna and Jared took Andy off to the Dodge House for their noon meal while Dora and Mayor Kelley strolled over to Ham Bell's livery stable. Bell doubled as the town mortician, and Dora was anxious to learn exactly what the funeral arrangements were.

"Suzanna seems happy," Kelley said in an attempt to distract Dora's thoughts.

"Yes, she does. She hasn't said anything about marriage, but I'm sure it's just a matter of time. Did you know Jared is from a wealthy family in Maryland?"

"I always figured he was quality. Do you suppose he'll take Suzanna back to the family mansion where she can live a life of luxury?'' Kelley asked with a sly grin.

"He certainly should," Dora replied without a hint of a smile. "I can't think of anyone who deserves it more, but it seems our Jared got himself into some kind of a scrape and doesn't think his family wants him to come home."

"Oh, a prodigal son, eh?" Kelley teased.

"Something like that, but can you imagine Jared doing anything truly evil?"

Kelley shook his head.

"I can't either, and I can't help thinking that if only someone would contact his family, everything would work out just fine."

"Dora, put that thought right out of your mind," Kelley said. "It's none of your business."

Dora smiled and patted his arm. "Of course it isn't," she said, but even then she was trying to remember what Suzanna had said the name of Jared's home was. Rosemont? No, Rosewood. Rosewood, Maryland. Dora wondered exactly where that was.

Chapter 9

"Suzanna?"

"Hmmm?" she answered sleepily. She and Jared had just made love in the feeble light of dawn and were curled up, spoon fashion, waiting for sleep, or at least Suzanna had been.

"What were you planning to do when the season ended?"

Suzanna's weary mind awoke instantly. In the ten days since Jared had come back to her, this was the first time either of them had dared broach the subject of the future. She eased over onto her back so she could see his face. 'I've been saving up so Andy and I could go home to Georgia. I thought I'd open a boarding-house or something."

"Oh," he said, troubled by the information, and he, too, rolled onto his back and threw an arm over his eyes.

"Jared?" She propped herself up on one elbow. "I'm not planning to go to Georgia anymore, not since . . . since you came back," she said, not quite certain how to refer to their relationship.

He lifted his arm and looked at her, his eyes as carefully guarded as if flesh and bone still covered them. "What *are* you planning to do?"

Suzanna hadn't really allowed herself to make actual plans, but she spoke the desire of her heart when she said, "Stay here with you."

"And what if I can't stay here? When the cattle drives stop coming, I'll be out of a job."

"Then I'll . . . *we'll* go wherever you go."

She stroked his chest, still damp from their loving, and silently willed him to turn to her again. Instead he sighed gustily. "Suzanna, I . . . Oh, hell." He bolted upright to a sitting position, clasping his bare knees and dropping his head to meet them.

Fear coiled in her stomach like a rattler ready to strike. "What is it, Jared?"

"I want to ask you something." He lifted his head to look at her. "But I don't have any right, not when I've refused to give you my name."

He moved as if to get up, but she grabbed his arm and held him there. "You can ask me anything, Jared, because I love you and I've given you the right."

When his dark eyes met hers again, they were wary but no longer guarded. She could clearly see his need, but she had no idea what he needed. Literally holding her breath, she waited for his request.

"Suzanna, I want you to quit your job at the Comique."

"*What?*" she asked, unable to believe he'd made such a fuss over something so minor.

Misinterpreting her relieved surprise, he hurried on. "I know I don't have any right to ask, and I know you're saving for Andy's future, whatever it might be, but I can't stand the thought of you in that place, night after night, dancing with strange men and—"

"Are you jealous?" she asked, delighted by the thought. He ran his fingers through his chestnut hair impatiently. "Of course I'm jealous. What man wouldn't be?"

Suzanna didn't mention the men she knew who actually pimped for their wives and mistresses. Instead she savored the feeling of being cherished by the man she loved. Leaning back on one elbow, she adjusted her nightdress around her legs and pretended to consider his request. "I don't know, Jared. What would I do with myself?"

"You could *sleep* for one thing," he snapped. "You're exhausted all the time."

"You work all night."

"Yes, but I don't have a child to take care of. Andy's too old for naps, which means you can't sleep in the daytime much anymore, and besides, I don't like the idea of you leaving him here alone every night."

Suzanna studied his earnest expression. "All right."

"What?"

"I said, all right. If you don't want me to work anymore, I won't."

He stared for a moment, not quite trusting her docility. "What about the money?"

"What about it?"

"You'll . . ." He hesitated, as if choosing his words carefully. "I don't want you to misunderstand what I'm going to say, so hear me out before you get angry. I can support us—"

"You already do," she reminded him.

"I can support us," he repeated doggedly, "on my winnings. I'll give you the money Dog pays me, a hundred dollars a week, to save for you and Andy."

"Jared!"

"I said not to get angry before you heard me out. I can't marry you because of my past and because I can't promise you a future. If anything happens, I want to know you and Andy will be provided for. There's money in a bank in St. Louis, too, almost ten thousand dollars—"

"Jared, don't!" she cried, throwing her arms around him. He clasped her to his chest and fell backwards against the pillows.

"We can't pretend we're going to live happily ever after," he said into her hair.

"Why not?" she demanded. Suzanna had no real reason to believe they couldn't. If no one had come after Jared in five years, surely no one cared about his

crime. She only needed a little more time to convince
Jared, then he'd feel free to marry her and everything
would be fine.

He pushed the hair off her ear and kissed it. "All
right, I'll let you pretend, but only after we get this
settled. I'll write out a will leaving everything to you
and Andy—"

"No!"

"—and then we'll never talk about it again."

Suzanna drew an unsteady breath. Anything to end
this conversation, she thought, and nodded against his
shoulder. His arms tightened around her for a second
or two, then gentled into a caress. "There now, try to
get some sleep before Andy wakes up," he whispered.

True to his word, Jared didn't mention the subject
again, although he came in a few days later with an
important-looking envelope which he told her to put
in her trunk for safekeeping.

Suzanna quit her job and joyfully took up the task
of making a home for Jared and Andy. Their days settled into a blissful routine. Each evening she and Andy
would see Jared off to his job at the Alhambra. She
kept Andy up later than most boys his age so he would
sleep longer in the morning and not disturb Jared.
Sometime near dawn, Jared would crawl into her bed
and awaken her with kisses. As if it were an extension
of a beautiful dream, they would make love and fall
asleep in each other's arms.

When Andy awakened later in the morning, he and
Suzanna would dress and leave the house to run their
errands until it was time to wake Jared for the noon
meal. The three of them spent their afternoons together in various ways, sometimes renting a buggy and
going for a ride, sometimes picnicking down by the
river, sometimes going someplace with Dora and the
mayor, but always together.

Suzanna had a desperate sense of foreboding which
she blamed on Jared's insistence on making his will,

but she doggedly ignored it, concentrating instead on making each day more idyllic than the last.

In September, the terrible heat eased somewhat, although the drought continued and billows of yellow dust still choked anyone attempting to cross the plaza on a windy day. The flow of cattle and cowboys into town had slowed to a trickle, and Suzanna could clearly see the end of the cattle season approaching. She and Jared carefully avoided any talk of what would happen when October came.

On the morning of September tenth, about three weeks after Jared had come to live with them, Andy and Suzanna walked down to Dog Kelley's house to see what plans Dora had made for visiting the sick children of the town.

"I'm so glad you're here," Dora said when she opened the door and invited them in. The place was identical in size and shape to Suzanna's house except Kelley had a bed in each room. Suzanna had discreetly refrained from inquiring who slept where. "Last night Jimmy was telling me there's a terrible epidemic of yellow fever in Memphis. People are dying by the hundreds."

"How terrible!"

"What's yellow fever?" Andy wanted to know. "And where's Memphis?"

"Yellow fever is an awful disease that makes people very sick," Suzanna explained, taking the boy into her lap as she sat down in one of Dora's straight-backed chairs. "But Memphis is a long way away, so we don't have to worry about getting sick here."

"Mrs. Hand is worried," Andy pointed out.

Dora bent and kissed his forehead. "Mrs. Hand worries about everyone's problems," she told the boy with a smile, "even if they're hundreds of miles away."

"Is there anything we can do?" Suzanna asked, frowning her concern.

"Well, I don't suppose it's practical to think about going to Memphis to help nurse the sick," Dora said wryly, "but Jimmy suggested we might take up a collection. He's over on the North Side now asking Reverend Wright and the other ministers if we can use the church to hold a meeting. You can help us spread the word."

Suzanna went home and woke Jared immediately. Within a few hours, over two hundred people had gathered at the Union Church. Jared, Suzanna and Andy had come early to get a seat, so they had a good view of the proceedings. Mayor Kelley called the meeting to order, thanked everyone for coming, and explained the situation in Memphis. Reverend Wright made an impassioned plea for those suffering from the dread disease, and several other ministers and a priest echoed his concerns. At last P. L. Beatty, Mayor Kelley's partner in the Alhambra, stood up.

"I've been a victim of this yellow fever, and I know how these people in the South suffer. Here's what talks!"

He held up a ten-dollar bill, and the crowd cheered. Someone grabbed a hat and began to pass it up and down the rows. Jared dropped a twenty-dollar gold piece into his bowler and began passing it down the row. Other hats appeared. Coins clinked and paper money rustled. The poor bootblack dropped in his nickel while diamond-studded gamblers and wealthy merchants put in large bills and gold coins.

"Three-hundred twenty-seven dollars and fifty-five cents," Mayor Kelley announced when the contents of the hats had been dumped and counted. "No one beats Dodge City when it comes to generosity!"

The crowd cheered and dispersed, the rougher element heading for the saloons along Front Street for some liquid celebration while the gentlefolk adjourned to congratulate themselves over tea and cookies.

Jared treated his party to cold sarsaparillas.

"You should have known the people of Dodge would be generous," Suzanna told a jubilant Dora.

"Yes, I guess if they'll give to bury a wax baby, they'll give for anything," she replied with a laugh.

"A wax baby?" Jared asked.

"Don't you know that story?" Suzanna asked in amusement. "Seems this family came to town carrying a dead baby—"

"Sorriest-looking bunch you ever saw, too," Kelley interjected. "Wagon falling apart, barefoot kids wearing flour sacks, mother in rags and holding this poor dead baby in her arms."

"Claimed they wanted to bury the child proper but didn't have the money," Suzanna added.

"So of course the softhearted folks in Dodge took up a collection for them," Dora explained with a sly grin. "Got enough to bury the baby and give them a start on their way."

"Next morning the grave had been dug up, the 'baby' was gone, and so was the family," Kelley concluded.

"The baby was a wax doll," Andy informed him, "not a real baby at all."

Jared groaned. "They must have played that trick on people all across the country."

"If everybody was as generous as the folks here, they're in California by now, too," Kelley said with an appreciative laugh.

"I'm surprised the people here are still willing to give money after being taken," Jared said.

"Oh, wicked folks like us are always willing to ease our consciences by throwing a few dollars into a hat," Dora said offhandedly, turning her attention to catching Andy's sarsaparilla bottle before he dropped it.

Jared frowned thoughtfully, and Suzanna noticed he didn't have much to say for the rest of the afternoon. When he left for work that evening, he kissed her absently, as if his mind were on something else entirely, and when he returned to their bed in the early hours of the morning, for the first time he did not reach for her.

Suzanna had awakened the moment he entered the house, but she continued to feign sleep, fear clutching her heart with icy fingers. Listening to Jared's breathing, sensing his wakefulness, she tried to imagine what could be bothering him. Had he tired of her already? Had another woman caught his eye? Had he decided the demands of a family were simply too restricting? Whatever it was, she didn't want to wonder any longer. "Jared?"

He started. "I thought you were asleep."

She wanted to ask why he hadn't wakened her, but instead she said, "Is something wrong?"

"No. Go back to sleep."

She winced at the lie and wondered what to do. If Jared were her husband, she would demand an explanation. Married people shouldn't have secrets. Andrew had refused to discuss his terrible feelings of failure. Instead of letting her help, he had sought solace in drink. Suzanna knew from experience it was far better for couples to share their problems.

But she and Jared weren't married, and she had no idea what her rights might be as his mistress. Did she dare confront him? And if she did, what would she do if he told her he was leaving?

"Jared, please tell me what's wrong."

He sighed, a sound she had learned to recognize as a warning. Her nerves instantly prickled in apprehension. "Something Dora said today got me to thinking. I've taken a long hard look at myself, and I don't like what I see."

"What did she say?"

"Something about wicked people salving their consciences by giving to charity. I suddenly realized she was right, that today I'd donated money to help people I'd never met because I felt guilty for what I've done to you."

"You haven't done anything to me," she protested.

"Haven't I? Here you are, a good Christian woman, living in sin. And what about your future? Before we met, I'd planned to spend the winter in St. Louis. I was glad when you said you'd go with me if I left here, but since then I've been doing a lot of thinking. Everyone here knows our situation, and, as you reminded me, you had no reputation to lose, but if we moved to a new place, things would be different."

"No, they wouldn't," she insisted.

"Oh, no? How would I introduce you in St. Louis? As Mrs. Prentice, the woman I live with? Or should I give you the appearance of respectability by pretending you're my wife? And if people *think* we're married, you'll be doubly disgraced if I'm arrested, first because you're my wife and again when people find out you're not."

Suzanna wanted to say that if they were married, there wouldn't be any problem, but so far she had never dared to broach the subject and this didn't seem like an opportune moment. She wanted to cling to him, to tell him none of this mattered, but pride forbade her. Instead, with pain twisting her heart, she said, "You could go to St. Louis without me."

He flinched as if she'd struck him. "No!" he cried, reaching for her as she'd prayed he would. "Oh, God, Suzanna, I could never leave you!"

Tears of relief flooded her eyes, and she hid them against his shoulder. They clung desperately for several minutes, his hands stroking over her back, his lips breathing kisses across her face. Slowly, his caresses became more insistent, and she felt his desire swelling against her leg.

Suzanna smiled against his mouth. "For a while there I thought you were too tired."

He rolled her over, pinning her to the bed with his body. "As long as I'm breathing, I'll never be too tired," he promised, lifting her nightdress and peeling it over her head. When she was naked, he adored her with his hands, touching all the sensitive spots he had discovered in the past few weeks until she writhed in mindless frenzy.

"Jared, Jared, Jared," she said, repeating his name like a litany.

"You're so beautiful," he whispered, "and I love you so much."

She loved him, too, more than she'd ever thought it possible to love anyone, and she wanted him close, as close to her heart as her own flesh. Urging him with hands and lips, she drew him in, welcoming him into the haven of her body with a sigh of ecstasy.

He groaned his response, easing out and in again with infinite care that drove her wild with wanting. "Jared, don't tease," she pleaded, but he smiled mysteriously.

"Teasing can be fun. I'll show you."

And he did, lifting her to the brink but denying her release, calming her, holding her, until her quivering ceased and the fiery need flickered down into a molten ache once more. Then he fanned the flames to life again, over and over, until Suzanna thought she might go mad.

In the last second of sanity, however, she recalled her own power, and as he brought her body trembling and burning to the brink yet again, she wrapped her legs around him and pulled her mouth to his. He resisted, but only for a heartbeat before his control shattered, releasing the full force of his desire.

His breath rasped as he drove into her. She lifted her hips to take him more fully, wanting all of him, wanting to join their bodies completely. The flames rose high and higher, and they strove together in the heat, bodies slick and panting, wanting, needing, loving.

The flames roared higher still until Suzanna saw the red glow throbbing before her eyes. In the last second she called his name, and then the flames engulfed them, melding them into one.

During the next week, Suzanna often thought it was a pity that making love couldn't solve all problems. If it could, she and Jared wouldn't have had a care in the world. Sometimes she even resented her own son for demanding her attention when she would much rather have been off somewhere alone with Jared. At other times, when she lay alone in the dark after putting Andy to bed, she would wonder what the future held for them. Unfortunately, she simply couldn't imagine anything at all.

About a week after the yellow fever meeting, just as Jared, Suzanna, and Andy were coming out of the Western's dining room, the fire bell began to clang.

The prospect of a fire in the flimsy wooden town was enough to send the entire population of Dodge pouring into the street. Jared lifted Andy to his shoulders to keep him from getting lost in the growing crowd.

"I don't see no smoke," Andy reported from his vantage point.

"It ain't a fire," a stranger nearby told them. "It's Injuns."

"Indians?" Suzanna repeated in alarm as Andy whooped his approval.

"Yes, ma'am. I heared they escaped from the reservation, but that's about all I know. Reckon they'll tell us at the meeting."

"What meeting?" Jared asked.

"The meeting at the fire hall. That's why the bell's ringing. Better hurry if you want to hear what's going on."

To hurry was out of the question, however, as the plaza quickly filled with people who had all heard the same rumor.

The fire bell continued to clang, grating on Suzanna's nerves. She spotted Maisie in the crowd and waved. The girl pushed and shoved her way over to them. "Have you heard? They killed a whole family just south of here, even scalped the baby in its mother's arms!" she reported before Suzanna could warn her not to frighten Andy.

"A baby!" Andy shouted in outrage. "We'll kill all them red devils, won't we, Jared?"

"Hush," Suzanna snapped, swatting him on the leg. "What Indians are they? How many are there? Where are they going?"

But no one knew the answers to her questions, so she allowed Jared to take her elbow and maneuver her through the crowd until they got within earshot of the fire hall where Dog Kelley stood on a makeshift platform of wooden egg crates trying to get everyone's attention.

After what seemed like hours of mind-numbing clanging, the fire bell ceased abruptly, although Suzanna could still hear it echoing in her head long afterwards. Several men in the crowd shouted questions, but Kelley motioned them to silence.

"We don't know much, but I'll tell you what we do know. Chief Dull Knife, who a lot of you will remember, has taken a couple hundred of his Cheyenne and jumped the reservation. They're headed back to their old hunting grounds up north, and seems like they intend to kill every white person who gets in their way. Dodge is right in their path."

A woman screamed, and several others wailed. Suzanna covered her mouth. Indians! The spectre of their savage killing had haunted her every day she had lived on the prairie, even though by the time she and Andrew had arrived, all the local Indians had been safely ensconced on reservations.

She looked at her son and agonized over every moment during the last weeks when she'd wished Andy away so she could be alone with Jared. She reached up and clutched the boy's bare leg where it rested on Jared's chest.

"Ouch, Mama, you're pinching," he complained.

"Sorry, darling," she murmured, wishing she could reach his precious face to kiss it.

"Will they attack the town?" someone wanted to know.

"I doubt it," Kelley replied, "but we ought to be ready anyway. I've talked to all the merchants, and they're willing to issue the guns they have in stock to any man who needs one. They'll issue ammunition, too. I've sent word to Fort Dodge for some troops, and I wired the governor to send us more men and two hundred stand of arms."

"I've got twenty drovers outside of town, holding my herd," a well-dressed rancher called from the crowd.

"Better get them in. We're sending riders out to warn farmers and ranchers, too. The trains will pick up anybody they see along the way and bring them to town, free of charge."

More questions were shouted and answered until at last Mayor Kelley instructed everyone to return home. Whenever he got fresh news, he would summon them back with the fire bell.

After the crowd had thinned somewhat, Jared and Suzanna made their way over to where Kelley stood surrounded by members of the city council. Suzanna noticed Kelley's face was gray, and she wondered if he knew more than he was telling.

"Anything I can do?" Jared asked.

Kelley looked up distractedly and grinned when he saw the boy riding on Jared's shoulders. "Seems like you've got your hands full already."

Jared did not return his smile. "I can ride out to warn some of the settlers."

"Jared, no!" Suzanna cried, grabbing his arm as if to physically prevent him from going.

His eyes were mild when he looked down at her hand. "If you were still living out there, wouldn't you be grateful to have someone warn you?"

She couldn't argue with his reasoning, but why did Jared have to go?

Fortunately, Mayor Kelley was as reluctant to send him as Suzanna was. "I've already sent out a dozen crazy cowboys, but we could use your help in town.

Get yourself over to Zimmerman's hardware. Tell him I sent you to make sure the distribution of guns is done in an orderly fashion."

"Won't Wyatt object?"

"He'll be glad for the help. He and his deputies can't be everyplace at once. And Suzanna, Dora said to tell you to get over to the church. They're collecting blankets and food for the folks who'll be coming in."

"*Look, smoke!*" someone shouted from the roof of the firehouse.

Everyone in town turned to see the dark cloud billowing up in the distance.

"Ain't that the Berry place?" a man nearby wanted to know.

"Yeah, they was one of the first to make it to town this morning. Injuns must've found the place empty and set it afire!"

The bell began to clang furiously as Kelley barked orders. "There's a locomotive at the station. We'll take as many men as it'll carry." He started calling names, and Suzanna cringed when she heard Jared's.

She turned to him to protest, but he was already lifting Andy off his shoulders. "I'll have to go to Zimmerman's to get a Winchester," he said. "You stay with Dora. You'll be safe at the church and I'll know where to find you. If I don't get back tonight, don't stay at the house alone. It's too close to the river."

"Jared, you don't have to go!" she cried, taking a struggling Andy, who was loudly proclaiming his desire to go and kill 'Injuns' too.

"Yes, I do, Suzanna." He pointed at the billowing smoke. "That might have been your home. I have to go." He bent and kissed her, and then he was gone, disappearing into the surging crowd.

Andy began to wail, and Suzanna comforted him absently, her heart in her throat as she pictured Jared maimed or killed by the rampaging savages.

The rest of the day passed in a blur. Suzanna went to the church, where she found Dora and several other women already at work sorting the donations the townspeople and merchants had sent over. One of the women took Andy outside with some other children, leaving Suzanna free to concentrate on the tasks assigned her. But while her hands worked, her mind was four miles away at the home of Harrison Berry where Jared had gone to fight Indians.

At intervals during the long afternoon, the fire bell clanged, summoning everyone to more meetings at which Mayor Kelley or one of the councilmen would read the latest telegram from the governor promising help or give the latest report from the refugees swarming into town. If one could believe these terrified creatures, the Indians were as close as two miles away, the dead and scalped bodies of their victims littering the prairie.

Dora kept telling Suzanna and the other women that such stories were almost surely exaggerations, but later reports named actual individuals. Southwest of Dodge, at Henry Kollar's camp, a herder named Warren had been killed, and near Sun City, two more men were reported slain. Whole families had been wiped out, their homes burned, their bodies mutilated.

By the time Mayor Kelley stopped by the church near suppertime, Suzanna was thoroughly terrified, and the sight of his haggard face frightened her even more. Dora rushed to him the instant he stepped into the door, and Suzanna was close behind her.

"Jimmy, you're ill. You should be in bed!" Suzanna heard Dora exclaim, making her realize for the first time that Kelley's sickly appearance might be caused by something other than the Indian attack.

"Somebody's got to be in charge, and I'm the mayor," he protested.

"You won't be the mayor if you drop dead," Dora scolded.

"People don't die from dyspepsia," he replied, gingerly rubbing his stomach. Then he noticed Suzanna behind her. "Suzanna, I'll be calling a meeting in a few minutes, but I knew you were worried, so I came to let you know. There wasn't any Indians at all at the Berry place. A rider just brought me the news and everybody else will be back in a little while, safe and sound."

Relief flooded thorugh her, and she resisted an urge to throw her arms around Kelley. "What caused the smoke, then?" she asked.

"The house was on fire when they got there, but if it was Dull Knife's bunch, they must've gotten scared off because they didn't loot the place and the stock was still there. Our men managed to save the outbuildings and the animals."

"Did they see any sign of the Indians?" Dora asked.

"No, but everybody else I've talked to has or at least so they claim," he said in disgust. "If every story I've heard today is true, the people in this town are the only ones in Kansas left alive."

Jared arrived home with the others about an hour later, tired and dirty and smelling of smoke both from the fire they had fought and their trip back clinging to the sides of the locomotive. He and Suzanna had time for only a brief reunion before Kelley put him to work again.

As nightfall approached, sleeping arrangements had to be made for the hundreds of people who had sought refuge in Dodge. Women and children, Suzanna and Andy among them, slept in the church. Others filled the livery stable and fire hall and lined the floors of the saloons and dance halls, while guards restlessly roamed the rooftops watching for approaching redskins.

The following day was more of the same. The fire bell clanged almost constantly. Groups of men ran to and fro followed by barking dogs. Fortunately, Suzanna had taken Pistol to Mayor Kelley's kennel where he had locked up his animals for safekeeping, so she only had to worry about keeping track of Andy. And Jared.

She caught glimpses of him as he carried out Mayor

Kelley's orders and helped to man the guard posts. Near nightfall he finally sought her out to bid her good night and make sure she was taken care of, but after a single kiss he was gone again.

The next morning, a train arrived carrying half the guns Mayor Kelley had requested and Adjutant General Noble from Fort Leavenworth. Dodge City's Silver Coronet Band turned out to greet him and his troops, as did most of the enlarged population of the town. Noble made a brief speech on how they would soon have the Indians under control again.

Only after the troops arrived did Mayor Kelley confess to Dora and Suzanna how truly worried he had been. When news of the Indian raid had reached them, Fort Dodge had only nineteen soldiers in residence to protect the entire area.

"I couldn't tell the people that, though."

"Of course not," Suzanna said, thinking what panic the news would have caused.

"No wonder you look so awful, carrying that secret around," Dora soothed. "I hope you'll go home and get some rest now."

"I think we all should," the mayor said. "Suzanna, why don't you go find Jared. You've certainly earned an afternoon nap." His suggestive grin brought the heat to Suzanna's face, but embarrassment didn't stop her from hurrying to do as he had suggested.

First, of course, she had to find her son. Andy was still being kept with the other children, and he was having too much fun to be dragged away, so she left him there and went to find Jared. He did not hesitate a moment when she told him what the mayor had said. Taking her hand, he hurried her across the plaza and down the alley and into the blessed silence of their tiny home.

They were in each other's arms even before they'd closed the door completely. The terrors of the past few days still lingered in their minds, reminding them of the fragility of life and the uncertainty of the future.

Desperation drove their passion as they tore away their clothes and fell onto the bed and joined their bodies in a feverish frenzy. Their loving was an explosion, bright and glorious, shaking the foundations of their souls, but over much too quickly.

Afterwards they lay entwined for long minutes as they sobbed for breath and savored the glorious privilege of being together.

"Oh, Jared, I've been so frightened."

"You needn't be. Even three hundred Indians wouldn't be bold enough to attack a town this size, and I don't think Dull Knife has that many warriors."

"I wasn't afraid for me and Andy. I was worried about you."

He smiled tolerantly. "I'm just as safe here as you are."

"Yes, but I knew you wouldn't *stay* here if the Indians came. When Mayor Kelley needed men to go to the Berry's farm, you were one of the first ones to go."

"Because I knew there wasn't any real danger," he told her with a smile.

"Liar." She kissed his nose.

"Did you hear the Berrys decided the fire was probably caused because they forgot to put out the fire in the stove before they left?"

"Yes, but nobody knew that two days ago. They thought a thousand Indians were swarming over the countryside, and you rode right out there."

"We had to protect the town. I had to protect you and Andy if I could."

She touched his face, tracing the line of his stubbled cheek with loving fingers. "I know, but that doesn't mean I have to like it."

"The danger isn't over yet, either," he warned with a frown.

"No, but the army is here now, and more soldiers are on the way. If there's a battle, you can stay here and guard the town."

He kissed her fingers as they drifted across his lips. "Yes, ma'am." He grinned, drawing her close.

He held her for several minutes in blissful silence. At last she sighed. "I'm sorry to nag you, but the whole time you were gone, I kept thinking we'd only had a month together. Just one short month, and there were so many things I wanted to tell you and share with you."

"Like what?"

"Like how much I love you, for one thing."

"Oh, I have a pretty good idea how much you love me. It's about half as much as I love you."

"*Half!*" she cried in feigned outrage.

"Yes, half. Maybe even one-fourth. You couldn't love me as much as I love you because you're too little."

"Little? What does size have to do with it?"

"There isn't enough room in this beautiful little body to hold all the love I have for you," he explained, his dark eyes glittering as his hand boldly measured the expanse of certain sensitive parts of her anatomy.

"Jared, you're crazy," she protested, trying unsuccessfully to capture his hands.

"Probably," he agreed cheerfully, at last allowing her to subdue him. She pinned his hands to the mattress. "I thought Dog suggested we take a nap. I'm never going to get any sleep if you don't leave me alone."

Suzanna sighed in disgust and allowed him to settle her against his shoulder, but in spite of her exhaustion, sleep eluded her. Having Jared so near after being separated for two terror-filled days was too stimulating, and her mind raced, considering subjects she usually didn't allow herself to think about. The future, her future and Jared's, their future together, and how she could guarantee they would have one.

Of course she could do nothing about Jared being wanted, but she couldn't forget Dora's suggestion that she contact Jared's mother. The idea had haunted her for weeks, and although she knew she could never go behind Jared's back the way Dora would undoubtedly have done in her place, perhaps she could encourage him to make the contact himself.

"Jared?"

"Hmmm?"

"Do you ever hear from your family?"

Even without seeing his face, she could sense his instant wariness. "How could I? They have no idea where I am."

"I was just thinking how frightened I was when you were only gone a few hours. Your poor mother hasn't seen you in years."

She waited, but he didn't respond. His breathing told her he was upset, but she couldn't resist just one more try. "Have you thought of writing to her? Just to let her know you're all right?"

The silence stretched on so long, Suzanna became alarmed. Slowly, she lifted her head and looked into his face, terrified she would see the anger he had every right to feel. Instead she saw the bleak despair she had thought her love had banished forever.

"Jared, I'm sorry!" she cried, not even knowing how she had hurt him.

His lips were white and his voice strained. "Suzanna, I think it would be better if we never spoke of my family again."

She opened her mouth to protest, but how could she refuse when she saw the pain it caused him? "All right," she murmured, wishing she dared defy him. The subject of his family was like a festering wound that would never heal unless exposed to the light of day, but she had no right to expose it. In fact, where Jared was concerned, she really had no rights at all.

He smiled slightly at her capitulation, a wan, sad smile that tore at her heart. Impulsively, she kissed him.

"Don't start that," he said in a hollow echo of his previous humor, "or we'll never get any sleep." He pushed her head back to his shoulder and touched his lips to her hair.

"I love you, Jared," she whispered.

"I love you, too."

For now, she knew, it would have to be enough.

As the days passed, so did the threat of Indian attack. People who had been reported massacred appeared in town unscathed. Investigation proved that a cowboy who had supposedly been killed by Indians had really been murdered by another cowboy. The army chased—or perhaps just followed—the maurading renegades into Nebraska. Settlers returned to their homes, and life in Dodge City settled back into a normal routine.

Except that Dog Kelley didn't get any better.

"Doc McCarty thinks it's his appendix," Dora told Suzanna privately one afternoon while Jared and Andy paid him a visit. The mayor had spent an unpleasant night and been unable to rise at all that morning. "He's running a fever, and he's in terrible pain." The two women were standing outside of Kelley's house.

"Can't they do anything?" Suzanna asked.

"They want him to go to the hospital at Fort Dodge for an operation, but he won't hear of it. I tried to explain how they'll put him to sleep with ether so he won't feel a thing, but you know how unreasonable men are. He's hoping he'll feel better in a day or two."

"Well, if you need any help getting him to the fort against his will, let us know," Suzanna offered with a grin.

"I'm afraid it may come to that," Dora said as Jared and Andy stepped out of the house.

"Mr. Kelley's real sick," Andy reported solemnly. "He can hardly talk."

Dora nodded. "When an Irishman can't talk, you know it's serious," she said in an attempt at lightness, but no one smiled at her joke.

"Dog asked me to look after you," Jared told Dora.

"I'll walk you to and from work and make sure you get from the Alhambra to the Comique all right."

Dora snorted in disgust. "When is he going to admit how sick he is? Couldn't you talk to him, Jared?"

"I told him they used ether on me, and I couldn't remember a thing, but he doesn't want to have surgery until he's sure he's not going to get better."

"I just hope he doesn't wait too long," Dora muttered, and Suzanna slipped an arm around her waist and gave her a hug.

"If he gets too bad, just holler. We'll help you get him to Fort Dodge, day or night."

Dora nodded despondently.

By the end of September, the cattle drives had almost ceased, but there were still enough cowboys and cattlemen lingering in Dodge to keep the saloons and dance halls operating for a few extra days of revelry. Eddie Foy and his partner had moved on to Leadville, but Dora and Fanny Garrettson continued to sing every night at the Alhambra and the Comique.

The mayor remained bedridden with his stomach ailment. Dora confided to Suzanna that she wanted to stay home with him, but he wouldn't allow it.

"Stubborn as an Irish mule," she said quite frequently.

Jared continued to escort her around town in the wee hours in Kelley's stead, and Suzanna suspected people were gossiping, but she didn't care. Gossip couldn't hurt any of them.

The first day of October dawned bright and golden. Suzanna was straightening up the house while she waited for Andy and Jared to return from the barber shop when someone knocked on her door. Thinking Dora might need help, she hurried to answer it and was surprised to see a strange man standing on her doorstep.

"Mrs. Prentice?" he asked.

Suzanna nodded, looking him over curiously. He

was a handsome fellow, tall and well-dressed, wearing a tailored suit and holding the bowler hat he had whipped off the instant she opened the door. His dark brown hair was carefully pomaded, and his brown eyes held pleased surprise as he eyed her calico-clad figure.

"Perhaps you can help me. I'm looking for my cousin, Jared Wentworth."

Jared *Wentworth?* Suzanna thought in confusion, then remembered Jared had told her he'd changed his name. Could this man really be his cousin? She looked at him more closely. Yes, of course, she could see a faint resemblance. Nothing striking, but they had the same mouth, the same smile. This man was Jared's *cousin!*

"Yes, I believe I can help you, Mister . . . ?"

"Covington. Booth Covington. Pleased to meet you." He nodded politely, his smile still slightly amazed.

"Won't you come in?" she asked, stepping aside so he could enter the tiny parlor.

He gave the room the same surprised scrutiny he had given her. She assumed he must have expected to find a different type of woman and a far different type of dwelling on this side of Dodge City.

"Please, sit down," she urged. "May I take your hat?"

He handed her his bowler which she hung on a peg by the door. He waited until she sat before seating himself across from her at the small table.

"I . . ."

"You . . ."

They both spoke at once and stopped, laughing self-consciously. "Ladies first," he said, his eyes twinkling the same way Jared's did.

"How on earth did you find me?" she asked, voicing the most pressing question.

"I . . . or rather my aunt received a letter from a friend of yours, a Miss Fanny Keenan."

Suzanna frowned. She knew no one by that name. The only Fanny she knew was Fanny Garrettson, Dora's friend. . . . Then she remembered. Dora's real name wasn't Dora at all. She'd taken it as a stage name when she'd married Theodore Hand. Her real name was Fanny Keenan.

"She wrote a letter? About Jared?" Suzanna asked incredulously. Oh, dear, how would she ever explain this to Jared?

"Yes, she told my aunt, Jared's mother, that he was well and living in Dodge City. She suggested we might be able to contact him through a Mrs. Andrew Prentice."

"So you came here? All this way?" she asked in dismay.

He smiled tolerantly. "Jared is my cousin, and I'm very fond of my aunt. She hadn't heard from her son in over five years, so naturally she was most anxious to know if this Miss Keenan was telling the truth."

"Your aunt could have written a letter."

"She already had a letter, Mrs. Prentice. She wanted firsthand information on whether or not her son was alive."

Suzanna placed a hand over her racing heart. Good heavens, what should she do? Jared didn't even want to discuss his family, much less meet one of them face to face. But surely once he knew how eager they were to contact him, he would change his mind. Imagine coming all the way from Maryland on the strength of a letter from a total stranger! How could Jared doubt their concern?

Of course she'd have to tell him about Dora's letter first and give him the choice of whether or not to see his cousin. She would explain to Booth Covington that she did know how to get in touch with Jared and would see if she could arrange a meeting between them. Unfortunately, before she could even open her mouth, she heard the familiar sound of Andy's laughter in the alley beside the house.

Jumping up in alarm, she almost knocked over her chair. Covington jumped up, too. "Is something wrong?'' he asked, following her stricken gaze to the front door where first Pistol, then Andy, and then Jared appeared.

The instant Pistol sensed Covington's presence, he began to bark a staccato warning, straining toward the intruder. Andy took a two-handed grip on the dog's rope and dug in his heels. ''Whoa, boy!''

''It's all right, Pistol,'' Suzanna said sharply, silencing him. She winced as she saw Jared's hand go instinctively inside his coat where his gun was concealed. He squinted, trying to make out the stranger in the dim interior light.

''Who are you?'' he demanded.

Covington blinked and stared. ''Jared?''

Jared took another step inside, pushing past Andy who still struggled with the dog. The two men were no more than four feet apart, and Suzanna watched in horror as Jared's expression changed from wariness to stunned recognition to anger.

''Booth?'' he said, as if hoping to be wrong.

''Jared, you're alive!''

Jared stiffened. ''How did you find me?'' he demanded.

''Your mother got a letter telling us where you were, so naturally I came . . .'' His voice trailed off in the face of Jared's growing rage.

''A letter?'' he asked, turning his gaze to Suzanna.

His dark eyes blazed with a fury she'd never seen before, and for the first time, Suzanna felt actual fear. ''Jared, let me explain.''

''Uh, perhaps I've come at an inconvenient time,'' Covington said hastily, sidling around Jared, stepping quickly past Pistol, who had begun to snarl, and reaching for his hat. ''I'm staying at the Dodge House,'' he added, slipping out the door.

''Who was that man, Mama?'' Andy asked, but no one paid him any mind. Suzanna couldn't tear her gaze from Jared's icy stare.

"You wrote to them?" Jared accused her. "You told them where I was?"

His deadly calm sent shivers up her spine, and she had to fight to keep from cringing before him. This is Jared, she reminded herself. Jared would never hurt you. "No, I didn't write. It was Dora."

"*Dora?* But how . . . ?" As the truth dawned, his expression became terrible to behold. "You *told* her! You told her all about me, didn't you?"

"No! I hardly told her anything at all! Jared, please listen to me! I only told her you'd gotten in some trouble and were afraid you'd disgrace your family, so you'd left home. I didn't tell her what it was, I swear!"

"You must have told her more than that if she was able to contact my family," he insisted.

"She'd already guessed you were from Maryland from your accent," Suzanna explained frantically. "And I told her your family had a place called Rosewood there. She said I should write and tell them where you are, but of course I wouldn't dream of—"

"That meddling bitch!" he shouted. "Do you know why he came here?"

"Yes," she hastily assured him, trying to remain calm. "Your mother wanted to know for sure that you were alive and . . ."

But Jared was shaking his head, his eyes brimming with emotions she didn't dare name. "No, Suzanna," he said coldly, "he's come to see me hang. You see, I didn't kill a stranger in a saloon someplace. The man I killed was my own father."

Chapter 10

$\sim\!\!\infty\!\!\sim$

Suzanna stared at him in mute horror. As if from far away she heard Andy demanding to know what was wrong, but she was too numb to respond. All she could see was Jared's tortured face. All she could hear were his words echoing in her mind.

He stood before her for what seemed an eternity, then he turned on his heel and stormed out of the house.

"Jared!" Andy called, his small face puckering, but Jared was gone. "Mama?" he tried, turning to her.

She opened her arms, and he ran to her. Sinking down into her chair, she took him in her lap, holding him close, needing comfort as much as he. "Why was Jared so mad, and who was that man?"

Drawing an unsteady breath, she managed a reassuring smile. "The man was Jared's cousin."

"Jared doesn't like him much."

"I'm sure he likes him fine. He was just surprised to see him."

Andy shook his blond head solemnly. "No, he was mad. I can tell. He was mad at you, too."

Tears stung her eyes, and she blinked hard. "He was upset. He thought I played a trick on him."

"Did you?"

"No, not . . . not exactly." Somehow she managed to calm Andy down and give him an explanation he would accept, but there was one part of the story she couldn't explain.

"Why did Jared say he killed his father?" Andy asked.

"I don't know," was all she could think of to say.

"Where did Jared go?"

Suzanna was wondering the same thing. "I'm sure he just went for a walk. When people get angry, they sometimes like to be alone to calm down," she said, wondering if Jared *should* be alone right now with his terrible secret and wishing she had stopped him from leaving.

Suzanna waited nervously for his return, but when he had not come back in an hour, she had no choice except to take Andy to the Western for a meal. Fear had knotted her stomach so she was unable to eat anything herself, and as soon as Andy finished, they went for a brisk walk around town past all of Jared's familiar haunts while Suzanna tried unsuccessfully to find him.

At last they came to Ham Bell's livery where Jared kept his horse. The stable boy told them he'd ridden out a few hours earlier and hadn't come back.

"Where did he go?" Andy wanted to know as they walked back to their house.

"I guess Jared thought a ride would calm him down better than a walk," she said, trying to convince herself that was Jared's only motivation for taking his horse and leaving town. He must be coming right back. He hadn't taken a stitch of clothing with him, and he certainly wouldn't simply leave her and Andy without a word.

Except that he thought she'd betrayed him.

By suppertime, Suzanna was frantic. She had to speak to someone about it, and Dora Hand was the most logical person. Unfortunately, Dora was equally frantic for an entirely different reason. When Suzanna and Andy knocked on her door, Dora stepped outside instead of inviting them in and closed the door behind her so Kelley couldn't overhear their conversation.

"Andy, why don't you and Pistol go back to the kennel and make sure the dogs have enough water?" Dora suggested, and waited until the boy was out of earshot. "Jimmy's fever is worse, and he's in constant pain. I'm afraid to leave him alone, so would you tell Jared I won't be going to work tonight?"

"Jared isn't here."

Dora frowned in confusion. "Where is he?"

"I don't know," Suzanna said, fighting to keep her voice steady. She could see Dora didn't have the energy to deal with hysterics right now. "We had an argument, and he left."

"What on earth did you argue about?"

"His family. Dora, you wrote a letter to his mother, didn't you?"

"Oh!" Dora cried, covering her mouth with her hand. "I'd forgotten all about it. Oh, dear, I can see by the look on your face that my little plan didn't work out very well. Did she write back and say she never wanted to see him again?"

"Much worse. Jared's cousin showed up at my house this morning, a man named Booth Covington. Dora, Jared is wanted by the law, and he thinks his cousin came to have him arrested."

"Oh, God!" Dora exclaimed. "Suzanna, I'm sorry! I had no idea."

Suzanna sighed. "I know. It's partly my fault for not telling you the whole story, but—"

"—but the whole thing was none of my business in the first place." She groaned in despair, covering her face with her hands. When she lowered them a moment later, she looked a decade older. "When will I ever learn to stop meddling in other people's lives?"

Instinctively, Suzanna reached out to comfort her. "Don't be too hard on yourself. If it wasn't for your 'meddling,' Jared and I never would've gotten back together."

"And I couldn't be satisfied with that," Dora berated herself. "If only I'd left well enough alone, but when you said Jared had gotten into trouble, I never thought it could be serious. Even Jimmy couldn't believe he was actually wanted. What on earth did he do?''

Suzanna couldn't tell her everything, at least not until she'd gotten the whole story from Jared, but she said, "He killed a man."

Dora's cry of anguish broke Suzanna's tenuous self-control. Tears flooded her eyes, and the two women threw their arms around each other, clinging for the meager comfort they could obtain from the physical closeness. They only had a moment before Andy and Pistol came racing back from their visit to the kennels behind Dog Kelley's house.

"I gave the dogs more water. They was out, just like you thought," he reported.

"I'll be sure to tell Mr. Kelley what you did," Dora said, wiping her eyes with her sleeve. "He'll be very grateful."

"Why're you crying?" Andy asked, looking from one woman to the other.

"Because Mayor Kelley is very sick," Suzanna hastened to explain. She turned back to Dora. "Is he going to Fort Dodge?"

"He's still refusing to, but if he's not any better by tomorrow, I'll take him if I have to hog-tie him to do it."

They stared at each other, momentarily overwhelmed by their personal crises. At last Suzanna said, "If you need anything, you know where to find me."

"Honey," she said, capturing Suzanna's hands, "I'm so sorry."

Suzanna managed a small smile. "Maybe it's all for the best," she said softly so Andy couldn't hear. "Jared wouldn't marry me because he was a wanted man. Maybe now we can get this thing cleared up once and for all."

Dora returned her smile, but it didn't quite reach her

eyes, and Suzanna could see she didn't believe her generous lie either. "I'll pray you're right."

"And I'll pray that Mayor Kelley gets well."

"I will, too!" Andy piped, making Dora smile for real.

"Maybe you should just pray that he'll allow the surgery."

Suzanna patted her arm sympathetically. "We're going for our supper now. We'll bring you back something," she promised.

Again Suzanna could hardly eat for worrying about Jared. She kept a watchful eye for sight of him in the plaza and in the hotel while at the same time also watching for his cousin. She knew she should do something, but she had no idea what action might be appropriate, particularly where Booth Covington was concerned. He'd seemed like a nice man, a perfect gentleman, and not at all like someone bent on exacting revenge for his family's honor.

Could Jared be wrong about his intentions? Could he have come simply to verify to Jared's mother that Jared was truly alive and well? There was really only one way to find out. When they had finished their supper, Suzanna asked Mrs. Galland for paper and pencil and wrote a note to Covington asking him to come to her house late that evening after she'd put Andy to bed.

Surely Jared would be back by then, and if not . . . Well, she wouldn't think about that now.

When Booth Covington came to her door at ten o'clock, Jared still hadn't returned. By then Suzanna had driven herself half-crazy with visions of renegade Indians from Dull Knife's band capturing Jared—even though the Indians were hundreds of miles away by now—or of Jared lying on the prairie somewhere with a broken leg and no one to help.

If only Mayor Kelley weren't sick, she'd ask him to send someone out looking for him. The only other people she knew to ask were Sheriff Masterson or Marshal Earp and neither seemed the appropriate person to consult if Jared really was a wanted man.

"Don't bark," she commanded Pistol at the sound of Covington's knock, and opened the door to her visitor. This time he seemed wary, and when she invited him in, he hesitated, glancing cautiously around the room. His gaze rested on the curtained doorway to the bedroom.

"Jared isn't here," she assured him.

"Do you expect him?"

Suzanna winced inwardly, but said, "No."

He visibly relaxed and came inside, allowing her to shut the door behind him.

"Please sit down, Mr. Covington."

Again he waited until she was seated, a courtesy she had known only from Jared until now. She studied Covington's face, looking again for signs of resemblance. His eyes were brown, but much lighter than Jared's, and his dark hair lacked Jared's reddish highlights. Still, his steady gaze reminded her of the man she might have lost forever. She had to clear her throat before she could speak.

"Until today, Jared never told me the real reason he left home."

"Oh?" he said, wary again.

"He told me he'd gotten in some trouble, but I never dreamed . . ." She stopped, folded her hands carefully on the tabletop and examined them for a few seconds. "Anyway, Jared thinks you've come to have him arrested."

He reared back in shock. "*Arrested?*"

"You didn't, did you?" she asked, elated by his reaction.

"Of course not!"

"I knew it! I tried to tell Jared, but he wouldn't believe me."

"I only wanted to see for myself if it was really Jared,

and tell him his mother and his sister are well and send their love. They want to see him, of course."

"Of course," she said with a sad smile. "I'm sure he'd like to see them, too."

Covington's finely molded features grew solemn. "Do you think there's any chance . . . ?"

Suzanna shook her head. "Not under the circumstances, but . . ." She hesitated, thinking of her original plan to have Jared go back and clear his name. She certainly couldn't promise any such thing on Jared's behalf, and without knowing the circumstances of the crime, she couldn't even be certain he *would* be cleared. "No, I'm sure Jared won't be seeing them."

He nodded slowly, his expression unreadable, and another thought occurred to Suzanna. "You won't tell anyone where he is, will you?"

His smile came slowly, and to her surprise, his eyes glinted flirtatiously. "Not if you don't want me to."

"I . . . I don't," she replied, feeling a blush steal up her cheeks at his frank male appreciation. He really was quite attractive, and if she'd never known Jared . . . But she did know him and love him, and nothing would change that.

Covington's gaze drifted over her, then slid away to examine the room's sparse furnishings, touching on Jared's faro layout stacked neatly in one corner. "If you don't mind my asking, how do you know my cousin?"

"We met in a . . . a dance hall," she admitted reluctantly.

Covington's eyes widened slightly, but his expression remained calm. "What on earth were you doing in a dance hall?"

Suzanna lifted her chin defensively. "I worked there, as a hostess."

Obviously nonplussed, he considered this for a moment. "And Jared?"

"Is a gambler."

Covington's eyes closed briefly, as if he needed a bit

of darkness in which to absorb this information. When he opened them again, he'd regained his control, reminding her again of Jared. "I'd really like to speak with Jared before I leave. If you'll tell me where he lives, perhaps I can . . . Is something wrong?"

Suzanna knew her face must be scarlet. "I . . . We . . . Jared lives here, with us."

He was too much of a gentleman to say anything, but she could clearly see his shock. "Us?"

"My son Andy and me."

"Oh, the little boy I saw this morning."

Suzanna nodded. "I'm a widow," she explained before he drew any inaccurate conclusions about her.

He leaned back slightly in his chair as if to gain a new perspective on her. His brown eyes narrowed slightly. "You said you didn't expect him back tonight. Is he gambling someplace in town? I could—"

"No, he . . . he left here right after you did this morning, and I . . . I don't know where he is."

"What do you mean, he left?"

"I mean he got his horse and rode out of town, but I'm sure he'll be back soon. He was just angry. He thought I'd told people what he'd done and . . . Well, anyway, even when he comes back, I'm not sure he'll want to talk with you."

Covington smiled wryly. "He certainly gave me that impression this morning."

"I'm sorry. He was just surprised."

"But I shouldn't have been. I probably shouldn't have come either. After all, if Jared had wanted to get in touch with us, he certainly knows where we are, and we haven't had a single letter from him in five years."

Suzanna sighed. "It must be terribly difficult for his mother."

"It is, but she's managed quite well, all things considered." He stared at her thoughtfully for a long moment. "Well, if you think it's best, I'll leave, and you can certainly tell Jared I won't betray his whereabouts if that's what he wants."

"Oh, thank you, Mr. Covington." Impulsively, Suzanna leaned across the table and laid her hand on his arm. "I can't tell you how grateful I am, and I know Jared will be, too."

Covington glanced down at her fingers resting on his sleeve, then looked up into her face. His slow smile came again, crinkling the corners of his eyes and making him look disconcertingly like Jared. He shook his head with profound regret. "Now isn't that just my luck," he murmured.

"I beg your pardon?"

His eyes twinkled with the same expression that warned her when Jared was teasing her. "I finally meet the most beautiful woman in the world, and my cousin has beat me to her."

"Mr. Covington," she scolded, snatching her hand away, but he grinned Jared's unrepentant grin.

"Please call me Booth."

"I don't think—"

"How can you deny me when you've already broken my heart?"

"Mr. Covington!"

"Booth," he insisted

"Booth!"

"What?"

"This isn't funny."

His grin turned rueful. "Nothing much is in this vale of tears, is it? But I've learned that if I laugh at times of crisis, the crisis seems less tragic. May I call you by your given name?"

"I . . . I suppose."

His eyes glinted, so like Jared's her heart ached. "What is it?"

"Suzanna."

"How lovely." He leaned across the table, closing the distance between them to inches. His voice was like a caress. "A lovely name for a lovely lady."

Suzanna quickly drew back to a discreet distance. "I . . . thank you," she stammered, not quite certain how to take Booth Covington's flattery. Reason told her he was only being charming, trying to put her at ease. Unfortunately, his charm was having the opposite effect.

"Jared is a fortunate man."

Suzanna felt certain Jared didn't feel very fortunate at the moment, and neither did she. "Booth, you're embarrassing me."

"And she's modest, too. How did Jared find such a flower in this barren wilderness? But then Jared always was lucky."

"I'd hardly call it lucky to be wanted for killing your own father," she reminded him sharply, wondering how he could joke about such a thing."

"Wanted . . . ?" he began, but stopped abruptly, his brown eyes narrowing again. He straightened in his chair and crossed his arms over his chest. Suzanna shifted uncomfortably under his intense scrutiny, even though he didn't seem to be looking at her at all. "I'm sorry," he said after a few moments. "You're absolutely right. Can you ever forgive me?"

Suzanna reminded herself Booth had already agreed to protect Jared. "Of course."

"I suppose I'd better go," he said brusquely, rising from his chair. "It's late, and besides, Jared may return at any moment. I don't think he would be happy to find me here."

Suzanna hoped he was right about Jared returning. She rose, too. "Thank you for everything. I just wish . . ." She shrugged.

"Yes, I wish we could have met under more pleasant circumstances," he finished the thought for her. Before she could guess his intention, he took her hand, lifted it to his lips, and pressed a kiss to it.

Suzanna gasped her surprise, jerking her hand from his. He smiled again.

"Not the least bit interested in being unfaithful to Jared, are you?"

"Of course not!"

"As I said, Jared is a fortunate man. I'll be leaving on the noon train tomorrow, so I doubt we'll meet again, more's the pity. Please tell Jared I'm sorry to have alarmed him, and assure him his secret is safe with me. As far as I'm concerned, Jared Wentworth is dead, and I certainly never saw him in Dodge City."

His promise should have pleased her, but she couldn't forget the other people who would be hurt by the lie. "Is that what you'll tell his mother?"

His smile flickered for an instant, then came back full force. "Don't worry, I'll think of something kinder for Aunt Lavinia and Cousin Ellie. Good-bye, fair lady."

He sketched her a little bow and was gone, closing the door softly behind him. Suzanna stared at the door and absently rubbed the back of her hand where his lips had touched it. Booth Covington was a strange and disturbing man, but at least he had agreed to help. When Jared came back, she could put his mind at ease.

If he came back.

After a nearly sleepless night spent listening for sounds of Jared's return, Suzanna spent most of the morning nursing a sick headache. When she couldn't stand the four walls of her house and Andy's relentless questions about where Jared had gone, she decided she had better find something to do to distract her. There was at least one person in this town whose problems were as serious as hers.

Dora seemed relieved to see her and Andy when they came to her door. "I've asked Ham Bell to fix up a spring wagon for me," she explained. "I'm taking Jimmy over to the fort hospital, and they'll operate on him this afternoon."

"Would you like me to go with you?" Suzanna asked, even though she was loath to leave town in case Jared returned.

Fortunately, Dora shook her head. "You've got enough to think about right now. I've asked Fanny to go with me. Jimmy didn't like the idea of me being in the house alone with him gone, either, so she'll be staying with me, at least until he comes home."

Dora's pale face belied her calm manner, and Suzanna knew Dora wasn't quite as sanguine about the upcoming operation as she was trying to appear. "Andy and I will be praying everything goes well, and if there's anything we can do, just let us know."

A whistle blasted, heralding the approach of the noon train and making Suzanna jump. Booth Covington would be leaving Dodge City in a matter of minutes, and with him would go the last danger to Jared's freedom. If only Jared knew it.

"It's noon already," Dora exclaimed. "I told Ham I wanted that wagon right away. Where could he be?"

"Andy and I'll go down and see if we can't hurry things along," Suzanna offered, grateful for something to do. She'd also have a chance to see if Jared's horse had been returned to the livery.

Half a block past the Comique on the south side of Front Street, Hamilton Bell's livery stable was a cavernous building redolent of horses and leather. Bell himself was hitching up a spring wagon when Suzanna and Andy arrived.

" 'Morning, Miz Prentice. Andy boy, you'd better tie that dog up outside before he scares the horses." When he turned his gaze back to Suzanna, his eyes glittered with amusement. "Your boy's getting as famous as Mayor Kelley for having a dog with him all the time. What can I do for you?" he asked.

"Mrs. Hand is getting anxious, so I told her I'd check on your progress."

"As you can see, we're just about ready to go. What slowed me up was fixing a soft place in the back for the mayor." Bell gestured toward the wagon bed where he had spread a thick layer of straw and covered it with a tarp and some blankets.

"You did a good job. I know Mrs. Hand will be pleased. I'll tell her you're on your way."

"Mama, can I look at the horses?" Andy asked, tugging at her skirt.

"Just for a minute. We have to get back."

Andy charged off toward the inner recesses of the building, stopping precipitously at each stall to clamber up and peer over the half-door.

Suzanna folded her hands and watched Bell finish with the harnessing, and wondering if she dared ask the question uppermost in her mind. "Mr. Bell?"

He looked up.

"Has . . . has Jared Cain brought his horse back yet?"

"Not yet." He frowned in concern at her obvious disappointment. "When did you expect him?"

"I don't. I mean, he didn't really say when he'd be back, but after the Indian scare, I'm a little nervous about him being gone at all."

"I know what you mean, but I doubt you've got much to worry about where the Indians are concerned."

"You're probably right," she mumbled, wishing the Indians were her only worry. Twenty-four hours had passed since Jared walked out her door believing Booth Covington had come to charge him with murder, and she was beginning to believe Jared was running for his life. From the end of the plaza she heard the whistle again, signaling the departure of the noon train. She felt the lifting of a burden. Now Booth was gone and with him any danger to Jared.

But how would Jared ever know?

Suzanna closed her eyes and whispered a silent prayer that somehow Jared would come back to her. When she opened her eyes, there he was, riding slowly into Ham Bell's livery. Her heart leaped to her throat.

"Well, speak of the devil." Bell chuckled. "Cain, you've given your lady friend a real scare. She had you figured for buzzard bait."

Jared's head jerked in her direction, his eyes narrowing as he attempted to find her in the shadows of the stable. Was he still angry? Did he still blame her for Booth's visit? A wave of apprehension dampened her initial joy, and she swallowed hard, trying to find her voice. "Jared," was all she could say.

He swung down and hurried over to her, carefully skirting the restless team Bell was hitching. His black suit looked almost brown from the thick coating of yellow dust he'd picked up in his travels, and his cheeks were stubbled with a day's growth of beard, but—thank heaven—his eyes were clear and calm, all trace of his former fury gone.

"Suzanna, what are you doing here?"

"Looking for you," Ham Bell offered cheerfully. "She figured you'd been scalped by Dull Knife's band or something."

Jared's eyes softened, and his beautiful mouth twitched into a smile. Suzanna went weak with relief. "Dull Knife's a thousand miles away by now."

"Don't matter to a woman. You know how they worry," Bell explained. "Well, now, looks like I've got this thing licked. I'd better get it on down to Mrs. Hand before she sends the dogs after me."

Chuckling at his own joke, Bell hopped up onto the seat and slapped the team into motion. Neither Jared nor Suzanna even heard him. They simply stared into each other's eyes, fighting the almost overwhelming urge to shock the entire town by embracing in public.

"Jared!"

They both turned at Andy's shout, just in time to see the boy barreling into Jared's leg. Staggering, Jared caught him and lifted him high into the air. "Hey, partner, are you trying to knock me over?"

"Jared, where've you been? Mama said you went for a ride 'cause you was mad, but then you didn't come back, and she started crying and . . ."

Jared's gaze cut to Suzanna, and she saw his remorse in the second before he smiled reassuringly up at Andy. "I went out to your old farm to see how things were doing," he explained, setting Andy back on his feet.

"Our farm?" the boy said in confusion. "Why'd you go there?"

"Let me get my horse stabled and some of this dirt washed off, and I'll tell you. Can you take my horse and find an empty stall for him?"

"Sure," Andy cried, running for the horse even before the word was out of his mouth.

Jared turned to face her.

"Suzanna—"

"Jared—"

They spoke in unison, but Jared silenced her with a gesture. "I'm sorry I walked out on you yesterday."

"You had every right to be angry. I never should have—"

"No, I never should have told you anything at all without telling you the whole story. I didn't want you to know the truth because I was afraid you wouldn't love me if you did."

"Oh, Jared, how could you think that?"

He grinned ruefully. "I've thought a lot of strange things since I met you, or have you forgotten?"

"You don't have to think them anymore," she said, taking his hands. "Your cousin is gone—"

"Gone? But I wanted to talk to him. When did he leave?"

"Just now, on the train, or at least he said he was going when I talked to him last night."

"You talked to him again after I left?"

"Yes, and Jared, he didn't come to have you arrested! He—"

"Shhh, not here," he cautioned, nodding toward the stable boy who was hurrying to help Andy with Jared's horse. "Let me wash up and get my horse taken care of, and then we'll go home and talk."

"Oh, dear!" Suzanna cried. "I almost forgot. Dora

is taking Mayor Kelley to the fort hospital. That was what the wagon was for. I've got to get back."

"Go ahead. I'll get Andy and follow."

Suzanna hurried back down Front Street to the alley that led to her house and the mayor's. She found Dora instructing several of the mayor's friends on how to place him in the wagon so he'd be most comfortable. Mayor Kelley alternated between groans and curses as he was jostled in the process. Fanny Garrettson had arrived and was helping Dora place pillows around him.

When he was situated at last and Dora stopped to catch her breath, Suzanna touched her arm. "Jared's back."

"Is he still angry?" she asked, placing her hand over Suzanna's.

"I don't think so. He said he rode out to our old farm, of all places. We didn't have much chance to talk. He rode up just as Mr. Bell was getting your wagon ready."

"Please tell him for me that . . . Oh, wait, here he comes now. I'll tell him myself."

Suzanna turned to see Jared, Andy, and Pistol hurrying toward them. Jared detoured to stop by the wagon where Dog Kelley lay groaning. He said a few words of reassurance, promising to help Beatty, his partner, run the Alhambra in his absence and to look after Dora for him.

They couldn't hear the mayor's response, but when Jared turned away from the wagon, he was smiling. His smile dimmed somewhat when he caught sight of Dora, but his step did not falter as he approached them.

"I'm sure he'll be fine," Jared said to Dora. "The post surgeon is excellent."

Dora nodded. "Jared, before I go, I have to tell you how sorry I am for writing that letter. I only wanted to help."

"I know. I realized that sometime in the middle of

the night last night. I realized a lot of things, but you don't have time to hear them right now."

Tears glistened in Dora's eyes. She reached out and squeezed Jared's arm. "Thank you," she whispered, and hurried away to join Beatty and Fanny on the wagon seat for the drive to Fort Dodge.

Jared took charge of Pistol's rope so the dog wouldn't follow the wagon. When the wagon rounded the corner toward Front Street, the rest of the onlookers began to drift away. Jared took Suzanna's hand in his. His eyes glowed. "Shall we go home now?"

Once inside their house, they still couldn't talk freely because Andy wanted an explanation, too. Jared stripped off his dusty clothes, washed up, and stretched out wearily on the bed clad only in his underdrawers. Andy clambered up and sat on his stomach while Suzanna sat down on the bed beside them. The sight of Jared's long, bare limbs in her bed again sent joy flooding through her. Everything would work out now, she just knew it.

"Why'd you go to our farm?" Andy wanted to know.

"Well, at first I was just riding around. Like your mother said, I was angry, and I needed some time to cool off. Then I started remembering where your mother told me the farm was, and I realized I was pretty close, so I headed for it. There's a family living there now. They've got three little boys. One's about your age."

Andy smiled in delight. "What're their names?"

"George, Peter, and Alvin. Their parents invited me to stay for supper and sleep in their barn, so I did." Jared's gaze drifted to Suzanna. "It was a way to be close to you even though I was far away."

Suzanna nodded her understanding and blinked at the sting of tears.

He looked back at Andy. "I didn't sleep much. Mostly I thought about how sorry I was for yelling at your mama yesterday. I figured I'd better get back as fast as I could to tell her.''

"She said you didn't mean it," Andy informed him. "I don't think she's mad at you."

Jared glanced at Suzanna again. "I hope not."

Suzanna's pulse quickened. "Andy, Jared's tired now. Why don't you take Pistol out back to play for a while so he can rest."

"Awww," he complained, but Pistol had jumped up at the sound of his name and the word 'play' had set his tail to wagging.

"Go on now," Suzanna urged, lifting the boy off Jared and setting him on the floor.

"Don't let Pistol run into the plaza," Jared cautioned.

"And if he does, don't run after him," Andy sing-songed in a parody of past warnings, trudging for the door.

After the door slammed, the silence seemed like a living thing inside the small house. Jared and Suzanna stared at each other across the narrow strip of bed between them.

"*Are* you mad?" he asked.

Suzanna shook her head.

Jared's mouth quirked into a relieved grin. "I was wondering, because you haven't given me so much as a hug . . .''

Suzanna threw herself into his arms, laughing and crying all at once as their lips sought and found each other in a lopsided kiss that quickly righted itself. They clung desperately for long minutes, reveling in the luxury of being together again after a separation that seemed much longer than twenty-four hours.

"Oh, Jared, I was so scared. I thought you weren't coming back," she said, between kisses.

Jared's expression grew solemn. "I did think about leaving for good."

"No!"

"Yes, but I didn't think about it long." He touched

her face, tenderly tracing the curve of her cheek. "At first I thought that would be the best thing. If I left, no one would find me, and you wouldn't be hurt."

"But I would've been hurt because you left me!" she argued, and he nodded his agreement.

"After I thought about it for a while, I remembered what you'd said on the subject before. Besides, I knew I couldn't stand to leave you even if it *was* the best thing to do. Before I met you, I was almost unbearably lonely, but I didn't know how truly barren my life was until you filled it. Without you . . ." Pain flickered in his eyes, and he closed them for a moment against it. When his eyelids lifted again, he was back in control. "I just couldn't face the thought of life without you and Andy. I might as well be dead."

"Don't say that!" she cried, pulling him close again.

He clasped her tightly to him until she could feel his heart thundering against her own. "I didn't get much sleep last night, Suzanna," he said against her hair. "I spent the time thinking about my choices, and I only came up with two. I could leave you and spend the rest of my life running, but I've already told you I won't do that. My only other choice is to go back and give myself up to the law."

Suzanna pushed away so she could see his face. "But you don't have to! Booth isn't going to tell anyone where you are. In fact, he said he would tell people he didn't find you here at all."

"Booth said that?"

"Yes! He only came because your mother wanted to know if Dora's letter was true and so he could tell you your mother and sister are well and send their love."

Jared frowned. "You must have had quite a conversation with Booth."

"He was very kind, and he's very concerned about you. He doesn't want you to get caught any more than I do."

"Then he's changed a lot in five years. I've never known Booth to care about anyone but himself."

"Maybe he grew up since you saw him last. I don't know. All I do know is that he promised to protect your secret. He said as far as he was concerned, Jared Wentworth is dead."

Jared drew a ragged breath and let it out slowly. "I've been dead for five years, Suzanna. I'm tired of it. Even if Booth keeps his promise, I'm still wanted for murder. I can't drag you and Andy around from pillar to post never knowing when someone might recognize me from a wanted poster and turn me in for the reward."

Fear tightened her stomach. "But you said you weren't going to leave us."

"I don't want to, you know I don't," he said, his arms tightening around her. "But the only chance we have for any kind of life together is if I go back home and stand trial. Once my name is cleared, we can be together forever."

Suzanna shivered. "But *will* you be cleared?"

He went completely still, and his eyes clouded with memories. "I guess you want to know what happened, don't you?"

She nodded, fighting the tremors of apprehension racing over her.

"I don't even know where to start. It's such a long story. My father was . . . a difficult man to live with. Nothing ever pleased him, especially nothing I ever did, and every time he got angry, he beat me."

"Beat you? You mean whipped you?"

Jared laughed mirthlessly. "Hardly. I mean he beat me with his fists, hammering on me until I was senseless."

"Oh, Jared!" she cried, tears blinding her. She tried to pull him close, but he resisted.

"Don't feel sorry for me, Suzanna. I don't want your pity."

"It isn't pity, Jared. I love you. What hurts you, hurts me."

She felt some of his tension ease, but he still held

himself away from her, so she used her hands to comfort him, running them over the satiny skin of his chest and shoulders as he continued his story.

"When I got older, I tried to fight back, but he was always bigger and stronger. My mother protected me as best she could, and she suffered for her trouble."

"You mean he . . . ?" Suzanna could hardly say the words.

"Yes, he beat her, too, but not as often or as badly. He always said a gentleman doesn't use a closed fist on a lady, and he tried not to mark her where it would show."

Tears streamed down her face now, but Suzanna ignored them, afraid to move lest she distract Jared from his tale.

"Finally, I was old enough to go away to school. They sent me to William and Mary College in Virginia. That was the happiest year of my life, and I never would have come home at all except to see my mother and my little sister." Jared's eyes grew bleak as he looked down the long dark tunnel of memory. "Ellie was about ten then, a delicate little thing just starting to show what a beautiful woman she would become. I never would have thought . . ."

Suzanna went cold at the ugly vision forming in her mind. "No, he didn't, he *couldn't!*" Suzanna protested, wishing she had the power to make it so, but Jared nodded grimly.

"While I was away, he'd started beating her, too. When I got home, her arm was in a sling. At first she told me she'd fallen from her pony. She seemed ashamed, and I thought it was because I'd taught her how to ride and she was embarrassed to have been so clumsy. Then, one night, I heard him yelling. I'll never know why he didn't take out his rage on me the way he always had before. Maybe it was because I'd grown so much in the time I'd been away and he was afraid of me. Whatever the reason, he was beating her, hit-

ting her with his fists, and she was screaming for me
to help her—''

"Stop!" Suzanna pulled his head to her breast and
held him there, absorbing his agony with her body,
cushioning his pounding heart against her own. For a
few minutes they lay together until Suzanna felt she
could hear the rest of it.

At last she said, "That was when you killed him,
wasn't it?"

Jared lifted his head. She could hardly bear the agony in his eyes. "Yes. I ran into the room and grabbed
his arm before he could hit her again and spun him
around to face me. He was in such a rage, I don't think
he even knew who I was, but I knew who he was: the
man I'd hated and feared all my life. I couldn't let him
do to Ellie what he'd done to me, so I hit him. I only
hit him once, but all the hate and terror I'd felt for
nineteen years was in that blow. He fell backwards,
against the fireplace. His head smashed into the marble
and . . .''

Jared shuddered, closing his eyes on the horrible
memory.

Suzanna held him close, cradling him against the
wrenching agony, but even through the horror, she
knew relief. "It was an accident! Jared, don't you see,
you were defending your sister and—''

"I killed him, Suzanna," he insisted, pulling out of
her embrace and taking her shoulders in a relentless
grip. "I didn't mean to, but he died. His skull was
crushed against the marble hearth.''

"But surely nobody would call it murder!''

"Not if they knew why I had done it, but how could
I tell the police what he had done to her? I couldn't
drag out all our ugly family secrets. I told myself I
couldn't humiliate Ellie and my mother like that.''

"Jared!" Suzanna took his face in his hands. "You
did the same thing to your family that you did to me!''

His look of despair wrenched her heart. "I know. I
realized it sometime last night. I left them so I wouldn't

hurt them, but I hurt them more by running away. Why couldn't I see it before?''

''You've seen it now. That's the important thing.''

''But will Ellie and my mother ever be able to forgive me?''

At least Suzanna could put his mind at ease on this point. ''I've never met your mother, but I'm a mother, too, and I'd much rather endure any kind of shame than lose my son. In fact, one reason Booth came here was to tell you how much your mother and Ellie miss you and want to see you again.''

''Don't they know my showing up will resurrect all the scandal again?''

''Maybe they hope to put it to rest once and for all.''

Jared smiled ruefully. ''That's what I'm hoping, and that's why I have to go back. Do you understand?''

Blinking back renewed tears, she nodded.

''I have no idea how long it will take, but you and Andy should be all right here. I'll leave you enough money to—''

''You most certainly will not! You aren't going to leave us anything, because we're going with you.''

''Don't be ridiculous, Suzanna. This isn't going to be a picnic. They'll probably put me in jail and—''

''All the more reason for me to be with you. Jared, do you really want to go through this without me?''

''No,'' he admitted, ''but it's going to be bad enough putting my mother and Ellie through it.''

''So you'd rather leave me here where I'll be terrified not knowing what's happening to you, thinking you'll even forget all about me and—''

''*Forget* you? Are you crazy?''

In the other room, the front door opened with a crash. ''Mama, when're we going to eat? I'm starving!''

Jared and Suzanna broke apart, and Suzanna scrambled off the bed. ''In a few minutes, as soon as Jared gets dressed,'' she called through the curtain.

Jared frowned up at her. "We'll finish this conversation later," he warned in a whisper.

"We most certainly will," she replied.

Later was much later since they couldn't discuss anything in front of Andy. Jared had promised to help out at the Alhambra, so he couldn't stay home very long after Andy finally went to bed.

"When do you plan to go back?" Suzanna asked when she had made certain Andy was asleep.

"As soon as we're sure Dog is going to be all right. Beatty won't really need my help much longer since the season is over. Dodge will be deserted in a week or two. It won't even be dangerous for you to live on the South Side, although I'll get you a room at the Western so I don't have to worry about you being alone."

"I won't be alone, Jared, because I'll be with you, and if you try to leave us here, we'll follow you."

He sighed in exasperation, and Suzanna smiled benignly. She just needed a little time to wear him down. After all, he really didn't want to leave her and Andy behind. He just needed to be convinced that taking them was the right thing to do.

"We have plenty of time to talk about this," she reminded him. "You'd better get along. The customers might get rowdy when they find out Dora isn't singing."

Early the next afternoon, Dora returned from the fort, weary but relieved. The surgery had gone well, and Kelley was recovering nicely.

"He was cussing a blue streak," she reported, "complaining how he felt worse now than before, but Dr. Tremaine said it was just the laudanum talking and he wouldn't remember anything later."

Jared raised his eyebrows and shot Suzanna a concerned look. "Did I swear at you when I was sick?"

"No, you were remarkably quiet," she told him cheerfully. "In fact, you were rather boring."

His eyes promised her sweet revenge later, and she silently accepted his challenge.

"Jared, I'm going to sing tonight," Dora said, ignoring the byplay with amused nonchalance. "Will you come by for me on your way to the Alhambra tonight?"

"Will you be going to the Comique afterwards?"

"No, I'm too tired to sing all night. They have Fanny and the other girls at the theater, and with the crowds they've been getting lately, they shouldn't need me."

The evening started just like all the others had since Mayor Kelley had been sick. Jared left Andy and Suzanna, went to meet Dora and walk her to work. Instead of taking her to the Comique when she was done, he took her home and returned to the Alhambra. Business was slow, so they closed down at about three o'clock.

Jared saw Fanny Garrettson walking down the alley ahead of him with several other girls from the Comique and remembered she was staying with Dora while the mayor was away. He couldn't help thinking how reluctant he was to leave Suzanna here alone while he traveled back to Maryland. God only knew how long he'd be gone, or even if he'd be able to return at all.

The thought depressed him. By the time he had undressed and crawled into bed beside Suzanna, his usual desire for her had grown into a desperate need. Even though she was asleep, she responded to him, coming eagerly into his arms and returning his kisses instinctively until she woke to a passion as fervent as his own.

They made love quietly, aware of Andy's presence on the other side of the thin curtain. When they had gasped out their release, they lay together, touching and savoring the closeness, vitally aware they might soon be separated forever.

They had just dozed off when a loud shot sounded close by. Jared awoke instantly. He was off the bed and reaching for his pants when the second shot rattled the glass in their windows.

"Jared, what is it?"

"Mama!" Andy cried from the next room.

Suzanna scrambled off the bed, but Jared grabbed her and forced her to her knees. "Stay here!"

He darted into the other room, crouching as a third shot shattered the night. Andy howled, but Jared muffled the noise against his shoulder as he scooped the boy up and carried him to Suzanna.

At the sound of the fourth shot, Andy literally jumped into her arms. She clung to him, rolling to the floor and tucking his body beneath her own.

"Mama!" Andy sobbed in terror.

"Shhh, it's all right. Mama's here," she crooned, stroking his face even as she braced herself for another shot.

Above her, Jared struggled with his clothes. "Get down!" she urged, but he ignored her, pulling on a shirt.

Outside they could hear men shouting and the sound of a running horse, and a woman screaming.

"Stay here," Jared commanded, and started for the door.

"Jared!" she called, but he ignored her, slamming the door behind him.

Suzanna lay trembling in terror, trying to soothe Andy's sobs while fighting her own and praying for Jared's safety. Who could have been shooting? It sounded as if they had been firing right at the house.

The men's voices got louder, and Suzanna realized the residents of the Western Hotel must have been awakened by the gunfire.

A woman's voice rose above the men's, screaming shrilly. "It was the Kennedy fellow, I saw him. Spike Kennedy. He fired right into the house!"

That was Fanny Garrettson! Suzanna struggled to her feet. "Lay still for a minute," she cautioned Andy, and hurried to the door.

The gunfire had stopped, and she surmised the gunman had fled on the running horse she'd heard. She opened the door and peered out. The street was full of men in various stages of undress, and Fanny stood in their midst wraithlike in her white nightdress.

"What is it, Mama? Who's shooting?" Andy asked, peering through the curtain.

"I don't know, but I think it's safe to go out now." She hurried past him back into the bedroom for her wrapper and slippers.

When she was decently covered, she scooped Andy up and headed out the door into the street.

"Where's the marshal?" somebody was wondering. "Somebody oughta fetch him."

"I'm right here," Wyatt Earp called from behind Suzanna. She turned to see him running toward the group gathered in front of Mayor Kelley's house. "What happened here?"

"Somebody fired into the mayor's house," a man explained.

"Where is he?"

The question caused confusion. Some in the crowd started to explain the mayor was at the fort hospital; others that the gunman had fled on horseback.

Suzanna, with Andy balanced on her hip, forced her way through the crowd to Fanny. "Where's Dora?" Suzanna asked, looking around with a growing sense of foreboding.

"Inside still asleep, I guess," Fanny said distractedly. Her eyes were wild in the feeble dawn light. "He fired right through the window. Glass went everywhere. I cut my foot running out, but I saw him, all right. Spike Kennedy. Why on earth would he do a thing like that?"

But Suzanna didn't hear a word. All she could think was that Dora couldn't *possibly* have slept through the shooting, not if the shots had awakened the men in the hotel.

"*Jared!* Where's Dora?" Suzanna shouted above the clamor.

Everyone stopped talking at once and looked around futilely.

A brand-new terror coiled inside Suzanna. "Dora was sleeping inside, too," she said, her voice rising with panic.

Jared broke from the crowd and ran into the house. Suzanna thrust Andy into the startled marshal's arms and followed, plunging into the darkness.

"Dora!" Jared called, shoving aside the curtain separating the two rooms. "*Dora!*"

But no one answered his call. True panic gripped Suzanna now, and she shoved Jared aside, darting under his arm into the back room.

"Dora, wake up!" she screamed frantically.

The figure on the bed didn't move.

"*Dora!*"

Nothing.

Suzanna froze, paralyzed by terror. Jared came from behind her, moving slowly as if afraid of disturbing Dora's slumber. He touched Dora's shoulder gently. "Dora?"

Suzanna literally held her breath as tears rose, burning her throat, scalding her eyes, roaring in her head, but she held them back, knowing if she let them fall, Dora would be dead, and Dora *couldn't* be dead, not Dora, not like this!

"Someone bring a light," Jared called, his voice flat, all urgency gone.

No, no, no, no, no!

Outside, Fanny screamed again, and Andy began to wail, but Suzanna couldn't go to him, not yet, not until she knew.

Behind her came footsteps and a blaze of light as someone struck a match and touched it to the lamp wick. Marshal Earp pushed the curtain aside and the shadows fled before him.

Dora lay just as Suzanna had known she would, still and silent and unmoving, her eyes closed, her face serene. She was only sleeping.

Earp lifted the lamp. "What the . . . ?"

Then they saw it, all of them in the same instant, the small hole in her nightdress and the tiny red stain.

Suzanna cried out, covering her mouth with both hands. No, no, no! her mind screamed.

Marshal Earp leaned closer. "My God, the bullet went in right under her arm. Must've killed her instantly."

Killed? Dora? No, there was some mistake.

Suzanna heard a sob, a choking sound of pure agony torn from the depths of someone's soul. Fanny, she thought, until the next one came and the sound was close, so close, too close . . .

"Suzanna!" Jared's arms were around her in an instant, lifting her off her feet, taking her from the room, from the house.

They passed through the crowd, and Andy called for her. Someone brought him along, but she couldn't see who it was because she was crying too hard, sobbing into Jared's shoulder. Fanny was screaming something about Spike Kennedy, and others took up the chant, but Suzanna could barely hear them over the roaring in her head.

Chapter 11

Suzanna listened to the unfamiliar sound of rain on the roof of her house. She hadn't heard the sound too many times during the past few months of drought, but she thought it only proper that heaven should be weeping, too.

Dora was dead. Dr. McCarty said the bullet had struck her right in the heart and she'd never felt a thing. At least she hadn't suffered, people were saying, but Suzanna could take no comfort from such a pathetic axiom. Certainly not with Dora lying dead, cut down so senselessly in the prime of her life.

Suzanna finished dressing and left the bedroom where she had wept out her pain and loss over Dora's death. When she stepped into the parlor, she found Andy and Jared waiting.

Andy sat on the floor surrounded by his toy soldiers, and Jared sat on a chair, pretending to watch him play. Both of them looked up when she entered, instantly ready to come to her aid, but Suzanna had finished crying. "How will they find him in this rain?" she asked Jared. Sheriff Masterson had organized a small posse composed of himself, Marshal Earp, ex-sheriff Charley Bassett, and Deputy Sheriff Bill Tilghman to chase down the killer.

"They aren't even trying to track him. He rode east when he left here, but Bat figured he was only trying to throw them off. His father's ranch is southwest, near

Tascosa. He'll go there eventually, so they plan to head him off at the Cimmeron, at Wagon Bed Springs Crossing.''

"The rain will slow them down," she pointed out.

"It's raining on him, too."

Suzanna felt the hot surge of tears threaten, but she swallowed them down. "Why did he do it, Jared?" she asked brokenly.

Jared jumped up and took her tenderly in his arms. Infinitely grateful for his presence, she leaned against him, drawing courage from his solid strength. "I told you, he wanted to kill the mayor. He didn't know Dog was at the hospital, and he certainly didn't know Dora was sleeping in the house. It was all a terrible mistake."

After the shooting, Kennedy and a companion had gone to a saloon in town. When Earp and Masterson found them, Kennedy had fled. After being told Dora Hand had been killed, the companion admitted Kennedy had attempted to kill the mayor as an act of revenge.

"Don't cry anymore, Mama," Andy begged, hugging her around the knees as she clung to Jared.

Suzanna drew a ragged breath. "I won't, baby," she said, leaning down to include her son in her embrace. After another minute, Suzanna felt in control of her emotions, and she drew away from Jared's arms. "I want to see her."

Jared opened his mouth to protest, but seeing her determination, he said, "The preacher's wife and some of the ladies from the church went over to . . . to . . ."

Suzanna nodded. "I'll help them." She wiped at her eyes and leaned down to Andy. "Sweetheart, Mama has to go out for a while. Be a good boy for Jared while I'm gone."

"Are you going to see Mrs. Hand?" he asked.

Suzanna nodded, not trusting her voice.

"Is she sick or something?" His blue eyes were so trusting, Suzanna almost lost control again.

"Yes, she's sick. I'm . . . I'm going to visit her."

"Can I come, too? She likes me. I can make her feel better."

Tears flooded up, stinging her nose, blinding her, but she blinked them away. "Not this time, dear." Grabbing her cloak, she fled into the rain where the drops would hide her tears.

Lamplight glowed from the windows of Kelley's house, incongruously cheerful on such a gray day. Inside, she found the women preparing to leave, having already finished their work. Mrs. Wright greeted her, taking Suzanna's hands in hers.

"We're all so sorry, my dear. It's such a terrible, senseless thing."

Suzanna nodded numbly, glancing toward the curtained doorway. "I'd like to see her."

Mrs. Wright stood aside so Suzanna could pass into the bedroom. Pushing the curtain back, Suzanna caught her breath. Once again Dora might have been asleep. Dressed in a modest gown of maroon silk, her hair done to perfection, she lay on the bed with her hands folded and her eyes closed. If she hadn't been so pale, Suzanna could almost have believed . . .

Mrs. Wright put her arm around Suzanna's waist. "We've figured out what happened," she said, talking just to fill the empty silence, Suzanna knew. "He fired four shots. Two of them went into the floor. The third one hit the bed where Miss Garrettson was sleeping. It missed her by inches. The fourth one went through the wall and . . . The doctor said she didn't even wake up. At least she didn't suffer, Suzanna."

Suzanna wanted to scream. What did it matter if Dora had suffered or not when she was dead? But then she remembered George Hoyt, the cowboy who had tried to kill Marshal Earp. Hoyt had lingered almost a month before dying of his wounds, and Dora had grieved over him. Suzanna supposed a quick death was a blessing of sorts, but . . . "Why did it have to happen at all?" she asked bitterly.

"We don't know, dear. These things are simply God's will, and we are not to question—"

"God's will?" Suzanna asked in horror. "Do you think it was God's will that a worthless skunk like Spike Kennedy killed a wonderful woman like Dora?"

Mrs. Wright flinched from Suzanna's vehemence, but her own eyes grew moist. "No, dear, I don't, but nothing else makes any sense either."

She was right, of course, and Suzanna couldn't hold back her tears any longer. Surrendering to her grief, she tried to turn away, but Mrs. Wright drew her close, letting her weep out her grief and frustration against her shoulder. After a long time, Suzanna straightened, swiping at her cheeks. "Will . . . will Reverend Wright preach the funeral?"

"Oh, yes, and you needn't worry about the arrangements." Mrs. Wright pulled out a handkerchief and wiped her own eyes. "I think everyone in town has already contributed toward the expense. You know how cowboys loved her, and she did so much good. The only thing we have to worry about is telling Mayor Kelley."

"Oh, no!" Suzanna had forgotten all about the mayor lying ill in the hospital. How would he bear the news?

"My husband is planning to go out to tell him," Mrs. Wright was saying, "and he was wondering . . . Do you think Mr. Cain would go with him?"

"I . . . I'll ask him." Outside, the rain poured down, harder and harder, clattering against the house as if it would beat it down.

"It's hailing," one of the women in the front room said. "The poor posse, out in this storm!"

Would the nightmare never end? How much more pain would this senseless act cause?

When Jared returned from Fort Dodge late that afternoon, his face was white. Suzanna didn't ask him what the mayor's reaction had been. She couldn't deal with anyone else's grief just yet.

The posse arrived back in town the next morning with Spike Kennedy in custody. Jared heard the story directly from Marshal Earp.

"The posse got caught in the hailstorm," Jared told Suzanna when he came back to the house. "They had to take cover under a cutbank, but as soon as it let up, they rode on. They'd guessed right. Kennedy was headed for the crossing, and the posse beat him there. There's a dugout nearby where a farmer lives, and they waited for him in the house. Kennedy was almost to the front door when he recognized the men waiting for him.

"He tried to run, and they fired after him. Bat hit him in the arm, and Wyatt shot his horse out from under him. He was pretty cocky when they got to him, not a bit sorry for killing Dog. When they told him he'd killed Dora instead, he went crazy, cussing Bat for not killing him when he'd had the chance. He's in pretty bad shape from his wound, and I guess he's hoping he'll die."

"He deserves to," Suzanna said bitterly.

Jared took her in his arms, but for once she found no comfort there. Not even Jared's love could heal this hurt.

Dora Hand's funeral was the most spectacular one Dodge City had ever seen, surpassing even those of Ed Masterson and Mac McCarty. Suzanna bitterly recalled the day Dora had remarked how she hoped for as lavish an interment as those lawmen killed in the line of duty.

They laid her to rest with the 'respectable' folks in the Prairie Grove Cemetery. Every business in town closed, and the procession that followed her coffin included dance-hall girls, gamblers, gunslingers, saloonkeepers, cattlemen and cowboys, businessmen and their ladies. Reverend Wright spoke the eulogy, concluding with the words, "He that is without sin among you, let him first cast a stone at her."

Too ill to attend the funeral, Mayor Kelley lay in the fort hospital refusing comment on the life and death of Dora Hand. When asked why the two women were sleeping in his house, he explained he'd given them the use of it while he was gone because their regular quarters were so small. Everyone graciously accepted the fiction.

Dora's old friend Fanny Garrettson, who had worked with her for years in St. Louis, also refused to reveal exactly who Dora had been in the years before she had become an actress, and all the rumors about her romantic past circulated once more.

The Dodge City *Globe* said, "the deceased came to Dodge City this summer and was engaged as vocalist in the Comique Show. She was a prepossessing woman and her artful winning ways brought many admirers within her smile's blandishments. If we mistake not, Dora Hand has an eventful history. She had applied for a divorce from Theodore Hand. After a varied life the unexpected death messenger cuts her down in the full bloom of gaiety and womanhood. She was the innocent victim."

Spike Kennedy underwent surgery on his wounded arm. The doctor removed four inches of shattered bone just above his elbow, rendering the arm useless. His arraignment was delayed until he had recovered from the surgery.

The night after Dora's funeral, the Alhambra was closed out of respect for the deceased. Jared and Suzanna lay awake into the wee hours of the morning, lost in their own dark thoughts.

At last Jared broke the heavy silence. "Suzanna, I have to leave for Maryland soon."

"I know," she said, bracing herself for an argument.

"I've been thinking about it ever since Dora . . . and I can't leave you alone here in Dodge."

She turned to him, slipping her arms around his bare

waist. "I already told you I'm going with you when you leave."

He continued as if she hadn't spoken. "I can take you to St. Louis. You and Andy will be safe there."

Suzanna pushed up, propping herself on his chest so she could stare down into his face. "The only place I'll be safe is with you, Jared. If you try to leave us somewhere, we'll come after you."

"Suzanna, I can't—"

"You certainly can! If I've learned one thing from Dora's death, it's that you can't plan on tomorrow. She was the one who told me to take happiness wherever I could find it. We can't be sure what'll happen when you go home. I pray every day that you'll be cleared and we can have a new life, but if we've only got a short time left, we'll spend every minute of it together."

For several heartbeats, Jared didn't speak, didn't move, didn't even breathe. Suzanna waited, tensed for the most important battle of her life, but when he finally spoke, he simply said, "Suzanna, I love you."

The train ride to Baltimore was an ordeal. During the day they took turns entertaining Andy, who grew increasingly restless, confined as he was to the train. After a while not even the changing landscape interested him any longer, and they lived for the brief rest stops during which they could go back to the baggage car and visit Pistol, who was making the trip in a large packing crate.

Only at night did they find peace. Lying awake in the narrow, swaying berth with Andy sleeping soundly above them, Suzanna and Jared told each other all the things they would have shared much sooner had they courted in the accustomed manner.

Suzanna introduced him to her family via memories of the life she'd had growing up in Georgia. Jared spoke of the happy times with his mother and sister at

Rosewood, and reassured her about his relationship with Claire.

"But you must have loved her a little," she insisted one night as the train sped through the darkness.

"I didn't love her at all, which is why I chose her. Suzanna, you have to understand how worried I was about being found out. I'd changed my name, and I thought if I didn't make any close friends, I'd be safe from discovery. What I hadn't counted on was how lonely I'd get. I thought a mistress would be the perfect solution."

"She must have loved you if she agreed."

"She loved the things I bought her, and I set her up in a nice house and—"

"You lived with her like you lived with me?" Suzanna asked in outrage.

"No," he replied, amused by her jealousy. "I couldn't live with her for fear she'd find out too much about me. I just . . . *visited* her."

"How often?" Suzanna asked stiffly.

"Suzanna!" he asked, feigning shock.

"Every day?" she demanded.

"I don't remember."

"Jared—"

"Suzanna," he interrupted her, "I already told you I didn't love her and that you're a much better lover than she was." He ran his hand provocatively up her leg. "Please believe me, what I had with Claire was nothing like we have together. Being with her was worse than being alone. It only made me want real love more. Can you understand?"

Suzanna nodded, satisfied at last.

"If either of us has a reason to be jealous, it's me," he pointed out. "The woman I love was once married to a handsome young farmer who gave her a son and—"

"Jared, don't," she begged, instantly sorry she had never told Jared the truth about her relationship with Andrew. "It . . . it wasn't like you think."

"What wasn't?"

"My marriage. Oh, I'm not saying I didn't love Andrew. I loved him very much when we got married, but we were awfully young and didn't know much about life. We'd both always been poor, so we didn't mind at first. Andrew had big plans, though. He wanted to own land. We saved and saved, but we couldn't seem to get ahead. Andrew grew angry and bitter, but then we heard about the free land in Kansas. I didn't want to borrow money to go, but Andrew was so excited about it, I couldn't refuse, and it probably wouldn't have made any difference if I had. Then when we got to Kansas . . ." She paused, resisting the memories.

"What happened?" Jared asked gently.

"He . . . he hated Kansas. He missed the trees, and he didn't like living in a dirt house, and nothing was right. We had a good crop the first year, but not good enough to get us out of debt. Andrew started collecting buffalo bones and selling them in Dodge. That's when he started drinking."

"Drinking? You never told me."

"The first time I thought it was just a celebration because it was the first cash money we'd seen in so long. Then he did it again and again. He spent all the money he made on liquor, and he started neglecting the farm and . . ." Suzanna paused, fighting tears at all the painful memories.

"Did he abuse you?" Jared asked after a moment.

Suzanna blinked away the moisture in her eyes. "He didn't hit me, if that's what you mean, but he didn't have to. He got nasty. He said the most awful things. Sometimes I almost hated him." She shuddered. "Andy used to hide under the bed when he came home."

"Oh, God," Jared murmured, pulling her close.

"We were so poor, sometimes we didn't have any food in the house, but still he spent every penny he could find on whiskey. I was terrified that one day he just wouldn't come home at all, and then one day he didn't. He passed out drunk and fell out of the wagon. He froze to death before someone found him.''

Jared's arms tightened around her as if his love could shield her from the past. "I'm so sorry, my darling."

She let him hold her for a long time, savoring the comfort she had yearned for all the lonely months before they'd met. Then she pulled away. "Jared, I didn't tell you all this so you'd feel sorry for me. I told you so you'd understand how it was between me and Andrew. I didn't want you to think that as soon as my husband died, I forgot all about him."

"I never thought that," he insisted.

"I grieved for him in spite of everything, but I just couldn't afford the luxury of mourning. I had to find work so Andy and I wouldn't starve."

"I know. I understand."

"So you see, you don't have any reason to be jealous either."

He didn't speak for a long time. Finally she said, "Jared? Is something wrong?"

He sighed wearily. "I was just remembering the reason why I tried to leave you in the first place. I wanted to spare you any more tragedy. Now I might be causing you even more than Andrew did."

Suzanna was terrified he was right.

By the time they arrived in Baltimore, the combination of Andy's irritability and her growing apprehension over the unknown situation awaiting them had scraped Suzanna's nerves raw. The sights and smells of the city, the huge buildings towering three and four stories above the street oppressed her. Not even the hot bath in the pleasant hotel room cheered her. The next morning they would leave for Rosewood in a rented wagon. Tomorrow Jared would face whatever fate awaited him.

What kind of reception would they receive? What would his family think of her and Andy? Had the loving mother Jared remembered been embittered by the

tragedies that had befallen her? Would the sweet little
sister he remembered be angry at him for bringing
scandal into their lives once again?

As if he shared her unspoken fears, Jared clung to
her that night, making love to her with a fevered desperation she shared. When their shudders of desire had
faded and Jared tried to pull away, she held him fast,
caressing his damp skin possessively. Neither of them
spoke of the possibility that this might be the last night
they would be together.

In the morning the hotel porters loaded their trunks
into the rented wagon, and they began the final leg of
their journey.

"Look how bumpy the land is, Mama," Andy observed, and Jared explained about hills and mountains
to a boy whose only memories were of pancake-flat
prairies.

"Look at all the trees, Mama. Why are the leaves
such funny colors?" He had seldom seen more than a
dozen trees at any given time and was overwhelmed
by the lush, verdant Maryland woods that autumn had
painted a rainbow of colors.

With each mile, Suzanna grew more tense. Andy,
on the other hand, grew more excited, uncertain exactly where they were going, or why, but knowing
something important was happening.

Oddly, Jared seemed to share his growing enthusiasm. Suzanna noticed it first in his voice which became
more and more animated as he pointed things out to
Andy, naming the flora and fauna of this strange new
world for him. Then she saw it in his eyes, which
brightened as they scanned the distance for familiar
sights. Whatever fate awaited him, Jared was glad to
be home.

At last, near noon, they rounded a bend in the road
and saw the house. Suzanna didn't know how she had
recognized Rosewood out of all the lovely homes they
had passed. Perhaps she simply felt Jared's shock of

recognition. In any case, when he said, "There it is," Suzanna was not surprised.

The house was exquisite, sitting on a hill overlooking the road on one side and a small tributary on the other. Constructed of red brick, it stood three stories tall, the windows long and shuttered, with whitewashed columns supporting the second- and third-story verandas. Weeping willows swayed in the yard, their leaves golden in the bright sunlight, and all around were the fenced paddocks where sleek horses grazed, flicking their tails with easy grace.

Suzanna hadn't even realized Jared had stopped the wagon. A hard lump of apprehension formed in her stomach, and her heart beat laboriously against her ribs. Everything looked so peaceful and serene, just the way Dora had looked when Wyatt Earp lifted the lamp to find where the bullet had entered her body. Things were not always as they seemed, as Suzanna had learned to her sorrow.

"It . . . it's beautiful, Jared."

"Is that your house, Jared?" Andy asked. "How come it's so big?"

"I always wondered that myself," Jared told him with a smile.

"Which room is yours?"

"The one on the middle floor, on that side," he explained pointing.

"Did you have your own horse?"

"I told you, I had lots of horses."

"Maybe you'd let me ride one," Andy asked hopefully.

Only then did Jared's smile falter. He could make no promises for the future. "Maybe," he said, patting Andy's leg. He slapped the team into motion again.

The drive curved around in a semicircle in front of the house, and Jared stopped the wagon at the foot of the steps that led to the massive front porch. Suddenly, Suzanna felt small and insignificant, unworthy to enter such a grand abode.

But Jared didn't hesitate. He climbed down from the seat, lifted Andy to the ground, and reached for her. Having no other choice, she surrendered to his arms and let him help her out. Taking Andy's hand, she allowed Jared to escort them up to the carved oak door.

The brass knocker echoed hollowly. Suzanna placed a hand over her churning stomach and glanced at Jared. His face was unnaturally pale, and his hands were clenched into fists, but he betrayed no other signs of agitation as they waited for what seemed an eternity for someone to answer their knock.

A young woman in a black dress and a stiff white apron opened the door. For some reason Suzanna had expected to see a dark face above the uniform, but the girl was unmistakably Irish, with red hair and snapping green eyes. Jared had explained that very few people had kept slaves in this part of Maryland, but she was still surprised. White servants were not something she had seen often in her youth in Georgia.

"May I help you?" the girl asked, obviously puzzled by their presence.

"Is Mrs. Wentworth at home?" Jared asked stiffly.

"I'm not sure. Was she expecting you?"

"Not really, but I think she'll want to see us."

The girl frowned her uncertainty. "Who's calling, please?"

"I'm Jared Wentworth, her son."

The girl's apple cheeks went scarlet, and her eyes widened in amazement. "Mr. Jared? Is it really you?"

Jared looked at the girl more closely. "Katie?"

She nodded vigorously, nearly shaking loose the cap she wore. "Yes, sir, it's me."

Jared smiled slightly. "You've grown up."

"So have you!" she blurted, then covered her mouth. "I'm sorry, sir, it's just . . ." She gestured helplessly.

"If you'd tell my mother we're here . . . ?" he suggested.

"Oh, yes! I'm so sorry! Do come in." She stepped back and motioned for them to enter.

If Suzanna had felt insignificant outside, she felt positively invisible inside. The entryway was an enormous cavern open all the way to the third floor. From the glass dome that formed the lofty ceiling hung the most magnificent chandelier Suzanna had ever seen. Tier upon tier of shimmering crystal sent the noontime sun dancing in a thousand different directions around the hall.

The floors were ivory marble veined in gold, and above the mahogany wainscoting, the walls were papered in what appeared to be gold leaf. Before them stretched a massive staircase, wider than a street it seemed, that split into two directions on the first landing.

Awed, Andy stared openmouthed. Suzanna tried to keep hers closed.

"If you'll wait in the parlor, I'll tell Mrs. Wentworth you're here," Katie was saying, almost babbling in her eagerness to welcome them. She scurried off ahead of them to open the doors to the room. "Your dear mother will be that pleased to see you, Mr. Jared. She talks about you near every day, she does, and Miss Ellie! She's out riding, and she'll be that angry she wasn't here, but who would've guessed?"

Before anyone could even think of answering her, she was gone, fairly running up the huge staircase. Suzanna glanced up at Jared again, but he was still looking at the house, studying every inch of the hallway as one would study the face of a lover. Attuned to his every mood, she easily sensed his longing and the bittersweet joy he must be experiencing at being home again.

As if he felt her eyes upon him, he turned and smiled reassuringly down at her, but his eyes were guarded, veiling his true emotions. Taking her arm, he led her into a room the size of the entire Comique Theater. A grand piano stood in one corner, but it looked like a toy against the huge scale of the room. Gold leaf furniture upholstered in red velvet alternated with mahogany tables and every imaginable sort of bric-a-brac. A marble fireplace dominated the far wall, and for one awful moment Suzanna wondered if this were the one of which Jared had spoken. She almost expected to see bloodstains on the hearth, and quickly averted her gaze.

"Why does that thing have eyes?" Andy asked, pointing toward an arrangement of peacock feathers stuck in a silver vase.

"They only look like eyes," she explained, picking him up lest he be tempted to touch any of the valuable objects in the room. "They're really feathers." To distract herself from her troubling thoughts, she carried him over to examine them, hoping Jared couldn't sense her inner panic.

She had been a fool to come. She didn't belong in a place like this. All her life she'd been nothing but poor white trash, and then she'd slipped even lower by working in a dance hall. Jared's family would know what she was the instant they saw her.

Then from the hall they heard the sound of hurried footsteps on the stairs. Suzanna froze, hugging Andy tightly to her. Her gaze flew to Jared whose attention was riveted on the doorway. He took a step as if he intended to meet whoever was coming, but he caught himself and stood fast.

The color came back to his face, mottling his cheeks, and Suzanna knew his fears were even greater than hers. Steeling herself for what was probably the most important meeting of her life, Suzanna held her breath and waited.

The footsteps were on the floor now, clicking across the marble, slowing as they approached the doorway. At last, a woman appeared, stepping tentatively into the room, perhaps as uncertain of her welcome as they were. Jared's mother. Suzanna would have known her anywhere.

She looked at them with Jared's eyes, her gaze touching Suzanna and Andy before moving on to find her son. At the sight of him, she gasped, one white hand fluttering to her throat. "Jared?"

"Yes, Mother. I'm home."

She cried out in joy, opening her arms as she flew to him. He met her halfway, catching her up in bear hug that seemed shockingly out of place in this formal setting. They embraced for a long time. Mrs. Wentworth's hands skimmed over his back and shoulders as if she were reassuring herself he was real. At last she pushed away, gazing up at him with shining eyes.

She was tall for a woman, several inches taller than Suzanna. The chestnut hair her son had inherited was touched with gray and artfully arranged in a neat chignon. Slender, although the years had obviously added some fullness here and there to her figure, she carried herself like a queen. Even in her simple brown day dress, she was far more elegant than Suzanna in her Sunday best.

"Jared, I thought . . ." Mrs. Wentworth began, but shook her head as if to deny any unpleasant thoughts. "But you're here now, thank God! You have so much to tell me, but first . . ." She whirled to face Suzanna and Andy. The dark eyes so like Jared's misted as a smile twitched hopefully around her lips. "My grandson?"

"Not exactly," Jared hastened to explain. "Mother, I'd like you to meet my fiancée, Suzanna Prentice, and her son, Andy."

Disappointment passed like a shadow across her face, but she smiled warmly and held out her hands as she glided across the oriental rug to where Suzanna stood with Andy.

"Welcome to Rosewood, my dear." She took Suzanna by the arms. "I can't tell you how happy I am to meet you since I'm sure you're the reason Jared has finally come home." To Suzanna's surprise, she kissed her cheek, enveloping her in a cloud of lavender. When Mrs. Wentworth pulled away again, a tear trickled down her cheek. "I'll give you the most beautiful wedding this county has ever seen!"

Before Jared or Suzanna could reply, Andy said, "You smell good."

Suzanna could have died, but Mrs. Wentworth only smiled. "Perhaps you'd like a kiss, too, young man. It's been a while since I kissed a little boy, and I wonder if I remember how."

"I'll show you," Andy said, reaching for her neck. She leaned toward him obligingly and allowed him to place a smacker right on her mouth.

"Andy!" Suzanna scolded. "I'm sorry, ma'am, I . . ."

Suzanna stopped when she saw Mrs. Wentworth was crying.

"Did I hurt you?" Andy asked in dismay.

"Oh, no," she replied, smiling through her tears. "You just made me remember things. What a delightful child," she told Suzanna. "You must be very proud."

Suzanna could only nod.

"Oh, dear," Mrs. Wentworth said suddenly. "Where are my manners? You must be exhausted after your trip. Please sit down. Katie!"

The girl appeared in the doorway instantly. "Bring us some tea, will you? And set three extra places for luncheon." She glanced at Andy again. "Or perhaps you're too hungry to wait for luncheon?"

Andy had never heard of luncheon. "I'm hungry," he allowed.

"Then Katie will take you right to the kitchen, if you like."

Andy looked at Suzanna, who nodded and set him on his feet. He made a dash for the door, but skidded to an abrupt stop halfway across the room. "What about Pistol?" he asked Jared.

"Pistol?" Mrs. Wentworth asked.

"My dog," Andy explained before anyone else could. "Mr. Kelley gave him to me, and we left him out in the wagon. He'll get thirsty."

Bemused, Mrs. Wentworth shook her head. "Katie,

have one of the stable boys take the dog out to the barn and feed him. They'll take good care of him out there," she assured Andy.

When Katie and Andy had gone, Mrs. Wentworth turned to Jared again. "I can't believe you're really here," she exclaimed, reaching for him again.

He came forward and took her hands, his eyes still guarded, not letting himself feel her joy completely lest it be snatched away.

"Come sit by me, both of you," she commanded, drawing Jared toward a long, low sofa. She motioned for Suzanna to follow.

Suzanna did so reluctantly, conscious of her shabby, travel-stained clothes. Jared's mother was the picture of elegance as she moved regally toward the sofa, and Suzanna felt like an interloper.

When Mrs. Wentworth had them seated on either side of her, she turned to Jared.

"Now tell me where on earth you've been all these years and why you've never written."

Jared frowned. "I think you know why I haven't written. I was in St. Louis mostly, but most recently in Dodge City."

"Then you *were* there! That woman was right and . . ." Her gaze swung to Suzanna. "Prentice! You're the Mrs. Prentice whom Booth was supposed to see."

Suzanna only nodded, conscious of her accent which sounded coarse compared to Mrs. Wentworth's velvet tones.

"Why couldn't he find you, then?"

"He did find us, Mother," Jared said.

"But he said—"

"We asked him not to tell anyone where I was, or at least Suzanna did."

Mrs. Wentworth turned to Suzanna, her dark eyes troubled. "I don't understand."

Suzanna bit her lip, wondering what she should say, but Jared was already replying. "At the time, Suzanna didn't know I'd already decided to come home," he told her grimly.

For some reason this pleased Mrs. Wentworth. "And I'm so glad you did! We'll have a wonderful wedding, although you'll have to give me some time to plan. We'll have a dress made, perhaps even a whole trousseau—"

"Mother!" Jared stared at her incredulously. "There can't be a wedding until everything else is settled."

"What needs to be settled?"

His amazement mirrored Suzanna's. Could Mrs. Wentworth possibly have forgotten why Jared had left home so long ago?

Jared's throat worked for an instant before he said, "Father . . ."

"Oh, my!" Mrs. Wentworth cried, jumping to her feet. "I've been so selfish! I never even thought to tell your father you're home! Don't move, I'll be right back. He'll be so happy."

Stunned, Jared and Suzanna could only stare after her. "Jared, what . . . ?"

"I don't know," he said, rising to his feet and running a hand through his hair. "She seems so normal, but . . . My God, she must have lost her mind."

His despair tore her heart, and she jumped up to comfort him, slipping her arms around his waist and laying her head on his chest. He hugged her fiercely. "I'm glad you're here," he whispered into her hair. "I don't think I could bear this without you."

They held each other for a few minutes, until they heard a disturbance in the hall, and his mother's voice saying, "Hurry, Jared's waiting."

"Jared?" a hoarse voice answered.

"Yes, he's come home."

Jared stiffened and jerked free of Suzanna's embrace. "My God," he said again, heading for the door.

Suzanna followed, careening into his back when he stopped abruptly in the doorway. Peering around him, she saw Mrs. Wentworth and an older man making their way slowly across the entrance hall.

The man was wearing a dressing gown over a dress shirt and trousers. His snow-white hair had been carefully combed. He had once been tall, but now his shoulders were stooped, his chest sunken, so he appeared only a few inches taller than Mrs. Wentworth, who held one of his arms. In his other hand he wielded a cane, and his steps were sure but cautious, as if he were not quite certain of his destination.

"Jared's come home?" he asked Mrs. Wentworth.

"Yes, there he is," she said, pointing to where Jared and Suzanna stood in the doorway. "Say hello to your son."

I'm dreaming, Suzanna thought. How else could she explain this. Beside her Jared gaped, too shocked even to react.

"Jared, aren't you going to say hello to your father?" Mrs. Wentworth said, her lovely face creasing into a concerned frown. "I know you quarreled before you left, but surely you don't still hold a grudge, not after all this time."

"I . . ." Plainly, Jared was speechless with disbelief.

Mr. and Mrs. Wentworth came relentlessly forward until they were face to face with Jared.

"Jared?" the old man said, his voice quavering.

"Yes, Father," Jared croaked. Suzanna slipped her arm around his waist, not surprised to feel him trembling.

The old man blinked, his eyes vacant and faraway. "Jared is my son, you know."

"Of course we know." Mrs. Wentworth laughed. "Jared, help me, please. Take his other arm."

Woodenly, Jared assisted his father into the parlor and onto the nearest chair. Suzanna stepped aside, feeling helpless and a little numb.

"Jared's come home to get married. This is his bride-to-be," Mrs. Wentworth explained, her tone the one Suzanna used when she explained difficult concepts to Andy. "Her name is Suzanna."

Mr. Wentworth looked up at where Suzanna hovered nearby. "Pretty girl," he said, nodding sagely.

Jared stood back, gazing at the man in the chair with wild-eyed amazement. "Mother, what—?"

"*Jared!*" a girl's voice cried from the hallway, and Suzanna looked up to see a lithe figure in an emerald-green riding habit charge into the room and straight into Jared's arms.

Her sparkling laughter broke the bizarre spell that had silenced them. "Jared, you're home! I thought Katie was teasing me! Oh, Jared, I can't believe it!" She rained kisses on his face until he put her forcefully away from him so he could see her.

"Ellie, you're a woman!" he told her in unabashed delight.

"Almost," she said, preening coyly. "I'll put my hair up in January." She flipped the long, chestnut braid dangling down her back and laughed up at him, smiling the way Jared smiled when he was truly happy. "Oh, Jared, I'm so mad at you for being gone so long! Whyever didn't you tell us where you were? Why didn't you write?"

"I . . ." Jared glanced at his parents who were looking on, his mother with smiling approval, his father with mild interest. "Because of what happened . . . I thought . . ."

He looked at Suzanna, his eyes pleading silently for help. "You must be Ellie," she said with forced brightness, resisting an urge to flee this strange situation.

The girl spun around, her shining eyes widening in surprise. "Who are you?"

"Jared's fiancée," Mrs. Wentworth said with obvious satisfaction. "We're going to have a wedding."

"A wedding!" Ellie cried. "How glorious. May I be a bridesmaid?"

"Uh . . . Of course," Suzanna said lamely.

"Oh, forgive me," Ellie said, swooping over to where Suzanna stood and taking her hands. "I'm Jared's sister, and I'm very pleased to meet you."

"I'm please to meet you, too," Suzanna said, acutely conscious of her accent, although the girl didn't seem to notice.

"You don't *look* pleased," Ellie accused her cheerfully. "You look overwhelmed, and I'm sure you are, but you'll get used to us. We're really harmless, aren't we, Jared?"

Jared's expression said he wasn't sure at all.

Everyone sat down, and for a few awkward minutes, Mrs. Wentworth made conversation, asking Suzanna where she was from and who her people were. While she responded to the embarrassing questions, she was aware of Jared sitting beside her on the sofa, tensely eyeing the decrepit shell of the man he thought he'd killed.

Katie came in with a tea tray and announced luncheon would be ready soon. Suzanna continued to answer Mrs. Wentworth's questions as best she could, giving an abbreviated version of her move to Kansas and her husband's death. "A few months later, I met Jared," she finished.

"And now that your mourning is over, you're going to get married. How romantic," Ellie declared. "Don't you think it's romantic, Father?"

Mr. Wentworth nodded gravely. "I'm tired," he said suddenly.

"Please excuse me while I take Father back to his room," Mrs. Wentworth said. "Ellie, refill everyone's cup."

As soon as they were gone, Jared turned to his sister. "Ellie, what the . . . ?"

Ellie's radiant smile vanished, and Suzanna realized she had been maintaining her ebullient high spirits only with great effort. "Oh, Jared, you thought you'd killed him, didn't you?" she asked bluntly.

"Of course! You know what happened. He fell and—"

"And Mother came in and screamed he was dead. Yes, I'll never forget it. I remember you telling me I'd be safe now, then you kissed me and left. But he wasn't dead, Jared."

She rose and hurried to the door, closing it softly.

Turning to face them, she explained, "We called Donald from the stable to help. We didn't know what to do, but Donald said he was still breathing, so we put him to bed and sent for Dr. Wilbur. He didn't think Father would live, but he did."

For a long minute no one spoke. At last Jared said, "Is he like this all the time?"

"Yes, he's simpleminded, although Mother refuses to acknowledge it. She pretends he's perfectly normal and that he's always been this sweet, kindly man. Jared, it's like she doesn't remember anything of what happened before he fell."

"Doesn't she remember I pushed him?" Jared asked incredulously.

Ellie shrugged. "She always calls it 'the accident.' She told people you left because you had a quarrel with Father. Everyone thinks he had a stroke from the shock."

"My God!"

Ellie rushed to him, falling on her knees before him. "If only you'd written to us, we could have told you! I prayed every day you'd come back and find out."

Suzanna could hardly believe it. This was everything she'd hoped for and more. The man she loved wasn't a murderer, wasn't wanted by the law. All the dreams she'd cherished could now come true. "Jared?" She laid a hand on his arm. "Do you know what this means?"

He nodded grimly. "It means I've wasted five years of my life."

He was right, of course, and nothing she could say could call them back. "But we have a future now," she pointed out. "You're a free man."

"And you're home," Ellie added. "And you're rich! Booth has been managing the farm since . . . since you left, and he's done a marvelous job."

"Booth?" Jared asked. "How did he . . . ?"

"I know you two never got along," Ellie said, "but he was absolutely wonderful to Mother and me when Father was so ill. He's really the only male relative we have left, so naturally we turned to him. He took care of everything, but now that you're back . . . Oh, Jared, I'm so glad!"

Impulsively, she leaned over and kissed his cheek, making him smile, but his frown quickly returned.

"Did you know Booth found me in Dodge City?"

"No! He said the woman who wrote the letter wanted money to help locate you and he thought she was a fake. He said he'd asked around the city, but no one had ever heard of you or Mrs. Prentice."

"He lied," Jared said, but Suzanna quickly jumped to Booth's defense.

"I asked him not to tell anyone where Jared was, not even his family. I thought . . . we both thought he was wanted for murder."

"But Booth knew I wasn't," Jared pointed out. "Why didn't he tell me Father was still alive?"

"You didn't give him much chance to say anything at all," Suzanna reminded him.

"He could have told you, then."

"Jared, you act like you think Booth did something wrong," Ellie said. "I'm sure there's some logical explanation."

"Of course there is," Suzanna said. "Is Booth here? We can ask him."

"He's away, delivering some horses, but we expect him back tonight." Ellie grinned mischievously. "Won't he be surprised to see you?"

At lunch, Mrs. Wentworth questioned Jared closely about his life for the last five years, exhibiting normal motherly interest in, and disapproval of, his activities. Yet she insisted on characterizing Jared's absence as the selfish whim of a spoiled schoolboy. Her inability to admit the truth lent an air of unreality to the entire meal.

Afterwards, Ellie got to meet Andy, an event that delighted them both.

"When your mother and Jared get married, I'll be your aunt," Ellie explained to the boy, "so you must call me Aunt Ellie."

"You don't look like an ant."

"I don't? What do aunts look like?"

Andy considered for a moment. "Well, some are black and some are red, but they're all real small and crawl around on the ground, and . . ."

Ellie dissolved into laughter while Jared and Suzanna managed to keep their composure.

"Well, they do," Andy defended himself, and Ellie proceeded to explain about the other kind of aunt.

Ever the perfect hostess, Mrs. Wentworth assigned her guests rooms upstairs. Jared got his old room, while Suzanna received a guest room with a large dressing area where Andy could sleep. To Suzanna's chagrin, Ellie went upstairs to help her settle in while Jared took Andy to the stables to find out how Pistol was doing.

"I really don't have very much to unpack," Suzanna said, hoping to discourage Ellie from accompanying her. She certainly didn't want the girl to see the meager contents of her trunk.

"Katie will do the unpacking," Ellie said, linking her arm through Suzanna's as they climbed the imposing staircase. "I just want to visit with you. We're going to be sisters, after all."

Suzanna wished Andy had come along as a distraction. The last thing she wanted was for Ellie to find out more about her. The less any of the Wentworths knew about her past, the better.

The room Suzanna had been assigned would have held her entire Dodge City house with space left over. The curtains and bedspread were pale blue, complementing the delft tiles adorning the fireplace. In one corner, an oriental screen concealed a hip bath, and the opposite corner held a settee where a lady could recline while reading a novel. The dressing area contained a narrow bed where a maid would ordinarily sleep. It would be perfect for Andy. Suzanna only wished Jared would be sharing the room with them, but of course propriety forbade such a thing.

By the time Ellie had finished showing Suzanna around, Katie had already emptied Suzanna's trunk and hung her few garments in the wardrobe. As Suzanna had feared, Ellie's natural curiosity demanded she examine the garments. Seeing Ellie's shocked reaction, she winced.

But Ellie was a well-bred young lady, and she had no intention of offending her beloved brother's fiancée. "You were smart not to bring too many things with you," she said cheerfully. "It's probably impossible to get the latest styles in Dodge City anyway, and now you'll have an excuse to get a whole new wardrobe."

"I don't think—"

"Don't bother to protest. Mother will insist, and since she likes nothing better than ordering new clothes, you'll actually be doing her a kindness."

Suzanna wondered vaguely how far her savings would go in purchasing the type of clothing she would need as Jared's betrothed. "I suppose I'll have to meet Jared's old friends," she murmured, thinking she couldn't possibly shame him by wearing her Kansas calicoes.

"Meet? My dear girl, Mother will probably hold a ball in your honor to introduce you to society, and then everyone else will hold one to make hers look shabby, and . . . Well, you'll need a lot of new clothes."

Suzanna forced a smile, feeling slightly sick. "I guess *you'll* enjoy the parties," she said to change the subject. "You must have lots of beaux."

"Not yet. I'm too young, but I don't care about beaux."

"You will in another year or two," Suzanna predicted.

"No," she said, flouncing down onto the bed. "I'll just marry Booth."

"Marry Booth?" Suzanna laughed, certain Ellie was teasing. "Does Booth know about this?"

"Of course," she said in perfect seriousness. "He asked me a long time ago."

"He asked you to marry him?"

"Yes, I've been in love with him for years, and one day I wrote him a love letter. It was a silly thing to do, but I was just a child. I tried to get the letter back before it was too late, but Booth had already seen it. I expected him to laugh, but he didn't. He said he loved me, too, and he hoped I'd still love him when I got old enough to pick a husband. I promised I would, so we decided we would be secretly engaged. Oh!'' she cried as if suddenly realizing what she had revealed. ''You won't tell Mother, will you? She'll approve, of course, but I wanted it to be a surprise, and if you tell her now, she won't believe I'm serious.''

''Ellie,'' Suzanna said gently, sitting down beside Ellie on the bed. ''Are you sure Booth really meant what he said? I mean, you're awfully young. Perhaps he was teasing you—''

''He wasn't teasing!'' Ellie insisted.

''Or perhaps he was just pretending so he wouldn't hurt your pride,'' Suzanna suggested, recalling how flirtatious Booth had been with her in Dodge. Ellie must have misunderstood his attentions. ''He may think you'll grow out of your infatuation with him.''

Ellie grinned smugly. ''He gave me a ring.''

''A ring?'' None of this made any sense. Why would a grown man be interested in a fifteen-year-old girl? A very unpleasant possibility occurred to Suzanna as she watched Ellie pull a long chain from inside her bodice. On the end of the chain was a small gold ring set with a red stone.

''It's a garnet, my birthstone,'' Ellie confided, holding the ring up for Suzanna's approval.

''It's lovely,'' she said, her throat tight. ''Uh, Ellie, has Booth ever . . . ?''

''Ever what?''

Her eyes were so like Jared's, only completely innocent. Suzanna had to swallow before she could speak. ''Has he ever . . . uh, kissed you?''

Ellie blushed with maidenly modesty and quickly stuffed the ring and its chain back into her collar. ''Once,'' she admitted shyly. ''He said it was to seal our engagement. It was so romantic! We were in the rose garden, in the gazebo, and his lips felt like two rose petals.''

Ellie sighed rapturously, while Suzanna's shoulders sagged with relief. Her worst fears for Ellie's virtue were groundless, but she still couldn't understand why a man like Booth Wentworth would encourage a child to believe she was engaged to him. If he was trying to spare her pride, he had gone much too far. Suzanna knew she should do something, but what?

With a pang, she thought of Dora. Dora would have known exactly how to handle the situation and wouldn't have hesitated a moment in doing what must be done.

"Suzanna, is something wrong? Your face went white!"

"Oh, no," she replied, covering her cheeks self-consciously. "I guess I'm just tired from the trip. Maybe I should rest a little before supper."

"You probably should, but first you have to come to my room for a minute."

"Why?"

"So you can pick out a dress to wear tonight. All your things are creased from traveling," she said diplomatically. "I've got dozens of dresses I never wear, and you're welcome to borrow as many as you need. We're about the same size."

This was true. Ellie was tall for her age, and Suzanna's delicate curves closely resembled those of a young girl. "Unfortunately, we are," Suzanna said with a disparaging glance at her small bosom.

Ellie laughed and bounced off the bed, taking Suzanna's hand and pulling her along. "I have this beautiful blue gown that looks horrible on me, but it'll match your eyes perfectly."

Ellie was right, and in short order Suzanna had 'borrowed' enough dresses to suffice until a dressmaker could be summoned to provide her with an appropriate trousseau. To Suzanna's dismay, a maid appeared later in the afternoon to help her dress, and Suzanna had to admit she had no experience with servants. The girl immediately put her at ease and helped her into her borrowed finery and arranged her hair in flattering upsweep.

Suzanna hardly recognized the woman staring back at her from the mirror. Ellie's gown was robin's-egg blue, cut modestly but designed to accentuate feminine curves. Suzanna's more womanly figure filled it out beautifully. The fine French cambric draped into a neat bustle and row after row of ruffles that made Suzanna loath to sit and crush them.

"Mama, you look pretty," Andy said, awestruck by her unusual appearance. He had been scrubbed by another maid and helped into his Sunday suit in preparation for the meal. "Are we going to a party?"

"No, dear, but in such a fine house, people get dressed up for supper."

"Why?"

Suzanna smiled. "For the same reason the house is so big."

Andy considered this a moment before understanding dawned. "Oh, I know! Just because!"

"Exactly. Now, shall we go downstairs?"

Jared had told her to come to the back parlor, a room less formal than the one where they had met his family. Armed with the maid's directions, she and Andy made their way down the long stairway.

Clad in Ellie's dress, Suzanna felt a little less uncomfortable, but she wondered if she could ever possibly feel at home with crystal chandeliers and servants shuffling in and out and furniture she was afraid to touch.

She and Andy had just reached the landing of the stairs and started down toward the main hallway when the front door opened and Booth Covington entered. He was wearing riding clothes and tall, dusty boots. Obviously, he had just returned from his trip. He didn't see them until Andy said, "There's that man who came to our house."

Booth looked up, but Suzanna couldn't quite make out his expression beneath the brim of his hat. She wondered if he'd even recognize her, but after a moment he said, "Suzanna?"

Something in his tone struck her as strange, but then he swept off his hat, and she saw he was smiling up at her.

"Good heavens, it really is you! What on earth . . . ?"

"Booth, you're home," Ellie cried, emerging from somewhere behind the stairway. She hurried to Booth, and Suzanna held her breath until she saw how he would greet the girl.

"Not a moment too soon, either," Booth said, giving Ellie his cheek for a chaste kiss that allowed Suzanna to breathe again. "I see we have company."

Ellie glanced up to see Suzanna and Andy on the stairs. "Oh, you ruined everything! I wanted it to be a surprise. Jared is here. He came home!"

Booth smiled, but Suzanna noticed his expression remained guarded. "And he didn't come alone. Suzanna, how delightful to see you again."

Suzanna and Andy continued down the stairs. "I'm happy to see you, too," she replied. "This must be quite a shock."

"It certainly is. I never thought . . . You were so certain Jared wouldn't want to come home. What changed his mind?"

"Your visit," Jared said, emerging from the depths of the hall. He was dressed as Suzanna had seen him so often before in the Comique, his dark suit and string tie immaculate. "Seeing you again made me homesick."

Booth laughed, but it sounded forced. "You can't be serious."

"No, I'm not," Jared assured him coldly. "If I were being serious, I'd ask you why you didn't tell me my father is still alive."

Chapter 12

Jared watched Booth's reaction carefully, using all the powers of observation he had honed during his years as a gambler.

Shocked surprise and perhaps a touch of fear flickered across his face before he could mask his reactions. He was good, Jared thought, but not good enough.

"Jared," Booth said, glancing at Ellie, then at Suzanna and Andy, "I don't think this is the time or the place to discuss this."

"Perhaps you'd like to retire to the library then."

Booth nodded, quickly assuming his natural charm. "Ladies, if you will excuse us," he said with a smile, gesturing for Jared to precede him. Jared felt uncomfortable turning his back on his cousin, but he strode into the library while Booth followed and closed the door.

Booth didn't wait to be questioned. "Jared," he began, lifting his hands helplessly, "Suzanna asked me not to tell anyone where you were, so naturally I didn't say anything to your mother or Ellie. What could I tell them, in any case? That you were working as a gambler in a saloon in infamous Dodge City? That you were living in sin with a woman who was not your wife, a woman you'd met in a dance hall?"

"Leave Suzanna out of this," Jared snapped. "All I want to know is why you didn't tell me about my father. You knew I'd left home because I thought I'd killed him—''

"*What?* I most certainly didn't know any such thing!''

"Why else would I have run away?'' Jared challenged.

Booth shrugged. "Everyone knew how you and your father quarreled. Your mother said the two of you had a terrible row and you left. Your father had a stroke, and—''

"Surely you didn't believe that fairy tale!''

"I believed what your mother told me,'' Booth insisted.

Jared sighed in exasperation. "You must have seen him. I practically crushed his skull!''

"His head was bandaged, of course, but I thought . . . Good God, I had no idea, and of course Aunt Liv always said . . . Jared, I'm so sorry! If I'd known, I would have told you at once. All these years . . .'' He shook his head as if unable to find words to express his emotions.

Jared drew a deep breath as he waited for his fury to subside. How frustrating to discover Booth was innocent. For a while there, he'd actually relished the thought of having someone on whom to vent the rage he'd been harboring all afternoon. The realization that he had wasted five years of his life and caused his family incalculable pain for no reason infuriated him. Unfortunately, he'd have to deal with the anger in some other way than by taking it out on his cousin.

"I beg your pardon, Booth,'' he said when he was in control of himself again. "I had no idea how thoroughly my mother had deceived everyone about what really happened.''

"I hope you aren't angry with her,'' Booth said with some concern.

"Of course not. She did what she thought was best. No one can fault her for protecting her family the only way she could.''

Booth laid a comforting hand on Jared's shoulder. "It must be a shock to you. I can't even conceive of what you must have gone through, thinking your father was dead and . . ." He shook his head again. "But look on the bright side. I see Suzanna is still with you, and if you hadn't left here, you never would have met her, now would you?"

"No, I wouldn't have," he conceded.

"What are your plans?" Booth asked heartily, withdrawing his hand.

"I really hadn't made any since I expected to be in jail by now. I know you've been running the farm—"

"Don't let that influence your decision!" Booth exclaimed. "This is your home, after all. I've only been filling in. Surely Aunt Lavinia will expect you to take your rightful place as heir apparent."

Jared couldn't help returning Booth's smile. He never would have expected his cousin to take this so well. "We'll keep you on as manager, of course."

"Don't be ridiculous! You can run the place without my help."

He was right, but good manners forbade Jared from saying so. "But what would you do?"

"I'll think of something," he said with a grin. "Like you, I haven't had much chance to make plans, but I'm sure I'll find a position without too much trouble. This is horse country, and I'm an expert, almost as good as you."

Jared frowned, feeling the first twinges of guilt over the upheavals his return would cause. Still, he couldn't help thinking how happy and relieved he was to be able to step back into the life he'd been born to. Having Suzanna with him made it perfect.

"We're keeping the ladies waiting," Booth reminded him, "and I still have to wash off the travel dirt before I'm fit to sit at Aunt Lavinia's table. Why don't you tell them to start without me, and I'll join you as soon as I'm decent?"

Jared nodded, but before Booth could leave, he stuck out his hand. "Thank you, Booth."

Booth shook his hand firmly but frowned in confusion. "For what?"

"For taking care of them for me."

Booth shrugged off Jared's gratitude. "You would have done the same."

Suzanna looked apprehensively around the ornate parlor—which, in spite of what Jared had said, was not noticeably less formal than the front parlor. Glancing at Andy, she wondered how much longer he would sit still. He'd been kicking his heels restlessly for some minutes, and now he shifted on the brocade sofa. Suzanna tensed to catch him before he could bolt and knock over one of the priceless treasures displayed on every available tabletop, but he contented himself with giving her a disgruntled frown.

"I'm hungry," he announced for at least the tenth time.

Suzanna shushed him nervously, terrified he would do or say something inappropriate. Her apprehension increased as she realized she had no idea what Mrs. Wentworth would consider inappropriate.

"I'm so sorry, Suzanna," Mrs. Wentworth said kindly. "I should have remembered. We used to feed the little ones earlier, but it's been so long since we've had any little ones to think about, I quite forgot."

"I think *everyone* should eat earlier," Andy said, making Ellie giggle.

Suzanna cringed, but Mrs. Wentworth graciously ignored the remark. "I can't imagine what was so important that Jared and Booth had to keep us waiting."

At that moment Jared appeared in the doorway, smiling. "Please accept my apologies, Mother. Booth said to tell you to eat without him. He'll join us as soon as he's changed his clothes."

Mrs. Wentworth glanced at Andy. "I suppose we should wait, but since we have Andy to think of, we'll go ahead into the dining room." She smiled down at the boy. "Andy, you may take my arm."

"Where should I take it?"

This time Ellie stifled her giggle as Mrs. Wentworth instructed Andy on the proper method of escorting a lady into dinner.

Jared watched in fond amusement for a moment before turning to Suzanna. What he saw took his breath. Out in the hallway, he'd barely even noticed her, as he'd been concentrating on Booth's reaction.

"Suzanna, you look . . . lovely," he said, unable to think of a word to adequately describe her. Suddenly she really was the fine lady he'd dreamed of making her when he'd watched her dancing in the Comique. Love swelled his heart, tightening his chest.

Suzanna rose, her hands fluttering uncertainly over the exquisite dress. He resisted the almost overwhelming urge to take her in his arms. For a moment he resented his family's presence and longed to be back in that little house in Dodge City. But only for a moment. No, he reminded himself, Suzanna belonged here, surrounded by luxury. Soon enough they'd be married, and then they'd have all the time in the world for doing what he wished he could do right this minute.

"Ellie loaned me the dress," she explained.

"You do wonderful things for it," he said, admiring the way it hugged the curves he knew so well. For a few blissful seconds, he fantasized about running his hands over those curves. Desire scorched through him, and he wondered how in the world he would manage to stay in his own bedroom tonight.

"Jared, what a scandalous thing to say," Ellie scolded cheerfully, but Jared hardly heard her. He was concentrating on the way Suzanna's golden hair brushed her satiny cheek and the way her azure eyes shone when she looked up at him. Still, she didn't smile, and he realized she must be worried about his conversation with Booth.

"Everything's fine," he whispered. "I'll explain later."

"No secrets," Ellie said, moving closer. "Are you going to take us into dinner or not?"

"My pleasure," Jared said, offering each of them an arm. "I can't remember ever escorting two lovelier ladies."

"Probably because you never have," Ellie replied, grinning smugly. "What did you and Booth talk about?"

"Business," he said. "Nothing you need to worry about."

Ellie made a face at him. "Booth will tell me later. He tells me everything."

"Does he?" Jared asked perfunctorily, returning his gaze to Suzanna. How natural she looked in her finery, moving gracefully through his home as if she had been born to the gentry. This was the kind of life he'd wanted to give her. Here no rough man would ever lust after her, no one would ever fire a gun in her presence. At Rosewood no unpleasantness would ever touch her again. She'd be so happy when he told her they would be staying here permanently.

Suzanna looked up at Jared and tried to return his smile. She wanted to believe that he and Booth had settled their differences. Jared certainly looked happy enough. After supper she would have to get him alone so she could find out for sure.

Then they entered the dining room, and every other thought fled from her mind. The table was set with more cutlery than Suzanna had ever imagined existed. At each place were more dishes than Suzanna used to feed Jared, Andy, and herself an entire meal. What on earth were they all for?

Jared seated her at his mother's right, the place of honor. Andy took the seat beside her, and Jared claimed the chair at the end of the table opposite his mother. Ellie sat across from Suzanna and an empty chair beside her awaited Booth's arrival.

Suzanna stared at the dishes in front of her in panic, wondering how in the world she would know what to do herself, much less help Andy. Beside her, Mrs. Wentworth rang a small bell, and the maid brought in the first course: oysters on the half shell.

"These are fresh from the Chesapeake Bay," Mrs. Wentworth informed her.

"I hate oysters," Andy informed everyone.

Suzanna blushed, but Mrs. Wentworth only looked surprised. "You have oysters out West?"

"Yes, they're brought in daily on the train, 'fresh from the Chesapeake Bay,' " Jared explained after instructing the maid to bring Andy some bread and butter. "Dodge City is quite civilized. Like everyone else, we have to settled for tinned oysters out of season, but we get them fresh when they're available."

At least Suzanna knew how to eat seafood, but the thought of eating made her feel sick. Her stomach still hadn't recovered from the poor fare they had encountered on their journey east, and she hoped she'd be able to choke down enough of her food to appear polite. To her right, Andy gobbled his bread and butter. Suzanna prayed silently that she would make it through the meal without disgracing herself or Jared.

The next course looked and tasted like potato soup, but it was stone cold. Suzanna looked up in alarm, thinking how furious Mrs. Wentworth would be with her servants, but everyone else ate theirs as if nothing in the world were wrong. Perhaps hers was the only bowl that had cooled, but then Andy said, "My soup is cold."

Jared coughed into his napkin, and Mrs. Wentworth smiled indulgently. "It's supposed to be cold, dear. It's French."

Suzanna silently thanked God she hadn't said anything and concentrated on making sure Andy didn't spill his soup and getting her own to her lips without soiling Ellie's gown.

By the time the maid had set down something that

looked like fish in front of each of them, Booth had joined the party. He made his apologies to his aunt and took his seat, quickly catching up with the rest of them.

"Suzanna and Jared are going to be married," Ellie informed him.

He glanced pointedly at Jared. "I certainly hope so," he said. Jared frowned, and Suzanna felt the heat rushing to her cheeks, but Booth's guileless smile soothed the sting. Certainly Mrs. Wentworth and Ellie saw nothing insulting in his remark.

"Suzanna said I can be a bridesmaid," Ellie continued, oblivious to the undercurrents. "We're going to have the wedding in the front parlor. Isn't it romantic?"

"Terribly," he agreed with an indulgent smile.

Suzanna forgot her own embarrassment and watched the exchange carefully, relieved to see Booth treated the girl exactly the way Jared did, as if she were his adored younger sister. She was sure now that Ellie had somehow misunderstood Booth's attentions. She'd have to speak to Booth and see if he couldn't undo the damage somehow without breaking poor Ellie's heart.

Ellie turned to Suzanna. "You never told me how you and Jared met."

Suzanna almost choked, but Booth made up for his earlier remark by coming immediately to her rescue. "Didn't you tell me you'd met at a dance?"

"Yes, it was a dance," she replied, gratefully grasping at this straw.

"Jared asked you to dance?" Ellie prompted when Suzanna did not continue.

"Yes, I . . ." Suzanna winced inwardly at the memory. This time Jared assisted her.

"I asked her to dance and promptly offended her. She didn't speak to me for weeks."

"Jared!" his mother exclaimed, shocked.

"He didn't offend me too much," Suzanna hastily assured her. "And it wasn't weeks, only a few days."

"It seemed like weeks," Jared said gallantly. The

glitter in his dark eyes made her remember so much more.

"Don't forget how you met me," Andy reminded him. Jared gave them a condensed version of Andy's rescue, then skillfully led the conversation to the safer topic of horses.

Suzanna understood little of the discussion, which was just as well since she had to give all her attention to pretending to eat the food that kept appearing before her. By the time the ladies retired to the parlor so the men could enjoy their cigars, Suzanna was a nervous wreck. How on earth would she ever adjust? She simply didn't belong here, and soon everyone would begin to notice. If anyone ever found out about her past, she would disgrace Jared before his family and friends, and he would be sorry he had ever brought her.

Even though she reminded herself of Jared's love, she couldn't seem to shake the doubts that multiplied with every minute she spent in this house. She longed to speak to Jared. They had so many things to discuss, and she needed reassurance that he still loved her. Fortunately, between keeping Andy from causing a disaster in the parlor and trying to participate in the conversation between Ellie and her mother, Suzanna had little opportunity to dwell on her anxiety.

At last Jared and Booth joined them, but by then Andy was exhausted.

"I think I'd better take Andy upstairs now," she said. "Tell everyone good night," she told her son.

When Andy had made the rounds, giving Ellie and her mother a kiss and clamoring for a hug from Jared, Suzanna led him to the door.

"Suzanna," Jared called, stopping her. "You're probably tired, too. There's no need for you to come back down after you've got Andy settled in."

"I . . . all right," she replied in dismay. Didn't he realize they needed to talk? Or did he simply want to get rid of her before she embarrassed him any more?

These questions haunted her as she got Andy tucked in and allowed a maid to help her undress and prepare for bed herself. Jared had been right, of course. The day had been one of the most trying of her life, and her body yearned for sleep. Her mind had other plans, however, and she found her eyes wouldn't close as she reviewed everything that had happened since they'd arrived at Rosewood.

She'd been lying awake quite a while when she heard a noise outside the door leading to the veranda. At first she imagined it was just the normal creaking of the house, but then the latch clicked and the door began to open.

Suzanna sat up, clutching the covers to her breast. "Who's there?"

"Now just who else would be sneaking into your bedroom, Mrs. Prentice?" Jared inquired as he slipped inside and closed the door behind him.

He was nothing more than a shadow in the darkened room, but Suzanna held out her arms and called his name joyfully. He hurried to the bed, sinking down beside her and drawing her to him in one motion. Even though they'd shared a bed just the night before, Suzanna felt as if they'd been separated for weeks, and she clung to him, savoring the security his nearness offered.

He moaned her name and buried his face in the curve of her neck. "Mmmm, did I tell you how beautiful you looked tonight?"

"I think you mentioned it," she replied against the warm spot just under his ear.

"I wanted to tear that dress right off your luscious body and make mad, passionate love to you right there in front of God and everybody."

"Jared! What a scandalous thing to say," she laughed, quoting Ellie.

"Isn't it?" he inquired. "That's why we'd better get ourselves married as soon as possible. This sneaking into your room is fun, but I certainly wouldn't want to get caught doing it. I don't want anyone to have reason to think badly of you."

Suzanna suspected his family already thought badly of her. Booth certainly did, and for good reason. She clung to Jared more tightly, needing the reassurance only his love could give her. "What did you and Booth talk about before dinner?"

Jared lifted his face from her neck and sighed wearily. "I'd been entertaining the notion that Booth had deliberately not told me my father was still alive, but it seems he'd always believed my mother's story about the stroke. He had no idea I'd caused my father's 'accident.' "

"He didn't?" Suzanna frowned. For some reason she, too, had thought he knew the truth.

"No, he didn't, and I don't want to talk about Booth any more." Jared's mouth closed over hers, effectively distracting her from thoughts of his cousin. Already his hands were moving over her, seeking out the sensitive places he knew so well.

"Is Andy asleep?" he asked against her lips.

She nodded, forgetting all the things they needed to talk about, and let him press her back against the pillows. She quickly discovered he'd discarded his suit coat and vest before coming to her, and she made short work of his shirt buttons. No sooner had her seeking hands bared his chest than he began to tug her nightdress over her head. Soon they lay flesh to flesh, and in the dark, the only differences between them that mattered were the ones that enabled them to join in the age-old quest for union.

Suzanna's need flared quickly, leaving her no patience with teasing caresses. At her urging, Jared filled her with his strength, sending shock waves of pleasure roaring through her. She bit back the moan struggling in her throat and clutched his slick, satiny back. Her blood heated, searing her as it raced through her body. She wrapped her arms and legs around him in a passionate attempt to make them one. Breathing his name, she strove for each breath, straining with every ounce of her strength for the unattainable prize.

He thrust into her, deeper and deeper, as if he would reach her heart or perhaps her very soul. Groaning out his need, he vowed his love for her in disjointed phrases she only half-understood. But her body understood and replied, enveloping him in the love for which no words existed.

They ended fiercely and suddenly, exploding in a shower of sparks and ecstasy that wrenched his name from her lips and sent her whirling into mindless oblivion. Afterwards, they clung to each other, breath rasping, loath to break the sweet bond between them. When Jared would have pulled away, Suzanna held him close, acutely aware again that a woman like her had no real claim to him and fearing he might have also realized it.

He chuckled at her possessiveness. "I'll squash you," he warned, and managed to shift them both until she lay on top of him. "There, now we can talk."

Fear sent a chill down her spine, and she wished she could see his expression in the dark. "What do you want to talk about?" she asked warily.

He laughed outright at her question. "Are you serious? We have a dozen things to talk about. My father, for one, and our future, of course. That should keep us busy for a while."

Suzanna swallowed the lump forming in her throat. "What about our future?"

"Well, the fact that we have one would be a good place to start. I've been so obsessed with the thought that I was a murderer, I never really let myself see things from your perspective. I've just begun to understand how abominably I've treated you, taking your love and refusing to give you anything in return. I can't change what's past, but I'm going to spend the rest of my life making it up to you, if you'll let me. Suzanna, will you marry me?"

How often had she prayed to hear these words? Considering they were lying naked in her bed, she should have been relieved at the proposal, but the things she had learned this day robbed her of the joy she should have felt. "Jared, I'm not . . . you shouldn't . . ."

"I shouldn't what?" he prompted when she hesitated.

"I don't belong here," she blurted.

"What do you mean? Of course you do—"

"No, I don't! Jared, I told you all about myself, but maybe you didn't understand. I'm not like you. The house I grew up in had two rooms for six people. When I married Andrew, we lived in a one-room shack with a dirt floor, and when we moved to Kansas, we lived in a hole in the ground. I've never even been inside a house like this before and—"

"Suzanna, none of that matters!" he insisted, but she knew he was wrong.

"It matters a lot. Tonight at dinner, I didn't know the soup was supposed to be cold or that you served two different meats or even which fork to use. There must be a hundred things I don't know. Jared, I'll make a fool of myself and disgrace you and your family and—"

"None of that matters to me! None of that matters at all!" He flipped them over so he was lying above her. "For God's sake, you can *learn* which fork to use."

"I . . ." How could she explain that the differences between them went far deeper than simple social graces? "Jared, what if your mother finds out how we really met? What if Ellie finds out I worked in a dance hall?"

"You never did anything to be ashamed of."

"But your family might think I did, and your friends . . . Jared, you'd be a laughingstock! And even if no one ever finds out I worked at the Comique, I can't change who I am. Every time I open my mouth, people will know I'm poor white trash."

The words seemed to hang there between them. In

the silence, Suzanna could hear nothing but her own pounding heart. Jared didn't speak, didn't move, didn't even breathe for what seemed an eternity. For one horrible minute she thought she'd actually convinced him they didn't belong together.

At last he said, "Suzanna, do you love me?"

"Yes! You know I do!" she exclaimed, blinking at tears.

"I thought you wanted to marry me."

"I do, but—"

"But nothing. Suzanna, I need you. Without you, I would never have had the courage to come back here, and when I think of the rest of my life . . . I can't face the thought of living without you. It doesn't matter what other people say or think or do, as long as you're with me, and I want you with me for the rest of my life."

Suzanna strained to see his face in the darkness, but she didn't need to see him to feel his pain because she felt the same anguish at the thought of a future without Jared. Maybe he was right. Maybe none of this really mattered so long as they were together. But . . . "Where would we live?"

"Right here," he told her happily, sensing her capitulation. "This is the kind of life I've wanted to give you ever since the day I woke up in your bed with a hole in my shoulder. Suzanna, you'll never have to worry about supporting yourself and Andy again. I'll give you everything you could possibly want, and nothing bad will ever happen to you. Please, Suzanna, let me take care of you. Be my wife."

"Jared," she protested, wishing she could find the words to tell him how living in this house made her feel. How could she ask him to leave his home, though, when he'd only just regained it? She couldn't, of course, and in any case, he wasn't going to give her the chance.

"Really, Suzanna," he said with mock gravity, running his palm over her bare hip. "Most women in your position would be *grateful* for a proposal of marriage. You're thoroughly compromised, you know."

"Don't tease me," she warned.

"I'm not teasing," he replied solemnly, easing his knee up to part her thighs. "If I have to, I'll call for help, and when everyone finds us in flagrante delicto, you'll have no choice but to accept my proposal. Shall I shout?" He drew a breath, and she clamped a hand over his mouth.

"Jared! This isn't funny."

"Not funny?" he echoed in feigned outrage when she removed her hand. "I've just robbed you of your virtue, and you're refusing to marry me because you have poor table manners. Some people would find that hilarious."

"That's not the reason, and you know it!"

"No, I don't," he said more seriously. "Suzanna, this has been a difficult day for you, and you're probably feeling pretty overwhelmed. I certainly am! This morning I thought I was a murderer with no home and no future, and now . . . My darling, we can have a life together. We can make a home for Andy. We can—"

"I'll never be able to give you children," she reminded him.

"I've already told you I don't care. You're all I want, and no man could want a better son than Andy. I'll adopt him, and someday Rosewood will be his."

Suzanna couldn't even imagine such a thing, especially if it meant she would be living the rest of her life here. "Then you're planning to stay here for good?" she asked tentatively.

"Where else would we go? This is my heritage, but without you, it doesn't mean a thing. Say you'll marry me, Suzanna."

She really had no choice. "I . . . of course I will, silly," she replied, trying for lightness and hoping her voice did not betray her doubts.

"At last," he breathed on a gusty sigh. "You can be awfully stubborn, Mrs. Prentice."

"Are you complaining?"

"No, because if you weren't stubborn, we wouldn't be here right now. You would have let me walk out of your life, I never would have told you about my family, you wouldn't have told Dora, and she never would have written to my mother."

Hot tears sprang to Suzanna's eyes at the mention of Dora's name. "We owe her so much."

Sharing her grief, Jared pulled her close. "I never even thanked her."

"You forgave her, which meant a lot more to her. I have to believe she knows how much she helped us."

"I hope you're right."

They lay together in silence for several minutes. At last Suzanna said, "Jared, I'm so happy your father is still alive."

"I still can't quite believe it, and when I think about all those years I wasted running and hiding—"

"Don't," she urged, laying a hand on his cheek.

"You're right, I shouldn't complain. As Booth reminded me this evening, if I hadn't been on the run, I would never have met you."

"No," she said with a pang. "You would have married the daughter of some wealthy neighbor—"

"And died of boredom before I was thirty. Suzanna, I don't want some neighbor's daughter. I want *you*. Now, not another word about it. And you're going to have to convince my family you're eager to marry me, too, because we can't delay the wedding until my mother has a whole new wardrobe made for you."

"Why not?"

"I told you, I want you in my bed, and I can't be seen sneaking into your room. I hope you find the prospect of sleeping alone as distasteful as I do."

"I do," she assured him.

"Then you'll have to convince my mother you simply can't wait. We'll have a quiet ceremony right away, then Mother can plan a reception for us later. You'll get to meet everyone in the county."

Suzanna nodded against his shoulder, glad he couldn't see the dread in her eyes.

They snuggled for a few more minutes while Suzanna reassured herself by recalling all of Jared's protestations of love. She should have known he'd never take no for an answer in any case. Imagine threatening to call for help and . . . "Jared?"

"Mmmm?"

"What's 'fragrant del . . .'? You know, what you said?"

She felt his grin against her cheek. "It's a little hard to explain," he said as his hand closed over her breast. "Maybe I'd better show you."

At first the distant screams didn't register. In Dodge Suzanna had often heard screams in the night. She snuggled closer to Jared, but the screams grew louder.

"Mrs. Wentworth! Mrs. Wentworth!"

Beside her Jared started awake, jarring her to full consciousness. She looked around, suddenly remembering where she was.

"What the . . . ?" Jared muttered, throwing back the bedclothes and reaching for his pants. Suzanna grabbed her nightdress from where Jared had tossed it on the floor the night before and pulled it over her head.

"Mama?" Andy called from the other room.

"I'm here," she replied, sliding off the bed and hurrying to him. The voice came closer as the person screaming for Jared's mother came up the stairs to the second floor.

"What's the matter?" Andy asked when Suzanna opened the door to the dressing room. He was sitting up in his bed, knuckling the sleep from his eyes.

"I don't know, sweetheart." She reached for him, lifting him onto her hip. By the time she turned back to the other room, Jared was almost dressed. He buttoned his shirt as he stepped, sockless, into his shoes and headed for the door.

He flung it open. "What's going on?" he asked of whoever was in the hallway.

"Mr. Wentworth is dead!"

Mrs. Wentworth lifted a soggy handkerchief and dabbed at her reddened eyes. "It was like he was waiting for you to come home, Jared, just hanging on until he saw his son again."

Jared nodded, automatically patting her hand. They were seated on a sofa in the pack parlor, waiting for the doctor to give them his report.

Suzanna and Ellie sat on the sofa opposite them. Katie had taken Andy away, promising to keep him occupied during the crisis. Left with nothing to do, Suzanna would have comforted Ellie, but the girl didn't seem to need it. Instead, she watched Ellie watching Booth, who paced restlessly back and forth in front of the French doors leading out onto the lawn.

"I wish you could have known him before the accident, Suzanna," Mrs. Wentworth was saying. "He was so vibrant and full of life."

Not exactly the description Suzanna had heard from Jared, but she had already realized Mrs. Wentworth's memories were less than accurate.

"I had no idea he was ill," Mrs. Wentworth went on. "He seemed fine yesterday, don't you think?"

Jared nodded, patting her hand again. Suzanna's heart ached for him. He'd barely had time to get used to his father being alive and now he was comforting his mother in her widowhood. Her own head was spinning, and she'd never seen any of these people before yesterday.

Someone tapped lightly on the parlor door, and Jared hurried to let the doctor in. He was a young man, not yet thirty. He'd grown a beard to look older, but without much success. Ellie had explained he was the son of the man who had been their family physician for years.

"I . . . I'm very sorry, Mrs. Wentworth," Dr. Wilbur

stammered, obviously ill at ease. Suzanna supposed he had little experience on which to draw in dealing with this situation.

"Thank you, Alexander. You're very kind to come so quickly."

He nodded and glanced nervously at the other occupants of the room. "I've examined the bod . . . Mr. Wentworth."

Mrs. Wentworth touched the hankie to her eyes again and stifled a sob. Jared laid a hand on her shoulder and said, "Was it his heart?"

"I . . . uh, no . . . I mean . . ." Wilbur looked around again, and Suzanna suddenly realized his unease was caused by more than inexperience. She stood up in response to an instinctive need to move closer to Jared, although she could not have said why.

"Doctor?" Jared prompted.

Dr. Wilbur blinked several times, shifted the black bag he carried from one hand to the other, and cleared his throat. "Mr. Wentworth did not die of natural causes."

"What?"

Suzanna was too shocked to notice who had asked the question.

Dr. Wilbur drew himself up. "I said, Mr. Wentworth did not die of natural causes."

"Then what . . . ?" Jared demanded, gesturing vaguely.

"There were . . . *are* bruises on his neck. He was . . . someone strangled him."

Mrs. Wentworth cried out, half-rose from the sofa, clutched at her throat, and collapsed in a heap. Lost in their own shock, no one noticed until she hit the floor.

"Mother!" Ellie cried, lunging for her too late.

In an instant, Jared had lifted his mother to the sofa and laid her gently down. Ellie chafed her wrists while Dr. Wilbur searched his black bag for a vial of smelling salts. When he would have put them beneath her nose,

Jared grabbed his wrist. His dark eyes glittered with fury.

"Wait. Before you bring her to, I think you'd better tell the rest of us exactly what you found."

Dr. Wilbur swallowed audibly. "As I said, there are bruises on your father's throat, and there are certain other . . ." He glanced at Ellie and Suzanna and cleared his throat again. "Other evidences that he died from strangulation. Mr. Wentworth, your father was murdered."

"This is ridiculous," Booth insisted, having taken his place at Jared's side. "Forgive me, Alexander, but you can't have much experience in these things. Perhaps you're mistaken."

Dr. Wilbur obviously took offense at the remark, but he was too well-bred to answer back. "If you doubt my opinion, I'm sure my father will be happy to examine the body."

"It's not that we doubt your opinion," Booth said diplomatically. "It's just . . . murder is such an ugly word. My God, who could have possibly . . . ?"

Plainly, everyone in the room was wondering the same thing. Why would anyone want to kill such a harmless creature as Mr. Wentworth? Suzanna had seen many deaths in Dodge City, but most had been crimes of passion, committed in the heat of argument or in self-defense. To strangle a helpless old man in his sleep was an act of such depravity, Suzanna could hardly imagine it.

"Booth . . ." Ellie called softly, reaching for him. She had gone white, and the hand she held out was trembling. He grasped it, hastily lowering her into a chair.

"Don't worry," he soothed her. "I'm certain he's mistaken. He should never have mentioned it at all until he was sure," Booth added, giving the doctor a dark look.

Wilbur flinched but held his ground. "I *am* sure, but I'll send my father out the instant he returns from his morning calls. Meanwhile, I'll have to notify the sheriff.''

"The sheriff!" Jared exclaimed. "Good God, man, have you no sensitivity at all? My mother . . ." He gestured toward her prone body.

"Oh, dear," Wilbur said, hastily offering the smelling salts again. When no one else moved, Suzanna took them and waved them under Mrs. Wentworth's nose until she coughed and her eyelids fluttered.

"Mother? Are you all right?" Jared asked, going down on one knee beside her.

"Booth? What . . . ? Oh, Jared," she said in relief, taking his hand. "For a moment I thought . . ." She glanced up and saw Dr. Wilbur hovering near the sofa. "Oh, no! It isn't true, is it?"

"We aren't sure," Jared said gently. "Old Dr. Wilbur will be out this afternoon."

Young Dr. Wilbur made a noise in his throat, and Suzanna realized someone had best get him out before he upset Mrs. Wentworth again.

"Dr. Wilbur, I'll see you to the door," she offered, indicating he should follow her. He was as eager to leave as they were to see him go. When she had shut the front door behind him, Suzanna leaned against it and closed her eyes. Dear heaven, she thought in despair, were she and Jared destined to tragedy?

In the early afternoon, old Dr. Wilbur and Sheriff Norwood arrived. The senior physician was approaching sixty, with white hair and a slight paunch and worry lines around his eyes and mouth, and his many years of experience made him everything one could wish for in a doctor.

Sheriff Norwood was a far cry from the dapper lawmen Suzanna knew in Dodge City. Short and built like a tree stump, he was dressed like a farmer and had a habit of pulling thoughtfully on his grizzled beard. Accustomed to judging people's characters at a glance,

Suzanna wasn't fooled by his homely appearance. She quickly noticed his pale eyes didn't miss a thing.

The men greeted Jared warmly and welcomed him home, both expressing regret over the circumstances of their meeting. Jared introduced Suzanna as his fiancée. Self-conscious under the sheriff's scrutiny, she simply nodded her acknowledgment.

When the two men had completed their examination of the body, they took Jared and Booth into the library for a private conference.

"I'm afraid Alexander was right," Dr. Wilbur began when they were all seated. "Your father was strangled, Jared,"

"How can you be sure?" Booth asked.

Dr. Wilbur smiled sadly. "The bruises on the neck, of course, the bulging eyes, protruding tongue—"

"It's impossible!" Jared exclaimed, unable to listen to more. "Who could have done it and why?"

"I was hoping you'd be able to tell us," Sheriff Norwood said with a faint smile. "But of course you've been gone for a long time. Maybe Booth would be a better person to ask."

"I'm just as puzzled as Jared," Booth said, leaning forward anxiously. "Most men have enemies, of course, but Uncle Ezra was . . . Well, you know how he was. He couldn't possibly have offended anyone at all, certainly not enough to make someone want to kill him."

Norwood tugged on his beard. "It's been my experience that folks kill for two reasons: hate and greed. We know nobody hated Ezra, at least not anymore. That leaves greed."

Jared frowned, and Booth snorted derisively. "Who stood to gain from his death?" Booth asked. "Jared is his heir, but the way things stood, he would have had control over the property for all practical purposes anyway."

"What about you, Booth?" the sheriff asked. "Aren't you mentioned in the will?"

Booth stiffened. "I have no idea," he snapped.

Unperturbed by Booth's vehement response, the sheriff turned to Jared. "What about your sister?"

"You can't think a fifteen-year-old girl would . . ." Jared couldn't even complete the sentence.

"One thing I've learned in fifty years of living is that people do things you just wouldn't believe," Norwood remarked blandly. "To answer your question, though, I don't think a girl would be strong enough to do it, but somebody who cared about her might do it for her. Does she stand to inherit anything?"

Jared glanced at Booth who shrugged and shook his head. "I'm afraid we'll have to find my father's will before we can answer your questions," Jared replied.

"Does she have any beaux?"

"She's only fifteen!" Jared reminded him in exasperation.

"She's a pretty girl and rich, too," Norwood pointed out. "Her age wouldn't matter much if a man had his eye on her fortune."

"If she *has* a fortune." Jared glared at the sheriff, but Norwood didn't seem disturbed.

"Ellie isn't even out yet," Booth said. "She couldn't possibly have attracted the kind of attention to which you refer."

"Aren't you going to ask about my mother?" Jared demanded sarcastically. "She's certainly mentioned in the will. Perhaps you think she stole into her husband's room in the middle of the night and choked the life out of him with her bare hands."

"I don't think anything at the moment," Norwood informed them all with maddening calmness. "I'll need to ask everyone in the house to account for their whereabouts during the night, however."

"Can't this wait?" Jared asked. "My mother is practically prostrate with shock and grief."

"Then I'll question her later. I'd like to see everyone else here in the library, one by one—the servants, too. Jared, I'll take you first."

* * *

Booth was pale when he joined Suzanna and Ellie in the parlor. Mrs. Wentworth had retired to her room, having taken the sedative Dr. Wilbur prescribed. Booth explained briefly that his uncle had indeed been murdered and that the sheriff wanted to speak to all of them privately.

A few minutes later, Jared joined them and instructed Booth to return to the library for questioning. Surrendering to impulse, Suzanna slipped her arms around Jared's waist and held him close for a moment. He did not return her embrace. Holding himself rigid, he drew a deep breath as if he were trying to control his temper.

Sensing his struggle, Suzanna released him and led him to the sofa. When they were seated, Ellie perched on the arm beside Jared and took his hand in hers. Unaware of their comforting presence, Jared continued to stare out into space for another minute or two. Then he said, "He thinks one of us did it."

"One of us?" Ellie exclaimed. "Why on earth . . . ?"

"It's a logical assumption," he said, frowning. "Unfortunately, since we were all alone in our beds, none of us can prove where we or anyone else was." His dark gaze sought Suzanna's. She easily interpreted his silent warning. He'd already told her he didn't want anyone to know he'd spent the night with her, and she was to maintain the fiction.

By the time the sheriff called her into the library, she was fairly sick with dread at wondering how she could fool the lawman. Her anxiety must have shown, because he smiled sympathetically and bade her be seated on the leather sofa under the window. Suzanna had never seen so many books all in one place before, and she found the tomblike silence of the room oppressive.

"You're engaged to Jared, is that correct?" he asked.

Suzanna only nodded, aware her accent would betray her background and raise all sorts of new questions in the sheriff's mind.

"How long have you known him?"

"A . . . a few months," she hedged, realizing they had lived a lifetime in less than three months.

"You met out West?"

Suzanna nodded again, wishing she knew exactly what Jared had told him. "In Kansas. Dodge City."

"Dodge City, eh?" he replied as if the information surprised him. "What on earth were you doing there?"

"My husband and I homesteaded some land near there."

"Your husband?"

"I'm a widow."

He pulled thoughtfully on his beard. "I don't suppose your husband left you well-off."

"He was a farmer, and after he died, I lost the land," she explained, knowing it would be foolish to try to conceal the truth from him.

"How did you live, then?"

"I worked."

"Doing what?"

Suzanna took a deep breath and placed a hand over her quaking stomach. "I worked as a maid for a while, then I started dancing at the Comique Theater."

"Dancing? On the stage?"

"No, I . . . we danced with the customers."

"Oh, it was a dance hall," he said, his eyes lighting with understanding. "What else did you do there?"

"Nothing," she said sharply, feeling the heat in her cheeks. "I danced and talked to the customers, nothing more."

"I've heard things about dance hall girls . . ." He let his voice trail off suggestively.

Suzanna swallowed her outrage, knowing it would only hurt her case. "You never heard anything about *me*," she replied.

He studied her for a long, uncomfortable moment. "So you worked in this dance hall, supporting yourself and your child. You have a son, I believe?"

Suzanna nodded stiffly.

"It must have been hard for you."

"No harder than being a farmer's wife."

He lifted his eyebrows to acknowledge her point, but he wasn't willing to let her go just yet. "You've had a hard life all along, then. You must've been real happy when you found out Jared Wentworth was rich."

Stung, Suzanna couldn't keep the fury from her voice. "I didn't know he was rich. I didn't know anything about him at all until . . ." She caught herself just in time. She'd almost revealed she and Jared had lived together.

"Until what?"

"Until I'd already agreed to marry him," she improvised. "But he told me we couldn't marry until he'd gone home and cleared his name. You see, he left home in the first place because he thought he'd killed his father."

"So he told me. Must've been quite a shock to find the old fellow alive."

"It was, but of course, we were very happy because it meant Jared wasn't a murderer."

"At least not yet."

"*What?*" Suzanna cried, jumping to her feet.

Sheriff Norwood didn't even blink. "I said he wasn't a murderer yet, but he must've started remembering how the old man had treated all of them and thinking how unfair it was his mother had to take care of him all these years."

"What are you trying to say?" Suzanna demanded.

"If the old man was dead, you and Jared would have the whole place to yourselves—"

"Except for his mother and sister!" she reminded him.

"Oh, he could turn them out if he wanted to since he'd be the owner of the property."

"Jared would never do any such thing!"

"But Rosewood is important to him, isn't it?"

"It's his home, but he'd never kill someone for it!"

"He killed his father once before, or thought he did."

"That was an accident!"

"So Jared says, but what if he decided to finish the job, once and for all—"

"You're crazy!"

"Am I?" Norwood asked, his voice still perfectly calm. He rose slowly to his feet as if they were discussing nothing more important than the state of the weather. "It seems awfully strange that Jared left home thinking he'd killed his father, and when he comes home five years later—the very day he comes home, mind you—someone really does kill him."

"Jared couldn't have done it," Suzanna told him triumphantly. "He was with me all night."

"Really?" Norwood said with mild interest. "He didn't mention it, and I asked him specifically."

Suzanna could have bitten off her tongue. The last thing she'd wanted to do was lie to this man, but now she was making Jared out a liar. "He didn't want his family to know because they'd think . . ." Once again her cheeks began to burn under Norwood's knowing gaze.

"They'd think you were a loose woman, the kind of woman Jared might meet in a Dodge City dance hall, the kind of woman who might goad him to get rid of his father—"

"*No!* Jared didn't do it!" Suzanna fairly shouted. "I told you, we were together all night!"

Sheriff Norwood smiled. "How convenient," was all he said.

Chapter 13

Several hectic hours passed before Suzanna managed to get Jared alone in the library. "The sheriff thinks you killed your father!" she informed him when she had pulled the door shut behind them.

"I know. He made it very clear when he questioned me." Jared's dark eyes held the bleak despair she'd hoped never to see again.

"I told him we were together all night, but he didn't believe me."

Jared stiffened with outrage. "You shouldn't have humiliated yourself like that, Suzanna."

"What good is my reputation if you're accused of murder! Jared, how can we convince him you're innocent?"

"We'll just have to find out who the real murderer is."

Suzanna's stomach turned over. "Do you know who it is?"

"Not exactly, but it's not too difficult to figure out. It has to have been someone in the house. I think we can rule out the servants. Even Sheriff Norwood admitted Ellie wasn't physically capable of doing it, and I can't imagine Mother . . ."

"No, of course not!" Suzanna felt as if someone were squeezing the air out of her lungs with a giant fist. "That only leaves Booth."

"I know, but as much as I've always disliked him, I

332

still can't imagine him being capable of murder. And what did he have to gain? When we found my father's will, we discovered Booth only gets a small trust, hardly enough to keep him from poverty and certainly not enough to kill for."

"Jared, I . . ." Suzanna hesitated, knowing she shouldn't break Ellie's confidence but realizing the information might be important. "Ellie told me she and Booth are engaged."

"*Engaged?*" he echoed incredulously.

"Yes, I was sure she'd just misunderstood his attention, but she showed me a ring he had given her. She wears it on a chain around her neck."

Jared snorted in disgust. "That's ridiculous. Even Booth would never bother with a fifteen-year-old girl! Ellie probably made the whole thing up. She's always been fanciful."

"I was hoping you'd say that," Suzanna replied with relief. "All I could think was Booth might've killed your father so he could get Ellie's inheritance."

"Ellie doesn't have an inheritance either," Jared told her with a sad smile. "Father only left her a small trust, too."

"Did Booth know the terms of the will?"

"He says he didn't, but Booth has always been a consummate liar, and he didn't seem very surprised."

"If he did know, then he didn't have any reason to kill your father either."

Jared sighed wearily. "It seems I'm the only one to gain from his death, and heaven knows there was never any love lost between us. No wonder the sheriff suspects me."

"But we know you didn't do it," Suzanna began, stopping when she realized the only proof of that was her word, the word of the woman who would most directly benefit if Jared became the sole proprietor of Rosewood. How ironic, she thought. If she could only convince the sheriff how unappealing the idea was to her . . . but who would believe that a woman who'd known nothing but poverty all her life didn't want to be wealthy? "Are you sure no one else had a reason to kill him?"

"No one. I'm the sole heir. I don't even share with Ellie or my mother."

"What is the sheriff going to do?"

"Nothing right now. He agreed my mother shouldn't be upset anymore, so he's going to wait until after the funeral tomorrow. He spoke to all the servants. Let's hope one of them saw or heard something."

"The maid would have noticed your bed wasn't slept in," Suzanna pointed out, but Jared shook his head.

"I took the trouble to mess it up before I came to you so no one would suspect."

Her heart sank. If only Jared wasn't so blasted concerned about her reputation. As the day wore on, Suzanna's spirits dropped even lower. She tried to help Ellie and keep Andy occupied so he wouldn't get in the way of the funeral preparations, but nothing she did distracted her from thoughts of the new murder charge hanging over Jared.

Late in the afternoon, she took Andy and Pistol for a walk in the rose garden. A few tenacious blooms still struggled for life in the dwindling autumn sunlight, and Suzanna gratefully inhaled their fragrance. Andy and Pistol soon outstripped her on the garden path, so she lolled along, admiring the many varieties of roses Mrs. Wentworth had cultivated. Up ahead stood the gazebo of which Ellie had spoken, the one under which she and Booth had supposedly kissed.

Suzanna smiled, thinking of what Jared had said. Surely the girl really had made up the whole thing. Why would a man like Booth want to court a mere child—and a penniless child at that?

Engrossed in her thoughts, she at first didn't notice the two figures standing in the shadows beneath the tiled roof, standing so close they might almost have been one person. Startled, she made a small sound, and the figures separated instantly, becoming two distinct people again.

"Suzanna," Ellie laughed breathlessly. "What are you doing sneaking around in the garden?"

"I'm not sneaking around," Suzanna said, staring at the man beside Ellie. Booth smiled a greeting. Nothing in his expression betrayed guilt, although Ellie looked as if she'd been caught with her hand in the cookie jar. "I took Andy and his dog for a walk. They're around here somewhere."

"Booth was trying to make me feel better," Ellie explained just a shade too casually. "I'm really dreading the funeral tomorrow."

Suzanna nodded, understanding completely. She'd been to entirely too many funerals herself. "You're lucky you have two men you can turn to for comfort."

Ellie smiled. "I only need one," she said, her eyes shining as she looked up at Booth.

He frowned in disapproval, but Suzanna couldn't be sure of what he disapproved. Was he annoyed because Ellie read more into their relationship than was there or because he didn't want her to reveal that relationship to Suzanna? Suzanna wanted to believe Jared's theory that Ellie had fibbed, but she could no longer be sure.

"Maybe you can help me track Andy and Pistol down," she suggested to Ellie, hoping to get the girl alone so she could question her.

"I'll find them," Booth offered. "Why don't the two of you go back to the house. It must be time to dress for dinner by now,."

Ellie looked disappointed by his suggestion, but she followed Suzanna meekly out of the garden and back into the house. As they walked, Suzanna frantically sought some way to broach the subject of Booth without seeming to pry. At last she settled for, "Booth seems very kind."

"He's wonderful," Ellie agreed fervently. "Everything a woman could want."

A woman, yes, Suzanna thought, but Ellie wasn't a woman yet. "Has he said . . . I hope I didn't interrupt anything important," she said softly.

Ellie shrugged with feigned indifference. "Like I said, he was just trying to cheer me up. I hate funerals and wearing black. Now it'll be a whole year until I can get married, and—oh, dear! It'll be a whole year until you can get married, too!"

Suzanna stared at her in horror. "What are you talking about?"

"We'll all be in mourning."

Although Suzanna had far more serious problems to worry about, the thought still depressed her. It certainly was a good thing Jared's family didn't know how recently Andrew had died. By their standards, she should still be wearing black even though Andrew's death seemed to have happened in another lifetime. She thought of the year ahead, of Jared sneaking into her room and . . . *If* he were free to sneak anywhere at all. She forced the thought from her mind. "Surely you weren't thinking of getting married so soon anyway," she said.

Ellie sighed. "We were going to announce our engagement when I turn sixteen this winter, and there's no reason to wait. I've known Booth all my life, after all."

"Isn't it illegal for first cousins to marry?" she asked.

"We're second cousins. Booth's father died when he was little, and his mother didn't have much money. She was my mother's first cousin and they were very close, so he spent a lot of time with us."

Suzanna nodded, wishing she could think of some valid impediment which would convince Ellie she shouldn't be thinking so seriously about her cousin. Or maybe she should be talking to Booth, she realized when she recalled the scene in the gazebo. Had he truly only been comforting her? Suzanna's instincts told her otherwise, but she had no real reason to doubt Ellie's word.

She wanted to discuss the matter with Jared, but the funeral preparations kept everyone busy until late in the evening. Jared sent her off to bed with a chaste kiss. She pressed his hand, trying to make him understand she wanted him to come to her room. His teasing grin told her he understood, but he made no promises, silent or otherwise.

In spite of the coolness of the evening, Suzanna left her balcony door ajar so she would hear Jared if he chose to approach. An hour passed, and she had just about decided she would have to go to him when she heard footsteps on the veranda.

Anticipation tingled along her nerve endings, raising gooseflesh. She stole silently out of bed and hurried to the door, ready to surprise Jared the instant he entered the room. Holding her breath so as not to betray herself, she waited while the footsteps came closer and closer and . . . kept on going!

Suzanna peeked out the open door. A quarter-moon illuminated the night sky, enabling her to make out the figure of a man moving swiftly down the balcony to Ellie's door! Without even bothering to knock, he slipped inside.

Horrified, Suzanna could only stare as she tried to think of some logical explanation for why Booth might be going to his cousin's room so late at night. Unfortunately, the only one she could find was unthinkable.

Had Ellie lied to her when she said Booth had never done more than kiss her? No, Ellie was too poor a liar, as she had proved this afternoon. But perhaps things had changed between them since yesterday. Suzanna was certain they'd been embracing in the rose garden this afternoon. Could Booth have been plotting a seduction even then?

But why? It simply didn't make sense, and Suzanna wasted several precious minutes trying to find some logical explanation. Whether or not she could explain it, she knew she had to stop it. For a second she considered getting Jared, but that would take time, and if she was wrong about Booth's intentions—please God!—then Jared need never know.

Quickly, she snatched her robe from the chair and pulled it on as she ran barefoot down the veranda. The night breeze puffed at the delicate material until it billowed out behind her. She felt a hysterical urge to laugh when she realized she would probably look like a ghost to anyone below.

Outside Ellie's door, she paused, listening, trying to hear sounds from within over the pounding of her heart and the rasping of her breath. For an instant she hesitated, uncertain whether she even had the right to intrude, but then she remembered her friend Dora. Dora had never hesitated to intrude in other people's lives when she thought it for the best. Although people sometimes resented Dora's interference, she never did any actual harm because her motives were always the best. Tonight, Suzanna's motives were the best, too. She threw the door open.

"Ellie?"

Ellie cried out in alarm, and as Suzanna had feared, Booth bolted from the bed.

"What's going on here?" she demanded with far more confidence than she felt.

"Nothing!" Ellie said, her voice high and frightened.

Booth muttered a curse as he fumbled with his clothes. Even in the darkness, Suzanna could see enough to know he'd been at least partially undressed already. Her blood went cold.

"I was hoping I was wrong about your intentions when I saw you sneaking into Ellie's room," Suzanna said.

"You're a fine one to talk," Booth snapped, moving toward her. "Ellie, did you know your brother and Suzanna have been living together for months? Living in *sin!*"

"At least I'm a grown woman," Suzanna replied haughtily, ignoring Ellie's gasp. "What kind of a man seduces children?"

"I'm not a child!" Ellie insisted, sounding very much like one.

Behind her, Suzanna heard more footsteps, ones she recognized. She stepped aside as Jared burst into the room. "What's going on?"

Suzanna waited, giving Booth a chance to speak for himself. When he didn't, she said, "I found your cousin in bed with your sister."

"You bastard!" Jared shouted, lunging for him, but Ellie was quicker, launching herself off the bed and straight into Jared.

"No! Don't hurt him!" she screamed, wrapping her arms around Jared's neck. They struggled violently, Ellie clawing and clinging to protect the man she loved while Jared tried to defend himself without hurting her. After a moment, Suzanna grabbed Ellie around the waist and tried to help separate the two.

At last they were able to pry Ellie's hands loose. Suzanna held her while Jared broke free, but when he looked around, the hallway door stood open and Booth was gone. In another second Jared was after him, racing down the massive staircase.

"Keep her here!" he called as he followed Booth out the front door.

Suzanna hung onto Ellie with all her strength, ignoring the kicks and scratches and howls of protest. "We have to stop him!" Ellie cried. "He'll kill Booth!"

"No, he won't," Suzanna said with more certainty than she felt.

"He killed Papa, didn't he?" Ellie shouted.

"Don't be ridiculous!" her mother said from the doorway. "What on earth is going on in here?" she demanded, moving toward the lamp on the bedside table.

At the sound of her mother's voice, Ellie quit struggling and went limp in Suzanna's arms. "Booth!" she called, but the sound melted into a sob.

Suzanna released her grip and pulled the girl into her arms. "Oh, Ellie, I'm so sorry!"

"Why did you come?" she demanded, resisting Suzanna's comforting embrace. "It was none of your business!"

Behind them, Mrs. Wentworth struck a match and lit the lamp. "What was none of her business? Why is everyone shouting and running through the house in the middle of the night? Don't you remember your father is lying dead downstairs? Doesn't anyone have any respect?"

Ellie broke free of Suzanna. Her eyes, so like Jared's, were full of hatred and defiance.

"I saw Booth sneaking into Ellie's room, so I came to investigate," Suzanna explained.

"What? Why was Booth sneaking into your room, Eleanor?" Mrs. Wentworth demanded.

"So we could talk in private," Ellie said, her eyes daring Suzanna to contradict her.

"That's highly improper," Mrs. Wentworth said. "Booth should know better, and so should you."

Suzanna bit back her anger. "Did you know he was coming?" she asked Ellie through gritted teeth.

"Of course I knew," she replied with a toss of her head.

"But why would you do such a thing? Ellie, your father's not even buried yet!"

"What do I care about him? He made my life miserable until the day Jared smashed his head in, and ever since we've all been waiting on him hand and foot as if he'd done something to deserve our devotion. I'm glad he's dead!"

"Eleanor!" her mother cried, clutching her heart.

Suzanna and Ellie rushed to her, supporting her on each side as her legs gave out. "My . . . medicine . . ." she gasped.

Ellie ran for it.

Jared raced across the lawn, searching the shadows for signs of Booth but finding none. He'd go to the stables, Jared reasoned, and saddle the fastest horse.

Sure enough, just as Jared reached the stable door,

he heard a horse galloping away into the night. Frantically, he tried to remember the horses he had seen on his visit here yesterday with Andy and decide which one he should take. To his left he heard a whinny, and his decision was made. Whatever horse was highstrung enough to be disturbed would do.

Grabbing a halter off the wall, he wrenched open the stall door. After a few wild minutes of wrestling with the bit, he was on the horse and away, gripping the animal's bare back with his knees.

Following instinct as much as anything else, Jared headed in the direction he had heard the other horse running. Trees and bushes flashed by, but Jared ignored them. Squinting into the night, listening for all he was worth, he strained after Booth, as if force of will could catch him.

Each stride pounded through him, threatening to jar him from his precarious perch, but he held on, hatred and fury driving him, the same emotions he had felt once before when another man had tried to harm his sister. He'd killed then, or thought he had. Tonight he was angry enough to kill again.

His mount broke stride, lurching violently. Jared grabbed the mane, half-sliding off and saving himself only by sheer luck. Then he heard the other horse scream a warning as his horse danced nimbly out of the way. By the moon's feeble light, Jared could just make out the other animal as it skittered away. Surely this was Booth's mount, but Jared saw no rider on its back.

Then his horse lurched again to avoid something in the road, a dark mass that Jared instantly recognized as a fallen man. Reining to a stop, he slid to the ground.

"God damn you, I hope your neck is broken!" he shouted as he hurried to his cousin and turned him over.

Booth groaned and tried to struggle, but lapsed into unconsciousness again. Jared cursed, knowing an overwhelming urge to choke the life out of this man who would have ruined his sister.

"Good God!" he said, instantly sobered by the horrible impulse. He was about to do the very thing the sheriff had suspected him of doing to his father!

But he wouldn't. He jumped to his feet and stared down at Booth's prone body. No, he *couldn't*, however much he might want to, however much Booth might deserve it—he simply couldn't attack a defenseless man. Slowly the rage began to drain out of him, leaving behind a cold, sickening lump in the pit of his stomach.

Thank God I didn't catch him, he thought, wondering what he might have done if Booth had been capable of fighting back. For a moment he actually felt weak, but only for a moment. Booth had some questions to answer, questions better asked in Ellie's presence.

Resolutely, Jared calmed the horses and proceeded to load his groaning cousin onto one of them.

Ellie and Suzanna stared at each other across the expanse of the parlor floor. After getting Mrs. Wentworth her medicine and seeing her safely back to bed, Suzanna had checked on Andy, making sure the noise hadn't awakened him. Then she and Ellie had adjourned to the front parlor where they would be sure to hear either Jared or Booth returning.

Suzanna pulled her robe more tightly around her against the evening chill and wracked her brain for something conciliatory to say to Ellie.

"Ellie, I know you didn't really mean what you said about your father," she said gently.

"Of course I meant it," Ellie replied, defiance still glittering in her eyes. "I was only sad because I'd have to be in mourning and Booth and I couldn't get married. But after dinner tonight, Booth told me he'd thought of a way we could get married without having to wait."

"Let me guess, it had something to do with him coming to your room tonight," Suzanna said, feeling a now-familiar nausea.

"You're smart, Suzanna, or maybe you don't need to be smart to figure out that if I was with child or even if we'd just been together and Mother found out, we'd *have* to get married."

Suzanna stared at her in horror. The more she learned about this situation, the less she understood it. Why would Booth be so desperate to marry a fifteen-year-old girl? "Ellie, it was wrong of Booth to try to seduce you, no matter what his reasons."

"He loves me!" she insisted.

"I'm sure he does," Suzanna lied, "but even still . . ."

Ellie was no longer listening. Her head came up as they both heard the sound of footsteps trudging across the front porch. Ellie jumped up and ran into the hall with Suzanna on her heels. Just as they reached it, the front door swung open, and Jared shoved Booth inside.

He staggered, but Ellie caught him, crying out in alarm. "What have you done to him?" she demanded.

"Nothing yet," Jared replied coldly. Suzanna was relieved to see he had control of his temper. "His horse fell, and he took a nasty spill, but I think he'll be all right, at least until he's finished answering a few questions. Take him in the parlor."

Ellie put Booth's arm over her shoulders and led him back into the room where she and Suzanna had been sitting. Suzanna and Jared followed, and Jared closed the doors behind them.

Booth and Ellie slumped down onto one of the sofas while Jared paced off a little of his anger. Finally he turned to the two of them. "Are you ready to talk now?"

Booth nodded gingerly, holding one hand to the side of his head where a nasty bruise was forming.

"Was Suzanna right? Were you trying to seduce Ellie?"

Booth's eyes narrowed with fury, but before he could speak, Ellie said, "We're going to be married! He asked me months ago, and he gave me this ring." She pulled the chain, drawing the ring from the neck of her nightdress, and held it up for Jared to see.

Jared's face went white, and Suzanna had already taken a step toward him when he said, "Would you like to explain yourself, Booth? And don't bother telling me how much you love my sister and can't bear to live without her."

Ellie gasped in outrage, but no one paid her any attention.

"I do love Ellie. I want to marry her."

"Obviously," Jared snapped. "The question is *why* do you want to marry her? She has no money, she's still a child—"

"I am not!" Ellie insisted, but Jared only glared her into silence.

"I could understand it if Ellie were destined to inherit Rosewood . . ." Jared mused, stopping as a new thought occurred to him. "Wait a minute. How long ago did you say Booth proposed to you?" he demanded of his sister.

Ellie blinked in surprise. "I don't remember exactly. . . . Oh, wait, it was last spring."

"Last spring," Jared repeated thoughtfully. "When everyone thought I'd disappeared for good. Perhaps I was even dead. In fact," he continued, turning to Suzanna, "isn't that exactly what Booth said when he found me in Dodge? That as far as he was concerned, I was dead?"

Suzanna nodded, her eyes wide as everything started to fall into place.

"Jared, you're crazy," Booth protested. "I only said that because Suzanna had asked me to keep your whereabouts a secret. I had no idea why you'd left home in the first place and—"

"Yes, you did!" Suzanna cried, suddenly remembering. "I *told* you, that night you came to my house. I told you Jared thought he'd killed his father, and *you didn't even tell me he was still alive!*"

The color flooded back into Jared's face. "You bastard! You were going to let me live the rest of my life thinking I killed my own father so you could have Rosewood all to yourself!"

Booth jumped to his feet, his headache forgotten. "I

deserve Rosewood! I took over when you ran away like a frightened little boy and your father was more dead than alive with the back of his head smashed in."

"So you knew he didn't have a stroke!" Jared challenged.

"Of course I knew! And I also knew you thought he was dead and you'd never come home. With you gone, according to the terms of his will, Ellie would inherit everything."

"But I'd have to be dead before she could inherit."

"You'd already been gone for five years. In another two, we could have you declared legally dead."

"And by then Ellie would be old enough to marry," Jared concluded, "and as her husband, you would take legal possession of all her property."

"No!" Ellie cried, jumping up and grabbing Booth's arm. "You love me! You told me so!"

Booth touched her cheek and managed a small smile. "Of course I love you, little one. I would have made you very happy."

Jared's face turned scarlet and his hands curled into fists, but Suzanna threw herself between him and Booth before he could strike. "Jared, please," she said, taking his arms.

For a few seconds, she was afraid he would ignore her plea, but gradually the furious glitter in his eyes dimmed. He stepped back, out of Suzanna's grasp, and folded his arms across his chest. "All right then, so when I came home, alive and well, to claim what's rightfully mine, you decided to seduce Ellie as some sort of revenge."

"No!" both Booth and Ellie cried at once.

"He wanted to get me with child so we could be married right away instead of waiting for a year!" Ellie informed him.

"Or so you'd be disgraced and our family would be humiliated," Jared retorted. "Now that you can't inherit Rosewood, he doesn't want you anymore."

"But she *can* inherit Rosewood," Booth pointed out with a sly grin.

"Not while I'm alive," Jared reminded him.

"You won't be for long, dear cousin," Booth replied triumphantly. "We still hang murderers in Maryland, you know."

This time Jared did lunge toward Booth, but Suzanna caught him, holding him back. "You won't get away with it, Booth! Suzanna and I were together all night. She knows I didn't kill Father!"

Booth's grin widened. "Nice try, but no one will believe her, not after I tell the sheriff what I know about her background and her conduct with you back in Kansas. Honestly Jared, I would've expected you to handle it more neatly. Did you hate him so much you couldn't wait at least a few days? To kill him the first night you were home—"

"But I didn't do it, as you well know," Jared reminded him. "It all makes sense now. *You* killed Father, knowing I'd be the one accused. When I was hanged, you'd marry Ellie—"

"Don't try to pin this thing on me!" Booth shouted, shaking loose of Ellie's grasp and taking a step toward Jared. "I'm not going to hang for a murder you committed!"

"Booth, stop!" Suzanna cried, again wedging herself between them. "Jared didn't do it! He really was with me all night!"

The two men stared at each other for several heartbeats as the truth sank in.

"You didn't . . . ?" Booth asked at last.

Jared shook his head. "And you didn't either," he said in dawning comprehension. "Then who . . . ?"

"I did."

They all turned to the doorway where Mrs. Wentworth stood. Her lips were bloodless and the hand she held out to them trembled.

"Mother?" Jared said, hurrying to her. "What are you doing out of bed?"

"I came down when I heard the shouting," she explained as she allowed him to lead her to a sofa. "I thought you were only angry because of what Booth did tonight, but when I heard what you were saying . . ." She shuddered.

"Mother, I'm sorry," Ellie said, kneeling before her. "I didn't really mean the things I said earlier. I wouldn't upset you for the world."

Mrs. Wentworth smiled. "If I'm upset, I have no one to blame but myself." She looked slowly around the room, allowing her gaze to touch everyone in it. "You see, I really did kill Ezra."

"What?"

"No!"

"You couldn't!"

"But I did," she insisted, her eyes glowing with a fire Suzanna finally recognized as madness. She covered her mouth to hold back a cry and listened, mesmerized, as Mrs. Wentworth told her story.

"After you left home, Jared, as soon as I realized Ezra was still alive, I vowed to keep him that way if it was humanly possible. As much as I hated him for what he'd done to you and to all of us, I couldn't let him die because that would be hurting you even more."

"So that's why you nursed him day and night," Ellie said, her eyes wide with amazement.

Mrs. Wentworth touched her daughter's cheek lovingly. "Yes, and that's why I cared for him every day since. I couldn't let him die, not until Jared's name had been cleared." She looked up at her son. "As soon as you were home, I knew I didn't need to let him live another day."

"But, Mother," Jared protested, "you couldn't have—"

"Yes, I could," she insisted, the fire in her eyes flaring brightly. "He didn't deserve to live, you know, not after what he did to all of us. By rights he should have died the night Jared left, but his death would have destroyed an innocent boy, so God preserved him all these years, preserved him by my hand. You don't know how I hated him for the things he did, the things no one else ever knew about, but I kept him alive for you. I took care of him every day, hating him more and more, until sometimes I thought I'd go crazy, but I'd remember you and somehow I'd go on. Then yesterday you came home, and I knew it was over." She smiled a terrible smile. "It was over at last."

Jared's face was pale, and his voice quavered when he asked, "Didn't you realize if he was murdered, someone would be accused?"

She smiled slightly. "Not if I had done it properly, but Booth was right, it was sloppily done. I had intended to smother him with a pillow. There would have been no marks . . ." She gestured helplessly. "But he woke up and started to fight me, so I had to . . . Still, somehow I thought no one would know."

"Oh, Mother," Ellie cried, tears streaming down her cheeks.

Mrs. Wentworth looked up at Jared again. "I did it so we could all be free of him once and for all."

"Why didn't you tell us before?" Jared asked gently.

"I would have told the sheriff, but he didn't question me, and by the time I woke up, he was gone. When you told me he wasn't going to do anything else until after the funeral, I decided not to burden you with it until then." She let out her breath on a quivering sigh. "I suppose they'll hang me."

Ellie sobbed and threw her arms around her mother, but Mrs. Wentworth's gaze never left her son. Jared stared back at her with moist eyes. "They won't hang you, not when they find out why you did it," he said.

Suzanna prayed he was right. Surely no one would hold Mrs. Wentworth responsible for her actions. She took Jared's hand, not surprised to find it ice-cold. Every one of them had sustained a severe shock. "Jared," she said softly, "perhaps we all ought to go to bed now. Your mother is exhausted, and we had to give her medicine tonight for her heart."

"Her heart?" Jared said as if waking from a dream. "Mother, you didn't tell me you were sick."

"Not sick," she replied, easing out of Ellie's embrace and rising slowly to her feet. "Just old."

"You're not even fifty yet," Ellie scolded, dashing the moisture from her cheeks.

"Tonight I feel much older. Suzanna, would you help me to bed?"

Somewhat surprised to have been selected, Suzanna instantly agreed, leaving the others to make whatever peace they could. Leaning heavily on Suzanna, Mrs. Wentworth made her way up the stairs and back to her room. Suzanna tucked her in.

"Can I get you anything?"

Mrs. Wentworth shook her head. "You'll take good care of Jared, won't you?"

"Of course."

She smiled. "And give him lots of children. This house needs some happy children."

Suzanna nodded, wishing she could make such a promise. "Don't worry. I'm sure everything will work out."

Mrs. Wentworth smiled but Suzanna could see she didn't believe her. When she bent to blow out the light, Mrs. Wentworth said, "Leave it on, please. I can't face the darkness just yet." Suzanna slipped quietly out the door.

Downstairs, Jared, Booth, and Ellie stared at each other for a long moment.

"Booth," Ellie began, but he cut her off with a gesture.

"Not tonight, little one. Suzanna is right. We'll all think more clearly in the morning." He turned on his heel and was gone.

Ellie lifted stricken eyes to Jared, who held out his arms for her. She went to him, clinging and sobbing into his chest. They stood together until Ellie's grief was spent.

"What will they do to her?" she asked her brother.

"I don't know," Jared replied, "but I won't let them hang her."

He saw Ellie to her bedroom door, then sought the solace he could find only in Suzanna's arms. They lay awake for a long time, sorting out all that they had learned and trying to make sense of it.

The next morning they found Booth's room empty, his clothes packed carefully into a trunk. He'd left word with the servants that he would send for his things later. Ellie locked herself in her room and would accept no comfort.

When Mrs. Wentworth didn't ring for her breakfast, Suzanna went in to check on her. No one answered her knock, so she opened the door, calling softly.

"Mrs. Wentworth?" The woman lay on the bed covered to the waist, her hands resting on the blanket. She didn't stir, so Suzanna tiptoed closer. "Mrs. Wentworth?" she tried again, growing alarmed when she remembered the woman's heart problems. "Mrs. Wentworth, can you hear me?"

No response, and Suzanna's own heart lurched in her chest as she remembered finding Dora lying just this peacefully in her bed. Tentatively, Suzanna reached out and touched one of the hands lying so still on the coverlet.

"No!" she cried as she felt the icy chill of death. Tears flooded her eyes, and she sank down on her knees beside the bed with an agonized wail that brought Jared running.

Only later did they find the empty bottle of laudanum and the letter Mrs. Wentworth had written to the sheriff.

Epilogue

Suzanna laid the last rose of summer on the freshly turned earth of Lavinia Wentworth's grave and offered up a prayer that the woman had finally found peace. The autumn wind tugged at her shawl, and she pulled it more tightly around her as she made her way back to the house from the family cemetery.

Lost in thought, she didn't notice the approaching figures until Pistol barked a greeting. He raced to her side and danced in circles until she scratched his head. Looking up, she opened her mouth to call a greeting to Andy and Katie, but the girl with Andy wasn't Katie at all.

"Ellie," she said, striving for nonchalance. "It . . . it's good to see you out." In the days since her mother's death and Booth's desertion, Ellie hadn't come out of her room. Only Andy had been permitted to visit her there, and now, apparently, he had finally been able to coax her out.

"Ellie's feeling better now, Mama," Andy reported. "She stopped crying and everything."

Ellie smiled down at him and ruffled his hair affectionately. "Thanks to you, rascal," she said. "Why don't you take Pistol for a run up the hill. I want to talk to your mother for a while."

Andy made a face as if he would refuse, but he ran off after Pistol who had trotted away to investigate a nearby bush.

When they were alone, Ellie and Suzanna stared at each other for a long moment. Suzanna tried to think of something to say to break the uncomfortable silence, but the only subjects she could think of were taboo.

Finally Ellie said, "I'm sorry for the things I said to you."

"Oh, Ellie! You don't have to—"

"Yes, I do. We're going to be sisters, and I know Jared wants us to be friends."

Ellie's dark eyes were bleak, the way Suzanna had seen Jared's too many times. Her heart ached at all the tragedy the girl had already endured. "I'm sorry, too, for everything."

Ellie smiled sadly. "It wasn't your fault."

"I just wish I'd been wrong about Booth."

Ellie's smile disappeared. "So do I. I'm just thankful you caught us when you did. If he'd . . ."

"Don't think about it anymore," Suzanna urged. "He isn't worth your tears."

"Of course he isn't. Why couldn't I see it before?"

"Women in love tend to overlook a lot of faults," Suzanna said quickly, linking her arm with Ellie's and starting them down the path.

"I wonder if that's why Mother married Father, because she was too much in love to see his faults."

"Or maybe he changed over the years," Suzanna suggested, thinking of her own Andrew.

Ellie sighed. "I guess I'm lucky I didn't find out about Booth after we were already married."

They walked along in silence for a few minutes, then Ellie said, "Suzanna, why do you think she did it?"

"Did what?" Suzanna asked warily.

"Killed him. I mean, she told us, but it didn't make any sense. Why not just let him go on the way he was?"

"Ellie, I think the strain of pretending all those years finally broke her. I don't think your mother was in her right mind. She couldn't have been thinking clearly or she never would have . . . left you and Jared."

Ellie shook her head. "She did it for us, so we'd be spared the scandal. Like the sheriff said when he read her letter, it wouldn't do anybody any good to make the story public. As far as anyone is concerned, Father died in his sleep, and Mother's heart gave out from the grief. I think she planned it very carefully. I only wish we'd been able to stop her."

Suzanna squeezed her arm. "Remember when I called you a child?"

Ellie nodded.

"Well, I was wrong. I think you're all grown up now."

Ellie laughed bitterly. "What an awful way to get there."

"Yes, it was, but now you know how strong you are, and you don't need to be afraid of trouble because you know you'll be able to bear it."

"Is that what happened to you?"

For an instant the painful memories assailed her, but Suzanna resolutely pushed them aside. "Yes."

That night Jared came to her room as he had every night since they'd been in the house. Usually they made love and fell asleep in each other's arms, unable or unwilling to speak of the tragedies they had endured.

This time, however, Jared sat on the side of the bed and lit the lamp and told her he wanted to talk.

"What about?" Suzanna asked, propping herself up on pillows.

"About everything. First about Ellie. She came to me today."

"I know, she found me on my way back from putting flowers on the graves. She's hurt, but she's going to be fine, Jared."

"I'm not so sure. It's almost like . . . This sounds crazy, but it's like this house is cursed. Every time I come home, something terrible happens to the people I love."

Suzanna's heart leaped. Here was the chance she'd been praying for. All she had to do was convince Jared he was right about the house, and he'd take them away. Then she'd never have to worry about facing his friends and pretending to be something she was not or . . .

But she couldn't rob Jared of his heritage, no matter how much she might want to. "Your father was the one who caused all the trouble, and he's gone now. You and Ellie can make this a real home now."

"Ellie and I?" he asked with a smile. "Where will you be?"

"Wherever you are," she told him solemnly, hoping he couldn't guess how little she wanted to be at Rosewood.

He nodded, his smile fading. "What if I told you Ellie doesn't want to stay here?"

"She doesn't have to, does she? I mean, you could send her to school or something. She's pretty upset right now, but I'm sure she'll change her mind in time. This is her home, after all."

"Is it? I'm not so sure. For a long time I thought it was my home, too, but now, with Mother gone . . ." He shook his head sadly.

"What are you saying, Jared?" she asked, almost afraid to hope.

He drew a deep breath and took her hands in his. "Suzanna, remember when I asked you to marry me, I told you I wanted to give you a life of luxury where nothing could ever harm you again?"

"Jared, nobody can keep a promise like that," she assured him with a smile.

"I realize that now, but I still want you to have all the things you've never had, money and clothes and jewels and servants—"

"I don't need any of those things."

He frowned. "You don't have to pretend. Every woman wants them, and you deserve them more than anyone I know."

"I'm not pretending. It's not that I don't want them, but I don't need them to be happy. Remember how happy we were back in Dodge when we didn't have anything at all?"

"Then you wouldn't mind if we left Rosewood?"

Suzanna stared at him in astonishment, fighting her burgeoning hope. "Left Rosewood? What do you mean?"

He frowned again, as if searching for the proper words. "Ellie and I talked about it this afternoon. We'd like to sell Rosewood and move away, *far* away."

"Are you serious? Rosewood is your home and—"

"No, we decided we only loved this house because Mother lived here and now that she's gone . . ." He shrugged. "We want to leave the past and all its terrible memories behind, Suzanna, and start over someplace new and fresh."

"Where?" she asked, her head fairly spinning.

"Anywhere you want. Ellie doesn't care so long as she never has to see Booth or hear his name again. I'm a wealthy man, so we can go anywhere we choose. How about Kansas?"

"No," Suzanna said, having no trouble with the decision. "I want to have trees."

"Then how about Texas, or maybe even California? They need horses everywhere, and I can raise the best in the country."

Suzanna laughed at his exuberance. "We don't need to decide right this minute, do we? Let's talk to Ellie and find out what she wants."

"And I'm sure Andy will have an opinion, too."

"I'm sure he will!" Suzanna laughed again, hugging Jared close, almost afraid to believe she'd gotten everything she could have dreamed of.

Yes, *everything.*

"Jared?" she said, pulling back so she could see his face.

"Mmmm," he replied, trying to nuzzle her ear.

"Do you know what your mother's last words to me were?"

He sobered instantly. "No, what?"

"She asked me to give you lots of children."

His eyes filled with pain. "Oh, God, I'm sorry, Suzanna. She didn't know—"

"Maybe she knew more than we did. Jared, I . . . I threw up this morning."

"Are you sick?"

"Not exactly. You see, my stomach has been upset for weeks now, but I thought it was just from everything that was happening, Booth coming to Dodge, losing Dora, coming here and all the rest. But when I threw up this morning, I starting thinking and . . . Jared, I haven't bled for two months."

"What does that mean?" he asked in alarm.

She smiled at his fears. "It means I'm going to have a baby."

"*What?* A baby? But I thought . . . You said you couldn't—"

"I said the midwife didn't think I could, but it seems she was wrong."

"God in heaven," he breathed before he took her in his arms again. This time he was gentle, too gentle for Suzanna's taste.

"I won't break. You can give me a real hug."

She was instantly sorry, as he put her to the test with a bone-crunching embrace. When he finally released her, she punched him in the shoulder, ready to chasten him when she saw the tears standing in his eyes. "Jared . . . ?" she said tentatively.

"Do you know how happy you've made me? When we met, I had nothing, no home, no family, no one who cared if I lived or died. If it wasn't for you, I might even *be* dead, but you were too stubborn to let me die, and when I tried to leave you, you wouldn't give me any peace until I came back. You loved me and stayed with me even when I wouldn't marry you, and when I decided to come back here and face my past, you wouldn't let me come alone. You've given me more than any man has a right to deserve, and now this."

His eyes shone with wonder and adoration. Suzanna savored the moment, but only for a moment.

"You've made me very happy, too, you know," she reminded him. "I didn't have a home, either, and all the decent people in town had turned their backs on me. You taught me how to love again, and you treated my son as if he were your own, and I suppose you'd give me the moon if I so much as hinted I wanted it."

"Do you?" he asked with a hopeful grin.

"No, but I would like to get married, the sooner the better."

He gave a long-suffering sigh. "I thought you'd never ask. I'll round up a preacher first thing tomorrow morning. But with your permission," he added, bearing her back against the pillows, "we'll start the honeymoon tonight."

She smiled sweetly. "Only if you say 'please.' "

Author's Note

When I researched my first book for Avon, *Rogue's Lady*, I learned a lot of things about Dodge City that simply wouldn't fit into that book, so I had to write another one set in the most infamous town in the Old West. Many of the events mentioned in this book actually took place and many of the characters actually lived in Dodge City in 1878.

The famous vaudeville comedian Eddie Foy did appear at the Comique Theater when he was a very young man just starting out in show business. A cowboy named George Hoyt (or Hoy) did fire several shots at Wyatt Earp one night as he stood outside the Comique listening to the show. The bullets penetrated the thin walls of the theater, where Bat Masterson was dealing Spanish monte to Doc Holliday, and sent the occupants scrambling for cover. Earp returned the fire, wounding Hoyt who died a month later after admitting he had tried to kill Earp for the bounty on his head. Hoyt was the only man Wyatt Earp killed in Dodge City during his time as a peace officer there. Many years later in his autobiography, Eddie Foy described the incident and claimed that when he retrieved the coat of his brand new eleven-dollar suit from where it had been hanging on a chair backstage, it had been ventilated with three bullet holes.

Eddie Foy also discussed the dance-hall girls he met during his stays in Dodge. Although many dance halls in the West were run as fronts for prostitution, Foy claimed many of the women who worked at the Comique were as "straight as deaconesses," to use his words. Some of the women were widows, some married with worthless or missing husbands. Their job was to dance with the men, talk to them, perhaps flirt a bit, and induce them to buy drinks. They were, of course, snubbed by the better element, and they were seldom virgins. Such women often took lovers and defied convention by living openly with their paramours.

During the summer of 1878 the Dodge City Council passed an ordinance prohibiting gambling and prostitution within the city limits. Their intention was not to outlaw such activities but merely to enrich the city's coffers by fining those who engaged in them. Two outraged Dodge City prostitutes hired an attorney in an attempt to have the law rescinded.

Sometime during the month of August, several soldiers from Fort Dodge were fleeced by a crooked gambler. Their commanding officer returned with a troop, which fired a round into the saloon where the soldiers had been cheated, aiming high enough to avoid hitting anyone inside but low enough to put the fear of God into them. There is no record of whether or not soldiers were cheated at any future time in Dodge.

In September, the citizens took up a collection for the yellow fever victims in Memphis and endured the panic I described as a result of Dull Knife's escape from the reservation. The story about the wax baby is also true.

Finally, my account of Dora Hand is as accurate as I could make it. Dora arrived in Dodge in the spring of 1878, joining her friend Fanny Garrettson. The two women had worked together in St. Louis theaters for two years, and Fanny had written Dora that she was earning forty dollars a week in Dodge, twice what they had been making in St. Louis.

Little is known of Dora's past. Her real name was Fanny Keenan, and she had taken the name Dora Hand when she married Theodore Hand. By the time she arrived in Dodge, they had divorced. Dora's professionally trained voice—a rarity in the Old West—led to rumors that she had been a opera singer back in Boston. The story was that she had left Boston because of a broken heart or maybe because she had consumption. In reality, she probably wasn't even from Boston.

Dora's beauty, charm, and lovely singing voice won her many admirers, foremost among whom was Dodge City's mayor, James 'Dog' Kelley. Dora was frequently seen riding with Kelley behind his "boss buggy team" or accompanying him and his hounds on a hunting expedition. Kelley arranged with the owners of the Comique, Jim Masterson and Ben Springer, to have her sing in his saloon for two hours every evening, thus enabling her to increase her income substantially.

Dora used her newfound riches to stake cowboys who had lost all their wages at the faro table and to provide for the poor children of all colors in Dodge City. Although the church ladies resented having a woman of Dora's questionable reputation showing them how to do their Christian duty (especially after Reverend Wright started having her sing in church!), most people in Dodge considered Dora a saint and overlooked her relationship with Mayor Kelley.

Dora's death occurred just as I described it. The newspapers of the time claimed Mayor Kelley had allowed the women to use his home in his absence because their own quarters were so cramped. Other sources said that Kelley had rented one of his rooms out to one of the women, although considering the size of the rooms, it seems unlikely two people of the opposite sex would be living in such close quarters unless they were romantically involved. I believe the discretion with which her presence in his house was handled by the press is a measure of the esteem in which Dora Hand was held by the people of Dodge City. No one wanted to besmirch her name even after she was dead.

Because Spike Kennedy had not intended to kill Dora

Hand, her death was ruled an accident and the charges were dropped. Rumor said that Kennedy's rich Texas friends had bought justice for him. His right arm was hopelessly crippled, but he learned to use his left one well enough to engage in several gunfights before someone a little faster finally killed him five years later.

I hope you enjoyed *Fortune's Lady*. If so, please let me know and include an SASE for reply:

Victoria Thompson
301 Union Avenue, Suite 372
Altoona, PA 16602

goodbye to happiness,' she ventured, remembering her own excuses about duty which had previously caused her to deny her feelings towards him.

Eadulf reached out to take her hands in his.

'You are fond of quoting the sages, Fidelma. Wasn't it Plautus who wrote that to an honest man, it is an honour to have remembered his duty?'

'The Law of the Fénechus says that God does not demand that a man give more than his ability allows,' she countered hotly, thinking that he was teasing her about her previous opinions.

There was a shout across the water and a small skiff was pulling away from one of the large sea-going ships which lay at anchor in the inlet. The rowers were pulling rapidly towards the quay and several people, carrying baggage, were gathering to await its arrival.

'The tide is on the turn.' Eadulf raised his head and felt the change of wind on his cheek. 'The ship's captain will want to get away. I must go on board now. It seems, then, that we are always parting. I remember the last time we parted at Cashel. You determined then that your duty lay in going on a pilgrimage to the Tomb of St James in Iberia.'

'But I came back,' Fidelma pointed out reproachfully.

'True,' he agreed with a quick smile. 'Thank God that you did or I should not be here now. Yet you told me then that I had a duty towards Theodore of Canterbury. I recall your very words: "There is always a time to depart from a place even if one is unsure where one is going".'

She bowed her head contritely. 'I recall those words. Perhaps I was wrong.'

'And do you recall me replying that I felt at home in Cashel and could find a means to stay in spite of the demands of Canterbury?'

She remembered his words very clearly and she also remembered how she had answered him.

'Heraclitus said that you cannot step twice into the same river for other waters are continually flowing into it. That is what I answered. I remember.'

'I cannot return to Cashel now, for honour's sake. I have promises to keep at Canterbury.'

He made to turn away and then swung back, seizing her hands again. His eyes were moist. He was on the verge of telling her that he would return to Cashel but he knew that he had to be strong if they had any future together.

'I do not want to be parted from you again so soon, Fidelma. One of your ancient triads asks – what are the three diseases that you may suffer without shame?'

She reddened a little and replied softly, 'An itch, a thirst and love.'

'Will you come with me?' Eadulf asked with rough enthusiasm. 'Come with me to Canterbury? There would be no shame in that.'

'Would that be a wise decision for me to make?' Fidelma asked with a ghost of a smile trembling on her lips. Her emotions wanted her to say yes, but logic held her back.

'I am not sure wisdom enters into such matters,' Eadulf said. 'All I know is that no wind will serve the sails on your ship of life unless you steer for a particular port.'

Fidelma glanced behind her.

Along the quay Dego, Enda and Aidan were standing, waiting patiently while Fidelma and Eadulf said their farewells. They were holding the horses ready to commence the journey back to Cashel. She thought for a moment. No decision would come immediately. Perhaps being unable to make a decision, *was* a decision in itself? She did not know how to respond. Her thoughts were too confused. Eadulf seemed attuned to her doubts.

'If you need to stay, stay; I will understand,' he told her, his voice soft in resignation.

Fidelma met his warm brown eyes with her fiery green ones for several long seconds before she squeezed his hand, smiled quickly, let it fall, turned and walked silently away.

Eadulf made no attempt to say anything else. He watched her walking with a firm step back towards her mare. Aidan and Enda mounted their horses in readiness and Dego moved forward, leading her mount. Eadulf waited, his mind in conflict, torn between uncertainty and anticipation. He watched as she spoke a few words to Dego. Then she took her saddle bag from her horse. When she returned to Eadulf her face was flushed but she was smiling confidently.

'Brehon Morann said that if reason cannot be satisfied, then follow the impulse. Let's go aboard the ship before the captain sails without us.'

Shroud for
the Archbishop

Peter Tremayne

Wighard, archbishop designate of Canterbury, has been discovered garrotted in his chambers in the Lateran Palace in Rome in the autumn of AD 664. The solution to this terrible crime appears simple as the palace guards have arrested an Irish religieux, Brother Ronan Ragallach, as he fled from Wighard's chambers.

Although Ronan denies responsibility, Bishop Gelasius, in charge of running affairs at the palace, is convinced the crime is political; Wighard was slain in pique at the triumph of the pro-Roman Anglo-Saxon clergy in their debate with the pro-Columba Irish clergy at Whitby. And there is also the matter of missing treasure . . .

Bishop Gelasius realises that Wighard's murder could lead to war between the Saxon and Irish kingdoms if Ronan is accused without independent evidence. So he invites Sister Fidelma of Kildare and Brother Eadulf of Seaxmund's Ham to investigage. But more deaths follow before the pieces of this strange jigsaw of evil and vengeance are put together.

'The Sister Fidelma stories take us into a world that only an author steeped in Celtic history could recreate so vividly – and one which no other crime novelist has explored before. Make way for a unique lady detective going where no one has gone before!' Peter Haining

0 7472 4848 6

HEADLINE

The Mask of Ra

Paul Doherty

His great battles against the sea raiders in the Nile Delta have left Pharaoh Tuthmosis II weak and frail, but he finds solace in victory and in the welcome he is sure to receive on his return to Thebes. Across the river from Thebes, however, there are those who do not relish his homecoming, and a group of assassins has taken a witch to pollute the Pharaoh's unfinished tomb.

Reunited with his wife, Hatusu, and his people, Tuthmosis stands before the statue of Amun-Ra, the roar of the crowd and the fanfare of trumpets ringing in his ears. But within an hour he is dead and the people of Thebes cannot forget the omen of the wounded doves flying overhead.

Rumour runs rife, speculation sweeps the royal city and Hatusu vows to uncover the truth. With the aid of Amerotke, a respected judge of Thebes, she embarks on a path destined to reveal the great secrets of Egypt.

'The best of its kind since the death of Ellis Peters' *Time Out*

'A lively sense of history' *New Statesman*

0 7472 5972 0

HEADLINE

If you enjoyed this book here is a selection of other bestselling titles from Headline